Carnal Acts

ABOUT THE AUTHOR

Sam Alexander is a pseudonym for a highly regarded crime novelist. Do you know who it is?

Tweet your guess: #WhoIsSamAlexander?

Carnal Acts

Sam Alexander

ARCADIA BOOKS

Arcadia Books Ltd
139 Highlever Road
London W10 6PH

www.arcadiabooks.co.uk

First published in the United Kingdom by Arcadia Books 2014

A catalogue record for this book is available from the British Library.

ISBN 978-1-90980-754-9

Typeset in Minion by MacGuru Ltd
Printed and bound by CPI Group (UK) Ltd, Croydon CR0 4YY

Arcadia Books supports English PEN *www.englishpen.org* and
The Book Trade Charity *http://booktradecharity.wordpress.com*

Arcadia Books distributors are as follows:

in the UK and elsewhere in Europe:
Macmillan Distribution Ltd
Brunel Road
Houndmills
Basingstoke
Hants RG21 6XS

in the USA and Canada:
Dufour Editions
PO Box 7
Chester Springs
PA, 19425

in Australia/New Zealand:
NewSouth Books
University of New South Wales
Sydney NSW 2052

Dedicated
to
Gill Plain
with
gratitude and admiration

Prologue

Somehow Gaz had managed to sleep, on his side with knees drawn up and arms folded over his chest. The bed was wide and the sheets fresh. The only light came from the crack beneath the door. It was enough for him to see the toilet through the other door, that one open. After drinking thirstily from the tap, he realised that his clothes had been removed. He was wearing some kind of loose gown, white. His heart missed a beat when he understood what it was – he'd seen his father in one when he was coughing his life away in hospital.

He ran to the door and banged on it, shouting. The wood was thick and the handle round, cold and immobile. Turning to the bed, he saw there was food – rolls, cheese, apples – and kneeled by the low table to satisfy the hunger that suddenly raged. Then he sat on the bed and tried to remember what had happened.

He'd been pissed, all right – the usual Friday night pints in the pubs he and his mates visited. It had been damp in Newcastle, but only drizzle so his nuts hadn't frozen off for a change. They'd gone for a curry and downed plenty of Indian beer. Then his memory got rough around the edges. They'd gone to the night-club, he remembered that, and he'd danced with a fit bird, long dark hair and a foreign accent. And after that? A big car. Had he passed out in the back seat? Must have done. But what the fuck was he doing locked up in a room that had blacked-out windows? Never mind the soft mattress and clean sheets, the place smelled damp and old, like a dungeon.

Gaz cried out again, a chill running through him. The place was warm enough – he couldn't work out how – but he was afraid. He might have been over six feet and the hardest centre back in the amateur leagues, but this was way beyond his experience. What could anyone want from him? His job at the warehouse didn't even pay enough for him to get his own place. He thought of his mother. She wouldn't be wondering where he was; he often spent the weekends at friends' places. She'd be at the kitchen table, smoking and throwing back voddie and orange. He held up his wrist in the dim light and saw that his watch had gone. How long had he been here? Another shiver gripped him.

Then he heard footsteps, heavy as they approached, boots like the steel toe caps he wore at work. He shouted, but his voice dried up as bolts were drawn and a key turned in the lock. There was a light in what he could see was a stairwell, stone steps leading upwards. A barrel-chested figure wearing a black bala-clava, thick jersey and jeans filled the space. What really scared him was the object in his captor's hands. It was long and metal-lic, with a sharp point.

'Lie down!' the man ordered.

'Fuck you!' Gaz said, making a dash for the door. He was poked with the pole and a jolt of electricity threw him to the stone-flagged floor.

'On the bed!'

Quivering, Gaz got to his feet and did as he was told.

'Arms out, legs open! I'm aiming the cattle prod at your cock.'

Gaz felt metal on his right wrist and heard a click as the cuff was closed. The same happened on his other hand and both ankles.

'Don't you piss yourself,' the man growled. 'That'll earn you an arse that'll sting for days.' The heavy head came close to his face, dark eyes boring. 'Aye, you'll do,' his captor said. 'I see you've stuffed your guts.' He straightened up and raised the gown so that Gaz's groin and abdomen were bare. 'One more thing.' He took a balaclava from his pocket and pulled it over his captive's head. This one didn't have eyeholes. 'Enjoy yourself,' he said, with a sick laugh.

Lying there immobile, blind and defeated, Gaz reckoned the chances of pleasure were less than zero.

He couldn't have been more wrong.

∞∞∞

1

Joni Pax was at the window of her flat near Corham Abbey. The street ran behind the ecclesiastical building. Its stone flanks were now even more like honey under floodlights, the square tower surmounted by the yellow-and-red-striped Northumberland flag. For the first time since she'd transferred from the Met to the newly constituted Police Force of North East England three months ago, the chill had left her bones. The rain and cold winds had been a shock, the snide comments of her colleagues in the Major Crime Unit less so; for some of them, black people, even mixed-race Caribbean and Caucasian like Joni, couldn't survive in the wild north. She'd proved them wrong about that and several other things, but she had a way to go before they accepted her fully. In the meantime, she was going to enjoy what was left of the first real weekend of spring. She'd got to know the city and had read up about its most famous custom, as well as picking her colleagues' and neighbours' brains. She'd also driven around it in the nine-year-old Land Rover Discovery she'd reconditioned.

All over Corham, midway between Newcastle and Carlisle, preparations for May Sunday were coming to an end. The evening of the first Sunday in that month was traditionally an unofficial parade. The real thing, with re-enactors playing medieval monks, Viking raiders, Border Reivers and Roman legionaries, took place the following Saturday, in daylight. May Sunday, despite the religious significance it used to have (pagan Beltane and Walpurgis Night, replaced by Christian Roodmas), had for decades been an opportunity for citizens, especially the young, to let off all the steam they could raise. It was a demographic fact that more Corham babies were born in February than any other month, particularly to underage mothers.

Springtime, fertility: Joni felt oppressed. Her mother, who lived half-an-hour's drive further north, regularly reminded her that time was running out. Joni was thirty-four and had never been interested in starting a family, but the maternal pressure was wearing her down. It would help if she had a man, especially one who could look past the crimped scars on her abdomen.

It was time to hit the streets. Earlier she'd been for a two-hour run near the Roman Wall. She was buzzing, invigorated and ready to take part in the local carnival.

2

Gaz heard the door open again – it could only have been a few minutes after the gorilla had left. Listening intently, he realised that it hadn't closed. He could see a blur of light through the wool of the balaclava. For a moment he forgot about his bonds and tried to get up. A soft hand was laid on his stomach. He breathed in through the damp wool and picked up a hint of perfume. It was more subtle than any used by the women he got his end away with.

Then the hand began to move slowly downwards. He gulped involuntarily as his body responded to a shock almost as violent as the cattle prod's. He was erect before the fingers closed around his cock. He tried to raise his arms, desperate to touch the woman's breasts. A thought struck him. Maybe it wasn't a woman. Maybe the shithead who'd tied him down got off on dabbing perfume behind his ears and slathering on hand cream.

He breathed out as he felt himself being guided into what was without any doubt a cunt, moist and welcoming. The woman began to move slowly up and down on him. The sensations were so overwhelming that Gaz came in seconds, thrusting his groin upwards in a series of jerks. He was still breathless when he took a hard slap on the cheek. The balaclava soaked up some of the force, but his head still whipped sideways. Obviously he had disappointed her.

He heard the door close. What now, he thought. This is fucking crazy. Despite the painful rubbing of the cuffs, he laughed. His mates weren't going to believe this. Tied down and used as a sex toy? It was like something out of a porn film. Then he remembered the man with the prod. What the bleeding hell was going on?

Some time later the door opened again. Fingers touched his damp cock again and worked it. Then he felt the woman's breath through the wool.

'Make it last this time,' she whispered, 'or I'll cut your balls off.'

Gaz made it last.

◇◇◇

3

Heck Rutherford spent a couple of hours walking on the Roman Wall on Sunday morning. He breathed in deeply, his heart thundering and sweat beading his forehead. Before the operation and subsequent chemotherapy, he could walk all day without losing his breath. The surgeon who told him that cancer changed everything had got that right. Then again, the scalpel-wielder's idiot colleagues had consistently failed to spot the tumour that had been growing in his urinary tract for years, gradually sapping his strength and intermittently nagging at his groin like a piranha with attention-deficit disorder. By the time they finally decided to operate a year back, the growth was a monster, one end rooting around in his left kidney and the other creeping towards his bladder.

'Hector Hugh Rutherford, you listen to me,' Ag had said, the night before the operation, one which the surgeon had been less than optimistic about performing. His lower abdomen and groin had been shaved and he'd been given an enema, both of which made him feel that he'd reached rock bottom in the human dignity stakes. He was an innocent back then.

'Don't lecture me,' he said to his wife. 'This is already bad enough.'

Agnes Rutherford, née Sweet ('You wonder why I want to take your name?'), was thirty-nine at the time, thirteen years younger than Heck, a primary school headmistress who took no prisoners but was loved by almost all her pupils. She was only a couple of inches over five feet, surprisingly full breasted, and the owner of long auburn hair that a Pre-Raphaelite would have killed for.

'I'm not lecturing,' she said. 'I'm just telling you what you have to live for.'

'I know what I have to...' He broke off when she squeezed his arm hard. She looked like a schoolgirl, but she had the strength of a wrestler.

'You have a wife who loves you more than she loves herself – unusual, that, you know.' She paused, waiting for him to smile, which he eventually did. 'And two kids who worship the ground you walk on and are wetting themselves about what'll become of you. Not forgetting a father who'd happily take your place in this bed, a dog who waits at the door for you to come every night and a cat—'

'That doesn't give a shit about me,' Heck interrupted, blinking back tears.

'Well, you may be right there,' Ag said, with a smile.

'All Adolf cares about is his food. The little bugger sleeps with his paws over the bowl, for Christ's sake.' Kat and Mikey, ten and eight at the time, had found the stray kitten in the garden and fallen for it immediately. They didn't know that the diagonal stripe of black above his eye and the black splotches beneath his nose that marred otherwise completely white fur had a historical connotation. The fact that the animal seemed to possess the dictator's character had also been beyond them back then, although both had done Nazi Germany projects at school by now.

'I'm serious, Heck,' Ag said, squeezing again. 'You're going to come through this and you're going to be fine. For yourself and for all of us.'

He drew his forearm across his eyes, ignoring the tissue she held out. 'Oh, yeah, big girl? Whatcha gonna do if I don't?'

'You're a detective chief inspector, not Philip Marlowe,' his wife said. 'What am I going to do? Take your pension and run?'

That made him laugh. As if Ag, most devoted of mothers, would ever desert their children. She'd even look after his father until his dying day, despite the fact that she often found David a serious pain.

She leaned over and looked into his eyes. He couldn't resist the grey-green of hers: they had enchanted him the first time he saw her, at a funfair of all places. After he divorced Lindsey, he used to go to places like that to pick up women. In Ag he'd found a lot more than he'd been looking for – he'd found his saviour.

'I wouldn't be here if it wasn't for you,' he said resentfully.

'True. You'd have a year of life, if you were lucky.'

'I might still only have a year. Shit, I might never come round from the anaesthetic.'

'Look at me,' Ag commanded. 'You *will* come round, you *will* recover, and you *will* be back with us, a better man than before.'

'Oh great. I'm having a personality transplant too, am I?'

'You *will* recover,' she said, smiling but transmitting her full intensity to him. He felt it course through him like a surge of electricity. 'For me. For us.'

And he did, though it was a close one. Grade three (four being terminal) – a belligerent sod – and stage three, one, zero. The last was good, meaning no metastases, the first less so: it showed the fucker was well advanced. Which meant four months of chemotherapy. At least his hair hadn't fallen out, but it had thinned, so he wore it close cut now. And, despite taking the pills they'd prescribed, he'd vomited like a student on the lash. Having spent most of his life as a six-foot-one hunk, he now resembled a vertical stick insect, as Ag had pointed out caustically when he declined one of the no-nonsense puddings she'd started making.

Heck stood on a rock. He had nothing to complain about, he thought, scanning the contours to the north, the last of the dew rising smokily in the sunlight. He was back at work, in a new job, with a new boss and new colleagues. His prognosis, although no better than fifty-fifty after the op, was improving by the month and he'd had no recurrent symptoms. His bladder was the most likely area to have been colonised by malignant cells, so he'd already had an unfeasibly large camera up his dick three times, with another cystoscopy scheduled next month. The first time he really did think he'd gone beyond all the shame barriers, but the cheery nurses and dexterous surgeon helped him through. It didn't even hurt that much, though the first pee afterwards would have delighted a masochist.

Heck had only been back for six weeks at the headquarters of the new Police Force of North East England – Pofnee as it was already widely known. Starting the Major Crimes Unit from scratch had been challenging and he hadn't fully shaken off the effects of his wound. He still had pains in his abdomen at the end of every week and walked to work them off. But that did nothing to help the fear that had gripped him. Being a northern man and an ex-rugby player, he hadn't told anyone – not even his wife. Had the cancer left him unable to do his job?

Ag Rutherford heard the sound of the Cherokee as her husband pulled into the drive. They had moved to a run-down farmhouse ten miles northwest of Corham five years back. Heck and her father-in-law had done a lot of work on it, despite the fact that the former's grasp of DIY was shaky. Their closest neighbours were fifty yards down the road, Henthaw being less a hamlet than a line of separate houses. She had never liked their home's name – Whiffler's Close – but had agreed to keep it because Heck, who was sentimental off duty, had a friend who'd lived there when he was a kid. Her husband wasn't great with change and he'd had to cope with a lot of it recently.

She went out as Heck was on his way to the garage, his hiking boots over his shoulder. He was trying ineffectively to push away Cass, their Golden Retriever.

'Catch any criminal Picts?'

He gave her a long-suffering look. 'The tribe that occupied the area north of the wall didn't paint themselves. They were the—'

'Votadini, aka Otadini,' Ag interrupted. 'I do know something about local history, sweetheart. 'She stepped closer. 'You look tired.'

'No worse than usual.'

'Well, that's something. Are you going into town later?'

'No chance. Morrie Sutton's on duty. Let's hope he doesn't cock anything up.'

'Dad!' Their twelve-year-old son Luke ran up and thumped his shoulder into Heck's thigh, his back bent in the approved rugby tackle stance. Cass jumped up, forepaws scrabbling on the boy's sweatshirt.

Heck winced as he returned Ag's wry smile, which said, 'You wanted him to play rugby, now take the consequences.' His own nose, broken when he was nineteen and not properly reset, was a permanent reminder of the sport's hazards.

'Very good, lad,' he said. 'What've you been up to?'

'A bit of this, a bit of that,' Luke said, acting the wide boy from some TV programme. Heck only ever watched the news, sport and the History Channel.

'Hi, Daddy.' Kat stood at the garage door, her black hair in a ponytail and pretty face damp beneath dark brown eyes.

'Not again,' Heck said. His daughter might only have been fourteen, but she was already showing a worrying propensity for affairs of the heart. 'I'll break his legs.'

She laughed. 'Don't be daft. He'll be on the phone again in a few minutes.' She held up the ludicrously expensive mobile he'd been talked into buying for her last birthday.

'Ah, the strider returns.' David Rutherford came under the retractable door, bowing his head with its bush of demented professor's white hair. 'See any interesting birds?' he asked, with a wry smile.

His father had an encyclopaedic knowledge of wild birds, but he also still had an eye for women.

Heck shook his head in resignation.

'Come on, you lot,' Ag said. 'Lunch is nearly ready.'

'Are you doing roast spuds?' Luke asked. His face was a mass of freckles and his red hair was cut short in imitation of his father's.

'I might be,' his mother replied, pulling him away from Heck. 'Leave your dad alone. He's knackered himself on the Wall. Come on, Cass.'

Kat slipped her arm under her father's. 'You should rest more,' she said. 'And spend more time with us.'

Heck nodded, his eyes meeting David's. 'I know, pet. I need time to get my head together, that's all. How about Monopoly after lunch?'

Kat shook her head. 'Grandpa always steals money when he thinks we're not looking. Cluedo?'

'Cluedo it is,' Heck agreed. If only catching real criminals was so easy; not that he often won the game. He'd been in love with Miss Scarlett since he was Luke's age and he cut her all kinds of slack.

4

Gaz was still panting five minutes after he'd come. He was trying to work out what the woman was doing. This time she hadn't slapped him. He was pleased with himself because he'd made her moan and scream, but what the fuck was she up to now? He could feel her head against his thigh, but none of the rest of her body. In the light from the open door, he made out a vague shape. Was she doing a head stand against the wall?

Then a familiar figure appeared in the door. All the pride and pleasure vanished. Heavy feet came close. He felt a sharp blade along his throat beneath the balaclava.

'You do anything except what I tell you and you'll be having a shower in your own blood,' the man said. 'You got that?'

'Yes, yes,' Gaz said, his voice embarrassingly high.

'Good. I'm taking your cuffs off, all right? After that, you're going to the bathroom. Clean yourself up, especially down there.' A gloved hand grabbed his balls.

When he was free, Gaz was led on unsteady legs to the other door and pushed through. The door was closed behind him and an external lock turned. The light was switched on. The room was small and there was no bath, only a shower without a curtain in one corner. There was soap and shampoo, but nothing he could use as a weapon – no razor, no mirror to be smashed; even the toilet lid had been cemented against the cistern.

At least the water was hot and there was plenty of it. When Gaz finished, he found there were no towels, only a pile of face cloths. What was the gorilla scared of? That he'd flick his eyes out? The bastard had the fucking cattle prod. Then he had a thought. Maybe they'd taken precautions against him topping himself. That made his stomach flip. What else was in store for him?

'I'm opening up,' came the gruff male voice. 'You don't need to wear the balaclava now.'

When Gaz came out, hands over his groin, the man was pointing the prod at him and his face was still covered.

'There are clean clothes for you and more food.' He laughed emptily. 'Get a feed down. She might be back any time.'

When he'd gone, Gaz huddled under the covers in the dark and ate more bread and cheese. He and his mates had often joked about being gigolos or toy boys. The reality wasn't funny at all. Even though the sex was amazing.

✧✧✧

5

Suzana – she could hardly remember her surname, the Noli family having so little significance for her any more – ran her finger across the tines of the fork. It was a heavy piece of cutlery, steel, she thought, one that must have originally belonged in a rich house. She'd found it beneath a floorboard in the room that had been her prison for months, filling the gap with hair and dust so it wasn't discovered during the daily searches. The second-floor window was barred and the glass covered with black tape, but she peeled back a corner ever day and had seen winter turn to watery spring, and now the first days of sun. She had no other means of telling the time, just as she had nothing of her own. Her captors had taken everything.

Although she could only vaguely remember her mother's tear-stained face and the defeated way her father had raised his arm in farewell, Suzana could still see the mountains around the village, snow on the peaks even in early October. She had grown up in their embrace and had been proud to be a 'child of the rock fathers', as the villagers called themselves. They were poor, but every family had strips of land on the terraced slopes and a few beasts. There were trees in abundance as well – almonds, chestnuts, even some hardy cherries. The river that rushed down the crack in the mountains kept the small valley fertile, while the ridge at the western end cut it off from the rest of Albania. Even Hoxha's functionaries had given the villages there a wide berth, in awe of the powerful clans that ran things the traditional way. Deals were done with the communist state, a few lanky boys sent to do their national service and some truckloads of logs driven to the capital.

Suzana, seventeen a month before she left, brought the fork close to her left eye. She could put it out, she could rip apart her cheeks and slash open her breasts – that would reduce her value to the men who pimped her. Only one thing stopped her, and it wasn't fear for her parents. Once she'd arrived in London – how she had dreamed of that moment – and passed legally through the border control at the airport, her passport had been taken by the shaven-headed brute Leka. Later that day he and three other men raped her. She understood why her father had looked at her the way he did; he knew she wasn't destined to work in a restaurant or as a cleaner. She had made her decision. The only way to save herself was to be harder than stone with everyone else. She had shed her last tear weeks ago.

There was no mirror in the room, only a cheap wooden bed, a chair for the customers' clothes – though many of them did nothing more than undo their trousers – and a small table. On it were a box of condoms, tissues, lubricating jelly and a pair of nipple clamps. Two men liked to attach them to her (she still hadn't got used to the pain), while there was one with breasts larger than hers who clamped his own nipples. There was also a metal waste bin. When she was working, it soon filled up with sodden paper and used rubbers. During the few hours she got to herself, it served as a chamber pot.

The absence of a mirror was a blessing from God, not that Suzana had any faith. There had been an imam in her village since the end of communism – the imposition of atheism had been one of the few things the state had been rigid about – but her family had not gone back to being Muslims. What faith would have helped her in these months of violent coupling, sometimes twenty times a day, often without protection because the customers preferred it that way: she hoped she had passed on diseases to them. The doctor Leka brought in regularly had given her antibiotics more than once, but she wasn't allowed to stop working.

Even without the mirror, Suzana knew how she looked. She

could feel the swellings on her cheeks and was sure that the bones had been broken that first night when she'd fought until she was subdued. The acne that had plagued her when she was younger was still there, made worse by the chocolate she was given as a treat – the only one. Her nose was broken too, though it seemed to have reset itself in a fairly straight line. The strands of black hair that hung in front of her eyes were greasy. She thought today was her turn for the shower. It didn't matter. The customers fucked her even when she stank of the previous ones. They were animals, as was Leka. He had looked at her after he stripped her that first night, ogling her breasts but mocking her skinny legs and thin arms. There was more meat on them now as the 'girls' – she wasn't sure how many others were in the house – were fed mostly white bread and tasteless yellow cheese, and on rare occasions salty sausage; but never fruit or vegetables. Her skin was pasty and slack, and she hated herself. But not as much as she hated Leka.

She heard heavy steps on the stair and darted across to the loose floorboard to conceal the fork.

'Up, bitch,' Leka said, slamming the door against the wall. He gagged. 'And take that shit-can with you. Make yourself decent. It's a festival. There'll be a lot of customers.'

Suzana carried the bin against her chest, hoping he wouldn't follow her into the bathroom. He had taken her in the shower more than once, forcing her to bend over until the top of her head touched the cracked tiles on the floor. Instead, he watched her from the door-less entrance as she emptied her waste into the toilet and flushed it, then got under the shower. There was no curtain, but she'd got used to being stared at. She scrubbed herself with the pungent brown soap and rubbed thin shampoo into her hair. She was thinking about what the bastard had said. Plenty of customers. That meant the house would be busy, Leka and his friends making sure the correct money was handed over and the drunken men kept in line.

It was her chance. Tonight. Suzana couldn't wait any longer.

If she wasn't free by this time tomorrow, she would mutilate herself beyond all use and recognition.

<><><><><><><><><><><><><><><><><><><><><><><><><><><><><><><><><><><><><><><><><><><><><><><><><><>

6

Joni looked at her watch, a cheap thing she'd bought from a street-seller in London who claimed he was from Nigeria though she thought his accent was more Brixton. Growing up with money permanently in short supply had made Joni oblivious to fashion and status symbols. Her mother, Moonbeam, was an art teacher in a comprehensive, but she spent most of her salary on robes and other Wicca impedimenta, rather than saving to get out of the council flat she'd been assigned when she was a single mother. Whence Joni's nine-year-old Land Rover, identical dark grey trouser suits and pairs of heavy-duty black boots. Her only weakness was for blinding blouses, though she generally kept to white for work. She pulled on a tan leather jacket and headed out.

From what Joni had learned, May Sunday was one of the few times of the year when there was a degree of harmony in Corham. Perhaps there had been a homogeneous population in Roman times, though the presence of legions raised in continental Europe and even Asia Minor suggested otherwise, but in the final decades of the twentieth century the divisions between the town's northern and southern halves had attracted sociologists from the universities in Newcastle, Durham and beyond. The medieval town, built on a strategically salient hundred-foot cliff above the River Derwyne, had become a centre of worship and commerce because of the large abbey and monastery. It encompassed the remains of the Roman town, an important camp servicing the Wall fifteen miles to the north. In later centuries, tanning and distilling developed outside the old walls, still on the northern side. There had also been a large sugar mill, owned by the ennobled Favon family. It was only with the discovery of iron ore a few miles south of the town that the steel works and surrounding workers' communities sprang up there. The area was called Ironflatts and Corham's burghers paid as little attention to the rapid development there as they could, until they realised they could make money – serious money – from the works and the workers, as well as turn their town into a nascent city. They even built a second bridge to supplement the still operational medieval one. Pride was swallowed and profits pocketed.

But not by the poor. They had always been Corham's problem, and the multitudes that colonised Ironflatts made it worse. The tanneries, sugar processing plants and distilleries needed more labour than was available locally, so families had moved from the Derwyne and Wear urban areas. The landowners, bankers, lawyers and preachers who controlled Corham saw them as a necessary evil, but made sure only a minimum of the town's wealth was spent on them. Cheap two-up, two-down houses in narrow streets ran outwards like the spokes of a wheel from the old town centre, the abbey and its environs occupying a teardrop-shaped peninsula that the river wound around in a 'u' bend.

Ironflatts and its neighbouring communities south of the river were even worse. Terraced houses to the west and sixties tower blocks in the east stood up to the disparaging gaze of the Northies, as the people beyond the Derwyne were known to the Southies. The blocks' expanses of glass reflected the red explosions from the foundries as well as the weak north-eastern sun. True Corham natives blinked before shaking their heads. The brief presence of Ironflatts Rovers in the 1970s First Division was also a shock, but the team plummeted along with the local heavy industry. When the works were finally shut down in the mid-eighties, thousands of people left the area, turning it into a social and industrial wasteland. Drugs were the only burgeoning commercial venture and generations of Southies had been raddled by heroin, crack and any other poisons the disaffected youth could get its hands on. AIDS took a swathe as well. Meanwhile Northie kids did alcopops, weed and Ecstasy at weekends, dutifully doing their homework when they'd sobered up. But not on May Sunday.

Joni went down into Corham Square, with the Abbey on one side and refurbished shops and pubs on the others. It was full of braying and squawking humanity. Her uniformed colleagues had cordoned it off, but that hadn't stopped some idiot dressed as a traffic light standing in the middle of one of the access roads. He had rigged up functioning red, amber and green panels, which he changed every so often. People paid due attention, egged on by his friends; waiting when he displayed red, and then moving on with green. The level of hysteria this provoked drew Joni closer, though she had to push her way through a group of men in bikinis with peacock feathers sprouting from their heads.

'Come on, Nick!' a short-haired youth with a red plastic fish on his head shouted. 'Beer time!'

Joni saw there was a slit in the tall cardboard rectangle the traffic light had erected on his shoulders. The eyes behind it were creased in amusement.

'A few more minutes,' he said. 'This is fucking brilliant!'

Joni wasn't sure whether impersonating a traffic light was illegal, but swearing in public definitely was, under section 5 of the Public Order Act 1986. Not that she particularly cared. There were no small children nearby to be harassed, alarmed or distressed and this Nick was hardly the only person using profane language. She watched as the red light above his head came on. Then his friends lost patience and grabbed him, holding him horizontally and driving him like a battering ram into the Coach and Horses. Not all of them looked over eighteen, but that wasn't her problem either.

The crush of people headed down Derwyne Street, the main thoroughfare, and Joni went with them. There was a lot of drunken bonhomie, mainly to do with the amount of flesh on display. A guy dressed as a mermaid, tail split, was sitting on a fat man's shoulder. The beast of burden was naked to the waist. On closer inspection, Joni realised the black-and-white stripes on his abdomen were a tattoo.

'Like what you see, lass?' the man asked, with a grin.

Joni glared at him until his bravado departed. 'Two things. I've got a judo black belt. And I'm a police officer.' She watched as he took a step back, provoking an angry yell from the man whose toes he'd trodden on. 'Fancy your chances?'

He patently didn't. She let them go, the mermaid bending down to find out what had happened. Maybe her mother was right, Joni thought. Moonbeam claimed that Wicca was about harmony and not doing harm to anyone. If only life – let alone police work – was so straightforward.

⬥⬥

7

Over the hours Gaz had worked himself into a state of serious anger. He was ashamed at himself for being used by a woman – he was used to telling the cows what to do – and he was fucked off big time by the gorilla who had rolled all over him. What the shithead didn't know was that Gaz had form when it came to dishing it out. He had knocked out plenty of guys behind night-clubs and pubs. He'd even lain in wait for a forward who made a fool of him during a football match and done major damage to his kneecaps. He wasn't going to take being kidnapped and used as a sex slave lying down.

When the door crashed open, Gaz was ready. The man in the balaclava wasn't carrying the cattle prod this time, though he did have the knife in his belt. Gaz stood up, his shoulders down to make it look like he was defeated.

'Sit down, fuck face,' his captor said.

Gaz thought about it, then complied. Anything to get the gorilla up close.

'You're in luck, bonnie lad. Her highness wants another dose.' He looked at Gaz's groin. 'I hope you're clean.' He laughed. 'If you aren't, that'll make a fine sausage for my dog.'

That did it. Gaz had no idea what the woman was planning for him, but he was getting a bad vibe from her enforcer.

'I'm clean, me,' he said softly, dropping his head.

'Lie down then. Cuff time.'

Gaz made his move, grabbing the knife and pressing the point against his captor's belly.

'Back!' he shouted. 'Get away from me! And take that fucking balaclava off!'

The man was a couple of yards from him now and the knife wasn't an immediate threat any more, but he uncovered his face all the same. It was that of a classic hard man, gaze unwavering, square jaw, nose broken, heavy moustache.

'You think you'll get far, bonnie lad?' he asked contemptuously.

Gaz had thought it through. He knew there would be more doors. 'Keys,' he said. 'Now!'

'You really don't want to be doing this,' the gorilla said.

'Oh, yes, I fucking do. Take off your boots an' all.' Although he'd been given clothes, Gaz had no footwear – not even slippers. 'Sit down while you do it!' The man's boots were thick-soled and heavy, and would do damage if he threw them.

A couple of minutes later Gaz had the keys and the boots, though he didn't waste time putting the latter on now. He took a step towards his former captor, the knife extended. 'I should cuff you and slash your wrists,' he said. 'But I'm not like you. I'll just lock you in here.'

He turned and ran for the door, slamming it hard and fumbling to get the key in the lock and turn it. He shot the bolts too. Then he laughed and sat down to put on the boots. They rang loudly on the first stone steps.

The whistle from inside the room was loud and high-pitched.

Gaz looked round, then turned to the front again. The dog – he recognised it immediately as a Doberman – was already in the air, its spittle-flecked jaws wide open.

Gaz's head hit the floor hard and he lost consciousness. In that, he was lucky. The dog tore his throat out.

◇◇

8

Joni had followed the crowd to the Old Bridge, where it split. The Northies hung around the riverside park, waiting for the firework display, while the Southies crossed the refurbished medieval structure, claiming that the view was much better from their side. She looked around, taking in the willows whose branches were touching the water, and the lights on the wall that had been built along the bank. Some idiot teenagers – the males dressed as well-endowed schoolgirls in short skirts and the females as mechanics in gaping overalls – climbed up, but they were soon shouted down by the few adults who weren't the worse for alcohol. Joni had only drunk from the water bottle in her pocket, not having a head for booze. That had been another thing that differentiated her from her colleagues in the Met. She had never smoked either, let alone touched drugs. Growing up in Hackney, she'd seen the damage they did.

'Hey, Nick, get up on the wall!'

She turned when she heard the shouts to her right. The guy in the traffic light rig was being carried towards the riverbank. As she watched the group of lively young people, a tingling started at the top of her spine and then invaded her mind. It wasn't the first time this had happened. A month after she'd started in plain clothes, she'd reacted without conscious thought. She'd become aware of a small boy at the edge of the pavement near her flat in Vauxhall. She got to him as he had one leg in the air, pulling him back as a white van flashed past.

'Let him go!' a thin woman with rat-tail hair shouted from a shop doorway. 'Help! The brown bitch is taking my son!'

Fortunately a well-spoken middle-aged man in a suit, white like the woman, had seen the whole thing and told the mother she should be thanking Joni for saving her boy, and what did she think she was doing letting him so near the road unattended? The woman eventually mumbled thanks. Back home, Joni sat down and closed her eyes. The boy was still there, his back to her as it had been before she'd clutched him. The boy. He was mixed-race too. Would she ever have a son or daughter? Her mother was forever pressing her. They said the stabbing hadn't damaged any of the relevant organs, but she was still wary.

The traffic light was on the wall now, showing green. The youth's mates were chanting, 'Red! Red! Red!' None of them noticed that his legs were unsteady and his back was angling towards the river. He was very close to falling.

Joni came at him from the side, leaping on to the wall before she grabbed him, and lowering her left shoulder so that he would topple towards the others. They were caught before they hit the ground.

'What the…'

'Jesus, Nick,' one of the boys laughed. 'What have you pulled now?'

The laughter died in their mouths when Joni got up and stared at them. She pulled the traffic light to his feet.

'That was dumb,' she said, peering at the eyes through the slit in the cardboard. 'Grow up before you do yourself an injury.' She looked round the made-up male and dirt-streaked female faces. 'Now go away.'

The young people started muttering but did what she said, moving eastwards along the bank. Joni watched them go, suddenly aware that she'd put her body on the line for the first time since the Met operation that had finished her career down south. She was expecting the tingling to fade. It didn't, and that hadn't happened before. She suspected she needed to see a shrink again. She should go to the police doctor, but that was the last thing she wanted so soon after she'd taken the job in Corham. Besides, the sensation seemed to have a purpose. It was some kind of warning. She moved through the jovial crowd, keeping the top of the traffic light in sight.

'Hello, lass,' came a soft voice to Joni's left.

She turned and saw the small figure of Maureen Hughes, her sixteen-year-old son looming behind.

'Maureen. How are you?'

'Oh, you know,' the woman said, grimacing. The bruises on her face had almost gone, though her right arm was still in a sling. 'Wayne here's been helping out.'

Joni nodded at the boy, who avoided her eyes. He'd been knocked out by his father when he came to the aid of his mother. It had been Joni's first significant case in Corham and the trial was coming up.

Maureen looked down. 'He'll ... he'll be sent away for a long time, won't he?'

'I'll make sure of that,' Joni said, though she knew how random the justice system could be.

'I canna ... I canna thank you enough for what you did,' the woman said. 'He's been hurting us for years.'

Joni nodded, trying to keep sight of the traffic light bobbing through the crowd. She had tracked Vince Hughes down to an abandoned shed on the moors and broken his arm after he laid out the DC accompanying her. She'd had her photo in the *Corham Bugle* and been door-stepped by a reporter from Newcastle, as well as being required to do a press conference by Assistant Chief Constable Ruth Dickie, who was keen to publicise the new force's commitment to gender equality and racial diversity.

'I'm sorry, Maureen, I've got to go.'

'That's all right.' The woman squeezed her arm. 'Work to do, no doubt.'

Joni did her best to conceal the shock of being touched, her skin hyper-sensitive even through the layers of leather and cotton. The intense feeling that something important was about to happen was making her jumpy.

'I'll see you soon,' she said, nodding to Wayne and his mother, and set off again through the crowd. What were Nick and his friends up to now? Surely they'd have learned from what had nearly happened on the wall. Some of them were drunk, but none was raving or raging; yet. She knew that could change at any moment. She followed the group down the road that led to the former tanning and distillery district, now being redeveloped but still the location of several dodgy bars and clubs. This was old Corham's dope-dealing centre, though most of the serious business went on across the river in Ironflatts. Was that what the kids were doing down here? If so, she was going to step in.

9

Suzana felt the weight of the man, then his prick. He was the eighth, she reckoned, and it was more painful than usual – as if her body, aware of what she was planning, was resisting the abuse it had become accustomed to. At least the man with long hair and moustache was the one wearing the nipple clamps, but he might soon attach them to her. The street light was making yellow rectangles around the blacked-out glass, but she had no clear idea of the time. Evening, and a lot of noise. Leka had been right. There was some sort of festival going on.

The man grunted and then cuffed the side of her head, saying words she didn't understand. Except she did. Bitch, whore, cocksucker, cunt. The tone meant they didn't need translation. She lay still for a moment and then something broke inside her, a zigzag crack across the surface of her mind. Using all her strength to shove him off, she went to the floorboard and pulled it up, then ran back and jabbed the fork at the pig's groin. He let out a shriek like a lamb that had been castrated, though she could see the fork hadn't done that much damage. She stood over him, the weapon quivering as she aimed at his eyes. He curled up in a ball and didn't see as she grabbed his jacket, the wallet weighing down the breast pocket.

Trying to control her breathing, Suzana opened the door. A burst of noise came from the men on the ground and first floors. Leka was standing on the top step down the hall. She was at him before he realised, ramming the fork into where she hoped his right kidney was and wrenching it out. He screamed and went down the stairs head first, his chin bouncing on the uncovered wood. She ran barefoot over his prone form, waving the fork around and making the men move back – many were dressed as women or what looked like old-fashioned fighters. One of Leka's pig friends was guarding the next stairs. He stepped forward to see what was going on. She missed his eye, but the fork pierced the side of his forehead. She let it go and it vibrated as he bellowed. That gave her the chance to pull the combat knife from his belt and slash it at him as she slipped past.

It was impossible to calm her heart or regulate her breathing now. She heard herself screech like a witch in the folk tales, men retreating in panic as she headed for the street door. There stood the skinny runt who gave Leka orders, a long knife in his hand. He had once made her stick a finger up his ass before he ejaculated over her breasts.

'What have you done, shit girl?' he said, in Albanian. 'You're dead meat.' He made a horizontal cut that drew blood on her upper chest, narrowly missing her neck.

Suzana lowered her head and charged him, straightening her right arm. The knife sank into something soft and she felt an expulsion of breath on her scalp. She tried to pull the knife out but the bastard had a hand on it. Stepping to the side, she screamed again to scare off the nearby men, pushed the bloodied whoremaster aside before pulling open the front door. There were more men on the steps leading to the street. She ran past them, shrieking, and bounced off a traffic light in the middle of the road. It was only as she made contact that she realised it was someone in a cardboard costume. Then she was running away across the asphalt.

After she turned several corners and found herself in a quiet area, she remembered that she was naked apart from the jacket she had stolen. Naked, with her feet and chest bleeding, but free. Then she heard pounding feet behind her and scrabbled for purchase on a high gate.

10

Joni kept her distance from the group of young people as they went past the high walls of a run-down factory. It seemed they'd lost interest in the fireworks – or perhaps they knew a good viewpoint down here. She looked over her shoulder. The golden abbey in its shroud of lights was still visible, but not much else of the town centre stood out. The tingling had turned into a more painful prickling sensation, as if insects were crawling around in her brain. There seemed to be some connection with the youth in the traffic light she'd tackled on the embankment. He and his friends turned left behind a dilapidated building. Others followed them. Joni kept her distance as they reached a narrow street of three-storey Victorian buildings that would have been occupied in the old days by people who had worked their way up from the slum housing further out from the centre of Corham. At the far end were the lights of a dingy pub, people standing outside to smoke. About a hundred yards before it, on the left-hand side, a crowd of men was gathered on the steps of one of the houses. The crawling sensation in Joni's head worsened, then she heard a high-pitched scream. A few seconds later the people outside the house, who now included Nick and his mates, parted suddenly and a slim figure appeared.

The woman had tousled black hair that reached down to an over-large leather jacket. She wasn't wearing anything on the bottom half of her body and her right hand was covered in blood. She shrieked and ran into the cardboard traffic light, then continued in the opposite direction, turning right at the corner thirty yards before the pub. Joni sprinted to the steps and saw a thin man at the top. He was on his back, groaning and clutching a knife in his abdomen. The words he spoke were in a strange language.

'Nobody move!' Joni ordered, pulling out her warrant card. In the first few weeks she had felt that it was someone else's despite the presence of her photograph – she was only gradually getting used to the Pofnee crest. She knelt by the wounded man, aware that people were rapidly taking their leave, brushing past her as she went. 'I said, nobody move.' She pointed at the traffic light. 'Especially not you, Nick. You're a witness.'

She called the dispatcher at Force HQ and asked for an ambulance, as well as for DI Sutton and the Corham Major Crime Unit. But the tingling was still with her. The woman – she had to find the woman. Looking through the open door, she saw other scantily clad females peering out. It was obvious what the house was. Then a man staggered along the corridor with what looked like the handle of a piece of cutlery sticking out from the side of his brow.

Joni glanced around. Heads down, men were hurrying away, including one with a beard and monk's robe and another she'd seen recently. She couldn't keep them all there, but Nick wasn't going anywhere. She pulled out her cuffs – she never went anywhere without them – and closed one round his wrist and the other round the railing outside the house.

The moment she started after the half-naked woman, the crawling in her skull faded. She was a couple of back streets away from the brothel when there was a series of tremendous cracks and booms. The night sky filled with coloured lights that briefly blinded her: fireworks just when she didn't need them.

When she could see again, she made out the woman climbing over a high gate and dropping into the dark.

◇◇◇

11

Heck and Ag were in front of the TV, paying minimal attention to the news. After tea, they had played Cluedo and Heck had duly lost. The kids had complained about their bed times, but Ag was firm. In the end they went mildly enough, Cass following them to the foot of the stairs, her tail thumping against the wall. Kat seemed to have made up with her current beau and was all smiles, looking forward to a chapter of Malorie Blackman before she dropped off. She picked Adolf up when her mother turned away and took him to her room. He would sleep half the night on her duvet and then go out the window to crunch baby rabbits' heads.

David had declined to play, preferring to consume a bottle of murky local ale while reading a book about industrial architecture. He had worked his way up to a low-level management position at the steel works before they were shut down and he hankered after the old times. At seventy-six, he still worked three shifts a week at a DIY store outside Corham. His wife, Olive, had died in 2001 after suffering from emphysema. When Heck had been seriously wounded, David had thought his world would end. But his elder son was tough, even if he wasn't yet what he had been. Peter, two years younger than Heck, was all right, but he was practising law in Chicago and rarely came home.

'I'm off,' the old man said, closing his book. 'Get to bed, lad. You're worn out.'

'Night,' Heck said, waving a hand. He was glad Ag had agreed that David could live with them after Olive died, but sometimes the old bugger got on his nerves. He had his own sitting room in what had been the cow shed, but he liked company. 'Don't forget to brush your hair,' he called after him.

David laughed. There was no brush in existence that could get through his tangled locks and that was the way he liked it. Heck had threatened to take sheep clippers to him when he was asleep, but he knew his son wouldn't dare. They lived to take the mickey out of each other and without the thatch Heck would be bereft.

'Honestly,' Ag said, squeezing her husband's arm. 'I've got boys in Year Three who are more mature than you two.' She smiled and kissed him on the cheek.

'It was Year Two last week,' Heck said, returning the kiss.

Ag settled back on the sofa and pulled him closer, then planted her lips on his. 'Fancy messing around?' she said, when she came up for air.

Heck frowned before he could stop himself. 'Well, Mrs Rutherford, this is most irregular.' In truth, it was. His interest in sex had gone walkabout when he was on sick leave and it hadn't really returned. On the few occasions they'd made love he struggled to reach orgasm, though he made sure Ag did. She was loving, imaginative, even daring in her suggestions, but he wasn't able to respond fully. The thirteen years he had on her and the surgical violence done to his gut were undermining him in the worst possible way.

Ag had managed to get his zip open and was doing things with her tongue that most men of his age would have to pay for. And she was definitely having an effect. Then his mobile rang.

'Ignore it,' Ag said indistinctly.

But, of course, he couldn't. He wasn't on duty, but he was still responsible for major crime across a huge area. And it was May Sunday...

'Rutherford,' he said, his voice rising as Ag applied her teeth.

'It's Morrie, sir. We've got a situation.'

Heck listened to what he was told and hung up. Five minutes later he was in the Cherokee on his way to the scene.

12

Joni's breath was even as she took long strides to the gate at the end of the street. The lighting was poor and she couldn't see a sign of anyone behind the metal bars. She looked around. The houses on both sides appeared to be empty, no lights showing. The residents would be out on the streets. The two-up two-down buildings didn't have basements so there was nowhere to hide. Besides, she was sure the half-naked woman had gone over. What she found harder to understand was how she'd done that. The gate was at least ten feet high. Joni was pretty sure she could make it, and even made an attempt to jump and grab the top. It would have been hard and she had to get back to the brothel in Burwell Street. Although she wasn't responsible for Corham major crime, she didn't want to hand the case over to Morrie Simmons completely.

Then she saw a trail of blood high up on the gate. The young woman hadn't looked much more than five feet eight. She must have either been as fit as a special forces operative or extremely desperate. Remembering the damage she had done to the men back there, Joni wasn't sure which applied.

'Hello?' she called. 'Is anyone there?' She paused, aware how ridiculous she sounded. 'I can help. Really.'

There was no sound in the derelict factory beyond the gate.

'Please, listen to me.' Joni thought of the woman, naked apart from the jacket she had presumably stolen from one of the men inside the house and bloody; perhaps she was injured. 'I can help. Please, come back.'

Stupid, she said to herself. The poor woman probably can't even speak English. The others looked distinctly foreign, with their dark complexions and the rings under their eyes. And she'll be scared of anyone who comes after her.

Then she had a thought. Could the wounded man have been speaking Albanian? She knew that many Albanians understood Italian. She took one of her cards from her wallet, turned it over and wrote in that language, 'I can help. Please call me on my mobile number. PLEASE!' She pushed the card under the gate.

As she jogged back, Joni was struck by an intense sadness. She knew exactly what deprivation and cruelty could do. It was one of the reasons she had joined the Met after Oxford. She was going to help the women, especially the one who had escaped. She was a victim, no matter what she'd done.

Joni, atheist that she was, had always been one for missions.

13

'What?' Heck said, surprised. 'Joni Pax is down here?'

DI Morris Sutton nodded, his comb over shifting precariously. He was forty-four, overweight and a recently reformed, and bad-tempered, smoker. ACC Dickie hadn't been keen on having him at Force HQ, never mind heading up the MCU in the Corham conurbation, but Heck had insisted when the initial planning was being done. Morrie was a good cop, even if his manner was abrasive and he had problems with women, gays and ethnic minorities. Ruth Dickie's idea, put into operation when Heck was on sick leave, was that Joni would erode the former and latter of those prejudices, even though she was DI responsible for major incidents outside Corham and thus had a much larger brief. The fact that both Simmons and Pax reported to Heck meant they would have to cooperate. Sutton was Heck's sop to the Major Crime Unit in Newcastle, where he and Morrie used to work. He wanted to show that Ruth Dickie didn't get everything she wanted, as well as build bridges with the officers, many of them senior, who resented both his past involvement in the anti-corruption unit and his new position. That was one reason he had declined promotion to detective chief superintendent – the others were that he wanted to stay as close as possible to investigations and that he was unsure how he would perform after he'd been wounded.

He had the impression he'd played into the ACC's hands. She was building her fiefdom and could exercise more control as he was still only a DCI. It also saved money from her budget.

'Where is she then?' Heck asked, looking around. There were few men in the street now, only some locals standing behind the crime scene tape that had been unrolled. The lad in the traffic light was still attached to the wall, but the cardboard box had been lifted off his shoulders. He looked longingly at the bystand- ers, waving listlessly at another young man who departed shortly afterwards.

'She went after the woman who wounded the victims,' Sutton said. 'I've tried her mobile, but she's not answering.'

'We'd better organise a search party. The fugitive is probably armed.'

'People say she wasn't, at least not any more. What about the knocking shop?'

Heck raised an eyebrow. 'Forgotten the procedure, Morrie? Search it from top to bottom. There are usually drugs and weapons in these places. This time we might get lucky and find something that'll incriminate the fuckers who run the dumps.'

'One of the women said she was from Albania. I think the wounded men were too – they don't look English – but I can't get confirmation.'

'Albanians, eh? Surprise, surprise.' Clan-based criminal organi- sations from that country had spread all over England, controlling prostitution and moving into the drugs trade. There had already been some vicious fights with long-established Newcastle gangs. 'If they're pimps or heavies, they won't open their mouths.'

Paramedics had removed the prone figure from the thresh- old, as well as another man who'd been found unconscious with a punctured kidney at the bottom of the stairs leading to the second floor. Both were alive but urgently needed surgery. The traffic-light boy had seen another man stagger off down the street with a piece of cutlery in his head. A couple of WPCs were looking after the five working girls, none of whom could speak much English. Social services and the Border Agency had been informed, but would take their time to show up on the Sunday night before a bank holiday.

'I can squeeze the women,' Morrie Sutton said. 'Get them to talk.'

'Talk?' Heck said, with a laugh. 'Know much Albanian, do you? Even if they speak English, they'll pretend they don't. Then a lawyer in a sharp suit will turn up and bail them out. Unless the girls identify the men, we won't be able to prove the scumbags were even involved with the place. You know how scared they'll be of saying anything. And none of the customers is going to talk voluntarily.'

'What if we find an interpreter?' Sutton asked.

'A lot of them speak Italian.'

Heck turned on his heel. 'Joni,' he said. 'DI Pax. Glad to see you're still in one piece.'

'I lost her,' Joni said, her breathing regular.

'Didn't you hear your phone?' Sutton demanded.

'I was undertaking a high-speed pursuit, Morrie.'

'Not high-speed enough.'

'That'll do,' Heck said. 'What was that about Albanians speaking Italian?'

'They get Italian TV from across the Adriatic,' Joni replied. 'And there's been a lot of trade between the countries since the end of communism.'

'A lot of illegal immigrants too,' Sutton added.

Joni looked at him. 'And legal ones, would you believe? I spent four months in Bari. Plenty of Albanians actually get their papers sorted and work in the city.'

'So you think you'll be able to get something out of the girls?' Heck asked.

'I can try. How many are there?'

'Five,' Sutton said. 'Plus the one you let get away.'

'Shut up, Morrie,' Heck ordered. 'All right, we need to make sure social services and the UKBA keep them in the vicinity. In the meantime, we'll take them into custody overnight so you can talk to them.'

'Em, hang on, sir,' Sutton said. 'This is a Corham MCU case.'

'Jesus, Morrie, no one in your team can speak Italian, right?'

'Don't think so,' the DI muttered.

'While DI Pax has an Oxford degree in the language. With French, if memory serves. What's your problem?'

Morrie Sutton shook his head. 'Nothing, sir.'

'You should be thanking your colleague for her offer of help, not glowering at her.'

'I'll wait till she comes up with something useful, if you don't mind, sir.'

Heck raised his eyes to the night sky.

'I'd like to have a word with the traffic light too,' Joni said. 'He's about the only witness we've got.' She looked at the faces behind the tape and saw none she recognised. 'His mates seem to have left him in the shit.'

'I can handle that,' Sutton said.

'Do it together,' Heck said. 'Joni cuffed the boy.'

'And followed him from the town centre.'

Morrie Sutton stared at her. 'Why did you do that?'

Joni raised her shoulders.

'Women's intuition?' Sutton scoffed.

'Maybe.' Joni smiled. 'You're forgetting something.'

'And what might that be?' Heck asked. He wasn't a female-cop hater like Morrie, but he didn't like being strung along any more than the next man.

'Traffic light – his name's Nick – didn't only see the woman close up. He saw the men who came out of the house – the customers. Judging by their rapid departures, I don't think they want their names in the papers.' Joni gave Heck a more expansive smile. 'Who knows? Maybe we'll catch a town councillor or a paragon of local business who had his pants down.'

Heck exchanged glances with Sutton. Neither of them looked hugely enthusiastic about the prospect.

14

Michael Etherington had watched as his grandson stowed the bulky costume into the back of his mother's Rover. 'I hope you aren't going to do anything illegal with that.'

'Cool it, General Gramps,' Nick said. He was a handsome lad, recently eighteen and taller than his father had been, his hair raven black and, to Michael's mind, too long. 'It's a bit of fun. Remember fun?'

His grandfather, who had commanded British forces in Bosnia and Kosovo before ending up at a desk in Whitehall, didn't have it in him to be strict with the boy. Not only was he in his last year at the Abbey private school and almost ready to leave home, but he'd lost his father. Michael's only son, Alistair, had died of a heart attack fifteen months earlier. In addition, Michael's wife Christine had died a few weeks later. She'd driven into a tree. Nothing had been found wrong with the car, though there was black ice on the road so suicide could at least not be talked about. Michael had realised Christine would never recover from Alistair's death, but he couldn't be sure if she'd killed herself. Helping out Nick and his daughter-in-law, Rosie, was a way of coping – that was why he had moved in with them. They needed help, too. Alistair, a lawyer, had invested badly and lost clients because of his drinking.

'Of course he remembers fun,' Rosie Etherington said, squeezing Michael's arm. 'That's why neither of us is going anywhere near the town centre tonight. Omelette aux fines herbes and a nice Chablis will do for us.'

Nick rolled his eyes as he closed the car door. 'Fun means a lot of things, but not those.' He smiled. 'Well, maybe the Chablis.'

'One beer, all right?' Rosie said, her tone hardening slightly.

'Yes, Mum.'

'And back by midnight,' Michael added.

Nick, dressed in a grey boiler suit, clicked his heels together and saluted. At least the afternoons he'd spent in the school cadet force had taught him something.

'Yes, Gramps.' He got into the car and reversed smoothly down the drive.

They watched him head down the village's main street.

'He didn't kiss me,' Rosie said, lowering her gaze.

Michael put his arm round her thin shoulders. 'He's eighteen. Kissing his mother isn't high on his list of priorities.'

Rosie gave him a serious look. 'He was unhappy recently.'

'You have to let him go,' Michael said, remembering what he'd got up to at his grandson's age.

'Yes,' Rosie said softly. 'I suppose I do.'

They went into the former merchant's house and turned on the lights.

15

Outside the brothel, Joni said, 'Go home, sir. You need your sleep and we've got this under control.' She glanced at Morrie Sutton, who nodded reluctantly.

'I want to interview the boy,' Sutton said.

'Both of you,' Heck repeated. 'Then DI Pax can talk to the women. You've got plenty on your plate, Morrie. The house search, canvassing the neighbours – they must have known what was going on here.'

'This street's full of squats and dope dealers,' Morrie said. 'You think they'll say anything to us? Plus, the Albanians will have put the shits up them.'

Heck ignored his objections. 'You've also got to organise the search for the missing woman.'

Sutton shrugged. He knew of old that when Heck Rutherford was in this mood, there was no arguing with him. He walked over to his senior subordinate, DS Nathan Gray, and went into a huddle with him and his DCs.

'Anything you want to tell me, Joni?' Heck asked, his eyes

on hers. 'I hope you didn't let the woman go. It looks like she's responsible for three serious attacks.'

'Having been forced to work as a sex slave for God knows how long,' Joni said, in disgust. 'No, she got over a gate and was away by the time I got there. I felt I'd be more use here. I gave Nathan the location.'

'Anything else?'

Joni ran her fingers over the scar that bisected her right eyebrow. It was the result of a knife attack in Hackney when she was seventeen. The boy responsible hadn't been able to walk for two weeks. She should tell her boss that she'd left her card with the message in Italian. 'There's blood on the gate. I'll let the techies know.'

'All right,' Heck said, leaning against his Cherokee. 'Don't step on Morrie's toes any more than you have to.' He frowned. 'And don't let yourself get emotionally involved with the women. We need to keep our distance, especially as they may be illegals.' He didn't mention Maureen Hughes, but he'd had to tell Joni that he thought she'd lost her objectivity in the battered woman's case. He'd been impressed that she hadn't allowed the publicity to go to her head. If it had been Morrie Sutton, he'd still be walking around like a pigeon with its chest puffed out.

'OK, I'm for my bed,' he said, opening the door of the Jeep. 'One last thing, Joni. Why did you follow the lad in the traffic light from the town centre?'

She looked at him, then dropped her gaze. 'I don't know, sir. Hunch?'

Heck looked at her dubiously, then got into the 4×4. There was something strange about her. At first he'd thought she needed time to get used to Pofnee and the north in general but, if anything, she was getting weirder – the faraway look; the intuitive leaps that usually turned out to be on the button; the quick reactions, like her pursuit of the woman earlier. Joni Pax wasn't like any other detective he'd met. And then there was the issue of why she'd left the Met. There was no way of knowing how much the last operation she'd run still preyed on her mind.

He watched as she swung her long legs into a patrol car, then started his engine and pulled away from the scene. He was heading for bed, but he wasn't sure how much sleep he'd get. He had hunches too, though he put them down to his years of experience. The people who controlled the now defunct brothel in Burwell Street wouldn't be happy and someone would have to pay. He hoped the missing woman turned herself in to the police before the men who saw themselves as her owners found her.

Driving through the now quiet town, Heck Rutherford told himself to get a grip. Maybe Ag would wake up when he slipped into bed. Then his phone rang. It was ACC Dickie, requiring a status update – and telling him that she wanted a meeting at nine the next morning. So much for the May Day bank holiday.

16

Suzana had waited for at least ten minutes after the footsteps retreated down the street, then slipped forward and picked up the rectangular card. In the light from the street lamp beyond the gate she made out a name she could pronounce – Jo-ni Pax – under a red and blue shape, something like an old-fashioned shield. The word 'Police' was easy enough to understand – it was almost the same in Albanian. So the woman police had nearly caught her. Why hadn't she tried to get over the gate? And why had she written in Italian that she wanted to help? It must be a trick. Her captors would have friends in the police.

She knew it wouldn't be long until other police started searching. Men from Leka's clan would be on her trail too. She retreated into a crumbling building, the remnants of its roof long collapsed to the floor. She cut the soles of her feet even more on the broken stone and wood. There was very little light, but she came across an old sack and tore it up, wrapping strips of the rough material around her feet. She shivered as she stood up, her naked legs and groin covered with goose pimples. She fumbled her way round a corner and stopped dead. Ahead was a light, the smell of woodsmoke in the air. Suzana waited, then crept forward slowly, feeling gingerly with each foot before putting her weight on it. Finally she made out a motionless figure wrapped in ragged blankets on the other side of the fire's dwindling flames. She clutched about with her hand and found a length of wood she could use as a weapon. Then she made her approach.

A loud snore broke the silence. Suzana waited, but there was no movement from the man lying on his side, the light playing over a long beard and filthy hands.

She saw an almost empty plastic bottle on its side by the sleeper, the smell of raw alcohol pricking her nostrils even through the smoke. It looked like she was in luck. The man was comatose. He never stirred as she went through the shopping trolley full of plastic bags to the rear. She found a pair of trousers that fitted her when she fastened an old tie round the waist, as well as a thick shirt with holes in the armpits, a pullover and – she stifled a shout of joy – some socks and a pair of trainers big enough for her rapidly swelling feet. Deep down she found a woollen hat that she pulled low, hiding her hair beneath it completely.

As the flames died, she took out the wallet from the jacket she'd stolen from the long-haired pig with the bristly moustache. She removed a couple of notes, both with the number twenty on them. She left them by his hand, hoping they would be enough to recompense her unknowing benefactor. Then she moved on, the length of wood still in her hand, and searched for a way out. She found one behind a makeshift door, climbed over another gate and hobbled painfully into the dark.

She had taken her revenge on Leka and his vile friends, she had escaped them, she had dressed herself and she had money. Now all she had to do was find out where she was. England, but where in England? There had been a long journey in a windowless van. Could she even be in Scotland? The men wore skirts there, she had seen on Italian TV – but none of her rapists had worn those. So probably England, but far from London. After she had fed herself, she would disappear. The world was big; they would never find her.

Suzana almost dropped the police card in the gutter, but she stopped herself. It might be that she could use the officer if she had no other choice. There was no harm keeping it in the wallet. But she did drop the rapist's credit cards through an evil-smelling grating, feeling another wave of exhilaration. The man, whatever his accursed name, was now in the sewer where he belonged.

17

Joni found Morrie Sutton in the entrance hall on the ground floor of Force HQ, arguing with a well-dressed couple. The man was quite a bit older than the woman. The building had been a tannery owned by the local big shot Favon family, but now it smelled of fresh paint and new carpets. Large windows had been cut into the walls and bushes planted outside. The conversion had been shortlisted for a prize, despite the fact that a committee had imaginatively decided to call it Force Headquarters – cue endless jokes about excessive force, forced labour, force majeure, forced entry and the like. Apparently top brass had also given serious consideration to Leather House.

'… call our solicitor,' the man was saying to Morrie. The wrinkles on his face and neck suggested he was in his early sixties, but his upright bearing and broad shoulders made him look younger. The woman he had his arm round was pale, her fair hair straggly. She looked like life had become too much for her.

Joni introduced herself, getting a glare from her colleague.

'Michael Etherington,' the man said, extending a hand. 'I'm Nick's grandfather. This is his mother, Rosie.'

'I've been explaining that Nick isn't under arrest,' Sutton said impatiently. 'We just need to talk to him.'

'But he said on the phone he'd been handcuffed,' Rosie Etherington said, her eyes damp.

'Ah,' Joni said, 'that was my doing. Just a precaution. I didn't want him to leave the scene. He's a witness.'

'The lad would have stayed put if you'd asked him to,' said Michael Etherington. His tone and body language suggested he was in the habit of giving orders – in the services, Joni surmised.

'His friends didn't,' Morrie Sutton said, with a slack smile.

'Bloody cowards,' the older man said, under his breath. 'Well, may we be present?'

'That wouldn't be helpful, sir,' Joni said, with an apologetic smile. 'If you wait here, we'll arrange some coffee.'

She headed for the secure door and punched in the code. Sutton caught up with her before it closed. 'You know he was a major general?' he said.

Joni had a dim recollection from the TV. 'Was he in Yugoslavia?'

'Allied commander in Bosnia. He was on the news all the time.'

'Right.' She turned to him. 'And your reason for disliking him so vehemently is?'

'Can't stand the army, especially officers. Arrogant shits.'

Joni let that go. Morrie stank of smoke and she tried to put some space between them.

'I'm handling the interview, OK?' he said.

'Whatever you like. It's not formal, is it?'

'Nay, lass. Meaning I can squeeze his nuts all the better.'

Joni stopped and put a hand on the arm of his cheap anorak. 'Call me "lass" again and I'll remove *your* nuts, Morrie. Without an anaesthetic. Lay off the boy. He saw some bad things and we need him.'

'I'm handling it,' Sutton repeated, spots of red on his cheeks. He suspected Joni could do him serious damage, but he wasn't going to let her scare him, at least on the surface. 'I know what I'm doing.'

They went into the interview room. Only a few months in service and already it stank of sweat and something worse – a mixture of fear and deep unhappiness. Nick Etherington was sitting on the other side of a table that was bolted to the floor. He was no longer restrained and Joni was sorry to see a red weal on his right wrist. He was supporting himself on his elbows, his head bowed.

'Bring him a fizzy drink, please,' Joni said to the custody officer. 'Are you hungry?'

The young man shook his head. 'When can I go home?'

'When I've finished with you, lad,' Morrie Sutton said, taking off his anorak, then rolling up his shirt sleeves.

Joni gave Nick an encouraging smile, but didn't speak.

'So, a traffic light,' Morrie said. 'What was that about? You know how many regulations you contravened, especially with those lights that actually changed?'

'Sorry,' Nick said, his eyes narrowing. 'But it's May Sunday. Everyone dresses up. Surely you aren't going to arrest the whole of Corham.'

Joni twitched her head. Giving Sutton lip was not a good idea.

'Don't try that on with me, boy,' the DI said, his rheumy eyes locked on Nick's. He broke away when the constable came in and put a can of cola on the table.

'Right, what were you doing in Burwell Street?'

Nick Etherington drank thirstily before answering. 'Heading for the Brown Bull. There was a band.'

'Aye, right. You and your mates were off to the knocking shop, weren't you?'

Joni closed her eyes, but otherwise sat still.

'No, we weren't!' Nick said.

'Don't raise your voice at me.' Sutton's fist clenched and unclenched on the table.

'No, we weren't,' the young man repeated at normal volume. 'Jesus, some of our girlfriends were with us.'

Joni nodded, having seen that herself. Her colleague ignored her.

'Been to the brothel before, have you?'

'No. I didn't even know that's what it was.'

'A likely story.' Morrie Sutton leaned over the table. 'If I find your fingerprints in there, you'll be in deep shit.'

The door opened again and DS Gray came in. He whispered to his boss, who stood up immediately.

'He's all yours, DI Pax,' Sutton said and left at speed.

Wondering what had got him so excited, Joni called in the custody officer before continuing. Although it wasn't a formal interview, she didn't want any complaints from the high-powered lawyer she was sure the ex-army man would bring in.

'Listen, Nick,' she said, smoothing her hair back with her hands. 'I was watching you even before I saved you from a dousing in the river.'

'Why?' the young man asked, his brow furrowed.

'I'd never seen a mobile traffic light before,' she said, with a smile. 'I know you were only messing around and I saw the girls. One of them yours?'

He shook his head, cheeks reddening.

'Never mind. I'm sure you weren't heading into the brothel.'

'I didn't even know there were brothels in Corham.' Suddenly he looked much younger.

'Are you still at school?'

'A-levels next month.'

'Bad news. I remember what they were like.'

'Really? What did you do?'

'English, French and Maths.'

'No way. That's what I'm doing too.' He paused. 'What did you get?'

This time it was Joni who hesitated. 'Three As.'

'Fu ... sorry. I hope I manage that. I have to if I'm to get to uni.'

'Where are you aiming for?'

'Cambridge.'

'More bad news. I was at Oxford.'

'Bleurgh.'

She laughed. 'All right, let's get this over with. I'm sorry I handcuffed you, Nick, but I had to be sure at least someone would stay put.'

'You didn't catch the woman?'

Joni shook her head. 'I need you to tell me exactly what you saw.'

The young man gave some thought to that. 'For a start, you have to remember I had no peripheral vision in the box. My mate Pe—' He broke off. 'My mate let me know if there was anything I had to look out for.' He looked at her entreatingly. 'You won't make me tell on them?'

'They'll have to be interviewed, Nick. It's not a problem. None of them did anything wrong except leave you in the lurch. Your grandfather isn't very happy about that.'

'Gramps is here? Shit. I'll be grounded for months.'

Joni smiled. 'I don't think so. He struck me as a reasonable type. Is your dad not around?'

'He … he died last year.'

'Oh, I'm sorry.' Joni stretched her hand across the table and put it on his for a few seconds. 'That must be really hard.' She paused before speaking again. 'Let's get on. What did you see through the slit?'

'Well, there were people hanging around the steps of the house. Then I heard a scream – really high-pitched, like when a fox catches a rabbit. The door opened and the woman came out. She was screaming too, but hers was more like a war cry. She only had on a leather jacket. I saw her face when she crashed into me. She was scary.'

'You didn't see any weapon?'

'No. There was blood on her hand and … and her chest, but I'm sure she wasn't holding anything. Then people pulled away and I saw the guy lying inside the door.' He paused and licked his lips. 'Is he dead?'

'I don't think so, but he's in a bad way.'

'I could see the handle of a knife sticking up from his … belly. Blood everywhere…'

'All right, take a deep breath. Now, this is important. Did you see anyone else run out?'

'Well, no. I mean, most people who were near the house got moving, but I don't think they were doing anything except getting clear before the co … before your people arrived.'

'There were two other men inside who'd been injured. Did you see anyone else with a wound apart from the guy with the fork in his head?'

Nick's eyes dropped. 'With a … with a wound? No … no, I didn't.'

'Nick?' Joni's voice was harsh. 'Don't lie to me.'

The young man's eyes stayed down. 'I'm not,' he mumbled. 'I didn't see anyone like that.'

Joni knew he wasn't being straight with her, but it was better to change tack than have him clam up completely. 'All right,' she said lightly. 'One more thing. Did you see anyone you know?'

The question made him rock back in the seat. 'That I know? You mean apart from my friends?'

'Obviously apart from your friends, Nick.'

'Em, no … no, I didn't.' He looked up at her. 'Can I go now?'

Joni studied him for longer than he was comfortable with. 'I'm going to have a word with your mother and grandfather.'

That made his eyes widen. 'Don't … I …'

Joni waited, but he didn't speak again. She left the interview room and went to find DI Sutton. She was told that he and DS Gray had gone back to Burwell Street.

She considered following them there – something interesting must have been found – but she had the women to deal with. Before that, she had one last go at Nick Etherington, but he stuck to his story. She asked one of Sutton's team to take his statement and went to tell his relatives that he'd soon be out.

What she really wanted was to ask the major general to put the squeeze on the boy, but there was no point. Nick would either keep what he wasn't telling her to himself, or he'd come clean to his family. Given that they were apparently upstanding members of society, she hoped they might pass the information to her, but there wasn't much she could do if they didn't. One thing was in her favour. Michael Etherington hadn't shown the least reaction to her colour. Perhaps the general had commanded some efficient black squaddies.

In the meantime, she would tell Morrie about the men she'd seen outside the brothel: the monk with the obviously fake beard and the guy with black-and-white stripes tattooed on his gut, who had asked her earlier if she liked what she saw. They both struck her as likely regulars.

18

While her parents were out doing their thing on May Sunday, the Honourable Evelyn Favon, Evie to her friends, had spent the day in the library, as usual. The table in front of her was covered in books, many of them over two hundred years old. She put carefully cut slips of white paper between the pages and made notes on her laptop. The family's history had become her obsession.

The door at the far end of the long room opened and Cheryl came in.

'Can I get you anything, Miss?'

'No, thanks,' Evie replied, glancing up briefly.

'I'll be off for the night, then.' The dumpy middle-aged woman turned away.

Evie didn't wish her good night. Although Cheryl Reston and her husband Dan had been with the family for over a decade, Evie had always sensed antipathy from them. It was a class thing, her mother explained. Lord and Lady Favon were the Restons' employers and provided them with a cottage on the estate. It was natural for them to feel resentment – the underprivileged always did – but completely unacceptable for them to show it.

'But, Victoria,' Evie had said – since she'd left school the previous summer, she occasionally used her parents' first names, much to their disgust. 'Isn't it natural for the dispossessed to feel aggrieved? We have the Hall and thousands of acres, not to mention stocks and shares and the wealth our ancestors built up so ... assiduously, while they have our grace and favour.'

That hadn't gone down well. Although Victoria wasn't born a Favon, her father had been Bishop of Tyne Tees and she'd been sent to the best schools. She was very defensive of the family name, though her behaviour could be what the mother of one of Evie's friends described as 'erratic'. Andrew, Viscount Favon, had given Evie a talking to, but she paid no attention to him. The accident had dissipated what little trust she had in him.

Although Evie was fascinated by the story she was transcribing, she couldn't help thinking about the foggy morning the previous October. It was a week before she was due to fly to Nairobi to spend her gap year teaching in a primary school in the Ngong Hills. She had skipped down the Hall's main steps for her favourite walk around the lake. The geese were honking louder than usual, probably because the factor Dan Reston's dogs were in the vicinity. Perhaps that was why she didn't hear her father's 4×4 reversing towards her at speed until it was too late.

Evie felt no pain in her legs initially. She was more aware of the gravel that had been embedded in her scalp when she hit the ground. Then her father tried to lift her and she screamed before fainting. She woke up in the ambulance with tubes attached to her arms. Her mind was mushy and she kept thinking of the cries of the outraged geese. Again, her legs were not hurting ... nothing was hurting at all.

That state of affairs continued in Corham General, at least until the physiotherapy started. Both her legs had been broken above the knees. Fortunately the fractures were clean, but months of agony in the hospital exercise hall had scarred her mind, turning her from a happy and enthusiastic schoolgirl to a sceptical and suspicious young woman. She still needed a forearm crutch, but at least the wheelchair had been sent back to the hospital.

Her parents had reacted in different ways to the accident. Victoria had been surprisingly supportive, at least during hospital visits. When Evie finally got home, her mother was openly less involved, even complaining when the sewing room on the ground floor, which she never used, was converted to a temporary bedroom. Andrew had never apologised for running into his daughter and was unhappy when the cost of the Kenya trip was not fully refunded. The burden of care fell on Cheryl. Evie had thought that might bring them together, but she was wrong. The factor's wife, heavily built with a face twisted from permanent scowling, resented what she saw as the extra work, even though Evie had insisted on doing as much for herself as she could. There were nearly five months to go until she started her course at Exeter. She had deliberately chosen a distant university for her history and politics studies.

Apart from the toxic atmosphere in the Hall – which was nothing to do with her – there was only one problem. Going to uni meant Evie wouldn't see Nick for many months. He was planning on spending his gap year in the Far East. She wasn't sure how she was going to cope with that.

19

Heck rolled over in bed, away from Ag's warm back. It had been against his abdomen all night and the residual pain from his wound had been soothed. Then he remembered the previous night. She had been accommodating, very much so.

'Where are you going?' she said, sleepily. 'It's a holiday.'

'Got to head in,' he said, heading for the en suite bathroom. 'People got stabbed in a brothel.'

'Oh, for goodness sake,' Ag said, sitting up and ruffling her hair. She usually confined herself to pupil-friendly expressions, though she could swear like a constable when necessary. 'Can't Joni and Morrie handle that?'

'They both need careful monitoring. No, Ruth Dickie's expecting me.'

Ag sank back on the pillows. 'We were going to do something with the kids.'

'I'll try to get back in the afternoon – take them for a kickabout.'

She laughed. 'Kat'll love that.'

'She will, actually. There's nothing she likes better than sending Luke running around like a rabbit on heat.'

'Go away, you silly man,' she said, a smile on her lips.

Driving to Corham, Heck took in the mist rising from the fields. It was another cloudless day, the sun already a bright orb. Birds flitted across the road between the trees like small coils discharging energy. Heck enjoyed the trip every morning. For years he'd gone through the drab suburbs of Newcastle, the traffic thundering along until it ground to a halt in tailbacks. Corham was an efficient place. On the northern side the roads could handle the traffic even during rush hour, while the wide roads in Ironflatts that used to service the steel mill and other heavy industry were never congested now. Besides, there weren't many cars around early on the first of the May bank holidays.

He saw Assistant Chief Constable Dickie getting out of her dark green Audi as he pulled into his parking place outside Force HQ. She waited for him, her black jacket and skirt immaculate and her briefcase as full as ever. Until she spoke, she appeared to be 'Mrs Normal', her nickname – average height, weight, looks; bobbed mousy hair in an old-fashioned Alice band; a couple of unshowy rings on her left hand. Her husband – she hadn't taken his name – really *was* Mr Normal: an insurance broker in New-castle, who played golf and looked after the garden. The only thing that marked them out was that they didn't have the stand-ard two children – they didn't have any. The general feeling was that the ACC didn't do sex.

'Good morning, Heck,' she said, a faint smile on her unpainted lips. Make-up was surplus to requirements unless there was a press conference. 'Busy night.'

'Ma'am.' Although Ruth Dickie had been a WPC when Heck was already a DI, her rise had been rapid. She was a shrewd operator, good at police politics – Heck's bugbear – and hard-working. She had taken the weight off her then superiors during the early planning of Pofnee and had been rewarded with responsibility for crime across the whole force area.

'Something major go down in one of the cities?' Heck found it unlikely that she was referring only to the brothel stabbings.

'Nothing worse than usual,' she said drily.

Heck knew that could mean anything from running fights in central Newcastle to student bashing in Durham to drug-gang violence in Sunderland.

'I'm interested in the Albanian connection,' the ACC said, as they went across the entrance hall.

'Is that right?'

'They're becoming a real problem in Newcastle.' She tapped in the door code. 'We don't want them operating under our noses in Corham, especially if they're being overtly violent. That wouldn't be at all good for the Force's image.'

Heck nodded. It was all about image. If it hadn't been a holiday, the local press would have been clamouring for a statement.

'My office in five minutes,' Ruth Dickie said, as the lift doors opened. 'You and your DIs will be sufficient.'

Heck swallowed a laugh. Why couldn't the ACC use normal words like 'enough'? He knew the reason – because she wasn't normal at all, no matter how she looked. She was a woman rock-eting through the glass ceiling, the chief constable's job in her sights. He admired her and he wasn't envious. He'd rather have walked the Roman Wall in winter wearing swimming trunks than occupy the sixth-floor corner office.

'Morning, Joni,' he said, as he walked into the fourth-floor MCU suite, having taken the stairs and almost lost his breath.

DI Pax was hammering away at her keyboard. 'Sir,' she responded, without looking away from the screen. 'ACC want us?'

'How did you guess?'

Joni shrugged.

'Where's Morrie?'

'At the brothel. He and Nathan are being very secretive.'

Heck called the other DI. 'Morrie? You have a minute to get over here. The ACC's office.' He terminated the call. 'That should get him moving. In truth he's got three minutes.'

Joni went to the printer and started collating papers.

'Anything you want to tell me before we get grilled?' Heck asked, dumping his bag in his glass-walled office. There was no one else around.

'Nothing that won't wait, sir.'

'Thanks a lot. Let's go then.' He looked at her. 'Aren't you knackered?'

'It's not the first time I've pulled an all-nighter.' Joni's face softened. 'Thanks for the concern, though.' She followed him to the stairs, knowing his habit of avoiding the lifts. 'There is one thing.'

Heck looked over his shoulder.

'The brothel. It's owned by a company based in Liberia.'

He groaned.

20

Suzana watched the birds swarm over the park. They were like the shoals of fish she had once seen on Italian TV, circling and clustering in a dance only they could understand. She had spent the rest of the night behind the thick bushes that lined a park by a river. In the early morning she had gone through the nearby rubbish bins, finding half-eaten meat and bread and unfinished bottles – she ignored the beer and drank water and juice. Then, clutching her bent legs in her arms and leaning against the wall behind the bushes, she managed to sleep; not deeply and only in short bursts, but enough to refresh her. The wound in her chest was painful, as were her feet. She had taken off the trainers and socks and unwrapped the bandages, pouring water from a bottle she had saved over the lacerated soles. She didn't know if it would be enough to fend off infection, but it was all she could do. When it got dark, she would see if she could find an unoc-cupied house to break into – there would be food and hot water, maybe even ointment and clean dressings. She wasn't going near any hospital. Leka and his stinking friends would be there if she hadn't killed them; she knew how unlikely it was that all three were dead. Even if they were, others would come after her. The clan could never allow a woman to get the better of it.

She kept still as children came close, a ball crashing through the foliage. Fortunately the clothes she'd stolen weren't brightly coloured and she wasn't seen. Eventually the shouts and screams grew distant. Suzana was thinking about the kids in her village. They had nothing, certainly not the sturdy shoes and good quality clothes these ones wore. They used the heads of hens that had been slaughtered instead of balls, the boys with their heads shaven against lice and the girls never allowed far from their mothers or elder sisters; until they became old enough to go the way of many sisters, the way that led abroad to the worst kind of slavery. She wished she still had a weapon. That would be her priority when she found a house: a knife she could use on them when they came for her, then draw quickly across her own throat.

As the day passed, she found that sleep evaded her. She was sitting on a sheet from one of the newspapers she had taken from a bin. The print was faded and the photographs blurred. The word 'Corham' appeared in the title and in many other places. Was that the name of the place she had been living in for months? Cor-ham. She pronounced the word under her breath, wondering if she was saying it correctly. Cor-ham.

Then she looked closer. There was a photograph of two women coming out of a house, one of them short and white, the other tall and dark-skinned. Suzana had never seen a black person in the flesh until she was in the airport in London. This woman looked powerful, as if she was a queen, but she was different. Even though Suzana would have nothing in common with her, she felt a strange connection. She peered at the words underneath. The ones that began with capital letters were probably names. Ma-ur-een Hug-hes, she voiced. Jo-ni Pax. This was the police officer who had left the card. Pax was like Albanian 'paqe'. Was that what the name meant? 'Peace'? Suzana laughed silently. Peace was the opposite of what she had experienced in this land.

She fumbled in her new clothes for the wallet and took out the rectangle of card. There was a telephone number and an address under Jo-ni Pax's name, but she wasn't going to visit any police station. Free was what she was now, free until death. Still, this Joni woman looked capable. Maybe she really could protect her...

Suzana slapped her cheek. That was weakness. Only she could save herself. She had to plan, she had to steal, she had to be forever on the watch for Leka's people and those who would betray her to them, she had to stay in the shadows. No police-woman, especially not a dark goddess, could help her.

Suzana put the card back in the stolen wallet and tried to understand why Jo-ni Pax was in the newspaper. She understood some words that were similar to her own language and to Italian, but not enough to make sense of the story. If Jo-ni Pax was anything like the Albanian police, she would be taking money from criminals. Ma-ur-een Hug-hes probably thought she had been helped by her, but she would be just another victim. The police helped no one but themselves.

When the sun sank and darkness gathered, mist rising from the river as it did in the mountains where she had grown up, Suzana crawled carefully out of the bushes, having waited until the last people with dogs had left. Then she slipped away, anonymous, no longer a slave but fully committed to remaining free. And to revenge.

21

ACC Crime Ruth Dickie leant against the window ledge and looked at the three officers sitting on the other side of her desk. She liked to have height advantage, even though she was no more than five foot five in her flat shoes.

'Let me recap. One of the men attacked in the brothel is dead from the head injuries he suffered. Another, who was stabbed, is recovering from surgery and out of danger. Predictably, he hasn't said a word. There's been no sign of the man who walked down the street with what was described as a piece of cutlery sticking out of his head. Apart from confirming they're from Albania, none of the women has said anything material to the investigation.' The ACC looked at Joni.

'Correct, ma'am. They're terrified for their families back home.'

'They didn't even give you the missing woman's name?'

Joni shook her head. 'They say they didn't know it. It may be true. They don't seem to know each other. The pimps probably kept them in separate rooms.'

'Vile but not unheard of,' Ruth Dickie said. 'As for you, DI Sutton, you found a safe at the house in Burwell Street. Unfortunately, raising a magistrate has been a slow process, but we should have it open in the afternoon.'

'Yes, ma'am,' Morrie confirmed, looking pleased with himself.

'But canvassing of the vicinity has been singularly unproductive.'

Heck struggled not to smile. Ruth Dickie's standard operating procedure was to skewer subordinates when they thought the pressure was off.

'Well, the people down there aren't exactly our biggest fans. A lot of the men would have been customers of the knocking shop. We did find one old lady willing to talk, ma'am.'

'The witness who said the man had a fork in his head because she recognised the distinctive handle? The forked man.' If the ACC was proud of her witticism, she didn't show it. 'She also told you that a very tall person in a red hat was outside the house in question.'

This time Heck had to raise a hand to his mouth.

'Yeah, she got confused by the lad dressed as a traffic light.'

Ruth Dickie turned her gaze back to Joni. 'Who told you little of substance, DI Pax.'

'I'm going to do a follow-up interview, ma'am.'

'No, you're not,' Morrie Sutton expostulated. 'This is my case.'

The ACC had no interest in turf wars. 'DCI Rutherford?'

'DI Sutton left the interview before it got going, so DI Pax will continue for the sake of consistency.'

'Thank you. Your priorities as of now are what?'

'Joni ... DI Pax will see if she can get anything out of the man in hospital when he's fit to talk.' Heck glanced at Morrie. 'While DI Sutton will act on what is found in the safe, as well as coordinate the SOCOs' reports.'

Ruth Dickie nodded. 'And the house? It's all very well it being owned by this Liberian company, but someone local must be paying the bills.'

'DI Sutton's team will look at that, ma'am,' Heck confirmed.

'Very well. I'll see you at the morning briefing tomorrow.'

Joni stood up and looked at the ACC. 'Pardon me, ma'am, but what about the women?'

Ruth Dickie showed little interest in the question. 'Didn't you say they were being looked after in a hostel until the Border Agency's checks are completed?'

'Yes, but it's not secure. They've been sexually abused for who knows how long, but at the same time they don't want to antagonise the men who brought them here. I'm worried they'll slip away.'

'We don't have the resources to babysit them, DI Pax. Unless you want to volunteer.'

'Maybe I will, ma'am,' Joni said, glancing at Heck. 'But there's someone else at risk.'

'I presume you mean the woman who murdered one man, put another in hospital and forked another.' This time the ACC did smile, but there was little sign of amusement. 'I should have thought the citizens of Corham are the ones at risk. Her description has been circulated, has it not, DI Sutton?'

Morrie nodded, giving Joni a sly smile. 'Yes, ma'am. We'll catch the ... we'll catch her soon enough.'

'That will be all,' Ruth Dickie said, looking at Joni doubtfully. Displays of emotion were not to her taste.

<hr />

22

'It's OK, Nick,' his mother said, handing him a plate of bacon, sausage and scrambled eggs. 'You didn't do anything wrong.'

Michael was already halfway through his breakfast. 'That's right, lad. But if I get my hands on those so-called friends of yours, they'll be sorry.'

His grandson looked at him blankly. 'Leave them alone. Pete hung around for a bit. Anyway, I'd have done the same.'

'I sincerely hope not. Friends are the most important thing in life. I still have...' He broke off when he saw his daughter-in-law's face. 'Come on, eat up. We don't want to be late for the fishing.'

'Not coming,' Nick said, pushing his plate across the table and getting up.

'Wait, darling,' his mother said, holding on to his arm as he tried to leave the kitchen. 'We have to talk about this.'

'About what?' Nick said, pulling gently away and walking out. They heard his footsteps on the stairs.

'I don't understand,' Rosie said, her eyes damp. 'He's never been like this before. Not even when ... when Alistair died.'

'He saw some bad stuff last night,' Michael said. 'And he should never have been handcuffed, let alone interrogated. I thought that black woman had her head screwed on, but now I'm not so sure.'

Rosie sat down and stared at her son's untouched food.

'Don't worry,' her father-in-law said. 'I'll go and have a chat with him when he's cooled down. You know what it is?'

'No ... oh, you mean girl trouble.'

Michael nodded. 'You know, I can understand the girls in his party clearing off, but his male friends shouldn't have run.'

'They're just kids,' Rosie said softly. 'Don't judge them as if they were in the army.'

The major general didn't respond. His daughter-in-law still hadn't got over the loss of Alistair, for all his faults, and letting go of Nick was proving difficult for her. He hated to imagine how she'd be when Nick went to the Far East. He found himself thinking about the female detective with the curious name. Pax. Good name for a law keeper. She reminded him of a sergeant who'd served in his communications unit in Bosnia. Mavis Westron. He'd never touched her – he didn't do that kind of thing with female personnel – but there was an aura about her, a strange mixture of 'come hither' and 'do so and I'll break your fingers'. DI Pax had something similar.

'I'll take him a coffee,' Michael said. He went to the cafetière on the sideboard, poured himself one too and put the mugs on a tray.

He paused outside his grandson's door. Usually there was ear-shattering music coming from it, but today he could hear the birdsong in the meadow behind the house. He knocked and turned the handle. To his surprise, the door was locked.

'Nick? I've brought you a coffee. Come on, chap. I won't bite.'

There was a pause and then the key clicked. The door still didn't open. Michael turned the handle, balancing the tray on his other hand. Nick was sitting with his arms round his drawn-up legs in the far corner of his bed.

'I don't want anything to drink, Gramps,' he said fiercely.

Michael raised his shoulders. 'I'm not going to pour it down your throat.' He smiled. 'Though I could if I wanted to.' That didn't raise even the ghost of a smile. They had always had a tactile relationship, the older man hugging his grandson and ruffling his hair. They still occasionally played touch rugby in the back garden, but it didn't look like that wouldn't be happening today.

'Spit it out, then, lad. Problem shared and all that.'

Nick remained silent.

'Your mum thinks it's girl trouble.'

'Why? What have you told her?'

Michael raised a hand. 'Nothing.'

Nick stared at him, his eyes bloodshot. He obviously hadn't slept much. 'You promised you wouldn't, Gramps. You know it'll upset her.'

'I won't. But you have to promise me something in return.'

'What?'

'Forget her. You need to concentrate on your exams. Then it won't be long till you're backpacking your way across the other side of the world.'

Nick blinked and ran his forearm across his eyes. 'I can't, Gramps,' he said hoarsely. 'I can't … I love her.'

The major general smiled. 'Everyone has that problem at your age. But you have to prioritise.'

'You know she's helping me with my English revision.'

Michael nodded. 'Evie's a great girl. But think about it. You won't see her for nearly a year. Then, if everything goes to plan, you'll be at Cambridge and she'll be ... where is it she's going?'

'Exeter.'

The major general laughed. 'As far away as she can get from her crazy parents.'

'That's what she says.' Nick looked up at him. 'Why are the Favons like that?'

'It's a long story and one for another day. Come on. The fish will be harder to hook the higher the sun gets.'

'Sorry, Gramps, I'm not coming.' Then Nick Etherington, captain of rugby and cricket, head of house and governors' prizewinner, pulled the covers over his head.

<><><><><><><><><><><><><><><><><><><><><><><><><><><><><><><><><><><><>

23

Joni got home in the late afternoon. She kicked off her boots and looked out at the birds in the garden behind the house. It had been an eighteenth-century merchant's home, with tiny servants' rooms in the attic and a dim basement with barred windows. Developers had bought the building when the last member of the family died ten years back and split it into six apartments. Joni's was one of two on the first floor. It had a spacious living area, a reasonably sized bedroom, and functional kitchen and bathroom. Her mother had told her she could get a detached cottage where she lived further north for half the rent, but Joni didn't listen. She needed to be in the town, even if it was tiny compared with London. The countryside still made her nervous.

A couple of female blackbirds were picking at the shared

lawn, tchook-tchooking as they went. She liked the birds. The females lacked the males' show-off yellow beaks and the feathers, especially on their chests, were mottled brown. They were like her – less dark and seemingly disconnected from their male counterparts. Joni had never felt much in common with black people of either sex. She didn't like black music of any kind, sticking resolutely to the classical recordings she had first heard on cassettes borrowed from the public library. She didn't like black dance, black literature or black cooking. A friend at Oxford told her she was in denial about her racial heritage. Joni brushed that off. She was in touch with her white heritage and that was enough.

DCI Rutherford had told her to take the rest of the day off, almost marching her out of Force HQ when he left. She played along because she needed a shower and change of clothes. There was plenty she still had to do, not least since the injured Albanian had been cleared to talk by the doctors. Putting Brahms's second symphony on as loud as was feasible – her neighbours above were retired doctors with the hearing of bats – she stood under the hot water for five minutes, before dousing herself with cold for another three. As usual, that concentrated her mind.

Morrie Sutton had got his warrant and gone off with DI Gray and a locksmith to open the safe in the basement of the Burwell Street brothel. Although none of the women had made a complaint, Joni had insisted social services have them examined by a doctor. No one was in any doubt that they'd been subjected to prolonged sexual abuse and their lack of possessions suggested they were hardly there by choice. Morrie hadn't told her what had been found in the safe, saying only that he'd meet her at the hospital later. The man was a dick, but she had to work with him. At least Nick Etherington lived outside Corham and she'd been given responsibility for him, though re-interviewing him would have to wait until he finished school tomorrow.

As she dried herself, Joni thought of the Albanian women. She had gone to the hostel and spoken to them again, telling them to stay there. They looked at each other, and exchanged sentences in their own language. Only two of them spoke Italian, saying the others came from Kosovo.

'We will look after you,' Joni said, even though she had no idea what social services and the UKBA would decide. 'Don't go back to the people who made you do that terrible work.'

There was more chatter in the language she couldn't understand.

'We have stay here?' one of them asked, in Italian. She was thin and physically underdeveloped – a girl still. 'We go?'

'Not yet,' Joni replied, with a sigh. Maybe moving the focus away from them would bear fruit. 'The other woman. Is there nothing you can tell me about her?'

The thin girl translated for the others, one of whom spoke at some length.

'OK, we say this. Her name Suzana. This woman here, she in room below. She many times hear screaming from woman. Much – how say? – banging on floor. She fight with man Leka.'

The others hissed at her. Joni looked as impassive as she could. It was the first time a male name had been mentioned.

'He kept you in the house?' she asked, her voice low.

'Yes, Leka bad,' her interlocutor said, ignoring the objections. 'He ... he hurt us, he beat us if not make men happy.' She paused, staring at Joni. 'This Suzana, she always fight. We ... we frightened.' She let out a sob.

Joni squeezed her knee, wondering if Leka was the dead man. The women had been given ill-fitting but clean clothes and the thin one was wearing faded jeans. 'Listen to me. You never have to work for this man or his friends again. You are safe now.'

The young woman shook her head slowly. 'We never safe. We work till old and ugly.'

Nothing more had been said, but Joni felt she'd established a link, albeit an indirect one, with the fugitive woman Suzana. If she'd found Joni's card, they knew each other's names. Suddenly they had become closer.

24

'Where the fuck's Gaz?'

'Dunno, Kylie. He isn't answering his phone.'

'I fuckin' know that, Pumpkinhead.'

'I called his mother. She told me he wasn't there and if I saw him to say she's thrown out his sweaty footie kit.'

'Jesus, he won't like that.'

'Then she told me to fuck off.'

'Get that a lot, don't you?'

'Fuck off.'

'Ha ha. You call the others?'

'Aye. Hot Rod was still asleep.'

'Bet he told you to fuck off too.'

'Aye. Jackie was shagging his lass. He told me to fuck off an' all.'

'What about Daryll?'

'He didn't tell me to fuck off.'

'That must have been nice. Anything else?'

'Nah. He was getting ready to go for a run.'

'He's too fucking healthy, that lad. So no one's got a clue then?'

'Including you.'

'Fuck off.'

'See you in the Grapes later?'

'Aye. Gaz'll probably turn up with some tart.'

'Aye. Got any pills?'

'I told you last night, those things'll mess your head up even more.'

'Aye. So have you?'

'Aye.'

'Good.'

'Fuck off.'

25

Morrie Sutton and Nathan Gray were waiting for Joni on the third floor of Corham General.

'What is it?' she asked.

'Nothing,' DS Gray said quickly. He was fair-haired and blue-eyed with a reputation as a skirt chaser, though he'd never had the nerve to try anything with Joni.

'What do you think about the fact that this is now a murder case?' DI Sutton said, smiling slackly. '*My* murder case.'

Joni eyed him with distaste. 'You've got even more reason to go after the woman who carried out the attacks. Despite the fact that she'd have been forced into sex slavery and was probably defending herself.'

The two male detectives avoided her gaze. She'd heard Gray refer to her as 'Pam' rather than the more common 'Jackie', but that didn't bother her. Pam Grier had done serious damage to numerous men in her movies, not that Joni enjoyed them.

'Are you going to tell me what you found in the safe?'

DI Sutton nodded. 'Passports for all the girls, including the missing one – Suzana Noli is her name. They all came in legally through Heathrow last October. The guy who died was called Leka Asllani. I asked DC Andrews to run him and the rest of them through HOLMES and the other digital databases.'

'What are the other women's names?' Joni asked.

They stared at her.

'I'm going to talk to them again. Can I have copies of the passport pages with their photos so I can match them to their names?'

Sutton nodded without enthusiasm. 'In the meantime, you and I need to talk to the surviving pimp.' He handed her an open passport in a clear plastic bag. 'Blerim Dost – Jesus, these people have crazy names. Born in some godforsaken hole called Bajram, 19 November 1976. Like all of them, he's got a ninety-day visitor's visa that expired in January. He probably has documentation in other names – most of the pimps and hard men do – but it wasn't in the house.'

Joni stepped back as a nurse hurried down the corridor. 'What else did you find?'

Morrie Sutton grinned. 'Over ten grand in well-used notes and a load of credit cards that are probably clones.'

Joni looked at the two of them impatiently. 'I can tell there was more.'

Nathan Gray held up another plastic bag, this one containing small sachets of white powder.'

'There was over a kilo of this. The rest's at the lab, though there's a skeleton staff till tomorrow. Cocaine, and it's pretty heavily cut.'

Joni decided against asking how he'd ascertained that. Gray didn't give the impression of being an innocent when it came to drugs.

DI Sutton took the bag from him. 'Oh, and there were three sets of knuckle dusters, all encrusted with blood, two combat knives and … what else, Nate?'

The DS grinned. 'Three Sig P239 9mm semi-automatic pistols and twenty-four full eight-round clips. The lab will check them for prints and draw up ballistic profiles.'

Joni knew that Nathan Gray was a guns freak who spent his summer holidays in countries where pistol shooting was legal. That didn't mean she was going to encourage him. She'd seen what guns could do in London. One of the big advantages of working for Pofnee was that she hadn't come up against firearms. Until now.

'See if you can borrow a photocopier and run off DI Pax's copies of the hookers' passports, lad.' Morrie Sutton felt the intensity of Joni's gaze. 'What? That's what they are.'

'Sex slaves is a more accurate term. All right, how do you want to play this?'

'Simple. I ask a question, you translate it, then you translate the scumbag's answer. If there is one, which I'm not holding my breath for.'

'Sure you don't want a fag first?' Joni asked. 'Good, because I'm pressed for time.' She had no intention of acting as Morrie's interpreter. How was he to know what she said to the Albanian? 'You brought the coke to loosen his tongue, I presume.'

Sutton nodded, turning away.

'I presume DCI Rutherford knows about these developments,' Joni called after him.

'Aye, he does. Wouldn't do to keep the senior investigating officer in the dark, would it, lass?'

Joni went after him, biting her tongue. He was nothing compared with the worst of the Met's male officers, but he still irritated her. Which, of course, was exactly what he wanted.

26

Michael Etherington's fishing trip was a waste of time. The sun brightened even more quickly than he expected and he gave up at midday. He went first to his own house to drop off his fishing tackle. It was a couple of miles west of the one he'd shared with Rosie and Nick after his son and wife died. He told himself he was doing that to support his daughter-in-law and grandson, but he knew that was only part of the story. The fact was, he missed Christine badly and didn't like spending the night in the house they'd shared. It had been his refuge and he thought of it daily when he was on active duty abroad; his wife too.

Rosie was preparing lunch. She gave him a sad smile. 'Nick still hasn't come down.'

He touched her shoulder. It was fleshless like much of her body. She'd always been slim, but since Alistair's death she'd become a wraith. The curious thing was she'd never given the impression that she cared much for his son, especially not when the drink took him over. She was an unfathomable woman.

'I'll go and talk to him.'

Nick was still under the covers.

'Bloody farce,' Michael said. 'You were right not to come. Not a bite all morning.' He sat down on the bed. 'Tell you what. How about we go up to Favon Hall in the afternoon. You can drive – you need the practice. We'll put your bike in the back so you can come back under your own steam. I don't want to hang around like a wallflower.'

Nick's head appeared. 'Thanks, Gramps. I'll call Evie.'

Michael winked. 'Why not make it a surprise? In my experience women like surprises.'

'OK.' Nick smiled tentatively. 'She never goes out anyway.'

The trip north was smooth enough. Nick was a decent driver but, to his embarrassment, had failed his test six months earlier. He was calm enough and his reactions were good. According to the examiner, he had pulled out twice without checking his mirror. Michael had been surprised by that, as well as concerned. Did his grandson's usually imperturbable exterior conceal roiling depths like those that had done for Alistair?

'Well done, lad' he said, as Nick turned into the gate of the Favon estate. A long, tree-lined drive led to the Hall. 'Smooth as … I don't know what.'

'An attack by Julius Caesar?'

Michael laughed. Clearly the prospect of seeing Evie had restored the boy's spirits. He looked at the buildings ahead.

Favon Hall had been built by the first lord in the 1760s. It was a rather ugly Palladian block. Behind it rose an older building, a medieval tower that had often been besieged by Scottish raiders under the original owners. The last scion of that family, an unmarried twenty-year-old, had been killed at Culloden, enabling the newly ennobled Favon to buy the tower and a large area of surrounding land, both arable and moor, at a bargain price.

Nick pulled up by the wide staircase that led to the main entrance, beside a black Mazda sports car.

'Looks like Victoria's home,' Michael said. 'I'll come in for a word.'

Nick was already out of the door, bag of books in his hand. There was no doubt he was passionate about the girl. Michael followed him, happy that his grandson was experiencing love but worried about the young people's future together. And they were very young…

Lady Favon answered the door herself.

'Nicholas!' she said, her meticulously painted red lips parting in a smile that was more than welcoming. 'What a lovely surprise! I'm so pleased to see you.' She looked past him. 'Hello, Michael. Babysitting?'

'Good afternoon, Victoria,' the major general said coolly, running his eye over the viscountess. She was dressed in a well-cut white blouse and a black skirt that hung just above the knee. As ever, her heels were high and her legs sheathed in black stockings or tights, he couldn't tell the difference. Knowing Victoria, he'd bet on the former. 'Nick would like to do some revision with Evie.'

'Oh, never mind her,' Victoria said, smoothing back strands of blonde hair. 'She's got her nose in the family secrets as usual. Come and sit down for a minute, the pair of you. I haven't had two good-looking men in the drawing room for weeks.'

Nick gave his grandfather a reluctant look and then followed him and their hostess across the black-and-white tiled floor. Portraits of Andrew Favon's ancestors hung in the hall and up the marble staircase, their faces bland but their eyes piercing and acquisitive.

Victoria opened the double doors that led into a spacious room with French windows and surprisingly chintzy decor. The furniture was a mixture of faded heirlooms and incongruous modern additions.

'Here, Nicholas,' Lady Favon said, sitting on a floral-covered settee and patting the cushion next to her. 'Tell me what you've been up to.'

Michael watched from across the low table as Victoria held her gaze on his grandson. Although she must have been forty now, she was still a striking woman – if anything, even more attractive than when she was younger. Her figure was stunning.

'Nothing much,' he muttered.

'What did you get up to last night?' Victoria asked, lighting a cigarette with deft movements.

The question brought red patches to Nick's cheeks. 'Well, I…'

'He dressed up like a traffic light,' Michael said, in attempt to distract the siren.

'Gramps,' Nick complained.

Lady Favon laughed. 'Don't worry,' she said, giving the older man a conspiratorial look. 'I'm sure we've all done much worse.'

I'm sure *you* have, Michael thought. Victoria's reputation was…

'Nick!' Evie came through the open doors faster than someone using an arm crutch would be expected to do. Tall, slim and with short brown hair, she was attractive, but not in her mother's class. She sat down beside the young man and kissed him on the cheek. 'What a lovely surprise!'

Michael couldn't suppress a smile. Victoria looked put out as the youngsters started to talk to each other in low voices.

'We're going to the library,' Evie said, standing up in a practised move that still made her frown. 'I've found the most amazing story.'

'I'm sure,' Victoria said icily. 'Have … fun.' Her eyes were fixed on Nick as the pair headed away.

'Andrew not around?' Michael said, breaking the silence that ensued.

'What? Oh, he's out on the moors with Dan Reston. Something to do with sheep.'

Michael stood up. 'I'll be off then. Nick's coming home on his bike. I'll leave it by the steps.'

Victoria Favon nodded, the smile returning to her lips.

27

'No more than twenty minutes, please,' the female doctor said.

Morrie Sutton brushed past her into the private room. A heavily built constable was posted outside on an inadequate chair.

'Look at this piece of shit,' Sutton said.

Joni took in the patient, tubes leading to him from drips and from him to transparent bags hooked on the side of his bed, one half-full of dark urine and the other collecting bright blood. The Albanian was small, the skin on his face tight, but his eyes were shiny and malevolent. She felt a frisson run up her spine. He hadn't been secured to the bed as the doctors said he was in a weakened state post-surgery. Besides, he hadn't yet been charged, given the reluctance of the women from the brothel to incriminate him.

DI Sutton held up the bag of drugs. 'What have you got to say about this, you arsehole?'

If Blerim Dost understood English, he kept it to himself. His eyes moved to Joni and she read the race hatred in them. Taking a deep breath, she opened her notebook.

'I think we'd better do this properly, Morrie,' she said. 'Shall I ask him to confirm his name?'

'Oh, all right.'

Joni spoke in Italian. The Albanian listened, but didn't respond. Sure that he understood, she motioned Sutton over and took the bag containing the open passport.

'Mr Dost,' she said, 'this proves your identity. Or at least the one you used to enter the country. Your visa has now expired.'

Nothing – not even a blink.

'Evidence we have found suggests you've been involved in operating a brothel.'

The cold grey eyes stayed on her, but the patient didn't speak.

'Tell him about his pal,' Morrie said.

Joni nodded but did not immediately comply. First she asked

Dost what he had to say about the women in the house. When he kept silent, she asked who had attacked him and why. Then she took the rest of the material from her colleague. The sample of drugs and photographs of the weapons found in the safe and the piles of bank notes were held up in front of him. Still no reaction.

Joni smiled to put him at ease, then leaned closer. 'Leka Asllani,' she said. 'I'm sorry to tell you that he died from the wounds he received.'

That did elicit a response. The Albanian's eyes opened wide, but still he remained silent.

'Tell him I'm going to rip the tube from his cock and wrap it round his neck if he doesn't talk!' Morrie yelled.

Blerim Dost was way ahead of him. He pulled the bag of urine off the bedstead and looped the catheter tube round Joni's neck, dragging her closer as he tightened it. Urine dripped on to her blouse.

'I kill her,' he said in English. 'If you not sit over there, I stop her breathing.'

Sutton took a few steps backwards, staring at Joni as she struggled for air. The Albanian may have been slight, but he was strong. Although there was some give in the tube, he reduced that by threading it over and under his fingers.

'Now, black bitch, you stand up.' Dost clenched his teeth as Joni complied, the stitches in the wound in his abdomen straining. 'We go to table there.'

Joni looked out of the corner of her eye. She could see a stainless steel tray with dressings, bandages and a pair of pointed scissors on it. The latter was what her captor was after. The tube was hard for him to handle, especially in motion, but the scissors would be a lot easier, enabling him to threaten her with instant death if he held them to her jugular. She had no doubt he would.

So she moved her left shoulder slightly, let the muscles across her body go slack – earning herself a gasp of air as Dost involuntarily released the pressure on her throat – and threw him over her shoulder. It was the first time since the stabbings and subsequent operations that she'd dared to try a judo move – the tackle on Nick Etherington on the riverbank was much less of a strain. The Albanian screamed as the catheter was ripped from his penis, urine spraying in all directions.

'Jesus Christ!' Sutton said, as Joni cuffed the Albanian to the bed, leaving him on the floor.

She unwound the tube from her neck and stood up. 'You'd better get the doctor,' she said. She squatted down by Dost, who was now whimpering, his free hand over his groin. 'You like hurting women, don't you?' she said. 'Now two of us have shown you what we can do. Wait till you meet a woman called Dickie.'

Her attacker stared blankly at the wall.

'This is all going to get official – lawyers, recorded interviews, jail. You have very little time to talk freely.' She loomed over his face. 'Who's your boss? He's in Newcastle, isn't he? Tell me his name and I'll do what I can for you.'

Blerim Dost looked back at her and then laughed, before grimacing in pain. Blood dripped steadily from the dressings on his abdomen.

28

Suzana had been waiting in the bushes outside the house for nearly two hours – she knew that from the chimes of the clock on a nearby church tower. It had been seven o'clock when she got there, flitting down the streets like a ghost and standing behind the equally spaced trees when people approached. There weren't many as the evening was surprisingly cold. The houses were joined together in pairs but large, light flooding from front rooms with wide windows. People in nice clothes were watching television, eating, drinking – one elderly couple was dancing.

There were rich people's cars parked on the street and in driveways, except by the house she had chosen. It showed no lights, apart from a small flashing one on a box between the first floor windows. Suzana had seen those on the clan leaders' homes in Tirana while they were waiting to be flown to London. If she tried to get in, alarm bells would ring.

That didn't put her off. She went down a passage at the side of the house in a crouch. There was a wooden gate, but she was agile enough to get over it in one bound. She found herself in a garden surrounded by trees and tall bushes, an expanse of grass in the middle. At the rear was a small building made of wood. She raised her eyes and checked the windows of the house. She had been hoping that someone might have forgotten to close one. She was out of luck. Everything was secure and there was another box with a flashing light on the rear wall. But at least there were no people around. The wooden outbuilding beyond the grass was her only hope. Did they keep chickens or rabbits there? She hoped they did – she would tear them apart with her bare hands, so great was her hunger. But she realised as she got closer that this was no animal shed.

She looked in the window. There was some light from the house next door and she made out a desk, a high-backed leather chair and, behind them, a low bed. There was also what looked like a small refrigerator. There were plastic boxes on shelves above it and – could it be true? – tins of food. Heart pounding, Suzana went to the door at the side of the building and examined the door. It was secured by a padlock. Again, she wished she'd had time to pull the knife from the pig's belly. Dropping to her knees, she felt around for a stone or a piece of metal. This time she was lucky. Round the corner her hand fell on an old screwdriver. A minute later she was in the shed.

Or rather, in paradise. There was a tin opener on the shelf and soon she was gorging herself on fish and beans, gulping down cold soup, cramming biscuits from one of the plastic boxes into her mouth. She had no idea how long she ate for, but eventually she sat back against the wall, panting. She closed her eyes and sleep took her, deep and drowning, into scenes from the last twenty-four hours – the soft stab of the fork in Leka's back and the crashes as he went down the stairs, head bouncing against the floor and wall; the split-second of terror in the other man's eyes before she planted the fork in his forehead; the feel of the last bastard's chest against her head as she stuck him with the knife; then the screaming, her own and others', the strange traffic-light person in the road, the slap of her bare feet on the asphalt, and the pounding of her pursuer's boots.

Suzana woke with a start and took a few seconds to work out where she was. Remembering, she raised her head above the bottom of the window frame. There were still no lights in the house beyond the grass. The neighbours were having a party, music blaring and the lights brighter than they had been. It seemed she was still safe. She looked around the wooden hut. It was like no outhouse she had ever seen. The ones in her village had been basic, walls unplastered, floors earthen and windows without glass. This place was like a second home – but why have one so close to the larger building?

Opening the long drawer under the surface of the desk, Suzana found a laptop computer. It was of no use to her, she had never learned how to use the machines. Some of the men who paid for her had them in their bags. She considered stealing it, but didn't want the trouble of finding a buyer – one who would remember the woman in ill-fitting clothes who couldn't speak English. There was a small knife, its extending blade sheathed in a plastic holder. She took that. There was also a bag like those carried by the men in suits who fucked her. She filled it with as many tins of food and packets of biscuits as it would hold.

Suzana weighed up her options. She could risk staying here overnight – the bed, though only a flimsy thing, was inviting. Or she could wait until the party was over – she didn't want to risk creeping back to the passage at the side of the house – and find somewhere safe to sleep under the stars. She swallowed a laugh.

When she was ten, her ambition had been to spend a summer night up on the mountain, looking at the stars until their patterns burned into her memory. When she asked her father, he had hit her with the back of his hand. It was not done for females of any age to sleep outside the family home and the guardianship of men. Now she found the prospect less inviting after shivering through the night before, shivering even in her brief dreams.

Then she saw the heavy garment hanging on the back of the door. She took it down and tried it on. It was thick and soft, a deep red colour, and it almost reached her feet. There was also a hat, a wide-brimmed leather thing that could have been worn by a cowboy. It would protect her from the rain that she had heard falling so often in this accursed place, even though it would make her stick out in a crowd. She found a plastic bag and stuffed it inside.

Then Suzana took off her trainers and unwrapped the makeshift bandages from her feet. The smell was bad. Fortunately there was some water in an electric kettle and she was able to bathe the wounds in a metal bowl. When she finished, exhaustion seized her and she stretched out on the bed. But she didn't allow herself to sleep, determined not to be caught and see again the faces of the men who had forced themselves on her and kept her captive. Maybe all three were dead and, if she was taken by the police, she would spend the rest of her life in prison. She laughed bitterly. Leka's friends would catch her first and her death would be drawn out and merciless. The same would happen in jail.

Much later, the lights went off in the house over the garden fence. Suzana put the tins and wrappers from the food she had consumed into a metal bin that reminded her of the one in her room in the house of slavery. Pushing the door shut after her, she made her way stealthily to the street beyond. It was quiet. Laden with bounty, she walked quickly away.

29

Heck Rutherford found Joni at Corham General. She was talking to the uniformed constable outside the Albanian's room.

'What the hell happened?' he asked, after he'd led her down the corridor. 'Morrie said you were almost strangled.'

'With a catheter tube, would you believe?' Joni gave him a crooked smile, but it was clear she'd been rattled. 'I'll survive.' There was a line around her neck, but the skin hadn't been broken. 'But I stink like a urinal.'

'Never thought of using mine to do that,' he replied. 'Though there was one ward sister…'

'They have a way, don't they?' Joni said ruefully. 'I had the riot act read to me about destroying hospital property and endangering a patient. As you can imagine, Morrie was a lot of help.'

'Is he all right? The Albanian, I mean.'

'Suddenly found his tongue, English-speaking version. After a lot of squealing – his wound reopened – he said I'd be hearing from his lawyer.'

'Aye, right,' Heck said, with a laugh. Then his expression changed. 'I remember these slime bags when I was in Newcastle. They were beginning to move in and they weren't afraid to use extreme violence. You'd better watch your back.'

Joni nodded. 'They're in London too. The problem is, they can't be infiltrated. Everyone's related and they only use outsiders for jobs they can't handle – or don't want to get fingered for.'

'Come on,' Heck said. 'I've been stalling her, but you'll have to report to the ACC. Don't worry, I'll make sure she doesn't steamroller you.'

'Good luck with that,' Joni said, under her breath. 'Sir, what about the women? They should be told that one of the pimps is dead, as well as that Blerim Dost is unlikely to be a danger to them for several years.'

'Ah,' Heck said, stopping on the stairway. 'I had a call from the hostel on the way in. They made a run for it.'

'All of them?'

'Afraid so.' He put a hand on her arm, then removed it when he saw her expression. 'There was only one staff member on duty and they were well away before a patrol car got there.'

Joni slapped the wall. 'I knew it. We should have had people watching them.'

'You heard what the ACC said about that.' He risked a smile. 'Maybe now she'll see the error of her ways.'

'And maybe she'll be wearing a see-through top. Where is Morrie, anyway?'

'He went back to the brothel. Now this is a murder case, the SOCOs are going over it much more carefully.'

'What do you expect them to find?'

Heck shrugged. 'If we're lucky, fingerprints that are in the databases. Hairs, male bodily fluids that can be DNA-tested, fibres from clothing – it's amazing the stuff they can pinpoint these days.'

'But we know who the killer is – Suzana, the woman I ran after.'

He shook his head. 'It's likely she stabbed Dost, though none of the few witnesses Morrie's has tracked down had a clear view. Her fingerprints will be on the knife if she did and they'll obviously be in at least one of the rooms, not that we have any originals to compare with. But we don't have any witnesses to the murder of Leka Asllani – he was at the bottom of the stair from the second floor, which suggests Suzana's room was up there.'

Joni pushed the door on the ground floor open and held it for Heck. 'No one's seen the Albanian with the fork in his head, I suppose?'

'No. He's a problem.'

'Because he'll bring the heavy brigade over from Newcastle?'

He nodded. 'Though Dost will also be alerting them via the lawyer. That third man – what's his name?'

Joni looked at the list attached to the bag with Blerim Dost's

passport. 'Elez Zymberi. Not that he'll be calling himself that
now.'

Heck stopped by his car. 'Doesn't matter what identity he
uses. He'll be back to track down the woman who forked him, as
Dickie so neatly put it. I suspect the disgrace of being bested by
a member of the opposite sex is massive for them.'

'Probably,' she said, flexing her shoulder. 'That means Dost
will be putting out a contract on me.'

'Yes,' Heck said despondently. 'It probably does.'

<hr/>

30

'You swallowed those pills, didn't you, Pumpkinhead?' Kyle
Laggan shook his head as his mate came back from the bog. 'I
fucking told you to wait till later.'

'Away wi' you,' Daryll said, slamming down his empty pint
glass. 'The Grapes is a free house.'

'Not if this pillock falls over in a trance.'

'Lay off him, Kylie.' Jackie had his arm round a girl whose
name he hadn't divulged. She looked totally out of it. 'Who
elected you president?'

Hot Rod guffawed. 'President. Nice one. Whose round is it?'

'Yours,' Kyle said.

'Aw reet, aw reet. I'm on ma way.'

'Hot by name, hot not by nature,' Kyle muttered. He looked
round the table. 'Where the fuck's Gaz? He's never missed a bank
holiday session since we were bairns.'

'Calm down, man,' Daryll said. 'He'll be pigsticking some tart.'

'Charming,' said the nameless girl.

'Yeah, mind your fucking gob, Daz,' Jackie said, glaring at
him.

'Here you go,' Hot Rod said, putting a tray on the table.

'Newkie Nectar,' Jackie said, putting the bottle to his girl's lips.

She drank reluctantly. 'What's the matter, lass? Fancy something more sophisticated?'

'Piss off.'

'Charming,' chanted all five males, before bursting into raucous laughter.

Kyle called Gaz's mobile again. 'Voicemail again,' he said. 'Yeah, Gaz! Answer your fucking messages, mon!'

There was a brief silence as they drank.

'Maybe he's gone fishing,' suggested Pumpkinhead. 'I ken he used to go wi' his old man.'

Kyle snorted. 'These days Gaz's old man can't lift his cock, never mind a fishing rod.'

'But Gaz could still have gone off to one a' they trout rivers by Rothbury,' Pumpkinhead insisted.

'He could have gone anywhere in the north-east,' Hot Rod said. 'I still think he's with some lass. You know how they go for him.'

There was a bout of nodding.

'Lucky bastard,' Daryll said. 'I wish I had a co—'

'Shut it,' Jackie interrupted, glancing at his girl. 'I'm the one with the python around here.'

'Oh aye?' she said. 'I was thinking adder meself. Baby adder.'

The outburst of hysteria that ensued led the long-suffering barman to consider barring the wankers, even though they were a major source of income.

31

Joni survived the meeting with Ruth Dickie, who was remark-ably solicitous about her well-being. Afterwards Heck reminded her how important gender and racial minorities issues were to the ACC. Joni asked if officers could be detailed to look for the Albanian women around the town. That was denied – there was insufficient personnel because of the bank holiday – though the ACC did agree that officers on patrol be apprised of the Albanians' potential presence on the streets.

Which meant that Joni went home to change her urine-spattered clothes, had a shower and then started driving around Corham. She was sure the women would be bewildered by their surroundings, having probably never been allowed out by their captors. They also had no money, though it wouldn't take them long to make some. She wondered if they knew to go to Newcastle to find other Albanians, or if they would try to get to London. Either way, it was likely they would be trying to hitch, probably having split up. She headed to the eastern edge of the town. The dual carriageway led to Newcastle in one direction and Carlisle in the other. Decelerating as she approached the last roundabout, Joni saw a shadowy figure in the twilight. It was one of them. She slowed down more, trying to keep her head back so she wasn't recognised. The woman was one of those who spoke Italian, but she must have worked on roads before because she leaned down to inspect the driver before coming close. The instant she saw who it was, she turned away and dashed into the undergrowth. Joni got out and shone a torch around, but a planner had located a pinewood by the roundabout and she had little chance of finding anyone in the deepening gloom. She considered calling a patrol car, but decided against it. The women would go to ground the moment uniformed officers appeared. Short of driving around the vicinity all night, there was little Joni could do. The last thing she wanted was to persecute the Albanian women. She would try to find some other way of helping them.

Back at her flat, she did half an hour of yoga. Then she prepared herself a vegetable stir-fry. She had given up meat and fish when she was thirteen, much to her mother's amusement. Moonbeam rarely cooked, preferring to be taken out by the men she was involved with, so Joni had taught herself how to make nourishing meals. After eating, she sat on the sofa with a cup of mint tea and tried to get her thoughts in order. It had been a strange day, and not only because someone had tried to kill her. The fact that she'd been able to overcome the fear of opening her wounds by throwing Blerim Dost was reassuring. The tackle that she'd made on Nick Etherington had been the first step, although her unwillingness to follow the runaway Suzana over the high gate had seemed to neutralise that progress. That reminded her. She needed to speak to Nick's mother in the morning to find out when he'd be home from school. He had definitely seen more outside the brothel than he admitted in interview.

Joni thought back to the conversation she'd had with the Albanian women. It was the first time she'd spoken Italian since she moved north. She could have gone to Newcastle at weekends easily enough. For some reason that didn't appeal, as if, having decided to move out of the big city, she didn't want to be drawn back into another one on her days off. She also hated shops, multi-storey car parks and pubs full of screaming pissheads. Heck and the others had told her Newcastle was well stocked with all of those. Corham was enough for her now, and she kept up her languages by reading French and Italian newspapers and criminology articles, and listening to news broadcasts on the internet.

She had a sudden flash of Aurelio Moretti, with the harbour at Bari in the background. He was the most beautiful man she had ever seen, dark hair running back in waves from his perfectly proportioned face, full lips revealing gleaming white teeth. She had been twenty-one when she went to Italy for the first time, for a teaching job arranged for her by the university during her year abroad. Aurelio was a games master at the same school and she fell for him the day she started work.

'Hey, beautiful brown lady, you want come for coffee?'

His English had made her laugh and she replied in Italian that was fluent though lacking any regional inflection. They ended up in bed that night. He wasn't her first lover. Having avoided sex completely when she was at school, she had slept with three men and one woman in her first two years at Oxford, but had never been satisfied. Aurelio did things to her body she had never imagined. She didn't even mind that he was married. He gave her the standard story about his wife not understanding him. A functioning feminist at the time, Joni knew she should have planted a knee between his legs, but she couldn't resist him. He was mad about cars and started her off on the tinkering with machines that she still did in her spare time. They were together until the day she left Bari to take up her next teaching job in Marseilles. He had begged her to stay, told her he would follow her, cried as she boarded the train. She still had the charm bracelet he had given her, but she never wore it. Not my style, she would tell herself. Maybe if he'd come to France she'd have put it on. But he never showed up, never wrote apart from one card declaring his love. She hadn't replied, seeing that her future was different and elsewhere, even if she didn't yet know the details.

And now she was reduced to using the language of love – not just of Dante and Petrarch, but of her stunning Puglian man – to question sex slaves and their pimps. The starkness of the situation almost made her weep, but she pulled herself together. At least there were no French gangsters in Corham, probably not even in Newcastle or Sunderland. She could keep that language for memories of love. In Marseilles, she'd been an instant hit with the teenagers in the run-down suburb where she was posted. She argued with the headmaster for more time with her pupils and eventually he agreed. Julien Sorel was divorced, bald and as different from Aurelio as it was possible for a man to be. He didn't even like bouillabaisse, but he was an intellectual and a kindly lover. Without him she would never have borne the harshness of the kids caused by the society they were forced to grow up in. Many were from immigrant or mixed-race families.

Looking back, Joni saw that her decision to join the police was rooted in the squalid streets of Marseilles, where drugs were king and prostitution queen, as much as it was in her Hackney childhood. She had lost touch with Julien soon after her return to Oxford. One of the other teachers sent her a note a few months later, saying he'd been killed by a hit-and-run driver after he had stormed into a café that sold drugs to teenagers.

That had made her even more determined to right society's wrongs.

32

Nick and Evie were at the table in the library, the afternoon light shining through the tinted yellow windows. Their shoulders were touching as they studied the laptop screen.

'Read it,' Evie said, tugging her ear nervously.

Nick turned and kissed her on the cheek before she could react.

'What … what was that for?'

'Don't know,' he said, his long eyelashes flicking.

Evie stared at him. She wasn't surprised – she'd had feelings for him for weeks, but she hadn't been sure what he felt about her. She'd liked him at school, even though he was in the year below. He was a star of the rugby and cricket teams. Everyone knew him and most people, girls, boys and even some members of staff, looked up to him. At first she'd thought he was a typical good-looking sporty type, but he was smart and hardworking too. And he'd been sweet to her after the accident, visiting her in hospital, though always with others from the Abbey.

'I know,' she said, and kissed him back, on the lips. It wasn't easy for her. Growing up in proximity to her mother had put her sexual development back by years: she'd become aware of Victoria's eye for men when she was still small. There was no way she wanted men to look at her the way they did at her mother – with desire, of course, but also with contempt. Finally it was Nick who had got to her.

'You're going to uni in the autumn,' he said, when they broke off. 'And I've got my gap year. What's the point?'

Evie laughed. 'For a start, there's the whole summer ahead of us. We're young, Nick. Every day counts.'

They kissed again and, pushing back their chairs, embraced.

'Did I hurt you?' he asked, seeing her brow furrow.

'Just my leg. Don't worry about it.'

So he didn't. They ended up on the floor under the table, caution tossed to a gale-force wind. Evie expected it would hurt and it did, but it was worth it. With Nick everything was good.

'I love you,' he said, when he'd got his breath back.

'I love you for saying so.' Her forehead creased. 'Love's a big word, but, yes, I love you too.'

They laughed, then got dressed. Sitting together, they were looking at the screen again when the door opened.

'Don't you two want to go outside?' Victoria said, her eyes on Nick. 'It's a lovely day.'

'We're working, Mother,' Evie replied.

'You're only young once.' The door closed behind her with a loud click.

'Cow,' Evie said. 'Now, read this. I put together a diary and letters from the first Lord Favon. God, this family makes me sick.'

Nick was surprised by her venom, but did as he was told.

This is the story of a slave called Jaffray. Today he would be seen as high-spirited if he came from a rich home and in prison if his family were poor. But in eighteenth-century Jamaica there was no mercy for black men who took what belonged to their masters. Jaffray was tall and strong, and he worked in the estate sugar-boiling factory. Temperatures were high and the slaves were frequently scalded by spits and splashes of the sweet liquid. Some lost eyes and fingers. Some even dropped dead from the shock of the blazing contact. Jaffray had been two years in the inferno and was trusted for his steady hand and quick reactions. But his fate was sealed when he fell in love with a black woman, a housemaid in the master's huge abode. Jaffray looked for her at night, climbing the wall to her garret room and charming her with his devotion. For a while – a month at most – they were happy. Then they were discovered when the master himself came for the woman. He had taken a fancy to her when she was cleaning the drawing room.

The master struck hard with the butt of his pistol before Jaffray could move – no doubt he was protecting his lover from their lord's violence. When the slave awoke he found himself in the sugar factory, stretched out on a makeshift St Andrew's cross. Through the steam from the cauldrons he saw his master holding the long shaft of a deep spoon, manoeuvring it over his naked, bound body. His genitals were first to go. He bore that without a sound. Then the boiling liquid was dripped over his belly and he felt it burn through the skin and reach his very entrails. Next went his eyes, but still he did not scream. Then he was left alone for over a day.

When the master returned he spoke to Jaffrey. He told him that his love, the housemaid, had been returned to the cane fields, where she would work until she died from exhaustion or disease. But Jaffray could save her. All he had to do was beg for mercy. His owner would rescind the order and bring the woman back into the big house. He had already had her, of course, had spent all night pleasuring her. He gave Jaffray the full details. 'So, my brave fellow,' he said, 'will you save the woman you love?'

But Jaffray, owner of a spirit considerably stronger than the white man's, would not speak. Perhaps he thought the woman was better in the plantation than near the master. Some said his mind had already broken, but that is disproved by the action Jaffray took next: he spat in the white man's face. The slaves at the cauldrons could not believe what they had seen. The owner's fury was terrible. He ordered the tongues cut out of the four men who had witnessed his shame. Then he had Jaffray smothered in hot but not boiling sugar, before hanging him from a gibbet by a rope tied tight around his midriff. There are no reports of how long he bore the attentions of birds and insects. No one knew when his ribcage finally cracked and his innards ruptured completely. The master, my ancestor, rode by the gallows frequently and taunted Jaffray, but the black man never responded. His silence was his power and his glory.

Nick looked at Evie. 'It's fantastic. I mean, the writing. This really happened?'

'So it seems.' Now that she had finally shown the first fruits of her research to someone, Evie felt drained. 'Like I said, the Favons are disgusting people.'

'Not you.'

'I … thank you.' She kissed him on the lips again. 'You'd better go. I'm very tired.' When she saw his face, she laughed softly. 'That isn't a brush-off. I really am ready to keel over.'

'It's OK.' Nick helped her up.

A few minutes later he was on his bike, his heart and mind ready to burst.

33

'Ow!' Luke Rutherford yelled, falling backwards as if he'd been axed by a particularly unbending pole.

'Bloody hell, Kat,' Heck said, under his breath. He went over to his son, who was clutching his lower abdomen and writhing on the lawn.

'Sorry!' Kat said, running across the grass. 'I didn't mean it, Luke. Honest.'

'Piss … off,' the twelve-year-old gasped.

Heck picked up the rugby ball that his daughter had accurately kicked into her brother's groin and chucked it at her without much force. 'Go and practise grubber kicks against the garage wall, will you?' He kneeled down. 'Come on, lad. Deep breaths.' He pretended he hadn't seen the tears in Luke's eyes.

'It was an accident,' he said, even though he suspected it wasn't. Luke had been winding Kat up and she'd let it get to her. She wasn't in any of the girls' teams at the local club – too worried about her looks – but she'd followed plenty of Heck's coaching sessions in the garden.

'I'll … I'll kill her,' Luke said, getting unsteadily to his feet.

'Don't talk daft. Come on, I'll test you under the high ball.' Heck sent up a few mini Garryowens, which his son took with aplomb. There was no doubt the boy had talent.

Ag appeared on the terrace with a tray of tea and biscuits.

'One of the usual injuries, I saw,' she said, shaking her head. 'Maybe you could let his balls drop before they get atomised.'

'If you were watching, you know your daughter's the guilty party.'

'I saw you hand her the ball and point in Luke's direction, Heck Rutherford.'

Her husband's head dropped. 'Well, he's got to learn how to—'

'Suffer?' Ag asked sharply.

'Ah, Dad,' Heck said, relieved by the distraction of the old man as he came out of his quarters. He had an amazing ability to detect sweet food – it was a miracle he wasn't diabetic. 'Fancy packing down against Luke?'

'He's seventy-six, Heck,' Ag said. 'This place is going to turn into Corham General.'

Activities on the lawn turned into a general rabble with no reference to the ball, David joining in. Cass ran across, chased by Adolf, who had also smelled food.

'Tea's up!' Ag called, pouring out the last of the pot. 'Get away, you stupid dog. And stupider cat. You can't have chocolate digestives.' But she surreptitiously broke one up and slipped pieces to both animals under the table.

'Ah bliss,' Heck said, stretching out his legs and taking a mug.

'I suppose this is what they call family time,' Ag said, watching as her son pushed his grandfather backwards, the old man slipping and falling flat. 'More like mad people time.'

Heck smiled at the kids. They were dragging his old man to the table, their faces wreathed with smiles. David was laughing, though it didn't sound too healthy.

Ag stood up. 'I forgot the cake.'

'Has it got cream?' Luke asked.

'Wait and see.'

'Oh, Mum.'

Kat repeated the words sarcastically.

'Calm down, jungle creatures,' Heck said. 'Where did you find that decrepit giraffe?'

His father gave him two fingers, dropping his hand rapidly when Ag came back from the kitchen.

'No cake for you then,' Heck said, prompting loud laughter from Kat and Luke.

〰〰〰〰〰〰〰〰〰〰〰〰〰〰〰〰〰〰〰〰〰〰〰〰〰〰〰〰〰〰〰〰〰〰

34

Joni's phone rang as she was getting ready for bed.

'Mother,' she said, seeing the number on the screen. 'I thought you'd be out on a blasted heath boiling up frogs' eyes and bats' spleens. It's late enough.'

'Very droll.' Moonbeam Pax, who had changed her name by deed poll from Mary Higgins during her hippy days, wasn't endowed with a sense of humour. 'For your information Beltane, also known as Walpurgis Night, was last Wednesday.'

'And did you go to a blasted heath?'

'If you'd ever shown the slightest interest in modern paganism, I'd answer your question. As it is, you mock things you don't understand.'

Joni heard plangent music in the background and felt her skin prickle. Moonbeam knew how much she hated Joni Mitchell's music, but she never missed an opportunity to play it when her daughter was in earshot. The fact that she'd been given the singer's assumed first name and her real one, Roberta, as her middle name was another sore point. Joni had sworn she'd change all three when she came of age but, in the end, she hadn't. The irony of her mother's hippy adopted surname being used by a cop amused her. But, for all the tension between them, her mother was the only person she'd had any kind of lasting relationship with. Her father, an African-American, had left before she was born and had never been in touch since.

'Turn that racket down, will you?' she said. 'So what have you been up to? No, let me rephrase that. What do you want?'

'Some idiots are riding motorbikes up and down my road.'

Joni took a deep breath. 'Is that so? And what do you want me to do about it?'

'Throw the dolts in jail.'

'That's hardly very liberal of you. Anyway, public order's not my responsibility. I'm a detective, remember?' Her mother had never come to terms with her choice of career or with her refusal to countenance any kind of illegal drug use.

'I know. Are you working on that brothel killing?'

'I can't discuss that.'

'So you are.'

'Wow, you really are a witch.'

'Oh, grow up.'

Joni laughed. 'Like you?'

'At least I had you. When are you going to—'

'Don't even go there. Did you really phone me up to hassle me about my fertility?'

'You aren't getting any younger.'

'I'll be thirty-five in July. Still quite a springy chicken. Can I go to bed now?'

Moonbeam sighed. 'We never see each other, even though I'm only twenty-five miles away. I thought you'd find somewhere closer to live when you came up here.'

Joni suddenly felt sorry for her mother. 'Why don't you come in one evening? We could have dinner.'

'You expect me to drive twenty-five miles, spend half an hour trying to find somewhere to park, all to eat overpriced food in the only vegetarian restaurant in Corham and disagree with you on every subject under the sun?'

'Or moon,' Joni muttered. 'What's the reason for this call, Mother?'

There was a pause. 'To find out how you are. Is that so strange?'

'It wouldn't be if you'd actually asked that.' Joni recognised the song that was being played, something about Amelia Earhart – it was one of the singer's less excruciating efforts. 'Fine is the answer.'

Moonbeam gave one of her soft but caustic laughs. 'If you're fine, I'm a member of the BNP. Why can't you tell the truth? You're still upset about what happened in London. It's time you let it go and got on with your life.'

Joni kept her mouth closed.

'I've been mentioning your name in spells, you know. I can feel your resistance, but eventually I'll break it down.'

This time Joni let rip. 'Leave me out of your crazy magic, Mother. Just because I came up to Northumberland doesn't mean I want anything to do with that side of your life. Goodbye.' She broke the connection. Moonbeam's experimentation with the occult had exasperated her since she was a little girl, leading her to declare at the age of ten – in a manner she now realised was horrendously precocious – that she was an atheist. She'd rehearsed all the arguments, but her mother had only shrugged and said, 'Whatever does it for you, babe.'

She got her breathing under control and told herself to calm down. For once, Moonbeam had been helpful when Joni was on gardening leave after she came out of hospital, coming down to stay in her flat in Vauxhall and cooking for her. She'd also worked on her daughter to leave the metropolis and its police force, and she'd been amazed when Joni agreed. The fact was, despite that brief period of solidarity, they had never been close and never would be. Moonbeam was only interested in herself and what she called her 'sexual being'. That meant Joni had borne witness to dozens of men entering the flat in Hackney when she was growing up, most of them departing rapidly and with hollow cheeks. One of them described Moonbeam to the teenage Joni as 'a terrifying lover'. That only made her more committed to her studies, the yellow brick road that led away from the ramshackle home she had done her best to clean and keep tidy.

But her mother had brought the worst night of her life back to her and she lay on the bed, certain that sleep would be long in coming. She ran her fingertips over the scars on her belly. The familiar twinge in the nerves, the automatic tightening of the skin...

... and she was back in the Homicide Division Southwest squad car in Brixton on the evening of 18 June 2012, talking to the surveillance team leader on the radio.

'All six are in the warehouse,' he said. 'We need to go in now. Who knows how long they'll stay?'

Joni glanced at blonde-haired Detective Sergeant Roland Malpas, who was at the wheel. Only a year in the unit, he had a tendency to lose his cool in action. She didn't have to, but she decided to mind his front as well as his back. He had potential, as well as a reasonably pretty face.

'Pax to Tinsley,' she said, calling her DCI, the senior investigating officer.

'Tinsley receiving.'

'All suspects at location.'

'C019?'

Joni confirmed that the Authorised Firearms Officers were in position.

'Uniform backup?'

'Ready to move.'

'OK,' Tinsley said, with a dry laugh. He'd never been a fan of Joni, viewing graduates on the accelerated promotion scheme as bogus police officers. She was pretty sure he suffered from institutional racism too. 'It's your call, DI Pax.'

Although it was standard procedure to hand operations over to the senior officer on the ground, Joni got the impression he was washing his hands of her but she knew she could be over-sensitive – after all, she was a woman in the Met. Maybe things weren't as bad as she thought.

'Pax to AFO commander. Ready?'

'Confirmed.'

Joni nodded to DS Malpas. 'Move in. Slowly.' She advised the other units that they were on their way.

The last of daylight was greying the walls of the former bonded warehouse. According to the council's records, it had been empty for five years and the rust on the gate suggested that was right. A young ex-con Joni had been cultivating for over a year told her that Peter 'the Cricketer' Souter's gang of hard men had recently taken to using it, a fact confirmed by surveillance from the abandoned scrap yard across the road. Souter was suspected of dispatching more than one of his enemies with a cricket bat, as well as organising the raid on a security van at Waterloo that had cost both driver and guard their lives.

Because the information came from her informant, Joni was given the responsibility of planning the operation. She'd taken advice from officers with greater experience – that was one of her strong points – and left nothing to chance. Except, as she knew well enough, things could always turn to shit when armed headbangers with little to lose were confronted.

She took a deep breath as the unmarked Mondeo, showing no lights, moved slowly down the street. Other members of her team were approaching from different directions, covering all the building's known doors – the original bars were still on all the windows.

Joni looked at her watch. The street lights in the vicinity had been disabled, her plan being to hit the gang when twilight was at its darkest without raising suspicion among the men inside.

'Ram squad?' she said.

'Ready,' responded the leader.

She nodded at Malpas, who was looking avidly at the wide door fifty yards ahead. 'Stay with me at all times, Ro, all right?'

'Sure, ma'am.'

She nodded, then ordered, 'Assault units, move in!'

Officers in dark blue overalls and helmets piled out of a van that pulled up in front of the warehouse entrance, tyres screeching. Two of them approached the doors and smashed the heavy steel cylinders against the wooden panels. When they gave way, AFOs rushed in, pistols raised in two-handed grips. There was immediately a lot of shouting, but no shots were fired. Joni held her breath, then slowly let it out. Her worry had been that Souter's men would have had time to reach the sawn-off shotguns they had used against the security guards – they had been loaded with magnum 12 gauge shells.

'AFO commander,' Joni heard. 'Warehouse secured. All six suspects apprehended.'

'Yay!' said Malpas, getting out of the car.

'Cool it,' Joni said, opening her door. 'Let the AFOs bring them out.' She looked over to the van. 'Lights on the doors!'

The driver manoeuvred the vehicle so it was facing the warehouse, dipping the headlights. Soon afterwards, men started to emerge, hands behind their heads and eyes towards the ground. AFOs had each of them covered.

Joni and Malpas went forward. Peter Souter was at the front, grimacing as uniformed officers seized him and fastened his wrists behind his back with plastic restraints.

'FUCK!' he yelled, provoking laughter from some of the uniforms.

'Quiet!' Joni shouted, looking at the faces on her iPad as the men came out. Five of them matched the photos from their Met and Prison Service files, while the sixth, Marcus Ainsworth, a twenty-eight-year-old Mancunian without a record, glanced at the police officers nervously, shoulders slumped. His face was spattered with acne.

'Read them their rights, Ro,' Joni said, as Ainsworth reached the officers with the restraints.

Malpas had moved close to the prisoners and was only a few feet from them when it happened. Suddenly a knife appeared in Ainsworth's right hand from behind his back and he brought it down in a blur, causing the policeman holding the plastic cuffs to scream and clutch his face. At the same time, Peter Souter stuck out a heavy leg and tripped Malpas, so that he stumbled forward into Ainsworth's grasp. He had his back to the wall as he held the knife against the DS's throat, shielding himself from the AFOs' weapons.

'Let him go!' Joni cried, putting down her iPad and stepping forward.

'Screw you, bitch!' Ainsworth replied. 'He's my ticket out of here.'

Joni looked at the AFO commander. His lips were tight, suggesting his men didn't have anything close to a clear shot. Then she took in Roland Malpas. He was bulkier than his captor, providing an effective shield. He was also visibly terrified.

'I'm Detective Inspector Pax, officer in command,' she said. 'Take me instead.'

Marcus Ainsworth drew blood with the knife and looked round Malpas's head, sizing Joni up. She was six feet, but a lot thinner than her colleague. He moved his head behind Malpas again.

'All right, DI Pax,' he said, his voice steady. 'Be my guest. But no fast moves or yer man here'll turn into a blood fountain.' He gave an empty laugh.

Joni gave Roland Malpas what she hoped was an encouraging look and moved nearer, taking off her leather jacket to show she was unarmed.

'You won't be needing that either,' Ainsworth said, thumbing the top of Malpas's stab vest.

'Wha…' Joni lost the end of the word as her heart leapt. 'I…'

'Come on!' Ainsworth yelled. 'I'm slicing this fucker up!'

Joni pulled away the vest and dropped it to the ground as more blood ran down her DS's neck. 'All right, it's off,' she said. 'Please don't cut any more.' She heard Malpas's breath coming in short bursts. 'How do you want to do this?'

'Simple,' said the knife man. 'Stand next to him and then push him gently in the other direction.'

Joni followed the instructions and Malpas moved sideways until she was where he had been.

'Guv...' he began.

'Fuck off now if you want her to stay alive,' Ainsworth said. 'Now, you brown bitch, tell these shitheads to stay where they are. You and I are going for a stroll.' Again the dead laugh.

'You heard him,' Joni said, the blade pressing against her throat. 'Keep your distance. I'll be OK.'

'Yes, she will,' her captor shouted. 'Unless anyone tries be a smartarse.' He circled her chest with his free hand and kneaded her breasts. 'Nice,' he muttered. 'What'd'you call them where you come from? Mangoes?'

'Coconuts,' Joni replied, trying to humour him. She knew she had a chance if she got him off his guard. She stumbled as her boots hit a rough patch of road.

'Careful,' Ainsworth said, drawing blood. 'Walk like a crab. It's not that difficult.'

But for Joni it was. Her long legs were awkward going sideways and she almost stumbled again. The blade cut deeper and she wondered how much blood she was losing. Mustn't lose much blood, need all I've got for...

'Keep going, DI Pax,' the knife man said, his breath strangely sweet. 'When we reach the corner, I might even let you go.'

Joni swivelled her right eye as far as she could. The junction ahead was in full darkness, out of reach of the lights from the van. No vehicles passed as the access roads had been closed by the traffic police.

'There's nowhere for you to go,' she said. 'We've got the whole area locked down.'

'Is that right?' Ainsworth laughed. 'Thanks for telling me. Now, round the corner.'

Joni made up her mind. Once she was out of view of the others, she would be completely at his mercy. She had a Judo black belt, she could easily take this joker. Except she might...

She threw him, simultaneously punching upwards to knock the knife from her throat. He landed heavily, but was on his feet in a flash, dragging her out of sight of her colleagues and kicking her hard between the legs.

'Stupid,' he said, coming close and narrowing his eyes. 'Really fucking stupid.'

Joni felt the knife pierce her gut once and then again. She tried to call out, but she heard no sound; felt only a rush of wind as she was shoved backwards and her head made solid contact with the wall.

Joni slapped herself hard on the cheek. She had been fighting for months to keep the memory of the raid out of her mind, but it still came back with as much intensity as ever. The tap was open now, events gushing out, swamping her. At first it had been a blank. She was in a coma for three days, the haematoma that had started to form in her brain from the blow she had sustained to the back of her skull gradually – to the surprise of the neurologists – subsiding. Then she had blurred vision and crushing headaches for a week. Then she went mad. They didn't call it that, and the Met was very understanding, paying for psychotherapy and granting her six months' convalescent leave. Although she had played the strong woman effectively towards the end of the course, even convincing the shrink that she was ready for duty, she had known from the beginning that she wouldn't go back to Homicide Southwest. London was dead to her and, despite a major manhunt, Marcus Ainsworth had never been found. He had seriously injured a uniformed officer after he left her, proving that her carefully planned operation had failed to cover every eventuality – a point DCI Tinsley emphasised in his report. She had to get out and, to her mother's amazement, she agreed to move to Northumberland: to Corham and the newly formed Police Force of North East England.

But she still felt Marcus Ainsworth's stony gaze on her every night before sleep begrudgingly came.

∞∞∞

35

Nick Etherington slept fitfully. He was too excited by what had happened with Evie. He hadn't really believed that she would return his feelings. It wasn't that he was inexperienced with girls – he'd spent the last couple of years fighting them off and had been in several short-term but fun relationships. But Evie wasn't like the others. It wasn't just that she was older. Although she'd had plenty of friends in her year, she maintained a distance from them. He suspected it was something to do with being as different from her mother as possible. Victoria, she just wouldn't give up. He felt like the flesh had been stripped from his bones when she looked at him and the way she called him 'Nicholas' – something not even his mother did – made him feel like a naughty child who needed punishment. Not that the punishment would necessarily be unpleasant…

And Evie was right. Who cared about the autumn? They had months to spend together, especially after he'd finished his exams. Evie. She was so sweet. Then he remembered the story of the slave that she'd written. No wonder she had problems with her family if that was how they had treated their workforce. 'Their slaves,' Evie had corrected. 'Favon Hall was built with blood money.' Nick agreed, but he didn't understand why she was so worked up about it. Britain was full of big houses whose owners had exploited workers and peasants. Such was life.

He hadn't felt so good for along time. Even gathering together his school books was a pleasure. He whistled a Coldplay tune as he went down to breakfast. His mother and grandfather smiled at him. Gramps had realised as soon as Nick came in the door last night that something had happened. His mother was less observant. She was still upset that he'd been questioned by the police.

'Back to work today, young man,' Rosie said, with unusual severity. 'You've had your fun. It isn't long till exams.'

'Yes, Mum,' he mumbled, mouth full of bacon and egg. He saw Gramps wink at him.

A few minutes later they were in the major general's Jaguar. An unofficial routine had set in after Michael had moved in: he took Nick to the Abbey in the mornings and Rosie picked him up in the afternoons, unless her charity work got in the way.

'Your mother's right, you know,' his grandfather said. 'You really have to nail those exams.' He smiled. 'Like you've nailed so many tackles and tries. Half-centuries too. That reminds me. Is it cricket practice as usual this afternoon?'

'Yes. I can get a lift home if you like.'

'No, one of us will come down.'

As they neared Corham, Nick found himself thinking about Sunday night. Even with his vision restricted by the traffic light, he'd seen things he'd rather not have – the man with the knife in his belly, the skinny bodies of the women, the one who'd run into him, her lower half bare and blood on her hand... But something else troubled him: the heavy man with no jacket who'd come down the steps after the woman left screaming. Was it really *him*? There was blood on the fingers of the hand he was holding over his upper thigh and his features were twisted in pain. No, it couldn't be right. What would a man of his status be doing in a brothel in one of north Corham's dodgiest areas? And then there was the hair. If it was him, he must have been wearing a wig. The problem was its length. Rather than disguising him, it made someone of his age stick out. Would he really have taken the risk of being recognised to screw one of those sad women? Nick's eyes had met his through the slit. His heart missed a beat. What if *he* found out who'd been wearing the cardboard costume? It wouldn't be hard for a man in his position.

'You look worried. Tell me what you're thinking.' His grandfather's voice was a mixture of command and concern.

'I … oh, it's nothing. Exam tension.'

'You can take it. You're a hard one.'

Nick struggled to keep his lips in a straight line. He'd certainly had a hard one with Evie, not that she'd complained. He hadn't expected her to be a virgin. That made him feel even more privileged. She had trusted him to be her first lover. He blinked away a tear.

'Listen,' his grandfather continued. 'You had a bad time on Sunday night. You should talk to me, get it off your chest. Believe me, you'll feel better.'

'OK, Gramps. Maybe later.'

'Whenever you want, lad.' There was hint of disappointment in the major general's voice.

Minutes later Nick was walking into the Abbey School. He was immediately surrounded by friends wanting to know what had happened with the police – he'd kept his phone off when he was with Evie and afterwards. He was embarrassed to find that he'd become even more of a hero. At least no one knew about him and Evie. That was one thing he was going to keep to himself. Some secrets were good.

36

'All right, people, gather round.' Heck Rutherford, grey-faced, was leaning against the wall at the front of the MCU. Morrie Sutton and his team were on his left, and Joni Pax with her people to the right. It was nine a.m. and the holiday weekend meant that things had piled up. Officers had been in since eight a.m., collating reports and making their own to-do lists for Heck's approval.

Heck looked at Joni. 'By some miracle the bank holiday weekend was pretty quiet – at least outside Corham.'

'So it seems,' she agreed. 'Uniform were out in force and there were several arrests for drunk and disorderly and damage to property.' She glanced at the young man standing beside her. 'DS Rokeby has something to report.'

Heck waited for Peter 'Pancake' Rokeby to speak. He'd had him on his team in Newcastle and found him a solid performer. He'd taken some stick when other officers discovered he was gay, but he stood up to it well. ACC Dickie had been keen to have him at Corham because of her diversity drive. His nickname referred to his predilection for the food item, though some smartass had claimed it referred to make-up. Pete whispered something that made the guy blush like a schoolgirl, refusing afterwards to say what it was. He was a good man, Pete – discreet but deadly.

'Em, yes, ma'am,' Rokeby said. One of his few weaknesses was discomfort with public speaking. He could question a suspect as effectively as the next officer, but he hated addressing the morning meeting.

'Come on, Detective Sergeant, we haven't got all day.'

Heads turned and people took in Ruth Dickie, who had slipped into the room.

'No, ma'am. I mean, yes, ma'am. Traffic police up in Alnwick stopped a driver in a BMW speeding on the A1. He was doing over a hundred. When they went to breathalyse him, one of the officers saw the grip of a pistol sticking out beneath the front seat. They managed to immobilise the guy and cuff him. He refused to answer questions, didn't even give his name – just said the name of a Newcastle brief.'

'What name?' Heck asked.

'Richard Lennox.'

There were groans around the room. Lennox was notorious for his list of criminal clients, many of whom he'd kept out of jail by practices that came close to getting him disciplined. He benefited from the criminals' large financial resources, which enabled him to hire the sharpest legal minds, as well as former detectives now working as private investigators.

'The superintendent at Alnwick let the driver call Lennox, who arrived an hour later. By then, as well as the pistol, nearly a kilo of cocaine had been found in the BMW. The man is foreign, probably Albanian. He's been charged with possession of the weapon and drugs and is in custody.'

'Interesting.' ACC Dickie walked to the front of the room and stood next to Heck, with whom she exchanged glances before continuing. 'Albanians seem to be flavour of the weekend.' There was a hint of excitement in her voice. 'DCI Rutherford, you'd better send our resident Italian speaker to Alnwick to see if she can get anything out of this latest miscreant.'

Heck nodded at Joni, then looked to her side. 'Pan … DS Rokeby, you go too.'

'Any further developments with the Albanians here, DI Pax?' the ACC asked.

Joni saw Morrie Sutton's cheeks redden – he resented being overlooked, but that wasn't her fault. She said that she'd spoken to the hospital and been told that Blerim Dost was in a stable condition. His room was still being guarded. Joni added that none of the Albanian women had been spotted overnight. 'After we've been to Alnwick, we'll stop off to interview Nick Etherington again,' she concluded. 'I'm sure he saw something at the brothel that he hasn't come clean about.'

Ruth Dickie kept silent, so Heck nodded to DI Sutton.

Unlike Pancake Rokeby, Morrie loved spouting to the gathered masses. The problem was, he had absolutely no talent for it. After several minutes of chaotic rambling, Heck cut in. The upshot was that DI Sutton was told to intensify the search for witnesses and for the missing female suspect, while DS Gray was assigned to liaising with the SOCOs and the lab over their findings in Burwell Street. DC Eileen Andrews – short, plump, in her mid-forties and with a look of mild amusement permanently on her soft face – was asked about her trawl of the databases.

'The Border Agency has Leka Asllani, Blerim Dost and the man last seen with a fork in his forehead—'

'Elez Zymberi,' Joni supplied.

'All the zeds, DI Pax,' Andrews said, smiling. 'As I was saying, the UKBA has the three of them plus the six women as having overstayed their ninety-day visas. Apart from that, none of them appear in HOLMES or any of the other databases.'

'Is it worth giving Interpol their names and mugshots?' Heck mused.

'Hold off on that,' the ACC said. 'We need to build more of a case.' She looked at him. 'On the other hand, DCI Rutherford, you should talk to your former colleagues in Newcastle – see if the names mean anything to them.'

Heck's shoulders slumped. He'd suspected she would suggest that.

37

Suzana had spent the rest of the night in a park. The walls of what she took to be an old church were bathed in yellow light about a kilometre away. The red coat, almost like the cloaks the women in her village wore in winter, kept her warm and the wide-brimmed hat protected her head from the drops of dew that fell from the trees. She woke early and thought about what to do. The longer she stayed in this town, the greater the chance of being found by Leka's friends. She was hoping he and the other pigs in the slave house would be out of action for a long time if they weren't dead. But leaving would bring its own dangers. Taking a bus or a train – she used to hear the sound of engines and carriages clacking from her room – would mean that other people would see her, other people who might talk. She could have tried to whore herself on the roadside, but she'd vowed that no man would ever touch her again. So she had to walk; but before that she needed to locate this Cor-ham place on a map and decide where to go. Then there were the bags of provisions. She needed somewhere to hide them after she'd eaten again.

Rolling up the coat, Suzana hid it and the bags behind a thick bush. She kept the hat on as, combined with the good-quality leather jacket, it made her look less like a person who lived on the streets. Her feet were still painful, but they were better than yesterday, as was the wound on her upper chest. As long as she kept the jacket buttoned, she would not attract too much attention. If she opened it, the sour stench of sweat and men's fluids would cause people to gag. Heading for the town centre was risky, and not only because of the Albanians. The police would be looking for her too. She knew that stabbing men wouldn't be seen as acceptable, no matter what had been done to her. She'd been brought up to understand that women did what they were told, respecting the superiority of their fathers, brothers and husbands. She did not think things would be so different in England.

For all that, a man with a small white dog said something to her in a friendly voice as she left the park. She kept her head down and mumbled something in return, keen to fit in. The buildings around here were smaller than the one with the small wooden house, but not as shabby as the ones in the streets around the slave house. There were trees and in daylight she saw that the leaves were bright green and that buds had begun to appear. She looked up at the sky. High cloud in narrow white strips – what her grandfather on her father's side called 'goose-feather heaven'.

There were few people around – did they stay in their beds so late? Then it struck her. Living in towns meant you didn't have to rise with the sun to tend the animals. Why did they put ropes around their dogs' necks? In the village they ran free, scavenging for food and receiving savage beatings if they nipped the goats and sheep. Here it seemed people looked after them. Why would they do that at the same time as depriving the creatures of their freedom? Truly this was a strange country.

She came to a wide road with cars moving slowly. The few
vehicles in her village were driven as if they were in a race,
even the big tractors that had appeared in recent years. Young
men rode motorbikes with their heads lowered, never with the
helmets she saw in Cor-ham and always at full speed. Two of her
cousins had been killed, one hitting a wall and the other cata-
pulting into a ravine. It had taken the men a whole day to bring
his body back for burial.

Suzana came to the first shop. It was closed, but she stood at
the window, her eyes wide. She had never seen so many toys:
dolls, grown-up dolls with short skirts and huge hair like the
street women in Tirana, trains and cars for boys. In the corner
was a house nearly as tall as she was, with furniture in every
room and tiny plates and cups on the tables. There was even a
toilet like the one in the slave house. The first time she had used
one like that was in the airport. She had asked one of the other
girls, who told her to put her feet on the seat and squat. Was that
what fat men and old women did too, she wondered. Leka had
laughed when she climbed up on the seat in the bathroom down
the corridor from her room. 'Put your skinny ass on the plastic,
bitch,' he said. 'You're not a peasant now.'

No, she'd been something much worse: a plaything of men; a
doll like the ones in the shop, despite her lank hair and pale skin;
a vessel for their seed. She looked around, suddenly afraid that
she stood out. But people walked past, the younger ones paying
little attention to her and the older ones giving her tentative
smiles. She nodded to them, wishing she could respond to their
words. She didn't even know how to say 'Good day' in English.

Moving on, Suzana came to a street full of shops and restaurants. There was a stone column in the middle of a broad square
and, beneath it, a map in a plastic display case. She headed for it,
jumping at the horn blast from a car and ready to bolt. The man
at the wheel shook his head at her and drove on. She berated
herself. This is not the mountains. Here there are many vehicles.
Be careful, idiot.

She spent a quarter of an hour making sense of the map. Beside it was a tall post with signs at different heights, pointing in various directions. She followed them with her eyes and spoke the names under her breath.

'Cor-ham Ab-bey. Riv-er Der-wyne. Tan-ning and Dis-tilling Mus-e-um. Ra-il-way Sta-ti-on. Bus Sta-ti-on. I-ron-flatts.' She didn't understand the words, but she found where they were on the map, seeing pictures of a train, a bus and three bridges. She worked out the location of the riverside park where she'd spent her first night of freedom. There was a red dot in the Ma-in Squ-ar-e. She realised that was where she was standing. She memorised as much as she could. Having been to school with one teacher for all the classes and very few books or writing materials, she had come to rely on her memory. In recent months it had grown weak from lack of use, but now she had a purpose. She would sharpen her memory and every other part of her mind. They would be some of her most important weapons.

That reminded her. The small plastic-covered knife she'd taken from the wooden house was in her pocket, but she needed something more lethal. Looking around and waiting until there was a gap in the increasing flow of cars, Suzana crossed back to the shops and looked for one that sold knives. She'd began to lose hope when, on a road leading to the river, she found a place with not only knives in the window, but also screwdrivers, pliers and other tools.

She went in to stock up.

38

'That was a waste of time,' DS Rokeby said as he and Joni Pax came out of Alnwick Police Station.

'Mm,' his boss replied absently. She was looking at the walls that rose above the town. 'What is that place, Pete?' She never used his nickname – never seemed to use anyone's if she could avoid it. That made him uncomfortable about calling her Jack or Jackie Brown behind her back, as some of the others did.

'Alnwick Castle. Where they filmed Harry Potter.'

She looked at him blankly.

'Haven't you read the books? The films have been on the telly.' Then Pete Rokeby remembered. He'd experienced Joni Pax's ignorance about popular culture before. He put it down to her being an Oxford graduate, the fact that she didn't know much about black culture reinforcing that conclusion. 'Sorry, I forgot you only watch the news.'

'And the Proms.' They reached the Land Rover. Joni tossed him the keys. 'You drive. I know you've been desperate to get your hands on her.' After she'd strapped herself in, fumbling with the passenger seat belt, she sat back and nodded as he successfully manipulated the gears. 'Yes, you're right. Visiting Mr Hekuran Kondi was probably not the best way to spend our morning.'

The Albanian hadn't responded to her attempts in Italian, while one of Richard Lennox's junior lawyers sat in, shaking her head when the questions were voiced in English. Kondi was in his late twenties, Joni estimated. He had no ID on him apart from a gym card, though his wallet was full of cash.

'On the other hand,' Rokeby said, manouevring through the narrow streets, 'you did seem to touch a nerve. What did he say when he gave you that look?'

Joni thought back to the stocky man with the clippered hair and dark-ringed eyes. His voice had been low and emotionless. 'He said that I would be raped and murdered.'

'What?' the DS said, glancing at her, then looking to the front and correcting his course. 'You should have told the lawyer.'

'I didn't want her to know.'

'Why the hell not?'

'Because that wasn't all he said. I told him that the missing woman had been too much for his friends in Corham, having killed one, sent another to intensive care and stuck a fork in the third guy's head. What kind of men were they, I asked. Child fuckers?'

Pete Rokeby shook his head. 'You fight dirty, ma'am. So what else did he say?'

'He let slip a name.' Joni glanced at him. 'The Popi. He said the Popi would fix me. Mean anything to you?'

'Afraid not. Albanian gangs weren't on my agenda in Newcastle.'

Joni called Heck Rutherford. He didn't know the name either, but would run it past his former colleagues.

'Actually,' she said, as they headed back down the A1, 'I have an admission to make.'

'Oh aye?'

'Em, aye. Child fuckers wasn't the only thing I called the Albanians.'

Rokeby looked at her and laughed. 'Let me guess. You used some choice homophobic terms.'

Joni nodded, her eyes down. 'Sorry about that. I read in an Italian criminology article that Albanian mafiosi have a thing about gays. A thing as in "they hate their guts".'

'Chill, ma'am,' the DS said, laughing. 'What did you actually say?'

'Well … I said I thought they must have been busy sticking their pencil-thin dicks in each other's soft pink anuses.'

This time Pete Rokeby guffawed loudly. 'I love it! Don't worry, it was in the line of duty.' He glanced at her. 'We Pofnee minorities need to stick together.'

Joni watched as a flock of small birds rose up and banked over a small wood. 'Are you talking about my colour, my gender or my sexual orientation?'

'Em, the first two.' The MCU had been rife with speculation about Joni Pax's sex life since she'd arrived. No one had seen her with a partner of either sex.

'To tell you the truth, I don't see myself as belonging to a minority on either count. Obviously there are fewer women in Pofnee than there should be, but the statistics show there are more women than men in the world. And, if you count most of the occupants of Africa and the eastern continents, you'll have a pretty large number of black people.'

Pete Rokeby accelerated past a lorry. 'But there aren't many blacks in Pofnee. I think you're the only detective if you discount people of Indian and Pakistani origin.'

'The chief constable would say that the police force should reflect the make-up of the local population. I haven't seen many black people in Corham, let alone in rural Northumberland.'

'True. Then again, gays make up between six and twenty per cent of the population, depending whose statistics you believe. I only know three other gays in Pofnee and two of them are lesbians.'

Joni laughed softly. 'Gays can keep their orientation to themselves. They probably *have* to in the more macho units. I don't have that choice, either as a woman or a person of colour.'

'So what you're saying is that different minorities shouldn't stick together?' Rokeby said testily.

'No, of course not.' She pointed ahead. 'Why don't we follow that sign and get something to eat?'

They found themselves at a pub called the Yellow Cat. A chalked board claimed it did the best value meals in the county.

'We can always do them under the Trades Descriptions Act if it's shite,' Pete Rokeby said. He parked and handed over the Discovery's keys.

They ordered toasted ciabatta sandwiches, Joni's with grilled vegetables and the DS's with spicy sausage.

'Good enough,' Rokeby said, after he'd finished well ahead of Joni and drained his pint of lemonade.

She nodded. 'So why did you come out, if it isn't too personal?'

'Haven't you heard the story?'

'No one gossips with me, Pete. The DCI gives me the odd bit of background.'

Not that Heck Rutherford was much of a gossip merchant, Rokeby thought. 'It was in the old Newcastle HQ about a year and a half ago,' he said, meeting Joni Pax's eyes. He felt completely at ease with her. 'Some of the guys got suspicious when I kept avoiding the weekly trip to a pub with strippers. The nasty remarks started. So one morning, at the end of the briefing, I stuck up my hand and DCI Rutherford gave me the nod. I said, "I'm gay. Anyone got a problem with that?" Strangely enough, no one did. I got slaps on the back for having the balls to come out with it.'

Joni wiped her mouth. 'But that wasn't the end of it?'

He shook his head. 'There's never an end to it, you know that. They call me Pancake because I like my food, but there are still comments. Jokes, like, but with razor blades in them.'

'Sounds familiar. You have to be stronger than everyone else all the time. It gets exhausting.'

'It does.'

Joni patted his arm. 'This is on me. We'd better get a move on. Nick the Human Traffic Light will soon be home from school.'

Pete Rokeby watched her while she paid. Until then he had thought DI Pax was a typical hard-bitten female cop – a taller, darker version of Ruth Dickie. Now he wasn't so sure.

39

'Is Gaz there?'

'No. The fucker isn't answering his phone. I've got three cars in for service and two MOTs. I've had it up to here with him.'

'Don't be too hard on him. He's been missing for nearly four days.'

'Who the fuck are you? His social worker?'

'His best mate, Kyle Laggan.'

'I suppose they call you Kylie.'

'Only my mates. Or scumbags who can run fast.'

'Hard man, eh? When you find Gaz, tell him I'm docking his wages and he'll have to make up the time.'

'I'm going to call the cops, report him missing.'

'Good for you. Won't do any fucking good.'

'I know. Still, I got to do something.'

'Here, now I come to think of it, one of the other lads said they saw him on Friday night. Oy, Johnnie, get over here. Talk to this lad. He's called Kylie.'

'Fuck off.'

'What?'

'Not you. Your boss is a pillock.'

'I noticed. What do you want?'

'He said you saw Gaz on Friday night.'

'Aye, I did. He was with this guy round the back of the Stars and Bars.'

'About two o'clock?'

'Probably. I was pissed and I was smoking something reet skunky.'

'So what was going on?'

'They were having a chat, nothing nasty that I could see. They got into a black Bentley Continental GT Speed and drove off. It had tinted windows so I couldn't see inside. Fucking brilliant motor, that.'

'What the fuck?'

'What?'

'Gaz in a Bentley? He's got a knackered old Micra.'

'Maybe he's got friends in high places.'

'I've known him since primary school. The highest place we've been is the Get Carter Car Park.'

'Shame they knocked that down. It was an ugly piece of shit though.'

'So, the guy Gaz was with. What did he look like?'

'Bouncer-type. Black suit, big, shaved head. Oh, and his nose was all flat.'

'Did you see anything else at the club?'

'Nay, you know what them places are like. Headbangers speaking funny languages on the door, local headbangers trying to get into the knickers of lasses inside.'

'What funny languages?'

'I heard that lot are from Albania. Hey, the pillock's giving me the death stare. Got to go.'

'Albania? Fuck.'

40

'Come off it, Heck, the ACC's having a hot flush.' DCI Lee Young was number two in the Newcastle MCU. He was in his early forties, had a chip on his shoulder about officers who'd been to university and didn't like the way the new force had been consti-tuted. 'Stabbings at a knocking shop in Corham, then an Albanian caught near Alnwick with a gun and a kilo of coke and she thinks the wankers are taking over the region? That's bollocks.'

'Maybe and maybe not. I don't see the weeklies you send her. Are the Albanians getting ahead over there these days?' Heck and Young had an up-and-down history. They'd worked together to nail a couple of violent gangs a decade back, but Heck had sent down one of his former colleague's best friends when he was in the anti-corruption unit. As a result, he had to squeeze hard for cooperation.

'Are they getting ahead? Not really. The local mobs still rule the roost, but it would be fair to say the Albies are making inroads.'

'Women?'

'Big time.'

'Drugs?'

'Medium time, I'd say. The Turks still control things up the east coast. The Albies have a go from time to time.'

'I saw there were three dead down by the river a few weeks back.'

'None of them Albanian. We caught one of the knifemen, who might well be, but he never talked. That dickhead Lennox was all over us the minute we turned the heat up.'

Heck looked out his office window and watched a pair of scowling teenagers being walked to the main entrance by uniformed officers. 'If they can afford Lennox, they must be making serious money.'

'Not necessarily up here. They could be being subbed by their big bosses in London.'

Heck paused for a moment, then pressed the phone against his ear. 'The Popi mean anything to you?'

Young was silent for more than a moment. 'The Popi,' he repeated, stretching out the syllables. 'Might do. What have *you* got for me?'

'The tip of ACC Crime Dickie's shoe – and she's taken to wearing winkle-pickers.'

'Ha fucking ha.'

The thought of Mrs Normal in anything other than sober flatties almost made Heck laugh too, but he restrained himself.

'Oh, all right,' Young said. 'But I want to see the file on the dead man and his crew.'

'Fair enough.' That was no concession on Heck's part – the files would soon be available to the Newcastle MCU on the Force database, but Lee Young had to keep face.

'The Popi have turned up the odd time in the last couple of months. The guy we caught on the riverbank mentioned them when he was talking to Lennox. The interpreter picked it up. Did you know Lennox can speak Italian? Apparently the Albanians understand it. And we ran a phone tap before we raided a knocking shop off the Gallowgate – the name was mentioned. We're guessing it's a family or clan, but we don't know if it's up here or down south.'

'None of the names we sent over rang any bells?'

'Only Leka. It cropped up half-a-dozen times on that phone tap. Then again, Leka might be their equivalent of John.'

'Aye, and Popi might be the Albanian Smith. OK, Lee, thanks. I'll be in touch.' Heck glared at the uniformed sergeant who was standing at his door. 'What is it, Len? I'm up to my ears.'

'It's a woman, sir,' the wizened officer said. 'She insists on seeing you. Says she knows you. A Mrs Alice Liphook?'

'Oh, Christ. What does she want?'

'Says she's been burgled.'

'Well, get one of your lads to take a statement.'

'Tried that. She started ranting and raving, even threatened to tear down some of the notices…'

'Sounds like you should have arrested her. All right, I'll talk to her. Bring her up, but don't leave me on my own with her.'

The sergeant stared at him. 'She doesn't look like she'd—'

'Don't even think that!' Heck suddenly looked bilious. 'She's one of the governors of Ag's school.'

'I did wonder, sir.'

'When I say the word "crow" in any form, usher her out at speed. I'll be about to tear her head off.'

A few minutes later Alice Liphook was sitting on the sofa that ran along one side of Heck's office. Sergeant Moody stood in the doorway like a sentry. There were several female officers visible through the glass windows, so procedure was more or less being maintained.

'Does your colleague have to be present, Hector?' Mrs Liphook asked, in her high-pitched voice.

'Standard practice, Alice,' Heck replied. 'We do everything in twos here.'

The woman peered at him through large round glasses. 'No wonder crime's going through the roof.' She lifted one thick thigh over the other, giving a flash of support stockings beneath her long tweed skirt. 'As in the case of my shed.'

'Your shed?'

'Yes,' Alice Liphook said, her small head tilting back and forth as if it was coming undone. It looked incongruous on top of her well-upholstered body. 'Someone broke into it and stole a valuable velvet dressing gown and my favourite hat, as well as a lot of food.'

'A velvet dressing gown…' Heck busied himself taking notes. Mrs Liphook – her husband had sensibly died over a decade ago – was Corham's number one busybody.

'A lot of food was consumed on the spot as well. And the place smelled like a sweatshop.'

'You live in Corham Gardens, don't you?' Heck remembered dropping Ag off once in the expensive suburb. 'And this was your garden shed?'

'My study shed. I need to get out of the house to read and write. I stay there all day.'

'I see. And had the house itself been broken into?'

'No, they hadn't even tried as far as I can see. I was at my daughter's up in Rothbury. I stayed the night and drove back this morning.'

'And you saw no sign of the culprit or culprits when you arrived?'

'No, luckily they'd gone. I'd have given them what for in no uncertain terms.'

Heck frowned at Len Moody, whose lips were twisting as he tried to swallow laughter.

'Did anything else catch your attention, Alice?' It was hard to be sure about her age because of the heavy layers on face, eyes and lips. Seventy-five was as low as he'd be prepared to go.

'Yes. These were no ordinary thieves. They didn't take my laptop or radio.'

'Why do you say "thieves" plural?'

Mrs Liphook stared at him. 'Because of the amount of food that was consumed, my dear man. Three tins of soup, two of beans, and two of sardines, as well as three packets of biscuits. And that's just what was eaten there. They took a lot more away with them.'

Heck glanced out of the window and prepared to make an ornithological observation.

'Oh, one last thing, Hector. There were rags in the bin, rags with blood on them. The smell ... just awful.'

Heck thought about the woman Joni had chased outside the brothel. She had bare feet and was in need of clothes; food and shelter too. Had she found some cast-offs and made it as far as Corham Gardens?

'I'll tell you what, Alice. I'll send some people down. They'll check for fingerprints. Please don't go back into the shed until further notice.'

The woman looked as if she'd been evicted. 'Oh, but ... but my work.'

'I'm sure you can manage in the big house for a day or two,' Heck said, standing up. 'Now, Sergeant, I have an appointment with Inspector Crow. Please have someone take Mrs Liphook's statement and fingerprints so we can distinguish them from those of the intruders.'

'Thank you, dear Hector,' the woman said, gathering together her possessions. 'Do give my best to Agnes.' She was one of those people who refused to use diminutives.

Dear Hector. That would be around Force HQ before the hour was out, Heck was certain.

<><><><><><><><><><><><><><><><><><><><><><><><><><><><><><><><><><><><>

41

Evie made her own lunch. She preferred it that way. Her parents were rarely in and, although Cheryl would have done something for her, Evie preferred not to ask. She took her fruit and yoghurt to the dining room. When Favon Hall opened to the public in the summer months, it was one of the high points. For that reason her father had spent what he described as 'a ridiculous amount of money' restoring it to its original condition. The mahogany table was long and wide, and covered with antique silverware, china and cutlery. A red sash separated the paying customers from the valuables and a security guard was hired to make sure nothing was taken. The walls were covered in paintings, including a Gainsborough, two Constables and a Stubbs. They used to be kept in a bank vault, but Victoria had convinced Andrew to bring them out to attract visitors. The security system that the insurers required cost 'an even more ridiculous amount'.

Apart from the library, the dining room was Evie's favourite. The family rarely used it – only when they wanted to impress people and persuade them to put money into her father's numerous business initiatives. Although the sugar mill, distillery, tannery and machine works had gone, Andrew had his fingers in pies all over Northumberland and County Durham. Evie knew that her mother kept a close eye on the companies and was a director of several.

But it was all rooted in blood money. Evie wondered how the story of Jaffray had affected Nick. She still wasn't sure why she'd shown him it. After they'd made love beneath the table, she should have changed her mind, but her mind and body had moved on to a different, unguessed-at level and she had lost control of herself. Maybe she'd scared him off. Imagine losing your virginity and then forcing your lover to read about the disgusting behaviour of your ancestors. But there was something unusual about Nick. On the surface he was the school hero, but deeper down he was vulnerable. She had the impression he hadn't found himself yet. Maybe she could help, though not by recounting the fruits of her latest research. She had run it past her parents and they had reacted violently, telling her not to waste her time with the past – hardly the most helpful observation to a future student of history. Andrew had obviously heard at least part of the story, probably from his notoriously unpleasant and fortunately long dead father. It was clear that Victoria hadn't. Although she was initially shocked, a look came into her eyes that Evie didn't like at all.

What she'd found was the description of a slave ship's voyage across the Atlantic in 1766. The *Esmerelda* wasn't just any slave ship, though. It was the first that the Favons had a share in. Twenty years later, the family owned three ships outright, as well as retaining an exclusive agent in the Bight of Benin. One of her forebears even crossed from Africa to Jamaica. Erasmus was his name. He kept a diary. The writing had faded, but she'd managed to make it out.

The blacks were secured in fetters below deck. All were naked, sea water hosed over them to get rid of their filth every day. They were fed gruel by the females, who were ravaged by the crew before they were chained up again. The poor women were abused even when they were immobile. Her ancestor took pleasure in servicing one particular slave from behind because he didn't like her 'impudent but reginal face'. In the middle of the crossing, the wind dropped and the Esmeralda *drifted for days. Fresh water had to be rationed and the slaves, more valuable than the crew, were given enough to keep them alive. They groaned under the resentful sailors' whips, groaned as their lips cracked and sores from the rough decks erupted on their backs and buttocks, groaned collectively like a huge expiring beast. Twenty-seven of them died, including nine females, and their corpses were tossed overboard. The woman with the queenly face, whom Erasmus, with characteristic lack of wit, had named Negra, was one of them.*

By the time the Esmeralda *reached Port Royal, the survivors were in an appalling state. Erasmus reported that his father was most displeased, ordering the slaves to be taken to the nearest of his estates to be fattened up. They were assets, he told his sons, vital cogs in the engine of the family's wealth. It was a shame they were not machine parts, easily and cheaply replaceable, and not susceptible to disease, sloth and rebellion. Machines like the cane crushers and the sugar boilers did not need feeding or housing other than simple sheds. The old man had laughed, saying that, on the other hand, there was no joy in coupling with an engine, or in beating it. Erasmus noted that the pater was in uncommonly good*

spirits, despite the partial loss of his cargo – he had been appointed
deputy governor of the island and commander of the plantation
owners' militia. A title was in the offing.

But Evie had not left the story there. She carried out more
research and discovered it was Erasmus who, on inheriting
the title from his father, had built the Hall beside the medieval
tower. By the time he died, a pox-ridden, dropsical balloon, he
had gambled away much of his fortune. It was the beginning
of the family's decline, though the profits from the Caribbean
were still enough to surpass many of the older aristocracy's
holdings. When Erasmus died at fifty-three, he weighed twenty-
three stone and had to be fed like a child. His wife, twenty years
younger and the personification of avarice, leaned towards
his blubbery lips to catch his last words. They were, 'Negra …
forgive me'. She had no idea who he was talking about. It was
fifteen years since he'd made a trip to Jamaica and there were no
slaves in Northumberland. No black ones, at least.

<><><><><><><><><><><><><><><><><><><><><><><><><><><><><><><><><><><><><><><><><><><>

42

'That's it,' DS Rokeby said, pointing at a detached house on the
village's main street. A dark green Jaguar and a yellow Saab were
parked in the gravel-covered drive. 'So, how do you want to
handle this?'

'What? Oh. How about I ask questions and you take notes?'

Pete Rokeby wondered where her thoughts had been for the
last quarter of an hour. She'd been on autopilot, reacting to his
directions and driving safely enough, but silent and absorbed.

They got out and approached the entrance. The house was
large, but by no means the most striking in the village. Rosie
Etherington opened the door, her face pale. She took Joni's hand
and then Rokeby's, smiling nervously.

'I'm sorry, Nick and his grandfather have been delayed. They'll be back shortly, something about a cricket net over-running?' She seemed to have little idea of what that meant.

'We can wait in the Land Rover,' Joni said.

'Don't be silly. Come into the kitchen.'

Joni let her start inside, then whispered to Rokeby to stay by the Land Rover until the other males arrived.

'Oh, has your colleague ...'

'He has some calls to make,' Joni said. 'I like this room.'

Mrs Etherington glanced around. 'Just the usual country kitchen. Aga, oak table, old-fashioned storage jars on top of the cupboards and...' Again, her words trailed away.

Heck had told Joni about Rosie losing her husband – she was a friend of a friend of Ag's. After that, the death of the major general's wife had brought them even closer together and there had been gossip when he moved in here. Even a few minutes with the woman convinced Joni that she was nowhere near getting over her husband.

'How's Nick been?' she asked.

'Tea? I usually just do a big pot of Darjeeling.'

'That's fine, Mrs Etherington.' Joni wasn't going to let her off the hook, but she could be diplomatic when necessary. 'Look, I'm very sorry about what happened on Sunday night. I wouldn't have handcuffed your son if I hadn't been on my own. It looked like a serious incident and unfortunately that initial judgement was correct.'

'Yes, I heard a man died.' Rosie was fiddling with the alignment of cups and saucers. 'But Nick couldn't have seen anything. He was wearing that silly traffic light.'

'Let's hear what—' Joni broke off as male voices came from the front of the house.

Nick Etherington walked in, looking surprisingly relaxed, with his grandfather behind. Pete Rokeby was further to the rear.

'Detective Inspector,' Michael said, extending a hand. 'Your colleague introduced himself. Sorry we're late.' He pulled a chair back and nodded to his grandson.

'Hello, dear,' Rosie said.

'Mum,' Nick said, with a smile.

'Sit down, everyone,' Rosie said. 'There's some cake...'

Joni sat opposite Nick, while Michael went to help Rosie. DS Rokeby took the chair at the far end of the table. After a few minutes there were plates and cups in front of everyone.

'This won't take long,' Joni said, ignoring her tea. 'Nick, I need to clarify some of the things you said on Sunday night.'

'Clarify?' the young man said, looking down.

'Nick,' his grandfather said firmly. 'Do the lady the courtesy of looking at her when you answer.'

Joni gave him a tight smile. 'I'd be grateful if you'd allow me to handle this, sir. Otherwise we'll have to take Nick back to Force HQ.'

'No!' Rosie said, giving her father-in-law an imploring look. 'Please, Michael.'

The major general nodded and sat back with his arms crossed.

'So, Nick,' Joni resumed, 'you told us you didn't see anyone you recognised in Burwell Street.'

'That's right,' the young man said. 'Apart from my friends.'

Joni locked on to his eyes – they were dark brown and had unusually long lashes. He was already a heartbreaker. 'The problem is, I don't believe you.'

Rosie's mouth opened, while Michael's brow furrowed.

'What do you mean?' Nick stared at her. 'I was looking out of the slit in the traffic light. It was dark. All I saw was a crowd of people, then that half-dressed woman.'

'The slit is almost two inches wide and over seven inches long.'

Pete Rokeby blinked. Had the DI actually measured it? He hadn't thought of doing that.

'Also, as I remember, the street lights were fully functioning. You could see perfectly well, even though you had reduced peripheral vision.' Joni pushed her cup and plate away and leaned towards Nick. 'You saw someone you knew. Tell me who it was.'

'I ... no, I didn't. You think the people I know go to prostitutes?'

'Tell me who it was,' Joni repeated.

The young man's face reddened, but he didn't speak.

'Why are you so sure he saw someone?' his mother asked. 'Why's it important?'

'Was it a teacher?' Joni asked, ignoring the parental intervention. 'One of your friends' fathers?'

'No!' Nick said immediately. 'No!'

Joni let him stew. Rosie Etherington's second question was harder to answer than her first, not that she intended explaining herself. She knew Nick was lying because it was her job to know when people lied. Why she thought it mattered was beyond her, but her subconscious, her soul, whatever name she wanted to give the workings of her inner being that were beyond her comprehension, was telling her to press the point. But the schoolboy wasn't answering. Why? Fear was the most likely explanation.

She took out her wallet and removed one of her cards. She slid it across the table and put her pen next to it. 'Write the name down. I can't guarantee there won't be consequences – you're bright enough to understand that – but I'll treat the information with the utmost respect and confidentiality.'

Nick Etherington's eyes dropped to the objects in front of him. He picked up the pen with his right hand and reached for the card with his left. Then he seemed to realise what he was doing and stopped, the pen dropping from his fingers.

'I didn't ... I didn't see anyone I know.'

The major general pushed his chair back, the legs scraping loudly across the stone flags. 'That's enough, DI Pax. The lad's given you his answer. If you take this any further, I'm going to call our lawyer.'

Joni got to her feet and met his gaze. 'No need to do that, sir. I've got what I came for. Come on, DS Rokeby. Thanks for the tea, Mrs Etherington.' She stretched across the table and retrieved her pen. 'Keep the card, Nick. You can call me any time, day or night.'

Back in the Land Rover, Pete Rokeby said, 'What was it you came for then, ma'am?'

Joni smiled. 'That would be telling.'

'Well, it wasn't the tea. You didn't touch it.'

She laughed. 'Excellent observational skills.' She reversed on to the road. 'The thing is, Nick Etherington lives a very protected life. Good school, grandfather chauffeurs him around, mates always with him. What's he got to be afraid of?'

'Maybe he's got in with some bad lads. Drugs, whatever.'

'That might explain why they went to Burwell Street, now we know the Albanians were dealing dope as well as pimping those poor women.' She glanced at the DC. 'Does he look like a user to you?'

'No.'

'Or a pusher?'

'No.'

'So we're back where we started. He saw someone at the brothel whose presence put the shits up him.'

Rokeby took his life in his hands. 'Seems a bit circumstantial, ma'am.'

'Everything's circumstantial, Pete. Until it isn't.'

'Is that what they say in the Met?'

Joni shook her head. 'They don't like instinctive policing any more than the next force.'

So it's just you, DS Rokeby thought. DI Joni Pax follows her instincts. If I want to get on in Pofnee, I need to make sure she doesn't influence me too much.

Joni looked at him. 'Don't worry. I'm not asking you to do as I do.'

Pete Rokeby sat back, wondering how the hell she knew what he'd been thinking.

43

Suzana was back in the park where she'd left her bags in the morning. She'd walked around the centre of the town, taking in the main features and memorising them. She now knew how to get to the train and bus stations, the quickest ways out of Cor-ham should someone pick up her trail. She'd gone into a bookshop and found a small dictionary of English and Italian. In the village she had followed the subtitles on the Italian news broadcasts and picked up some words. She had also bought a map of the area. She looked up other words in the Italian part of the dictionary and mouthed their English equivalents.

'Cash. Go a-wa-y. On-e sing-le tick-et to Lon-don.'

She was so engrossed that she didn't notice the figures approaching her from right, left and straight ahead.

'Who's this then?'

Suzana looked up, her stomach clenching. A young man in a shirt with vertical black-and-white stripes was standing about five metres in front of her. She immediately felt nauseous. Many men in that shirt – she guessed it was a football team's – had been to her room in the slave house. This one had short hair brushed to a peak above his forehead and a spotty face.

'Le-av-e me a-lon-e,' she said, pulling the bag with her weapons closer.

There were bursts of laughter from him and the two other youths she'd failed to notice on each side of the bench.

'What did she say?' yelled one.

'Le-av-e me a-lon-e,' repeated the young man in front of her. 'What are you? Chinese?'

'Go a-wa-y,' Suzana said firmly.

'Go a-wa-y!' repeated the three, collapsing in mirth.

'Go 'awaii 5–o?' said the one to the left.

'Not from round here, are you?' black-and-white shirt said, moving closer. 'Maybe we can show you some of the local, er...' He looked at his mates and grinned. '...cock.'

That was a word Suzana had heard before, too often. The men said it when they wanted her to touch their penises or put her mouth on them. She slipped her hand into the bag beside her.

'The bushes behind'll do,' the youth to her right said.

'Hey, bitch, what's in the bag?' black-and-white said, making a grab for it.

'Go-od bla-d-e,' Suzana said, slashing the carving knife at his hand.

He leapt back and landed on his backside, blood flowing copiously.

'Grab the cunt,' he gasped, clutching the wound with his other hand.

Suzana pulled another blade from the bag. This one was shorter, but honed on both sides. The other young men tried to grab her, but they weren't quick enough. One nearly lost the tip of a finger and the other had his shoulder run through.

'Go a-wa-y!' she screamed, waving the blades like a Celtic warrior maiden.

Her assailants backed off, cursing loudly. She leaped at them and they ran down the slope like terrified sheep.

'Thank yo-u,' Suzana said, wiping the knives on the grass and gathering her things together. She was over the wall and out of the park in less than two minutes. For now she was safe, but she had to get out of town tonight.

44

In his office, Heck wasn't doing well. He had the cancer blues and he was trembling. He took some deep breaths and managed to get a grip, disgusted with himself. He'd turned into a coward and he didn't even have the balls to tell Ag. Then he saw Joni Pax and DS Rokeby come into the MCU. He picked up his mobile phone and put it to his ear, raising his other hand to buy himself some time. When he was on more of an even keel, he beckoned Joni in.

After giving him a questioning look, she reported about Nick Etherington.

'Sounds like a dead end to me,' Heck said, when she'd finished. 'Maybe he saw one of his father's friends. That wouldn't make him too happy, what with his Dad having died.'

'Why didn't he say so, then? Even if he didn't give the name.'

'Dead end,' Heck repeated. 'Besides, you don't want to mess with Michael Etherington. He was one of the few NATO people to get the Bosnian Serbs to negotiate.'

Joni sat down on the sofa. 'Was he in Kosovo, sir?'

'No idea. Why do you ask?'

'Well, I'm not a Balkan expert, but I know that Kosovo shares a border with Albania and that the majority of Kosovo's population is Albanian.'

Heck sat back, his hands behind his head. 'What are you suggesting? That General Michael was at the brothel?'

'No, he's got an alibi from his daughter-in-law. But he still may be involved.'

'Bloody hell, Joni, what are you on about? You think Michael Etherington has some connection with the Albanians.'

She raised her shoulders. 'Maybe Nick saw someone his grandfather knows in Burwell Street.'

'All this from a hunch? The ACC will tear it to shreds.'

'Not if I find out more. For a start, we can check his service record right now. There'll be plenty of newspaper reports.'

Heck looked at his computer screen with ill-disguised aversion. 'Be my guest. I have enough trouble with the Pofnee system.'

Joni went round to his side of the desk and pulled the keyboard closer. Within seconds she'd found a newspaper report marking the end of Michael Etherington's service in the Balkans.

'He was in Kosovo from June 1999 to April 2001.'

'Which proves nothing.'

'No, sir, but it piques my interest.'

'Oh, it does, does it? Well, take that pique to your own desk and get on with something useful. See what you can find out about this Popi clan or whatever it is. Ruth Dickie's already squeezing my nuts.'

'Yes, sir.' Joni turned at the door. 'I don't suppose Morrie's turned anything up.'

'Not a lot, but listen to this. A woman I know in Corham Gardens had her shed burgled last night. I sent the SOCOs down – don't ask, the woman can make Ag's life difficult – and guess who'd been there?'

'General Michael?'

'No, the Albanian woman you chased. What was her name?'

'Suzana.' There was sudden tingling in Joni's upper spine. 'Suzana Noli.'

'Aye, that's it. Her fingerprints were all over the place. She stole food and clothing. DC Andrews has got the report.'

'She was long gone, no doubt.'

'She was indeed.' Heck peered at her. 'What is it, lass?'

Joni ran her hand over her forehead. 'Nothing.' She turned to go and cannoned into Eileen Andrews.

'Oops, sorry, ma'am. You both might want to hear this. Uniform responded to a call from a lady who lives on the west side of Star Park. She saw three lads approach a young woman who was sitting on a bench. There was some kind of set-to and they ran off. She saw blood and, she thought, knives. The woman chucked plastic bags over the rear wall of the park and climbed after them.'

'When was this?' Joni asked.

'The call was logged at 3.39 and the officers called it in after they finished talking to the woman at 4.43.'

'She'll be well away by now,' Heck said.

'Uniform have got a description of the woman and it's been issued to all patrols. Not a huge amount to go on. Dark hair in a ponytail under a woolly hat, a dark leather jacket and mud-coloured trousers.'

'It has to be Suzana,' Joni said. 'She knows her way around knives.'

Heck nodded. 'Thanks, Eileen. Let us know if anything more comes in.'

Joni went to her desk and stared at the blank screen. She was seeing Suzana Noli walking into the darkness, lugging her bags and looking around constantly. She was friendless, wanted for murder and very far from home. It was likely she'd never been allowed out of the brothel and had no idea where she was. Aged seventeen, the target of the enraged and merciless bastards who had enslaved her and now the sworn enemy of local yobs. Joni wished she could rescue her, clean her up and let her sleep on her sofa.

She shook the thought away and switched on her computer. The only way to save the Suzanas of the world was to cut off the head of the gangs that abused them. She had a rendezvous with the Popi.

<hr />

45

Moonbeam Pax dropped a bay leaf into the vegetable stew she'd prepared and put it in the oven. It was good to be cooking for a man again. Her recent conquests hadn't lasted long enough to merit dinner. The last had been a twenty-year-old she'd given a lift to on her way back from Alnwick a month ago. She'd immediately seen in his eyes that he fancied her, despite the wrinkles on her face and her sagging breasts – she'd given up wearing a bra when she left school and, despite numerous battles with headmasters and mistresses, had stuck to that decision throughout her teaching career. He was an amusing enough diversion, not least because he'd looked like he was going to faint when she let him in the back door. She'd forgotten she had a frog and a bat stretched out to dry on the kitchen island. That hadn't stopped him grabbing her still firm buttocks as she led him upstairs. She'd guessed how it would be, so she stroked him to climax before he'd got his trousers off. A quarter of an hour later, he lasted long enough for her to orgasm. She always used her own fingers to do that, regardless of what her knuckles might do to the men's bladders. She hadn't been surprised when he'd reneged on his promise to call her. She liked it when she scared them and, besides, she wouldn't have had him back. He was weak.

Looking across her small back garden, Moonbeam took in the moors to the west. She'd given up teaching before she got her full pension, so she hadn't been able to live any nearer her childhood town of Corham. Not that she was bothered. It suited her to be on the outskirts of the small village twenty-five miles to the north. Billham was perfect. The old people accepted she was an odd one, the middle-aged found her amusing (not that they invited her into their homes, even though, or rather because she'd had sex with several of the husbands and one of the wives) and the young people bought the drugs she brought from Alnwick every week. She used to do her pick-up in Corham, but there had recently been disruption when some brutal new gang forced its way in. Besides, she didn't want to compromise her daughter. The cottage she rented from the Favon estate was cheap and had its own free water supply, even if the colour was sometimes a bit disturbing. It didn't matter. Moonbeam had a herbal remedy for everything, dodgy water included. And now the spells she'd cast for years were finally working. All would be as it had been and all would be well.

She had strong hopes that Joni would see the light, despite the twin barriers of rationalism and prejudice she had erected when she was still a little girl. Things were different now. After years of rejection, of claiming in the piping voice she used to have that she was an atheist, of going to the snobs' university and then throwing it all away to become a servant of the oppressive state, Joni needed Moonbeam. The fact that she'd moved to Northumberland was proof. Her daughter had become a victim. She'd been damaged physically and mentally, and was struggling to cope. That brought her closer to being one of the elect. Only through suffering could true wisdom be obtained, but you had to be born with the powers to move higher up the scale.

Moonbeam never asked herself what suffering she had undergone. She'd never had much money, but that was down to her spending the reasonable salary she earned on expensive herbs and ritual accessories. She'd been collecting grimoires – books of spells – since her twenties and some of them now had great monetary value, but she would never sell them. She'd lived in a run-down flat in Hackney for nearly thirty years, filling it with the necessities of her craft and rarely cleaning. She used a room as a studio too, occasionally selling art works, though they were too exotic for most people. And she had been on her own, deeply, painfully, since Joni's father Greg left her. Joni had never reached even the lowest level of natural understanding, for all her studies and certificates, while the men Moonbeam allowed in her bedroom were nothing but substitutes, none of them capable of giving her anything but fleeting physical pleasure. Not that she had any objection to that.

She had always been sure that Joni would come back to her, wounded and desperate for healing. Moonbeam was in a position to provide that now she had cleansed herself and achieved access to the true knowledge contained in the earth, the sea, the moon, the trees. Fertility was all around if only you knew how to set it in motion. Joni needed help to understand that.

46

Joni spent the afternoon carrying out searches for the Popi. What little there was in the databases was insignificant: mentions in statements by frightened minor criminals who were trying to take the heat off themselves; the name shouted in open court by a Turkish heroin dealer who claimed he'd been framed; the corpse of a headless young woman with the letters 'POPI' cut into her back.

Morrie Sutton came into the MCU with Nathan Gray. They asked her about the Albanian who'd been caught in Alnwick and she told them his mouth had been zipped up by one of Lennox's minions.

'No sign of Suzana Noli?' she asked.

'Who?' they said, in unison.

She stared at them with intent.

'Oh, the tart with the cutlery,' Gray said. 'Nope. She's gone, DI Pax. Turn your electric eye on someone else.'

Joni would have ripped into him, but she had more important things to do. The first of them, she wasn't looking forward to. Since she'd left London, she hadn't had any contact with her former colleagues in Homicide South-west. It was time she re-established relations, but she didn't want to do it in the open-plan office.

Picking up her pad and pen, she went over to DCI Rutherford's glass box. He was bent over a pile of papers.

'Sir, I'd like to call someone in my old squad in the Met. Could I do it from here? I don't fancy DI Sutton overhearing.'

Heck looked at her. 'What's Morrie done now?'

'Nothing egregious by his standards. He's not exactly setting DS Gray much of an example, though.'

'Not really your business, is it, Joni?' Heck said, then he relaxed. 'I take your point though. Gray's an arse, but the ACC wanted him here.'

'Blonde, blue-eyed boy minority representation?'

Heck laughed, then coughed and clutched his lower abdomen.

'Are you all right, sir?'

'I'll live.'

Joni knew about his cancer, but he didn't talk about it. Like much of Heck's past, it was off limits. Even when they'd been in his car for hours on surveillance, he hadn't opened up much. Then again, neither had she. But her boss would have seen her service record. He knew all about what she'd been though.

'The thing is,' she said, 'I need to ask about the Popi. I want to see if the Met's working on anything linked to it or them or whatever the hell the words refers to.'

'Don't jump into a heap of shit. I can call someone senior. Anyway, they should be updating the databases.'

'With respect, sir, you know that they'll give you, for want of a better word, shit. A DCI from the north of England is hardly going to make them open up. Besides, you know the databases are only updated with sensitive material when forces are desperate for help. The Homicide Units don't do desperation.'

'All right, have it your way.' Heck stood up.

'No, sir, stay. I'm not kicking you out of your office.'

Heck shrugged and sat down again, pushing the phone over to her.

DS Roland Malpas wasn't answering either his mobile or his office number. His voicemail kicked in, but Joni didn't leave a message. She suspected he wouldn't return her calls. The last time she'd seen Ro was at a squad party when she was on sick leave. He had avoided her all night and she heard from one of the secretaries that he blamed himself for putting her in danger. She eventually tracked him down by asking the same secretary to connect her without saying who it was.

'Ro,' she said, when he picked up, 'this is Joni Pax. Don't put the phone down!'

There was silence before he spoke. 'DI Pax. I wouldn't dream of cutting you off. How goes it in the frozen north?'

'I'm in Northumberland, not Norway. We've got spring here, same as you.'

'Oh, right.' Malpas sounded distracted.

'Is this a bad time?'

'It's always a bad time. Was there something in particular?'

Joni wasn't letting go of the chance to put him on the back

foot. 'I'm fine, thanks for not asking, Ro. Wounds healed, brain back in gear.'

'Shit, I'm sorry, ma'am.'

'Call me Joni. Forget it, Ro. I need you to check something for me.'

'Oh yeah?'

'You come across any Albanian gangs down there?'

There was a pause. 'Albanians? Well, they're on the rise all over the place. Have you got them up there?'

'Uh-huh. There's one particular name – I'm not sure if it's an individual or a family.'

'Have you run it through HOLMES?'

'What do you think? Nothing of any significance.'

Malpas paused again. 'Let's have it then.'

'Popi, or rather *the* Popi.'

This time the response was rapid. 'No bells ringing.'

'All right. Do you think you could ask your mates in other units, Ro? It would mean a lot to me.' She didn't want to ratchet the emotional pressure up too much – at least, not yet.

'OK,' Malpas said. 'I'll see what I can find out for you.'

'You're a star.'

'Yeah, right.'

She gave him her new mobile number and rang off.

Heck looked up from his paperwork. 'He's calling back?'

Joni smiled. 'Don't worry, I'll stay on him.'

'Is that it?'

'Yes. Well, not exactly. I was thinking about the international agencies. I know the ACC said no to Interpol, but there's Europol as well.'

'Have you got a contact there?'

Joni shook her head. 'I could put in a request for information.'

Heck ran a hand over his closely cropped head. 'This conversation isn't happening, DI Pax.' He lowered his voice. 'Of course, I can't control what you do off your own bat.'

Joni had never been good with sporting metaphors apart

from those originating in athletics, but she understood the risk was hers. There was no way she was going through the Pofnee international liaison officer. He was Ruth Dickie's tame chief superintendent.

47

Nick and Evie were in the back of Lord Favon's Toyota Land Cruiser, on the way back from the Hall. Nick had cycled up and done a couple of hours' revision with Evie. Although English was the only subject they shared, she had a great system for consolidating notes that was helping him with all his work.

They held hands in the dark, but kept a distance between them, aware that Andrew Favon was glancing at them in the mirror. Neither was keen on her parents knowing that they were together. This time Evie had turned the key in the library door before they made love. Nick trembled as he remembered what they had done to each other and squeezed her hand. He heard her inhale deeply and understood she was thinking about their time under the table too.

'I hope you appreciate this, Nick,' the broad-backed driver said. He was wearing the wide leather hat he favoured. Baldness was spreading over his large head. 'I don't normally drive around at this time of night.'

'My grandfather would have come to pick me up.'

'It's all right.' He looked in the mirror. 'Anything for my Evie.'

Evie laughed out loud. 'I should think so. If you hadn't broken my legs, I'd be driving this thing myself. Except I'd be in Africa.'

Nick stared at her. He'd never heard her be so sharp with her father.

'Steady, girl,' Favon said. 'It was an accident.'

'And what do you mean you don't normally drive around this

late?' she continued. 'I've often woken up in the middle of the night and seen no sign of the Land Cruiser in front of the Hall.'

'You know I sometimes park round by the tower.' Her father's tone, normally abrupt, had hardened even more.

Evie pushed her fingers between Nick's. 'Whatever,' she said, leaning back. Her body remained tense.

'What did you get up to on Sunday night, Nick?' Andrew Favon asked.

Nick was immediately suspicious. Was this why Evie's father had offered to drive him home?

'I went as a traffic light.'

'What?' Was the surprise genuine, Nick wondered.

'With fully functioning red, amber and green panels. The problem was, I got picked up by the police.'

Favon's laugh was high-pitched, like a donkey in season. 'That must have gone down well with the general.'

'He was OK about it.'

'Where did this happen?'

Nick was unsure if the question was as innocent as it sounded. 'Somewhere in the old industrial area. I don't know where exactly. I had the odd pint.'

'You weren't charged, though?'

'No.'

'Experiences like that are part of growing up.'

Nick didn't answer. He was trying to decide if Favon had lost interest or if he was playing a more subtle game. He gave the impression of being a dim-witted aristocrat, but Nick had never been convinced by that. Just as he'd never believed that Lady Favon was the man-eater she was said to be – until he found out otherwise. The way she looked at him was embarrassing. Tonight Evie had noticed and, later, told him to ignore her mother. She was an airhead and besides, Evie would look after him.

They didn't kiss when he got out of the 4×4. Nick watched as the bulky vehicle turned outside the house and went back the way it had come. He wasn't only sad to have parted from

Evie; he was worried about leaving her alone with her distinctly strange father.

◇◇◇

48

Heck and Ag often went to sleep spooned against each other. That night she dropped off quickly, but he was restless. He slipped away and went down to the kitchen. Since he'd come out of hospital, he regularly had disturbed nights. The only thing that helped was a mug of chamomile tea and honey – recommended by Ag – and recourse to his armchair. He had to manhandle Cass off it, the dog's eyes fixed on him pathetically. As he finally sat down, he felt a twinge in his abdomen. That was what this was all about. He'd been recommended counselling after the operation, but had declined, much to Ag's exasperation. He had to work through it himself, he told her. What he didn't say was that he had to confront his fear.

Heck had been a good amateur rugby player into his late thirties, captaining the Corham team for eleven years. He wasn't some fly-boy winger who kept himself out of the action; his place was at the back of the scrum and he was renowned for the devastating hits he made. He'd never been afraid of anything on the pitch, nor in Newcastle, a city that wasn't short of head-bangers, many of them in street gangs or more organised crime operations. The problem was, he'd allowed himself to be moved up the ladder in the Force. When he was in his early thirties, he spent six months undercover. They'd been the most exciting of his life.

His first marriage, which he hadn't thought about for years, was already on the rocks. He'd suspected Lindsey of shagging the next-door neighbour when he was on night shift, so the offer of taking on an assignment that would look good on his record came at the right time. He was taken off normal duties and treated like a VIP rather than a detective constable with only a few arrests. They briefed him about the crew of armed robbers he was to infiltrate, giving him basic firearms training and a fake background as a London heavy who'd moved north after five years inside.

'Like Jack Carter?' he said to the DI who was monitoring him.

'Fuck Jack Carter. He only got shot once, at the end of the film. If MacLean's crew get on to you, they'll turn you into a sieve before you've finished your popcorn.'

No Lard MacLean was a hard man of the old school, his nickname referring to his muscle-bound frame. His team was experienced in emptying banks, security vans, post offices, even a North Shields to Norway ferry's safe. What Heck – nom de crime, Jimmy 'the Juice' Joyce – brought to the party was a foolproof plan. He'd been supplied with the architects' drawings for a bank in Gateshead that had recently been completed.

'Where did you get these, bonnie lad?' No Lard asked, after Heck had been plied with spirits. Years of post-match boozing meant he could hold his drink.

'Nicked 'em,' he said, in the best London Irish accent he could manage. 'From the guy who got me sent down.' He grinned. 'He won't be using his legs again.'

'Tell us more,' said No Lard, with a sick grin.

Heck held his nerve and ran through the story he'd memorised. No Lard made some calls which checked out, thanks to the undercover squad's careful planning.

'So you'll be coming with us then, Juice,' the muscle man said, a statement rather than a question.

'Sure I will,' Heck replied. He didn't get much sleep that night, or the following three. The squad wasn't contacting him and he was only to use the dead letter drop if he was in immediate danger – this was in the days before mobile phones.

And so he found himself in a beaten-up van with No Lard and his men at two in the morning. They thought they knew exactly where to lay the explosives and they were tooled up with sawn-offs and semi-automatic pistols in case things went pear-shaped. Heck himself was carrying a Browning High Power he'd been supplied with by the Northumbria Police armourer. No Lard gave the word and they took up their positions, Heck by the leader's side – it had been made very clear that was a condition of his involvement. As the guy with the Semtex headed for the rear wall of the building, the undercover squad, bolstered by an armed response unit, moved in.

The subsequent inquiry found that two of the gang members had decided this was the perfect opportunity to dispose of No Lard. He hit the ground, riddled with bullets in his back. Heck threw himself to the side and managed to get round a corner as the rest of the gang started firing at each other. When the shotgun and pistol blasts ended, no one was left standing. Heck peered out and was met with a scene from a Peckinpah movie. Only the shooter who had disposed of No Lard was still alive. He had three bullets in his abdomen and only lasted two hours in hospital, but he managed to brag about what he'd done, saying his name would last longer than his victim's. Heck had forgotten it a few weeks later.

He hadn't been taken off the job. His celebrity status as the only survivor of what became known as the Gunfight at the Gateshead Corral meant he was soon recruited by another gang. Heck was involved in several big busts until things got too dangerous and he was withdrawn. But his knowledge of Newcastle's most dangerous crews was second to none and he ended up running operations against them. His target was the Bad Shepherds (they hated the former owner of Newcastle United). This lot were careful, taking months to set up a bullion raid. Heck had an undercover man participating in the planning, as well as in a post office robbery to keep the gang in ready cash. That officer, a DC playing the part of postmaster, managed to warn his colleagues and the takings were kept below five hundred quid. There was no shooting and no one was injured.

As time passed, Heck got more and more excited. Lindsey

commented on it, saying not entirely in jest that he must have a mistress. In a way she was right. Heck loved the danger, even at arm's length. At the same time he was repelled as never before by the brutality, the complete lack of humanity shown by the Shepherds and their kind. They treated each other like animals, they beat up their women – years back Heck had intervened and took a heavy blow to the side of his head – and they ignored their kids. But they knew how to behave when it counted. The Bad Shepherds' leader, a vicious streak of piss called Ned Sacker, kept them in line.

The operation ended with a whimper and only one bang – the blank round fired at the undercover man by an armed response officer when the gang was caught and disarmed as the members moved in on the shipment in the docks. They were all sent down for long stretches. Heck had been threatened outside court by Sacker's brother Ian, a waster known as Not So Lucky because the outsiders he habitually bet on never even placed.

Cass gave a quiet bark when Heck stifled a cry. He was shaking, his belly on fire: he was terrified of sustaining more damage to his abdomen and he was sure he could never face another suspect in the field again.

49

The darkness was not her friend. Suzana had known that since she was a small girl, when she had hidden in the most outlying of the village's abandoned houses. Bad things went on around her, bad men gambling, fighting, hurting women.

The problem now was getting away from Cor-ham without being seen. She tried several roads, but all had cars passing along them. Even though she wasn't wearing the dark red robe, she was aware that the bags she was carrying made her look like a person of the streets, and therefore someone that people might report to those who were after her, including the police. She presumed her description had been broadcast on TV and radio, and printed in the newspapers.

So she got off the road she had chosen, the one signposted to Jed-burg-h, and followed it from the field beyond. It was slow work, especially once the last of the light had gone, but she kept her eye on the shifting headlights as she moved. Eventually she walked into one barbed wire fence too many and decided to stop for the night. There were only the lights of the cars in the distance to help and, with difficulty, she opened some tins with the largest of her knives, having forgotten to take the utensil from the hut or buy a new one. She ate quickly, stopping herself before she used too much of her supplies. She had enough for two more days at most. Then she would have to buy or steal, both of which could bring her into the open.

Wrapping herself in the robe and pulling the hat down low, she tried to sleep. Her legs were aching from the kilometres she had covered, but she knew they weren't enough. Even if the police hadn't alerted everyone in the area, her own countrymen were relentless. They might not be expecting her to head north, but that didn't mean they wouldn't be on the lookout up here. For all she knew, they ran brothels in Jed-burg-h and the towns on the way or were selling drugs like the ones she'd seen Leka hand to the men who abused her. They would pour the white powder on her chair, then separate it into lines with plastic cards like the ones she had thrown away, before sniffing it up their noses. One of them, a fat man with black and white on his belly like the boy in the park's shirt, had tried to make her take some. When she struggled, he licked his finger, dabbed it in the powder and rubbed it between her legs. He seemed to think she would feel something, but that part of her body had lost sensitivity. She thought it would be that way for the rest of her life. Better like that if they caught her...

The night grew colder and Suzana couldn't stop shivering. She sneezed three times and searched for something to wipe her nose. There were broad leaves on some of the ground plants.

The cold got worse and, for the first time, she thought about giving up. She remembered the policewoman's card. Jo-ni Pax. Would there be any peace for her if she got in touch with the policewoman? They would send her to jail, even if she hadn't killed any of the animals. She was sure that stabbing people was not acceptable in this country. In the mountains men would fight when their honour was brought into question. As a child, she had witnessed several such blood-matches, the combatants surrounded by a wide ring of villagers. They would strip to the waist, the men, though they were often little more than boys, and slash at each other until one would collapse from loss of blood. Once, when a senior man's wife had been caught with another man, the fight had ended in death, the guilty lover castrated and left writhing his way to death. The authorities – police, local politicians, army commanders – had stayed away and the wife was never seen again.

No, Suzana thought, she would not surrender. The clan would track her down in jail and she would have no means of fighting back. Out here, despite the cold and the damp, she had her weapons and she was free. She breathed in the air. Despite the tang of car exhaust, she was in the country again, the smell of plants and soil in the air. She heard the hooting of an owl and took some comfort from it, though she knew the creature was a merciless hunter. She remembered the pellets she and the other children would find under the trees beyond the village – tiny bones, pieces of skin and tail.

She knew she would end up a sack of rotting flesh and broken bones herself, but she would take the men who'd enslaved her into the darkness with her.

50

'That must be him. Look at that splattered nose.'

'If you say so, Kyle,' Hot Rod said from the back of the car. He had a baseball bat between his thighs like the rest.

'His mate and him'll be carrying.'

'If you keep the bats behind you, we'll have them down before they can do anything about it. Besides, we've got the knives an' all.'

'How are we going to talk to this guy if he's Albanian?'

'He's on the fucking door, Pumpkinhead. He's gonna speak some English. Anyway, all he has to do is take us to where they've got Gaz.'

'What if he won't?'

'Jesus, Daryll, look on the fucking bright side. Anyway, we have ways of making him talk.'

'Very fucking funny.'

'What, you too, Jackie? Suppose you'd rather be sticking it up that skinny lass.'

'Fucking right I would. Then again, I like good barney, especially when we outnumber the cunts.'

'Look at that mob of students. Fucking ponces. Probably play rugby and think they're hard. Get in behind them, quick.'

'Hurry up, Pumpkinhead.'

'Fuck off, I'm coming.'

'Ow! Watch that bat, Daryll.'

'Kylie, cool it. You look like you're going to explode.'

'I fucking am. These fuckers taking our mate…'

'Deep breathing, you cunt.'

'Ready, everyone?'

'Aye.'

'Aye.'

'Aye.'

'Aye.'

'Good evening, gentlemen.'

Crack.

'Ach!'

Thud.

'Fuck, Jackie, you've busted his head.'

'Get him in the car.'

Thunk.

'He's coming quietly now, Kylie.'

'Where are we going?'

'Somewhere quiet, wait for the fucker to wake up.'

'Shit, that went well. Ale, anyone?'

'Aye.'

'Give it here.'

'Aye.'

'Aaaaah!'

<hr />

51

Joni lay awake, listening to the movements of the Abbey clock. Her thoughts were at surface level initially – the Albanian women, her mother, Heck, Pete Rokeby. Then she found herself recalling the first time she'd gone for a run by the Roman Wall. It was cold and she was pumping hard to keep warm. When she hurdled a low wall, a voice came out of nowhere.

'Careful, lass!' called an elderly man, sitting in the lee of the wind.

She raised an arm as she turned to the front again. Solicitude had never been a feature of the remarks directed at her when she ran in London. Lust and casual racism were the norm. When she was new on the job, she would stop and flash her warrant card, but she soon learned that was more trouble than it was worth. Ignoring the tossers was the best option. The old guy she'd passed was taken aback to see a black woman, she was certain. As a shopkeeper had pointed out the first week she was in Corham, there weren't 'many of her kind around here'; though there didn't seem to be any malice in the words.

…then Zak Cotter came back to her. They had been lovers for five years. He was seven years older and six inches shorter; a black man who successfully produced black music acts – mainly hip-hop and rap, not that she appreciated either the sounds or the distinction. She met him via an online dating service, having decided against getting involved again with any of her colleagues in the Met; when she was on the beat, she'd had a short and uncomfortable relationship with a white guy who boasted to his mates that he'd bedded a black woman.

Zak, the man she'd loved, the man she'd shared a flat with for two years – until she'd come home early one afternoon and found him in bed with his latest discovery, a seventeen-year-old singer called Kimalia. The girl was shameless, calling Joni by her Met nickname 'Pam', which Zak, a fan of blaxploitation movies, had obviously passed on. Joni would have broken her nose, put her in an arm lock and thrown her out, but she managed to keep her cool. She got rid of her by staring icily and saying nothing. Afterwards, Zak started to gabble about how Joni didn't want him in bed any more and she was only interested in her career, and look where that was heading. She grabbed him by his detumescent dick and hauled him outside, slamming the door and locking it. He rang the bell, begging for his trousers and his phone, but she ignored him, turning Wagner's 'Liebestod' up to full volume. The last time she saw him was when he moved out his gear, including the expensive stereo system. Love was dead in every sense, though she soon bought a cheaper music centre. Life without the classical composers wasn't worth living. Their music kept her going in the bad times; the music and the thought that something intangible lay over the horizon, calling to her and biding its time.

'Come on,' she muttered, turning over.

Then she found herself thinking of the time she'd met her boss up by the Wall…

'Hallo, sir,' she said, as Heck Rutherford approached.

'Hallo, Joni,' he replied. 'I told you to use first names when we're on our own, especially off duty.'

She looked away. 'I'm … I'm not comfortable with that. Sorry.' She felt his eyes on her and turned to the lake. 'Did you see the swans? The cygnets are growing fast.'

'Aye. You like the birds, don't you?'

Joni wasn't sure if there was innuendo in the question. People at work had soon found out she didn't have a boyfriend and inevitably had started wondering if she was a lesbian. She found her superior's tone hard to read. 'City girl,' she replied. 'It's a whole new world up here.'

Heck laughed. 'I'll take your word for it.' He shivered. 'You don't find it too cold?'

This time Joni didn't give him the benefit of the doubt. 'Black people can handle low temperatures perfectly well.'

'Shit,' he said, shaking his head, 'that's not what I meant. London's far off and, anyway, cities are warmer.'

Joni raised a hand. 'Sorry, hair trigger. Can we let it go?'

Heck nodded, though he looked aggrieved.

They parted at Joni's nine-year-old white Land Rover Discovery.

'Can't you find a newer model?' Heck demanded. 'You make the Major Crime Unit look like a bunch of farmers when you arrive at crime scenes in that thing.'

Joni caught his eye. 'Ar,' she said, before getting in and reversing away at speed.

At last her eyes closed. There was a smile on her lips.

52

Brian Sweeney had been trying to keep up with his two-year-old red setter since he'd parked the car by the River Coquet west of Rothbury. He was sixty-nine and only slightly overweight, but his knees had started playing up and the dog pulled the retractable lead to its limit before he could react.

'Bristle!' he shouted. 'Come back! Come, girl!'

He hobbled down the rough path, oblivious of the beautiful setting: willows bowing to kiss the water, birds singing in the trees, the sunlight casting its shafts between the leaves.

'Bristle!'

Brian came here most days – that was why the dog was so quick to find familiar smells – and he was sick to the back teeth of it. They'd got Bristle because his doctor had told him to walk regularly and Beryl used that as an excuse to get him out of the house so she could sit in front of the telly knitting for their three grandchildren. Brian had been a bank teller, never ambitious to rise higher in the company, which he had little affection for. He'd never had much affection for anything. Drinking was for louts, football for morons and smoking for those with a death wish. He liked to look at art books; they were his primary pleasure. He'd even developed an interest in abstract expressionism and was particularly fond of Arshile Gorky. No small part of his enjoyment came from the fact that Beryl, a former pay clerk at Corham Steel, couldn't stand the weird, bright paintings.

Brian heard a bark from Bristle. She was standing at the edge of the riverbank, her muzzle lowered. At first he thought someone had dumped a mattress or large sack in the water. Then he understood and moved forwards as fast as he could, dropping the lead.

'Back, Bristle!' he panted. 'Back, girl.'

The red setter walked around in circles and then sat down a yard away, whining softly.

Brian Sweeney extended a hand tentatively. The naked body

was on its front, feet towards the bank. He gritted his teeth and put his hand round one ankle. He tugged and the lumpen object turned over. Brian jerked back in horror. The man – that much was obvious – had no head. After he'd vomited his breakfast on the path, he looked back and realised that the hands were missing too. He heard a lapping sound by his side and gagged again. Bristle was avidly consuming the contents of his stomach.

∞∞

53

ACC Dickie didn't slip into the MCU morning briefing as before. She stood next to Heck from the start.

'DI Sutton?' Heck said. 'You've given a preliminary report to the CPS?'

'He has,' said a bright-faced young man from the rear. Roger Underwood was one of the Crown Prosecution Service's rising stars in the area. 'Blerim Dost has been transferred to the medical wing of Durham Prison while a full list of charges is prepared. High on that will be attempted murder of a police officer.' He gave Joni a predatory smile.

Morrie Sutton stood with his mouth open, registering his displeasure at being pre-empted. He thought Underwood was a premier league smartarse and was envious of the way female officers fawned over him. At least Jackie Brown wasn't doing that.

'Go on, Morrie,' Heck prompted.

'Thank you very much, sir,' the DI said, pushing the sarcasm as far as he dared. 'The SOCOs have finished in the Burwell Street brothel. We've run the fingerprints through the system and have got seven matches – mostly minor charges, affray that kind of thing, but we'll be following all the men up. None of the six women has been sighted. I'd say there's a good chance the five we had in the hostel went to Newcastle to hand themselves over to the Albanian pimps there. I've circulated descriptions to our colleagues.'

'You've included the killer of Leka Asllani in the first number,' Ruth Dickie said. 'Surely you don't think she'll go back into the fold?'

Joni was impressed by the intervention. She was convinced that Suzana Noli would stay free as long as she could.

'Er, maybe not, ma'am,' Morrie stuttered. 'No one's reported seeing her, that's all I know.'

'What about the lads she sliced up yesterday in Star Park?' Heck asked.

'We caught up with them in Corham General,' Sutton replied. 'They claim they only asked her for cigarettes. One of them has a record – six months in young offenders' for mugging an old woman – so we don't believe much he says. But you can't argue with the damage the woman did. He had twenty-three stitches, another of them seventeen, and the third had to have the tip of his little finger reattached. She's dangerous, but we knew that already.'

'It's hardly surprising,' Joni said, unable to hold back. 'She was a sex slave. If I was a man, I'd keep my distance.'

The ACC gave her a studied but not entirely cold look.

'We've got a Pofnee and neighbouring forces alert out for her,' Heck said. 'Anything else, Morrie?'

'Yes. An ironmonger on Haydon Street called in. He recognised the woman when he saw her passport photo in the *Bugle*. He sold her a carving knife and a boning knife in the morning. Said she didn't speak and smelled bad. She was wearing some kind of cowboy hat – we reckon it's the one taken from Mrs Liphook's shed. We're also checking the council CCTV.' He nodded at Heck.

'Right, thanks.' He turned to Joni, but before he could speak, DS Gray raised his arm. He was holding a desk phone in his other hand.

'DI Pax, I think you'd better take this,' he said, with a smirk.

Joni picked up the nearest phone and pressed the button that was flashing. She identified herself and listened intently. Then she put the phone down and raised her head.

'That was Inspector Parris in Rothbury. A man walking his dog found a male body in the river outside the town.' She looked at Heck and then at Pete Rokeby. 'It's definitely a suspicious death.'

'Why?' demanded the ACC.

'Because the head and hands have been removed.'

For a few seconds no one spoke, then Heck took charge. The Force HQ car park soon had several free spaces.

54

Evie was making coffee when her mother walked into the kitchen. Victoria was wearing a powder blue jacket and skirt, and a white silk blouse that left little to the imagination.

'God, these heels,' Victoria said, lifting one leg and adjusting the shoe.

Evie was in jeans and an Abbey School sweatshirt. 'Why on earth do you wear them?' she asked.

'Some women like to look their best.'

'Some women need the attention.'

Victoria laughed. 'For goodness sake, darling, lighten up.'

Evie took her crutch and limped over. 'I'll lighten up when you stop staring at Nick like he's your next meal.'

'Darling! He's a handsome boy, but he's far too young for me.'

'Is that right? Charlie Terry was only nineteen.'

Victoria waved her hand. 'That was nothing. I was expanding his experience.'

Evie shook her head and headed for the library. Having spent so much time in close proximity to her mother since the accident, she had seen a side of her that was deeply repellent. On the other hand, she couldn't really believe Victoria would try to steal Nick from her. Maybe she shouldn't have mentioned it. Her mother was very competitive. Oh hell.

She sat down at the table and opened the books she had marked up. One Favon ancestor had turned out to have more of an artistic bent than all the others put together. She switched on her laptop and opened a new file.

Imagine you're someone else, she told herself. That's the essence of the writer's skill. Imagine you're a beautiful, inno-cent girl on the threshold of womanhood, whose parents die in quick succession. You are sent to live with your aunt and uncle in a remote castle on a cliff, a river snaking through the valley far below. Your uncle makes advances and your aunt pretends not to notice. There is a sympathetic maid, who hints of family secrets and a curse. The old woman's son will help. He's a forester on your uncle's estate and hates having to destroy the trees, hun-dreds of them cut down every year for firewood and building materials. Your uncle is forever ordering tunnels supported by fresh beams to be dug under the castle.

You don't have to *imagine* this at all. Your ancestor Walter wrote it in the novel that scandalised the country in the 1780s. He called it *The Seeker* and it was never seen in respectable homes, though many a Victorian burgher kept it locked up. The title refers to the uncle, Baron Amherst, who makes a pact with a hooded figure he knows is an emissary of the devil. Although the baron is enormously rich from his sugar plantations in the Caribbean, he wants more. He seeks the mythical treasure brought back from a jungle El Dorado by a Spanish explorer and buried beneath the castle before it came into the family's hands. The emissary of evil knows the exact location, but he extracts a price – the niece. She must be sacrificed, her blood drenching the earth above the treasure's resting place.

Evie was sure her parents hadn't read *The Seeker*; they had probably never even heard of it. Andrew leafed through the papers and scanned the farming magazines, but she had never seen him with a book in his hands. Victoria read the novels on the Booker shortlist every year, without any sign of enjoyment.

But *The Seeker* was integral to the Favons' history. The family name was embossed under the title on the spine. The book was well known in academic circles and there were articles about it. Although the story was melodramatic – gypsies shouting curses at the Baron and his wife when their carriage passed, witches casting spells from ancient grimoires, the heroine tortured in a pit with something far nastier than a pendulum – there was power in the words. Once the heroine, unnamed for reasons known only to the author, realised her uncle's wicked plans, she became a strong character. She stabbed him with his own dagger when he came to rape her on the black altar and her bonds fell away. She watched as the Devil, in the form of a snake with the head of a crocodile, revealed the treasure sought by the Baron. It proved to be a box of rank earth containing the bones of numerous fingers. The wicked uncle screamed and was then devoured by the Devil. The hooded figure approached the heroine and said that his master admired her courage. She could go in peace or enter into a bargain that, because of her purity of spirit, would have real earthly value, though her soul would still be forfeit. The book ended with the young woman considering the choice. Would she become the next Seeker?

Evie felt that the writer was a kindred spirit. Walter had a club foot and was despised by his relatives. Evie was pretty sure her parents had little interest in her and had never got over the fact that she was a girl. On the other hand, Walter was sent down from Oxford for setting a servant on fire; the man later died and a large sum had to be settled on his widow. Dispatched to the plantations, Walter dared to take the side of the slaves, improving their living conditions without asking his father's permission. He was stricken by malaria and spent the rest of his short life in the mountains of Switzerland, whence the alpine landscapes of *The Seeker*. He died at thirty-three, his friends claiming he had been poisoned by agents of his family.

Evie was sure that was what happened. She sometimes thought her father would like her to suffer a similar fate. She shivered. Not for the first time she wondered if the accident with the Land Cruiser really had been an accident, as he always claimed.

55

Heck and Joni, wearing coveralls and bootees, stood side by side and looked at the body in the water. The right leg had been secured to a nearby tree trunk. The sun was high in the sky, but the light was blocked by the tall trees where the river took a bend northwards. Birdsong rang out over the softer rush of the water. They had looked at the map when they arrived. The crime scene on the Coquet was twenty-eight miles north of Corham and a couple of miles west of Rothbury.

'What's that on what's left of his neck?' Heck said, squatting down by the tape lain by the SOCOs on the grassy path.

Joni was trying to make sense of the torn skin below where the Adam's apple would normally be. 'A bite?' she wondered aloud.

'You know who cuts off heads and hands.'

'Bad people.'

'Yeees. What kind of bad people?'

'The professional kind.' Joni glanced at her boss. 'I know what you're thinking.'

'Do you now?'

'Gangsters like the Albanian kind would have no problem doing this.'

Heck shook his head. 'I did think that for a few seconds. Then I told myself not to jump to conclusions. The Newcastle gangs did worse than this often enough. It isn't so easy to hide the victims' identities these days with DNA testing.'

'But that isn't the point of mutilation. They're sending a message to the enemy.'

'Right.' Heck peered at the corpse again. 'This fellow was young. Even after some time in the water– not too long, I'd guess – his muscle tone is pretty firm.'

'The skin isn't worn much either,' Joni put in. 'Except around the knees. Those look like keyhole surgery scars.'

'A sportsman, maybe.' Heck drew her away as the photographers finished and men in wet suits started getting the corpse out of the river. 'Let's hold off on the speculation for a bit, Joni. We need to get things organised here.'

Tasks were given to the officers on scene. Pete Rokeby led a group of uniformed officers combing the woods for tracks and other trace evidence. Eileen Andrews interviewed Brian Sweeney. He was twitchy but calm, keeping his red setter on a short leash and eyeing her dubiously. He had little to tell. He had seen no one else on his brief walk, nor any vehicles parked near the river. Soon people in the local houses, which were few, would be canvassed and the pathologist and SOCOs would give their preliminary impressions.

Doctor Bertha Volpert was kneeling by the body, which was now on a rubber sheet on the bank. She was suited up, her hair in a matching white hat. The apparel gave her the look of an over-inflated Michelin woman. She shook her head after taking temperature readings.

'I'll have to do the calculations back at the lab,' she said. 'The river water is cold and it has reduced that of the body.' She looked up at Heck and Joni. 'So don't even think of asking about time of death.'

'I don't see any lacerations or other marks,' Joni said.

'You are observant, DI Pax. I do not know if the Coquet is a river full of fish, but he hasn't been nibbled at. That could suggest he hasn't been in the water for many hours.'

'The question is, did he have his throat ripped out before his head was taken off or afterwards?' Heck said.

Big Bertha gave him one of her trademark crooked smiles. 'It will be very hard to tell, DCI Rutherford. The bite or bites

– the tearing of teeth is unmistakable – would result in massive loss of blood, but brain function may have been terminated by severe head injury. Alternatively, he may have exsanguinated from a wound higher up the throat. He looks to have been in good physical shape.' Dr Volpert nodded at Joni. 'Going back to DI Pax's earlier point, it is suggestive that there are no defence wounds on the hands or arms. The animal – probably a dog, though I have to check the wounds in the lab – might have been on him before he could react.' She paused. 'Or perhaps he managed to keep it at bay with some implement for a time.'

'It didn't happen here, of course,' Joni said. 'The bank is undisturbed.'

'Assuming there are no blood deposits in the wider vicinity, no,' the pathologist said.

'The killer, or rather, the owner of the killer dog who muti-lated the corpse, took a chance dumping the body here,' Heck said. 'Although it may have happened under cover of darkness. Why take the risk?'

'So that DNA and other trace materials were washed away, of course,' Big Bertha said tersely. 'Fingerprints on the body will potentially have been compromised as well.'

'Let's hope we find some footprints then,' Heck said.

Joni glanced around. 'It's obviously not a path many people use – there's no signpost on the road – but I suspect there'll be plenty of prints to be excluded before we find those of the person who dumped the body. And the ground is dry.'

'I'm glad I don't have your job,' the pathologist said.

Heck and Joni picked their way over the markers left by SOCOs to a secluded spot between two sycamores.

'First question,' Joni said. 'Why was the victim put in the river? If he'd been buried on a moor or in one of the numerous forests around here, we'd never have found him.'

Heck nodded. 'Our dog-owning friend either wanted him to be found or didn't care.'

Joni looked away. 'The latter's even more worrying than

the former.' She waved a blowfly away. 'Second question. How many people in Northumberland own dogs trained to go for the throat?'

'How long's a piece of string? This is the country, Joni. Most people have dogs and plenty of farmers have vicious ones.'

'Not ones that would do that kind of damage.'

'Probably not. The average sheep dog'll give you a nasty nip at worst. I'd say that wound was caused by a large hound, but there's still no shortage of them. And there's no point going through the dog licence archive because, a) not every bugger buys a licence and, b) there's no record of training. Obviously there's the Dangerous Dogs Act, but that only covers a few breeds.'

'We need to check the missing persons register.'

'Aye, put one of your people on that.'

Joni stepped over the crime scene tape and took out her phone. Before making the call, she turned back to Heck. 'Of course, there is another possibility. The victim might be an Albanian pimp that Suzana Noli caught up with.'

'That's bit far-fetched,' Heck replied. 'Where would she find a dog?'

'Maybe she didn't. Maybe she tore his throat out herself.'

Heck watched Joni as she started to speak into her phone. Sometimes her human side was to the fore and at others she was colder than a sea trout.

56

'So what do we do with him, Kylie?'

'What do you think, Pumpkinhead? Squeeze his nuts till he tells us where Gaz is.'

'It's quiet enough around here.'

'Aye, Daryll, it is. When we've finished, we can dump him in the sea.'

'You what? You mean kill him? He's a fucking Albanian.'

'That's the point, Jackie. He's seen all our faces. Do you think we'll keep *our* nuts if we let him loose? These people are animals.'

'Still, Kylie, killing him because he … oh, I get it.'

'Glad to see one of you's got more than half a brain, Hot Rod. Right, let's get started. Hold him still.'

Thwack.

'Fuck, that hurt.'

'Why don't we take him outside and use the bats on him?'

'Good idea, Daryll. Right, dickhead, out. Keep a tight grip on him. Aye, lean him against the car. So where's Gaz, you fucker?'

'Don't know no Gaz.'

Crack.

'Sure about that?'

'Fuck you.'

Crack.

'Jesus Christ, Kylie. You've broken his fuckin' arm.'

'Who cares? He's got another one. For the time being.'

'Yeah, but…'

'Yeah, but what? This is our mate we're talking about.'

'All right, but you canna kill the guy.'

'Watch me, Pumpkinhead. Listen, you twat. We know someone who saw you put Gaz into a Bentley.'

'Aye, a Bentley Continental GT Speed.'

'Shut up, Jackie. Where was he going?'

'Fuck you. Aaaah!'

'Dinna worry, man. One of your balls is probably still OK. Pick the bastard up, Hot Rod. No! Shit! Fuck! Get after him!'

'What about Hot Rod?'

'Stay with him, Daryll. Come on, the rest of you.'

'Fuck. Where did he get that knife?'

'Good … fucking … question, Jackie. I thought … you … searched him?'

'I … did.'

'Come on, he's getting … to the road.'

'Ah … ah canna run … any more.'
'Useless tosser … Pumpkinhead…'
'Oh fuck, he's … stopped that car.'
'Oh fuck. He's … fucking … gone.'

57

Heck went back to Corham after a couple of hours and Joni stayed to supervise the canvassing and search in the woods. Officers from Rothbury had been drafted in and were going through the undergrowth on their hands and knees. None of the people in the cottages had seen anything, but some had gone to work. Interviews were being arranged, but one woman lived on her own and the neighbours didn't have her number. Pete Rokeby was trying to track her down.

'I'll tell you one thing,' the chief SOCO said. 'Whoever dumped the body was strong as an ox. I measured the victim's feet and there aren't any prints as big as that. He must have taken a size twelve.' He looked around disconsolately. 'Then again, there aren't many useful prints on this dry ground.' He tapped his nose. 'Unless you've got really sharp eyes.' He pointed to an area on the bank that had been taped off.

Joni kneeled down by it and stared at the grass. It had been trampled, but as the growth was fresh, there wasn't much damage to it.

'See that?' the SOCO said, extending a hand.

'Sort of. Medium-sized shoe?'

'Aye. It's only a partial, but I estimate it at a size ten. It's fresh and close to the water, so there's a good chance it's our man's. Unlikely to be a woman's, is it? It's an Adidas trainer, I recognise the sole pattern.'

'It could be a woman wearing whatever shoes she could find.'

'Well, she'd have to be bloody strong to have carried the victim this far from the road. Big Ber—, I mean Dr Volpert, estimated his weight at over twelve stone.'

Joni had a flash of the half-naked woman running away from the brothel. Could Suzana Noli have carried the tall man along the path? How would she have got him here? In a stolen car? Or the victim's own car? Had she been hitching and killed the man who'd picked her up? She had murdered one of the Albanians, seriously injured another and forked a third. She'd already shown she was capable of anything. On the other hand, she was skinny and probably undernourished, like the other Albanian woman. This case might not be connected to her at all.

'Whoever it was wanted the body to be found,' the SOCO said. 'This isn't exactly the middle of nowhere.'

'Perhaps the killer didn't know the area,' Joni said, arguing against herself out loud. 'Perhaps the victim's killer wasn't the same person as the person who dumped the body.'

'Could be. Then you've got to wonder which of them cut off the head and hands. If there are two people involved, you've got more on your plate, haven't you?'

Joni nodded, ignoring the SOCO's evident delight as Pete Rokeby walked up.

'I've spoken to the last potential witness,' he said. 'Violet Crichton. She sounded pretty doddery. She said she didn't notice anything out of the ordinary. She's coming to Force HQ in the afternoon to give a statement.'

'The body was probably dumped first thing in the morning – maybe even in the dark if the guy – or woman – knew the area.'

'Woman?'

Join told him her thoughts about Suzana Noli.

Pete looked dubious. 'She's a slip of a girl, isn't she? I mean, I can see *you* carrying the victim down here, but her...?'

'Thanks,' Joni said, unsmiling. She looked around the sylvan scene, the sun now glinting off the river and the birds still loud. She had just got her bearings. Her mother's cottage was less than three miles to the west.

58

Ag Rutherford had driven to work the long way round. Every Wednesday she took her father-in-law to his friend Gavin's place. The idea was that they played music – David on the Northumbrian pipes and his pal on acoustic guitar – but she suspected they nattered most of the day, consuming numerous mugs of tea laced with whisky. The old man was usually the worse for wear when she picked him up in the late afternoon, making the kids double up with his less than politically correct comments. Most of the time she let him get away with it.

'Lovely morning,' he said, struggling to push the Fiat's seat back as he looked out over the fields.

'Spring has blown in with its full and glorious palette.'

'You should write poetry, lass,' David said, with undisguised admiration.

Ag didn't tell him that she did, not that she'd ever had anything published. Even Heck was unaware of what she wrote in the leather-covered book she locked away each night. It wasn't that she was embarrassed by her writing – rather, it was the only thing that was hers and hers alone. She loved her husband and kids, she loved her job, she even loved the old reprobate sitting beside her, but she needed something for herself. She'd always been good with words, but it was only since Heck's cancer that she'd started putting her thoughts down in free verse. Although the diagnosis and treatment had been hard for all of them and she knew her husband wasn't clear of it by a long way, some of its effects had been positive. They were closer as a family and Heck had a better grasp of who he was; at least some of the time.

'He'll be all right, won't he, Ag?' her father-in-law asked, his voice cracking.

She wasn't surprised by the question. David asked it almost every day. Answering had become a kind of ritual, the words forming a protective sheath around the man they both loved.

'Course he will,' she said. 'He's a tough one, your son. It was bad, but he's over the worst. At least he's got a grip on his stomach these days.'

David laughed. 'Aye, it was tricky in the beginning. Remember the time he threw up on that toffee-nosed woman's shoes?'

Ag shot him a warning glance. 'Alice Liphook was very good about it. She said her husband had done much worse.'

Her father-in-law shook his head. 'Poor Alf. Thirty years with that dragon and then a stroke turned him into a vegetable. Just as well he didn't last long after it.'

Ag wasn't going to defend Alice, the 'Dame', as she was known by the other governors. She'd worked out how to handle her – massage her ego frequently – and she could be a useful ally.

'I remember when she was young,' David continued. 'By God, she was a stunner. She liked Olive because she was handy at bridge.' He fell silent.

Ag knew he felt guilty about how he'd treated his wife in the years she struggled with emphysema. He was a kindly man, perhaps too kindly, and he couldn't stand to see her suffering. He'd done more than the average man of his generation, but he'd taken every chance to meet up with his pals, often driving when he was way over the limit. Heck had been forced to have several words. Ag herself hadn't found Olive easy. She was over-protective of her elder son and always gave the impression that he could have found a better woman to marry, meaning a woman with more style and less commitment to her work. Ag had never been one to apologise. She was a teacher because she had a vocation and she bought clothes for the family in Marks and Spencer because they were good value, end of conversation.

'Poor buggers,' the old man said, pointing to a line of people walking from an open-backed lorry to the gate of one of the large fields by the road. There were men and women, most of them young, their clothes ragged and dirty. They looked defeated, their faces blank and their shoulders slumped. 'Poles, I should think, or other Eastern Europeans. Doing the jobs our benefit scroungers won't touch. The Poles and Czechs, they were heroes during the war. Now see what their grandkids have got.'

Ag let that invitation to political argument pass. Her father-in-law had voted Conservative since his thirties, his lowly management position at Corham Steel representing an upward move in society from his coal miner father's class. Her own family had always been liberals, many of them insufferable do-gooders if truth be told, but she felt betrayed by the Lib Dems' decision to form the coalition government with the Tories. She didn't agree with her father-in-law's harsh attitude towards the twenty per cent of society that were locked in the benefits spiral – some of the kids she taught came from such families and many of the parents were as honest as David.

'I certainly wouldn't want to work in the fields,' Ag said, 'even now the weather's better.' She'd caught a glimpse of the hard-faced ganger at the lorry's door. These workers wouldn't have a lunch hour and would only be taken back to the lodgings where they slept ten to a room when the sun was well down in the west. The *Corham Bugle* had run several stories about the appalling conditions migrant workers were forced to accept, both those from EU countries and from further afield. Nothing had happened, of course. The estate owners were in bed with agri-business and couldn't give a damn about the people on the ground. She'd read enough local history to know there had always been such accommodations.

'Looks like one of them has done a bunk,' David said, as they approached a slim figure on the narrow road.

Ag slowed down, thinking about offering a lift. As they passed, she saw it was a young woman, her high cheekbones brought into relief by the woollen hat she had pulled down low. She was wearing what looked like a good quality leather jacket, but her trousers were grubby and she was limping along in battered trainers. There were plastic bags in both her hands and a laptop bag across her chest. She doggedly refused to look at the car and its occupants.

'I wouldn't pick her up,' her father-in-law said. 'She probably stinks.'

'While *you* are a paragon of cleanliness,' Ag murmured. Her father-in-law had become erratic in his bathing habits and Heck had been forced to make that point to him.

She accelerated, seeing from the clock on the dashboard that she was in danger of being late, a cardinal sin for a head teacher. But there was something about the woman – girl, really, probably not many years older than Kat – that bothered her. Then David started coughing and she had to pound his back when he leaned forward. He'd been getting these fits more and more often, but he wouldn't go to the doctor. Men. Heck had been the same. She'd had to drag him to the GP and then to Corham General for preliminary examinations. If he'd put it off much longer … that didn't bear thinking about.

<><><><><><><><><><><><><><><><><><><><><><><><><><><><><><><><><><>

59

At lunch time, Ag went to her office and called Heck on his mobile.

'Hello, love,' he said, surprised. 'To what do I owe this enormous pleasure?'

'I think I've made a mistake.'

'You? Don't be silly. You're perfect.'

'I'm serious, Heck.'

'All right.' Had his father been thrown out for setting the sheets on fire with one of the roll-ups he swore he never smoked? 'Tell me.'

'That girl, woman, you're looking for who killed the Albanian. You know, the one Ruth Dickie was on the telly about last night.'

'Aye?'

'I think I saw her on the way to school this morning – well, on the way to David's music and whisky session.'

'Really?'

'I'm not sure. That's why I didn't call till now.' She sighed. 'To be honest, I forgot about it till classes ended.'

Not perfect after all, Heck thought, then immediately felt guilty. 'What did she look like?'

Ag described the young woman.

'It could be her. She probably reckons Alice Liphook's big hat is too obvious in daylight. Where was this?'

His wife told him. 'There was a gang of field workers on their way into the kale,' she added. 'I suppose she could have been one of them who'd had enough.'

'All right, pet, don't worry about it. I'll get on to it. Bye.' He grabbed his rain jacket and went into the MCU. 'Eileen, with me, now!'

DC Andrews, who had recently arrived back from the headless body scene to open the file on it, picked up her own coat and followed the DCI to the stairs. She was smiling. It wasn't often she got the chance to impress Heck Rutherford up close. She told herself to behave. Fancying your boss wasn't a brilliant career move if it was spotted, and he was the most uxorious man she knew. She'd learned that word from the *Sunday Express* crossword.

60

The ganger had got his slaves – that was how he liked to think of them, the pieces of foreign shit – into the field and told the head man what he wanted: the fresh side shoots of the kale, nothing else. He'd be checking the boxes later. As soon as the men and women had their heads down, he went back to the lorry, took a mobile phone from beneath the driver's seat and turned it on. This one he only used for important messages and he would turn it off as soon as he finished.

'Yeah, this is Wayne Garston. That tart you're looking for. I think I might have seen her.' He listened, holding the phone away from his ear. 'Er, not long ago,' he said, suddenly aware that he'd fucked up by not calling immediately. 'Maybe fifteen minutes. On the road between Haston and Wallington, heading north.' He listened again, shaking his head. How the fuck was he meant to... 'Yeah, all right, I'll head up that way. I can't leave the slaves for long, though.' There was more shouting, then the connection was cut. 'Well, it's the estate's land, you cunt,' he continued, to thin air. 'Think I care if they hack the kale to buggery?'

He went back into the field and told the headman he'd be away for a bit, but no fucking slacking or he'd kick his arse. Oh, and he wanted the blonde one again when he came back, the one with the big tits. No, he couldn't give a shit if her husband didn't like it.

61

Elez Zymberi, delayed by the clan's tame surgeon, drove the black BMW K1300GT motorbike out of Newcastle, observing the speed limits and avoiding the eye-catching overtaking that he often went in for. He'd had difficulty getting on his helmet – orange rather than the usual black to avoid looking too much like the angel of death – because of the dressing on his head. The fork that the bitch had jammed into him went deep and the clan's doctor said he was lucky he hadn't suffered at least minor brain damage. Suzana Noli – he knew her name from the copies of the passports kept in the clan's Newcastle premises – was going to suffer multiple organ damage when he caught up with her. It was a race, he knew. The English cretin in charge of the work gang didn't only work for the clan. He was also loyal to one of the local figures who were being drawn into its web. The police might show up as well, not that he was worried about them. English police were children. They didn't carry anything more than extendable clubs. He had a Glock 17L with a nine-cartridge clip under his leathers, and five more clips in his left pannier. There was a four-inch skinning knife in his right boot, while the right pannier contained rope, plastic cuffs, lengths of cloth for use as gags and to wipe up excessive mess, and a small axe. Suzana Noli was going into the ground jointed.

Zymberi, known in the clan as 'Fingers' because of his propensity for removing his enemies' digits, with his teeth on one occasion back in the mountains, turned off the dual carriageway and followed the signs as he'd been directed. The road quickly narrowed and he was forced to cut his speed because his vision was impeded by low-hanging branches. He soon found the field with the slaves bent double over plants that he wouldn't feed to cattle. There was no sign of the lorry or of Garston. He stopped and called the ganger's mobile.

'Where fuck you?' he demanded. 'I at field.'

'I'm about a mile further up the road. The woman went into a clump of trees and hasn't appeared again.'

'I come now.' Zymberi gunned the engine and went down the road at speed. The bitch must be hiding, though he wouldn't be surprised if the greasy Englishman had been tricked and she had slipped away. She was cunning as well as vicious. He hadn't forgotten what she'd done to Leka, may he enjoy virgins for eternity. He saw the battered old lorry up ahead and decelerated, manoeuvring the bike on to the verge at its side. He didn't want it to be obvious, never mind get hit by a passing tractor. He had worked for three months to buy the machine, even at the clan's reduced price – it had been stolen, of course, and repainted. The number plates were real, duplicates of those on a bike in Cornwall, wherever that was.

Keeping his helmet on, Elez Zymberi raised the visor. He saw Garston waving from a patch of trees about a hundred metres away. Opening the right pannier, he took out a set of plastic restrainers and a length of cloth. He didn't expect to need them as he would knock the bitch unconscious as soon as he found her. Other members of the clan would come to pick her up when he called. By then he'd have fucked her up the arse as a starter for the feast that would ensue back in the city.

Crouching, he went along the fence separating two fields until he reached the edge of a patch of trees.

'I think she must be by that stream,' Garston said, pointing to the shallow water at their feet. He pointed through the trees. 'See that red pickup?'

Zymberi nodded.

'You know who he works for?'

Another nod.

'It's been there for three hours, so you can be sure she hasn't got out that way. There isn't enough cover in the fields for her to have escaped us both. He must have been told not to go in because she's yours.'

The Albanian grabbed the ganger by the throat. 'Hope that true, Mr Garston. Or I take you fingers.'

The Englishman collapsed, gasping, when he was let go.

'Stay here. I find cunt.' Zymberi pulled the knife from his boot. Then he stepped into the water and started to move forward slowly, his head bending beneath the branches.

Wayne Garston watched him go, trembling like a boy on his first date. Then he took out his phone and called the man at the other end of the stream.

62

Heck drove along the narrow road and slowed as they reached a field of kale with workers bent over the tall stems. There was a patrol car behind them carrying four uniforms.

'They must be the ones Ag saw,' Heck Rutherford said, pulling up. He got out and looked around. The trees by the road were thick with leaves and the hedges high, but he could see a large fallow field on the other side. 'Can't understand where she'd have got to here.'

'Maybe she crossed that field to the road on the other side,' Eileen Andrews said. She'd been told what they were doing on the way.

'Maybe she did.' Heck walked to the patrol car that had stopped behind them. 'One of you lads come with me,' he said, through the driver's lowered window. 'You, turn round and go to the road over there.' He pointed through the trees.

'She could have cut across the kale field,' Andrews added.

'You're full of helpful suggestions, Eileen.' Heck looked beyond the workers with their bent backs. The field was vast and he doubted the woman would have risked being visible for the time it took her to cross it – unless she was crawling. Which raised the question of what she was doing in broad daylight, even on this out-of-the-way road. Perhaps she'd spoken to the kale pickers. He looked at his watch. Time was getting on. She could be several miles away by now, but they still needed to check the vicinity of the sighting.

'Constable...?'

'Jackson, sir.'

'Right. Get in there and find any of that lot who speaks English – there's usually at least one. Should be a ganger around too. Ask if the girl said anything to them. They probably saw her. We're going ahead, but we'll be back for you. Keep in touch.'

'Right, sir.'

Heck went back to the squad car. 'Come on, Eileen. Let's check all the way to the road end. I reckon she's long gone, but we need to be sure. She might have stopped for a kip. You drive, but keep the speed down. I don't fancy more time in hospital.' He stood on the sill, holding the door partially open and looking over the hedges.

After a few minutes, Andrews called up to him. 'Lorry ahead, sir.'

Heck turned to the front and told her to pull up behind it. He waited until the car had stopped before stepping on to the asphalt and closing the door. DC Andrews was already out and on the prowl.

'Look at this bike, sir.'

Heck went round the side of the lorry and took in the gleaming BMW. Its juxtaposition with the rust and mud on the old vehicle was striking. And interesting.

'You know what I'm thinking, Eileen?'

'That the ganger in charge of those kale pickers called for reinforcements.'

'Clever lass. Run the bike's plates, will you?' Heck crossed the road and looked at the stream and fence that divided the fields, as well as at the clump of trees in the middle. As often happened in the past, rocks from the soil would have been dumped there, making the removal of the trees around them more trouble than it was worth.

He thought he saw a heavy figure move back into the wood.

Andrews was back in a couple of minutes. 'Registered to a Mr Stanley Doolan of Penzance. Aged eighty-three.'

'Unlikely to be crawling around the undergrowth, is he? There's someone in that stand of trees.'

'At least two people, assuming the lorry driver's there too.'

'We're outnumbered here, Eileen. Go back and get Constable Jackson and call the squad car. No, hang on, we need them to secure the other side. Tell them to wait over there. They should be able to see the lorry.'

'What about you, sir?'

'What about me? Get moving.'

Heck waited until Andrews turned the car round, then took off his coat, folded it and put it under the hedge. Ag had given it to him last Christmas and there would be hell to pay if he tore it. Then he had another thought. He went back to the motorbike, took out his key ring and opened the small penknife on it. It was a struggle, but he managed to puncture the front tyre. That would stop the rider going anywhere. He left the lorry untouched – it couldn't outrun Eileen and, besides, the poor sods in the kale field needed to get back to their hovels somehow.

He debated waiting for the others, then decided to set off alone. His heart was pounding and his stomach full of bile. He was glad there was no one there to see how much he was trembling. Do it, he told himself. Prove you've still got the balls.

63

Suzana had been overwhelmed by exhaustion and had taken refuge in the deepest part of the wood. She hadn't been able to keep sleep at bay, but when she woke up she immediately took precautions. There were heaps of stones between the trees and she gathered some that fitted the palm of her hand. Her knives were fine for close work, but she might need to discourage the men's approach or distract them. She knew the ugly man in charge of the workers had seen her and would be looking out for her. Perhaps he would only want to see if she would work in the fields or sell herself, but there might be others on her trail. She looked at the fence that divided two huge expanses of ground, one covered in fresh grass and the other with shoots of barley. As she reached the last trees, she saw a red pickup on the road beyond, a man standing this side of it and staring into the trees. That couldn't be a coincidence. The word had gone out about her. She wasn't surprised, but angry with herself that she'd succumbed to sleep.

The lorry had stopped where the fence ended behind her. The driver was standing beside it. Then the furious sound of a motorbike approached. She shivered, having heard it before, racing up the slave-house street and screeching to a halt. One of her captors was on her tail. She guessed it was the pig whose head she'd stuck the fork into. He wouldn't show any mercy.

Taking the red velvet gown out of the plastic bag, she draped it over her other possessions, adding stones to them and placing the cowboy hat at the top. She stepped back and looked at her work. It looked convincing enough, a copy of how she was when she'd lain down to sleep against the boulder. She clambered over the rocks and took up a position as close to her dummy self as possible, the knives in her pockets. Then she looked behind. She couldn't see beyond the profusion of new leaves, but she was open to attack from the man on the other side. She crawled away from that heap of stones and took refuge behind another. Now she was concealed from both sides – unless another attacker cut across the field to her rear. There wasn't much she could do about that except keep looking over her shoulder.

There was a rustle to her right and she saw a tall figure in body-hugging black leathers creeping forward. He also wore an orange helmet, the visor raised to reveal eyebrows that joined in the middle and what looked like the corner of a surgical dressing. She recognized him immediately, the pig. He was carrying a knife and some pieces of plastic. She knew what they were – a kind of handcuffs. He was planning on taking her alive. That made her even more determined to overcome him. She knew that long agonies would precede her death.

An engine roared to her left and she caught a glimpse of the red pickup driving away at speed. Some seconds later a white car roared past, a siren suddenly ringing out. It seemed she had only one opponent now. Her fellow Albanian was close to the figure she'd made, ducking behind a fallen tree. She picked up one of the stones she had collected and waited. The helmet was a problem. She would have to hit him somewhere in the abdomen and rush him before he could react.

Suzana felt sweat drench her armpits as the man slid over the tree and approached the dummy on all fours, the knife between his teeth. Suddenly she realised what she had to hit: his right hand. All the children in her village had learned how to throw accurately and with power. It was a question of survival, as the sheep dogs responded only to their masters and savagely attacked anyone who strayed close to the flocks. She swallowed hard and waited, watching the orange-headed figure draw closer.

She needed to get the timing exactly right. If the pig got too close to the dummy, he would realise what it was. So she tossed another stone into the undergrowth to his left. He looked that way and she stood up, launching the stone at the hand with the knife. The crack on the knuckles was loud. The man screamed, which gave her a lot of satisfaction, and rolled on to his back, clutching his injured hand. She was on him in a flash, kicking the knife away and dropping a larger stone on his groin. The pitch of the second scream was markedly higher.

Someone was crashing about in the trees behind the man in leather. She leaped over the rocks, leaving her belongings behind, and ran in the opposite direction. As she approached the end of the fence, she saw cars passing on the road, but there was no sign of the pickup or the police car. The low branches clutched at her hair and scratched her face. All she had were the clothes she was wearing and her blades. That would have to be enough. She still had her freedom and she'd hurt another of the men who had abused her.

Suzana Noli was smiling as she jumped over the fence, crossed the road and disappeared into the steep woodland beyond.

64

Heck had gone over the hedge and alongside the fence with his heart doing a Keith Moon drum solo and his arms quivering. The fact that he'd picked up a damp length of four-by-two that had absorbed plenty of water over the winter didn't help. It wouldn't be much use in a fight with anyone serious, but he was buggered if he was going in barehanded on his own. On the other hand, the Albanian girl deserved the protection of the police even if she was a murderer and he wasn't going to delay. That was how his mind worked, but his body wasn't in agreement. There were jabs of pain in his lower abdomen and he was shaking all over.

He heard branches crack ahead and caught sight of a bulky man running across the fallow field to the south – the lorry driver, presumably. They'd catch up with him later, though he had the feeling that he wasn't a key player. He moved on, then stopped abruptly. He fiddled with his phone, putting it on vibrate mode; the last thing he needed now was a headbanger coming at him because his phone had rung. The quickest way to make progress was by walking through the stream. The water only came halfway up his calves, but it was surprisingly cold. He knew he'd catch another chill, let alone an ear-bashing from Ag about the state of his suit and shoes. She might let him off about the socks.

Come on, he told himself, mind on the job. You haven't been in a clinch with a villain since the op, so you need to keep your wits about you. He peered through the foliage, hearing the sudden blast of a siren. The patrol car must have gone after the red pickup, but he didn't have time to call them now. He moved on through the water, his office shoes slipping and sliding in the glaur. The phone started to throb in his pocket, but he ignored it. The motorbike rider might already have caught up with the girl. Then he heard a scream and he broke into run. There was another, more highly pitched scream. He clambered out of the stream and pushed through the branches, feeling their sharp points on his scalp and hands. It couldn't be much further now, the cries had been close. What had the fucker done to the woman?

Heck came out into a small clearing and took in the scene. A figure in dark red was lying motionless, head bowed forward under a leather cowboy hat. He remembered what had been stolen from Alice Liphook's shed. Jesus, was this the Albanian girl? He ran forward, the bottoms of his trousers slick on his legs. As he approached he saw marks on the ground and skirted them – some kind of struggle had taken place. Then he got to the figure in red and touched it. A frisson of shock ran up his arm before he realised it wasn't flesh beneath the long gown. He lifted the hat and a large stone rolled on to the ground. Smart, Suzana. But where's the scumbag who was after you?

He looked around and saw a bush to his left that had taken some serious damage. He went to it and parted the leaves. A leather-suited figure in an orange biker's helmet was staggering over the fallow field beyond, upper body bent and hands over his groin. Heck turned to the right. The woman must have gone that way and she might slip past if the lads in the patrol car didn't come back. What to do? This time he answered his phone when it started to vibrate.

'Where are you, sir?' DC Andrews asked. 'Are you OK?'

'Aye. Listen, our biker's stumbling across the field to the south of me. I'm going after him. Get through the hedge and you'll see us. Oh, and call the patrol car. I think the woman went in their direction.'

He cut the connection and pushed through the bush, feeling thorns tear his suit. Jesus, he was in deep shit with Ag now. Too bad. He got over the fence and gauged the distance between him and the biker. A hundred yards at most. He could make it, but not carrying the club. He ditched it. Only after he was twenty yards into the field did he remember that the specimen would probably be armed. His stomach did a somersault. If the piece of shit had a gun, it would be curtains. He considered giving up and letting Andrews and the constable do the dirty work, but that went against the grain. He kept going, breath rasping and lungs struggling to inflate sufficiently. As he got closer, the man turned. Heck saw that there was blood on one hand. In the other was a knife. His heart missed several beats. Was Suzana lying in a welter of her own guts in the wood? He upped his speed, shoes sliding on damp patches that the sun hadn't yet burned off.

The biker yelled something in a foreign language.

'Stop!' Heck shouted back. 'Police!' That might not have been the best thing to say. The bastard knew what he was up against now.

The man in the helmet stopped, then transferred the knife to his other hand. 'Come … English fuck. I cut … cock off.'

Heck looked at the way he was staggering, the bloody hand on his groin. 'Is that what she did to you?' he asked, realising that his fear had disappeared. He went for him, running hard and then diving through the air like he used to do on the rugby pitch. His head slammed into the biker's lower abdomen with satisfying force, hitting something metallic. He heard a rapid expulsion of breath. The man sprawled backwards, moans emanating from the open visor. Heck made a grab for the knife and tugged it from the weak grasp, tossing it over his shoulder. To his surprise he saw plastic cuffs sticking out of the guy's jacket pocket. He quickly applied them to his wrists, trying unsuccessfully to avoid the blood. Then he took out a handkerchief and removed a semi-automatic pistol from inside the biker's jacket.

'Bloody hell, sir,' he heard Eileen Andrews say from behind. 'That was some tackle.'

'Misspent … youth,' Heck said, gulping in air. 'The … woman?'

'They're looking, but there's a large forest on the other side of the road. If she's got in there, they won't find her easily.'

Heck watched as Constable Jackson went after the fat man at the far end of the field. He took him down with a decent though rather high tackle. 'The … the pickup?'

'They lost it. Local guy, obviously – knew the farm tracks. Probably up to no good as well. The rear registration plate was plastered with mud. Red, Japanese make probably, they weren't sure which one.' Andrews stuck out her hand and helped Heck up. 'Who's this, then?'

'Ask … him.'

She did.

'Fuck … you,' came the reply.

Heck and Eileen looked at each other.

'A real charmer,' said the DC.

65

'Hello, Nicholas,' Victoria Favon said, when she opened the door. 'Isn't Michael coming in?'

'No, he's got something to do in Corham, Lady Favon.'

'You know you should call me Victoria.' She took his arm and led him into the hall. 'Vicky, if you like.'

Nick glared as her right breast pressed hard against his arm. 'Stop it!' he said firmly, pulling away. 'Hello, Evie.'

Nick!' There was a smile on Evie's lips, but her eyes took in her mother with suspicion. 'Come into the library. I've got something to show you.'

'I'll bet you have,' Nick heard Victoria say.

'What happened?' Evie asked, closing the library door behind them. 'I've seen that look on Victoria's face before.'

Nick avoided her gaze. 'I don't know,' he mumbled. 'She ...'

'I'll rip her head off.'

'No,' he said, grabbing her arm. 'Turn the key, won't you? I don't want her walking in.'

Evie laughed. 'Neither do I.'

Afterwards, they got dressed and sat at the table.

'I've discovered something else,' Evie said.

Nick leaned against her. 'So have I. Not only do I love you, but you're wonderful.'

Evie turned and kissed him on the lips. 'You're sweet.'

'I mean it. I've never said that to a girl before.'

She laughed. 'But you have to a boy?'

His eyes widened. 'No, I haven't. I'm ... I'm a rugby player.'

Evie nodded. 'Who spends a lot of his time grappling with members of the same sex on the pitch and horsing around in the showers afterwards.'

'Horsing around?'

'You know what I mean.' Evie's expression grew more sober. 'I'm touched, Nick. I am, really. But this is the beginning of things for us. Let's not get carried away.'

'You mean … you don't love me,' he said, devastated.

'I think I just showed how I feel about you on that prickly rug. I'm only saying we shouldn't get ahead of ourselves.'

Nick's head went down. 'I'm telling you how I feel. Isn't that what women want?'

'I appreciate it, I do. To be continued, OK?' She waited until he nodded. 'Now, look at this.' She brought a document up on the screen. 'Remember Jaffray, the slave one of my disgusting ancestors tortured?'

'How could I forget?'

'Well, I've been doing some research into the slaves' religious beliefs.'

Nick read what she had written:

Native religions were banned in the plantations and celebrants mercilessly hunted down. In recent years, people's attention has been drawn to voodoo and the transformation of the old religions into spell-casting and the like, largely in the melting pot of New Orleans and by means of its music. The gris-gris rhythms and the blues singers who howl about their mojo and John the Conqueror root have become known around the world. But that's superficial. The real thing is vodoun, the ancient religion of West Africa, which was taken west by the slaves. The spirits, the vodoun, govern the world – the sun, the earth, the wind, the rain, the trees, the plants and the birds, intermediary creatures that move between earth and sky.

The vodoun, or loa, were joined with Christian deities and saints on the Caribbean islands. Even though Christianity was the religion of the oppressor there, many believers were driven to accept it, at least in part. But others served only the loa, in particular the rada loa, the benevolent ones: Legba, who stands at the crossroads and communicates between mortals and the other loa; Loko, the patron of trees, plants and healers; Loko's wife, Ayizan, the archetypal mambo priestess who controls initiation and the markets; and Damballah, the sky spirit, guardian of the cosmic egg, protector of the crippled, as well as young children. The loa *helped the slaves survive their awful lives, instilling in them an understanding of the world beyond the plantations.*

But there were darker powers, the spirits of the dead. To keep them at a distance, worshippers turned to the ghede loa. *They were dangerous, loud of speech and rude in their behaviour. They wanted sex and, in the paradoxical way of* vodoun, *were full of laughter and life despite their experience of the grave. They brought fertility and childbirth, especially under cover of night, but with a bright moon. They worked magic and trickery, but they were not witches – the* ghede loa *were far more powerful than humans who dabbled in the black arts.*

One of the best known was Baron Samedi in his top hat and dark suit, flashing a grin from his skeletal face. He brought with him his wife, Maman Brigitte, who was pale-skinned and had the same green eyes. She swore and shrieked at the Baron's jokes before they copulated, bones rattling and tongues slipping in and out of the gaps in their faces. Baron Samedi protected the faithful from any spell or danger, but he was always short of time. The dead were many and he had to escort each one to the world below. There were times when he and his alternates – Baron Cimitière, Baron La Croix and the cruel Baron Kriminel – absented themselves.

The Favons hated vodoun *with all the passion they could muster and, as always, were inspired by selfish motives. They were hypocritical Christians, happy to read the Gospels on Sunday and exploit their slaves on Monday. They thought worship of the old religions fomented rebellion. That was why* vodoun *was criminalised. But the slaves and their descendants needed retribution for the thousands, the hundreds of thousands, who had lived and worked in extreme hardship and had died because of the estate owners' greed. A terrible revenge would be exacted.*

'I don't understand,' Nick said, standing up. 'Who will take revenge? You really do have a problem with your family, don't you?'

Evie's face hardened. 'Doesn't everyone? Your grandfather killed innocent people in the former Yugoslavia, didn't he?'

Nick pushed his chair back and it hit the wooden floor with a crash. 'He did not!'

'All right, maybe he didn't personally, but the soldiers under his command did. I've read about it.'

'It was war,' Nick said, gathering up his books and papers. 'Sometimes I don't get you, Evie. What's all this got to do with us? I tell you how great I think you are and you make me read about some crazy slave religion. And then you insult my grandfather. Thanks a lot.'

'No, Nick, wait…'

But he was already out of the door.

'I'll ring the general and ask him to meet you on the road,' Evie called.

'I'm going on my bike,' Nick said, over his shoulder.

Evie went after him, then stopped. She wanted to grab him by the arm, pull him round and kiss him on the lips. Who cared if Victoria was watching? She wanted to tell him she loved him and that nothing else mattered, but she couldn't. Sincerity and openness weren't in her genes.

66

Heck and Joni were standing by the lorry. The Albanian's motorbike had been winched on to a tow truck, but not before the panniers had been opened. The contents, as well as the Glock and the knife taken from the prisoner, were in sealed evidence bags in the boot of the patrol car.

'You'll catch your death,' Joni said, as her boss shivered violently. She had come over when Eileen Andrews reported what had happened. 'Let me take you home and get you a change of clothes and shoes.'

'No, I need to get over to the search site. The Albanian woman—'

'Suzana.'

'Suzana,' he repeated. 'She might be hurt.'

'I'll do it,' Joni said, feeling the familiar tingling at the top of her spine and desperate to pick up the scent. 'One of the constables can take you home.'

They watched as DC Andrews came through the hedge with evidence bags full of the clothing and other gear that had been left among the trees.

'It's mostly stuff that was taken from Alice Liphook's shed,' Heck said. 'Maybe she was heading for Scotland.'

'Or the moors. Plenty of places to hide out there.'

'But not many places to find food and shelter.'

'What about the knives she bought?'

Heck shook his head. 'She's still got them. Then again, judging by what she did to the tosser I caught, she doesn't need them. It looks like she smashed his hand with one rock and inflicted serious damage on his groin with another. That isn't all. When we took off his helmet – God, he's an ugly bugger – there was a dressing on the side of his forehead.'

'Fork Man, aka Elez Zymberi.'

'I'd say so.' He frowned. 'How did you remember that name?'

'It's hardly common. He isn't talking, of course.'

'You can try him with your Italian back at HQ, but I doubt you'll get more than curses. I'll wager Dick Lennox or one of his sidekicks will be over to hold his unbroken hand.'

'And the other man?'

'Ganger,' Heck said, coughing. 'There's a bunch of Poles and the like in a kale field down the road.'

'I saw them. You think the ganger alerted the Albanians when he saw Suzana?'

'They're into people trafficking and anything else you fancy these days, so I wouldn't be surprised if there's a connection.'

'What about the pickup that was seen at the other side of the field? More Albanians?'

Heck slapped his chest and turned away to spit. 'Sorry. I don't know. Doesn't exactly match, having a luxury motorbike on this road and a muck-covered pickup on the other.'

'Plus I heard the driver knew the back roads like a local.'

'Hm. Maybe they weren't working together. We'll take the fat man back and question him. See who he's in with.'

'If he talks.'

Heck grinned. 'He'll talk. He's already quivering like a jelly.'

'Speaking of talking, do you think the patrol cars have a loudhailer?'

'Aye, at least one of them should. What are you thinking?'

'I'll give her some blasts of Italian,' Joni said. 'You never know, she might turn herself in now she's without food and warm clothing.'

'Worth a try. What's going on with the headless man?'

'Nothing earth-shattering. I'll brief you tomorrow.'

'All right.' Heck's face was damp with sweat.

Joni called to the constable who was standing by the patrol car. 'Take DCI Rutherford home, please.' She turned to Eileen Andrews. 'Go back to Force HQ and update the case files, please. I'll get Pete Rokeby over here.' She waited for Heck to sign off on the orders, but he didn't. He looked like he was about to keel over.

67

Pine trees were the worst, especially when they were close together. The forest was on a slope and Suzana struggled to get past the thick branches, the soles of her trainers slipping on the thick carpet of needles. The branches were obscuring the sun and she was cold, bitterly regretting the loss of her robe, let alone her provisions. Not that she could have worn the long garment now and stopping wasn't an option. Her blood was still up after the pain she had meted out to the bastard in the helmet. Close up, she recognised his beady eyes, full of anger and hate, and the single eyebrow. When she'd dropped the rock on him, pain and horror convulsed him. That made her feel good. But the enemy had got very close. She had to be more careful – and always be ready to use the knives on herself rather than fall into their hands.

Suzana stopped to catch her breath, crouching on all fours like a dog. She was as much of an animal as the ones who wanted her – she knew that and it didn't concern her. She'd been a human being until the first rape. Everything that followed had turned her into a ravening beast, a creature she didn't understand or even recognise in the cracked mirror when she was in the slave house. But since she'd been free that feeling had begun to recede. She was still far from being a person who could function in a town like Cor-ham – buying the knives had been the limit of her abilities, and she had become a wild creature again when the young men came at her in the park. Could she ever hope to be a woman? She'd been a girl before the horrors started. She had no idea what it would be like to be a grown woman.

'Su-za-na!'

She tensed when she heard the magnified voice, only realising that her name was being called after the fourth or fifth time. She had almost forgotten it, having had no one to talk to on first-name terms for so long. Leka never called her Suzana, he called her whore or bitch.

'Su-za-na!'

The voice was a woman's, she understood with a shock. What was a woman doing coming after her?

'Suzana, my name is Joni.' The language was Italian, spoken slowly and carefully. 'Suzana, this is Joni. I'm going to help you.'

Suzana took out the wallet and found the card. Jo-ni Pax – the policewoman who chased her to the old factory.

'Did you see my card, Suzana? I am Joni Pax from the police. I will save you from the men who are chasing you. Please, Suzana. You are in very great danger.'

She thought about it while moving further up the slope. The police wanted to save her. If that was true, they were very different from the police in her home country. *They* took bribes and answered to the clans. Could it be so different here? Also, nothing was said about her crimes. She had injured the pigs, maybe even killed the other two in the slave house. She'd also slashed the youths in Cor-ham. The policewoman would save her by putting her in prison, but there would be no safety for her there – or any weapons.

Suzana pushed on through the branches, her face now scratched all over.

'I am Joni Pax,' came the voice behind her – she couldn't tell how far. 'I can help you, Suzana.'

'No, you can't,' she muttered. 'Only I can help myself.'

Ignoring the pleading, tempting words in Italian, Suzana Noli pushed herself up the slope and deeper into the mass of trees.

68

'What the fuck do we do now?'

'The same as we've been doing all day, Daryll. Keep our heads down.'

'Aye, but we can't stay off work for long, Kylie. My old man's already giving me shit.'

'Jesus, Pumpkinhead, tell him the Albanians are after you.'

'He won't know what Albanians are. Neither do I, except they're hard bastards.'

'And what about Hot Rod? We can't just leave him in the hospital.'

'Aye, we can, Jackie. He's safer there than anywhere else. Christ, he was lucky. That blade nearly cut his throat open.'

'Maybe we should go to the cops.'

'I've already been, Pumpkinhead. Remember?'

'That was just to report Gaz missing. Maybe they'll give us protection.'

'Ha-ha-ha. Protection? They'll use us as bait, you arsehole.'

'So what are we going to do?'

'Sit tight. No one knows we're here.'

'Except the locals who saw us climbing in the back window. Anyway, this dump fucking reeks.'

'Oh, I'm so sorry, your majesty. If I could have, I'd have found us a squat with four bedrooms, a wine cellar and a fucking jacuzzi. Wanker, Jackie.'

'What are we going to eat?'

'You're going to the chippie later.'

'Aye, right.'

'Hey, Kylie, do you no' think we should call in the heavy mob?'

'Very good, Daryll. I've been thinking about that. Like a full-on, balls-out war between the Christies and the Albanians is going to be good for Gaz's health. Grow a brain, will you? It's an option for later, but we've gotta make more of an effort to find Gaz.'

'How are we going to do that? Grab another headbanger from the Stars and Bars?'

'You think that's funny, Jackie? That's exactly what we're going to do.'

'You're joking.'

'Come on, Kylie, man.'

'Fuck.'

'Fuck.'

'Fuck.'

69

'What's happened, Heck?' Ag cried, running to the door when she saw the state her husband was in. A constable was supporting him and between them they lowered Heck into an armchair in the sitting room.

'No,' Heck gasped, shivering. 'I'm dirty.'

Ag saw the trousers stuck around his calves and the soaked shoes. 'It doesn't matter,' she said, glancing at the officer. 'What happened?'

'Better if he tells you, ma'am,' he said, turning to the door.

'Thanks,' Heck said after him, then went into a coughing fit.

'Are you hurt?' Ag asked, pulling off his anorak. 'You look like you've been through a hedge backwards.'

'Forwards, actually,' her husband replied, smiling weakly.

'What is it, Mum?' Kat said, from the door.

Luke pushed past her. 'Ew, Dad, you've been in a bog.'

'Out, you two,' Ag ordered, having ascertained that Heck wasn't at death's door. 'Tea'll be ready in a minute.'

'I'm hungry too,' Heck said mildly.

'Come on, you,' his wife said, heaving him to his feet, though to be fair, there wasn't much meat on him these days. 'Get those trousers off.'

'Oh aye?' David was standing in the doorway. 'Bit early for that, isn't it?'

He disappeared after Ag turned her eyes on him.

'What have you been doing, for the love of God?' she hissed. 'You've only had that suit a few months.' She went over to the sofa and picked up the blanket he used when he watched TV.

'Got cold,' Heck said, sitting down and trying to reach his shoes.

'I'll do that.' Ag put the blanket over his shoulders and undid his laces. 'These shoes are only fit for gardening now.'

'I'll put in a claim.'

'It's all a joke to you, isn't it, you stupid man,' Ag said, pulling off his socks. Then she looked up at him. 'Don't tell me. You were chasing that girl, weren't you?'

'No.'

'What then?' Ag shook her head at his skinny legs. When he'd played rugby, they were like columns of wound steel.

'Confidential,' he said, clutching the blanket tighter.

'Don't give me that, Heck.'

He saw the look in her eyes and decided against that line. 'All right, if you … if you must know, I caught an armed gangster.' He laughed. 'Bloody great tackle, actually. He went down like a—'

'You caught an armed gangster?' Ag repeated incredulously. 'You were in a fight with a criminal?'

'Em, sort of.'

'You're a DCI, Heck. Young lads like the one who brought you home are meant to do the tackling.'

'He did, actually. He brought another one down.'

'Oh, for God's sake.' Ag went upstairs to get him dry clothes. When she came back, he was leaning back in the chair with his mouth open, snoring gently. She tucked another blanket around his bare legs and kissed him on the forehead.

What an idiot her man was. What a hero.

70

ACC Dickie walked into the MCU and looked towards Heck's empty office.

'DC Andrews, where's the DCI?'

'At home, ma'am. He got soaked when he caught an Albanian gangster.'

'What?'

Eileen Andrews told her everything, surprised that DI Pax hadn't contacted Mrs Normal. Morrie Simmons and Nathan

Gray were openly eavesdropping, but there wasn't anything she could do about that.

'What about the man in the river?' Ruth Dickie asked.

'The post-mortem's tomorrow morning, ma'am. The SOCOs are putting their report together, but they haven't found anything very useful. The canvass didn't come up with anything, either.'

'Where's DI Pax?'

'Chasing the Albanian girl from the brothel. She may have been involved in the headless man's death.'

'Really?' said the ACC sceptically. 'Quite a little killer, stress on the word *little*. What are you smirking about, DI Simmons? Have you anything to tell me about the Burwell Street brothel?'

'Yes, ma'am. The bills were paid monthly by direct debit from a bank in London. It's in the name of the Liberian company that owns the place.'

'Very helpful. And you, DS Gray? How have you been spending your time?'

'I interviewed Blerim Dost in Durham Prison, ma'am. The Albanian who tried to throttle DI Pax with his...'

'I know who he is. What did he tell you?'

'Nothing, ma'am. One of Lennox's people was there and they both put a zip on it.'

ACC Dickie shook her head. 'That must have been a lengthy interview, then. What are you doing now?'

Nathan Gray hurriedly moved his computer mouse. 'I've been talking to Newcastle MCU about the Albanians.'

'Have you? On DCI Rutherford's instructions, I presume.'

'Er, no, ma'am.' Gray looked at Morrie Simmons, but the latter's face was set in stone. 'On my own initiative.'

'Kindly keep it in check. DCI Rutherford alone is responsible for liaison with other MCUs. Understood?'

DS Gray's cheeks were red. 'Yes, ma'am,' he mumbled.

The three detectives watched the ACC's departure.

'Thanks a lot, boss,' Gray said, glaring at Simmons.

Eileen Andrews eventually stopped laughing. 'I don't know what came over me, she said.

71

Joni continued broadcasting though the afternoon as she pushed through the dense foliage. She had ten officers with her in a line, but none had found any trace of Suzana. When they got to the top of the forest, the sun had already sunk behind the hills ahead.

'What's up there?' she asked the constable on her left.

'Nothing much, ma'am. The odd farm, sheep, some of those wind turbines.'

She called DS Rokeby. He and another constable had gone up the solitary track in her Land Rover. 'Anything, Pete?'

'Afraid not. We've spoken to the farmers on the way, those that were in. They haven't seen her, but they'll keep a look out.'

'All right. Get as high as you can and survey the terrain.'

'The light's going fast.'

'I know. We're heading back through the forest now. See you down at the main road.'

One of the officers pointed to a firebreak between the trees and they walked back more easily.

'Do you think she doubled back on us?' Joni asked.

'We'd have heard from the fellas on the road, ma'am.'

She nodded, unconvinced. Suzana was showing unexpected survival skills. Halfway down, her mobile rang. Heck's home number was on the screen.

'Yes, sir?'

'I'm used to Miss,' Ag said drily.

'Oh, hello.' Joni had never felt comfortable addressing her boss's schoolteacher wife by her first name.

'Hello, Joni. What on earth has Heck been up to? He told me he caught a gangster.'

'That's true.'

'By rugby tackling him.'

'So I heard. I wasn't at the scene then. Is he all right?'

'Nearly caught his death of cold, but he's sleeping like a very long baby now. Look, Joni, I know this is probably irregular, but can you try to stop him putting his life on the line? We nearly lost him once and he's not over the wound, whatever he says. He should stick to his desk.'

'The DCI does the job his own way, Mrs Rutherford.'

'Ag.'

'Em … Ag. I can't nursemaid him, but I'll see what I can do.'

'Good, thanks. Come to lunch on Sunday. 12.30.' The connection was cut.

Joni put her phone back in her pocket. Lunch would be OK, but she was glad she wasn't one of Ag Rutherford's pupils.

Back on the road, waiting for Pete Rokeby, her phone rang again. She groaned.

'DI Pax, what exactly are you doing?' Ruth Dickie's voice was level, but there was the usual steely undertone.

'Searching for Suzana … for the Albanian woman, ma'am.'

'It sounds like you haven't been successful.'

'Not so far.'

'It's dark. Give it up.'

'We have, ma'am.'

'As for the man DCI Rutherford apprehended, Richard Lennox has already sent one of his lawyers to look after him. I'll see you at the morning briefing.'

Again, the call was terminated. What was it with people up here, Joni thought. Weren't they familiar with the word 'goodbye'?

She looked round as the familiar sound of her vehicle approached, its headlights making her drop her gaze.

'You've got full beam on, Pete,' she shouted, as he pulled up.

'Shit, sorry, ma'am.' He turned off the lights and engine.

'Anything?'

'No sign of her. It's a wilderness. I wouldn't fancy spending the night up there without a tent and sleeping bag.'

Joni remembered something that one of the constables had mentioned. 'Those people who were picking kale – whatever that is – did they talk to Suzana?'

'Apparently not. She walked straight past them.'

'Talk to the officers we left down here. She may have doubled back.'

Joni watched him go into the gloom and shivered, thinking of Suzana.

72

Suzana had come out of the forest and was looking at the grass-covered slopes ahead. They didn't inspire awe in her; these weren't the savage peaks of her home country. She ran on, into the last of the sun. There was a line of monstrous metal columns on the ridge, a blur at the top of each one. She had no idea what they were so she excluded them from her thoughts. Her feet were aching, but the carpet of needles beneath the trees had been much better than the hard roads.

What was she to do now? She could wait for full darkness and head back through the forest, starting at least three kilometres away from where she'd ascended, or she could press on across the upper ground. She stopped by a stream and cupped water to her mouth with her hand. Thirst wouldn't be a problem, but hunger was already attacking her. She looked around. There were no buildings in sight, but below the saddle between two hills was a cluster of white dots. She knew immediately what they were.

Her good grandfather had sometimes taken her with him to the high pasture in the summer. Her parents didn't approve, but the old man had seniority and they had to obey him. They set off before sunrise and reached the plateau by midday. Her grandfather's dogs accepted her presence, though they wouldn't allow her to stroke them. She didn't mind. She had a twisted crook in her hand and the smell of grass and herbs was on the cooling wind. After an hour she was gasping for breath. Her grandfather told her to keep going and eventually she found that breathing came more easily and the ache in her thighs passed.

'Wait,' the old man said, touching her bare forearm. His eyes were still good and they had caught movement in the trees behind the flock of long-tailed, shorn sheep.

'What is it?' she whispered.

'The Popi,' he answered, spitting. 'Those brigands always take what they want.' He unslung his rifle and shifted the bolt.

'The Popi are dangerous,' Suzana said, spouting the words she'd often heard from her parents. 'We don't get involved with them.'

'The Popi are louts,' her grandfather said. 'They're too lazy to tend to animals, so they steal. I've had enough of them.'

She followed the direction of his gaze. 'Grandpa, there are three men. They're young.'

'I don't care.' The old man looked down the rifle and fired.

She saw a man fall back, his arms outspread. The others looked in their direction, ducking when Grandpa loosed off another four shots. He changed magazines. By the time he raised the weapon again, the survivors had disappeared into the trees.

After waiting a while, the old man got up. 'Come, girl. Not only are they thieves, but they're cowards.'

They crossed the meadow, the animals having run off as soon as the first shot echoed out.

'See?' Grandpa said, pointing at a sheep carcass, the rear legs cut off close to the spine and the belly open. 'This is what the dishonourable scum do.' He turned to the man lying a few metres away. The top of his head had been taken off by the bullet. 'And this is what they get.'

Suzana trembled as the old man knelt by the sheep, knife in hand. He hacked away and held out a bloody mass to her.

'Here, the liver. It gives great strength if you eat it raw.'

Although she hadn't thought she could, she swallowed it all, blood covering her face. And Grandpa was right. For the rest of the day she ran around ceaselessly as he checked the other animals. She wasn't even tired when they got back to the village. The family ate the meat the old man had butchered. The next day he was stabbed in the throat as he walked down the street and the Popi came for the rest of them. She didn't know what was said and only much later did she understand. Her father was forced to give up his children. The Popi waited until the time was right and took her, passing her on to the men of the larger Spahia clan. They'd have come for her sister by now too. And maybe they'd killed her parents just for the sake of it.

It took her some time, but Suzana caught a sheep shortly before the last light died. She knew her way around a carcass and soon satisfied her hunger. Out of necessity she had become a thief like the Popi. She retreated – for all she knew, the shepherds here came every morning to check on their charges – and curled up in a hollow by a stream. The blood on her face had dried and she didn't bother to wash it off. Besides, there would be blood all over her clothes, even though she slept with the skin she'd removed with the fleece facing inwards.

In her dreams she was slashing at the men who killed Grandpa. When she woke up in the chill grey of dawn, she thought she might be in luck. Maybe the Popi, who specialised in retribution, were on her trail now and she'd be able to avenge the old man's murder. Before she put a blade to her own throat.

73

Back home, Joni called Roland Malpas on her mobile. This time her former Met colleague answered immediately.

'Guess who, Ro.'

'Pam! I've been a fan for ages. I loved you in *Coffey*, but *Foxy Brown* was the killer for me.'

Joni let him have his fun. The bits she'd seen of the Pam Grier blaxploitation movies had left her cold because of their casual violence.

'They call me Jackie up here,' she said. 'Tarantino's film is even more patronising if you ask me, but that's not why I called.'

'No, I guessed not. Just out of interest, what is your favourite movie?' Ro was exacting as much as he could from the situation – she could imagine him telling the rest of the homicide squad what she said. She could only hope he had something about the Popi for her.

'I'm not really a big film watcher,' she said. 'Maybe *The Leopard*?'

'What? I don't know that one.'

Una vera sorpresa, she thought. If Roland Malpas had sat through Visconti's three-hour version of di Lampedusa's great novel, she'd have eaten the hat that Suzana left behind in the wood.

'The Popi, Ro,' she prompted.

'Ah, right. I've asked around. Looks like you've got trouble.' He couldn't completely disguise his satisfaction. Joni knew that, deep down, he was resentful she had put her life on the line for him. 'The Popi aren't just any old Albanian gang.'

'Clan,' she put in, deciding to pick him up on anything she could.

'Yeah, I mean clan. The family that stays together et cetera'

'Get on with it, Ro. We have homicides up here too, you know. Clock ticking…'

There was a pause as he took in her tone. 'Of course. Anyway, the Popi seems to be a clan within the clans. They're mainly connected with a family called Spahia.' He spelled the name out. 'They've made it big in Italy and even in the States. They're into drugs, people trafficking, porn, smuggling, armed robbery, hostage taking – anything you like, really. A few of them have been caught, but no one important. In recent years, the Spahia have moved into the UK. They're based in London, but it seems they're setting up shop in the major provincial cities.'

'The Spahia?' Joni checked the spelling. 'So what about the Popi?'

'Ah, that's where it gets interesting. As in, "May you live in interesting times".' Roland Malpas waited for her to respond, but she let the Chinese cliché go. 'Er, the Popi are like the SAS of the Albanian clans. They get sent in when the ordinary guys – who aren't exactly shrinking violets – need support. The thing with them is they leave no trace.'

'What do you mean? SOCOs can always pick up something at a scene.'

'Yeah, but they never leave anything that leads to them. You know how they do that? By killing everyone present, usually as messily as possible. Remember those dope dealers who got taken out in Epping Forest a year back?'

The case had caused a lot of talk, even though Homicide South-west wasn't involved. Four Essex wide boys had muscled in somewhere they shouldn't. They were found with their intestines wound round each other's necks.

'That was the Popi?'

'So the rumour mill says. As you can imagine, there isn't much to go on and people – even ours – don't discuss them willingly.'

Joni sat back, one hand on her scars. 'Thanks, Ro.'

'Before you rush off, one more thing. Another way the Popi leave no trace is that they hire outside killers to do their dirty work. Not necessary Albanians.'

Joni thought about that. 'Interesting. Thanks again.'

'That's OK. But we're even, right?' He rang off – proving that 'goodbye' had gone missing in action down south as well.

Joni spent half an hour preparing and eating a bean salad, then sat down with her laptop. Several Italian criminology journals she subscribed to stood between her and sleep. It was as she finished taking notes on the last one that she found herself querying Malpas's motives for passing on the information. Joni had called him, but she had a feeling Ro would have been in touch himself. Although he hadn't disguised his dislike for Joni, he'd still come up with the goods. Why? As a last gesture of support for a former colleague? Unlikely. To scare her? That had the undeniable ring of truth.

Joni smiled and, ten minutes later, was in bed. Roland Malpas didn't frighten her. Her default mode was to respond well to challenges. Sleep came almost immediately.

74

Moonbeam Pax didn't usually watch the television, not least because her set was old and the signal in the foothills was poor. That evening she had been making an offering to the Great Mother and channelling all her positive energy into it had exhausted her. She turned on the late news and slumped in her single, cat-shredded armchair.

'…search for the killer of the unnamed male victim found in the River Coquet has started. The body was found this morning by Brian Sweeney, who was walking his dog.' The screen showed a man whiter than the most starched sheet. 'Unconfirmed reports say that the victim's head and hands had been removed.'

Moonbeam sat up straight. The decapitation of enemies and display of human skulls had been prevalent in Celtic times and still played a large part in certain forms of magic. Not hers, of course. She looked around the cottage's main room. On the walls she had a crocodile skull that a friend had brought back from Egypt – it had been blessed by a wise woman who followed the old religion there – and one of a small monkey. She used them in spells. It had never occurred to her to seek out a man's skull, though there was a certain temptation to do so. Human heads had great power. She wondered if there was a way she could get her hands on the one that had been taken from the man in the river. The idea that it may have been cleansed in running water made it even more enticing.

Then she tuned into the news again.

'…that the head and hands may have been used to prevent the victim's identity being discovered, as criminal gangs have been known to do.'

Moonbeam sat back as another, much more run-of-the-mill story was reported. A human head. Hands too – they had numerous ritual uses, especially if the dead man had used them in significant ways.

No, she told herself, getting up and going into the kitchen. The liquid in the pot was covered in a grey-pink scum now and she scooped it away. The skeleton of the salmon was almost clean of meat. The next day she would bury it in the garden, consigning the remains of the lithe creature to the earth mother. No, it was too risky. The man she'd got the fish from could obtain anything, or so he said. He'd never let her down and the steel in his eyes suggested he was capable of anything.

Moonbeam concentrated on lifting the flesh on to a plate with a strain. The man she'd attracted would love it. Joni had no idea, but her mother could cook very well when she had to. Joni. She'd be involved in the headless man case, though she hadn't appeared on TV. A tremor ran through Moonbeam's body. Yes, she thought. Everything is coming together. I've finally found a compliant man in the right place. Joni will come to understand the power of nature and its manifestation in her. And the rich, thieves and destroyers of their fellow human beings, will see their stratagems come to naught…

75

The morning briefing: Heck, feeling much better, started with the search for Suzana Noli. He ran through the events of the previous day, underplaying his own part in them.

'Great tackle, sir,' Pete Rokeby said, grinning at the double entendre.

Even Mrs Normal laughed – for a couple of seconds.

'Anyway,' Heck said, when the noise died down, 'the fork wound to the head and comparison of the photo in the passport from the brothel safe confirm that the biker is Elez Zymberi, the third Albanian attacked by the missing girl at the house in Burwell Street. He kept his mouth shut till Lennox's legal eagle turned up – DI Pax tried him in Italian – and, surprise, surprise, afterwards. None of the three Albanians has any form on HOLMES or the other databases.'

'We've got this Zymberi for illegal possession of the hand gun and ammunition clips,' Roger Underwood piped up. The Crime Prosecution Service lawyer was wearing a flash pinstriped suit. 'There won't be any problem getting him remanded.'

'What about the motorbike?' Heck asked.

DC Andrews raised a hand. 'The engine number and other identifying marks square with one stolen in Cornwall.'

'So we can do him for that too,' Heck said.

Underwood nodded.

'None of which gets us very far since he isn't talking,' the ACC said. 'Let's move on.'

Heck looked at his notes. 'Wayne Garston, the ganger. Where are we with him?'

'He was released yesterday evening,' Pete Rokeby said, giving Ruth Dickie an unimpressed look. 'Got a slap on the wrists for running from us.'

'He thinks we've lost interest in him,' the ACC said. 'When we go back, he'll be vulnerable.'

Heck nodded, resisting the temptation to say 'Good

thinking' to his boss. 'Are Garston's workers legit?'

'Yes, sir,' Pete said. 'EU nationals. The Border Agency cleared them.'

The briefing continued with tasks being allocated, but there was a definite air of sluggishness. The investigations were stalling and everyone knew it.

Heck and Joni attended the autopsy of the man without head and hands in the mortuary at Corham General. Unlike the old days when detectives had to wear surgical garb and stand in close proximity to the deceased, they were now able to observe from behind the glass screen in the viewing gallery. Dr Volpert's voice was coming through speakers in the ceiling.

'...of approximately thirty years ... head and hands severed by a well-honed, single, serrated blade ... genitalia normal ... height estimated at six feet and one inch ... weight twelve stone ... both knees show small healed incisions from what appears to be laparoscopic surgery ... both feet display recent contusions, both big toes bent inwards, indicative of tight shoes...'

'He's a sportsman,' Heck said to Joni. 'Skinny to be a rugby player and Big Bertha hasn't said anything about marks elsewhere on his body, which you'd expect. Footballer's my guess.'

Joni shrugged, out of her depth with contact sports.

'At that height he was probably a centre back. Not a pro or a high profile amateur because we'd have heard he'd gone missing. Probably a Sunday player. He's got a bit of a gut on him.'

Dr Volpert's voice droned on as she performed the Y-incision and removed the victim's internal organs. Her minions moved around quickly, collecting and weighing what she held up. The diminutive pathologist had a reputation for savaging fools and insubordinate inferiors. Joni watched impassively, while Heck shifted from foot to foot. He never used to be bothered by the insides of dead folk, but since his operation he'd become squeamish. That would teach him. He thought tackling the Albanian yesterday had dealt with his fear of going one on one and it had, but a sense of his own mortality was strong in Big Bertha's realm.

His phone rang.

'Heck, this is Lee Young.'

'Aye, aye, what's up?'

'I think I might have found out who your headless guy is.'

Heck took a deep breath. Being in his former colleague's debt was not a pleasant prospect. Still, if it got the job done…

'So?'

'You'd better come over to the MCU here. It's complicated and guess what?'

Heck had a bad feeling about where this was going.

'The Albanians are involved.'

'That's interesting. Have you nailed them?'

'That's the complication. Come on over.'

Heck stared at his phone when the connection was broken. Lee Young had always been one for power games and now he had Heck at a disadvantage. But he could hardly not go over to the building he'd worked in for years.

'Fancy a trip to the big city?'

'What, London?'

He gave her a glare. 'No, Newcastle.'

'No.'

'Well, you're coming anyway.'

'OK, but I want to talk to the ganger first. Pete can come with me on his way up to the moors.'

'All right, but be quick about it.'

'Later on I'll tell you what I found out about the Popi.'

'Good?'

'Very much not.'

76

Michael Etherington was worried about his grandson. Given that he had A-levels in a month, he was too bloody happy, though less so this morning. It was obviously because of Evie Favon. He couldn't fault Nick's taste. Evie was a delight and she had guts. Coming back from multiple leg fractures wasn't child's play and she'd started walking before the doctors had expected. She was smart too.

When he'd run Nick to school, his grandson talked about Saturday's cricket match. It was the last he was going to play for the Abbey and he needed to score over fifty to keep his three-year average in the sixties. It was a needle match with Moorden and they had a pair of handy fast bowlers.

'Can you take me up to Favon Hall again this afternoon, Gramps?'

Michael glanced at him. 'Are you sure that's a good idea? How much work are you getting done there?'

'Plenty. Evie's a big help.'

'Yes, but you've only got English in common. What about your other subjects?'

'I've got them covered, don't worry.'

'All right. I trust you, lad.'

'Thanks.' Nick looked out of the side window for a while. 'Lord Favon, is he right in the head?'

'What's Andrew done now?'

'I'm … I'm not sure.'

Michael took the road into Corham. 'He's not the brightest star in the galaxy, if that's what you mean.' He glanced at his grandson. 'What is it?'

'I … oh, it doesn't matter.'

'If you're sure. We can talk about it later.'

'So you will take me?' Nick said, grabbing his bag. 'Great.'

Michael watched as he got out of the car and was immediately surrounded by admiring schoolmates, male and female. God, he envied him.

77

'Do you think they'll still be working in that field?' Joni asked Pete Rokeby, as she turned off the main road.

'Maybe. At this time of year they only take the shoots off the kale. Apparently they're used in expensive restaurants.' He looked at his superior. 'That Garston's a spineless slob. If he was the one that alerted the Albanian headbanger, he'll clam up tighter than a—'

'Don't worry, I've got plans for him. Just play along.'

Rokeby raised an eyebrow. 'There's the lorry.'

Joni stopped the Land Rover behind the stationary vehicle and they got out.

Wayne Garston was leaning against a gatepost. He didn't look happy to see them. 'Er, morning, officers. Is there a problem?'

'No, sir,' Joni said cheerfully. 'We have a few more questions. Would you step into the Land Rover?'

'I can't leave my—'

'Slaves?' Joni said. 'You didn't have any problem doing that the other day.'

'All right, but not for long.' Garston yelled at one of the men bent double, telling him to keep everyone hard at it.

When he was in the back seat, Joni started the engine, reversed and drove past the lorry.

'Where are we going?' Garston asked, in alarm.

'We need some privacy, Wayne,' Joni said. 'I'm taking you back to the scene of the crime. I mean, where a skinny Albanian girl reduced one of their hard men to a squealing ponce.' She glanced at Pete, who remained impassive.

'Right, out,' she said, after she stopped where the lorry and motorbike had been parked the other day. She grabbed Garston's arm and led him to the fence on the left side of the road. 'And over.'

Pete stepped up, giving the fat man a heave over the wire. They followed, walking him to the stand of trees where stones were heaped.

'Take a seat,' Joni said, motioning Garston to the nearest pile. She picked up a stone that fitted her palm and tossed it from one hand to the other.

'What … what is this?' the ganger said, looking at them anxiously.

'Your mobile phone,' Joni said. 'Now!'

He started fumbling in the pocket of his filthy overalls. 'You can't—' The stone cracked as it impacted with another, a few inches below his groin. He handed the phone over.

Joni gave it to Pete. 'Open the contacts folder. Right, Mr Garston, you're going to tell us who all these people are. If I get the slightest hint that you're bullshitting, we'll call the number and tell them you're cooperating with a police inquiry into organised crime.'

'No!' Wayne Garston got to his feet, but sat down again heavily when Joni put pressure on his shoulders. 'You can't … you can't do this. I want my lawyer. No!' The last word came out as a shriek. Joni had picked up another weighty stone.

'On the other hand, if you answer my questions, we'll give you your phone back. After DS Rokeby's finished copying the contacts, of course.'

'You don't understand,' Garston said. 'These people are killers. I've got a wife and kids.'

Joni was tossing the stone from hand to hand. 'Not if we catch them and put them away. Your kids – what are they? Girls, boys?'

'Tracey's fifteen and … and Joey's twelve.'

Joni moved closer. 'You know what they do to fifteen-year-old girls, don't you, Wayne? The seventeen-year-old who escaped from here was probably forced into sucking cocks and taking it up the arse when she was your Tracey's age. No way they'll kill her. They'll work her to death and that'll take twenty years, maybe more. And they'll do the same to your Joey – plenty of demand for virgin male arse. As for your wife, yes, they'll kill her, but they'll gang rape and mutilate her first.'

The burly ganger was sobbing, one arm over his eyes. Joni felt Pete Rokeby's eyes on her, but ignored them.

'I can't,' Garston gasped. 'I—'

This time the stone clipped his upper thigh, making him yelp.

Joni picked up another. 'Last chance. Tell us which number you rang to get the biker up here.'

The ganger's eyes were on the stone moving between Joni's hands. 'A … alpha.'

'Very good. Alpha for Albanians?' She stopped tossing the tone. 'Have you ever heard of the Spahia clan?'

'There's an entry for "sierra",' Pete said. 'Shall I call it?'

'No!' Wayne Garston's eyes were wide. 'Please. That's only for emergencies. They … they don't like me using it.'

'So you do know the Spahia clan.'

'I … I know that's their name.'

'And how about the Popi?'

Garston shook his head, his eyes blank.

'The only "p" is for a pizza place,' Pete said.

'All right,' Joni said, taking a step back. 'That wasn't so hard.'

The ganger started to get to his feet. 'Can I go…'

Joni raised her hand and he sat down again quickly. 'We're not quite finished. There was a red pickup at the far end of these fields. What do you know about it?'

Wayne Garston's gaze dropped. 'Nothing,' he mumbled.

Joni's voice was steely. 'This time your bollocks will be squashed, I guarantee it.'

'Reston,' the ganger said. 'Dan Reston.'

'There's a "DR" on here,' Pete confirmed.

'Who's he?' Joni asked.

'Mate of mine.' Garston shrank back. 'No! All right, all right. He works for Lord Favon.'

Joni kept her expression neutral. 'And you called him as well as the Albanians when you spotted the girl?'

A brief nod.

'You're going to have to explain why.'

Wayne Garston let out a long sigh. 'All the fields here are part of the Favon estate. When there's work needing done, Dan Reston lets me know and I sort it.'

'And what interest would he have had in a runaway Albanian girl?'

'He … he likes girls … likes doing things to them. I send him the younger ones from the work gangs.'

'But this one wasn't from a work gang.'

'No…' The fat man caught Joni's gaze. 'Look, I felt sorry for her. The Albanians told me to keep an eye out and I read the papers. They'd have cut her to pieces.'

'So you decided to hand her over to a "mate" who "likes doing things" to young women?' Joni was standing over him now, spittle flying. 'What kind of things?'

Garston's head was low. 'He … he hurts them … ties them up and … shit, I don't know the details. He doesn't kill them. When they come back, they walk in a funny way and there's blood on their blouses. Sometimes on their jeans too.'

Joni took a couple of deep breaths. 'As I understand it, you're in the middle here. You do contract work for Lord Favon and at the same time you answer to the Albanians. Why's that?'

'They … they own my company. Bought me out when things were bad a year or so ago. They can pull the plug on me any time.'

'And they provide you with workers?'

Another brief nod.

'Mr Garston, we thank you for your cooperation.' She turned to her colleague. 'Add my mobile number to his contacts next to the pizza place, please.' She looked back at the ganger. 'Every time you hear from the Albanians or Dan Reston, I want you to call me. Agreed? A nod is not acceptable.'

'Agreed,' the fat man said sullenly, jerking backwards as the third stone landed a fraction of an inch below his crotch.

'Take a hike back to your "slaves",' Joni said, after Pete had given him his phone. 'You need to work off all that tension.'

Pete Rokeby waited until they reached the fence. 'You didn't exactly follow the manual back there, ma'am.'

Joni stepped over the wire gracefully, then extended a hand to her shorter colleague. 'Just using my initiative. Don't tell Mrs Normal.'

'I won't. Actually, I was impressed.'

'Don't patronise me.' Joni's expression softened. 'Sorry about the homophobic vocabulary.'

Pete laughed. 'Now I've seen what you can do with a stone, I'm not going to make a complaint, formal or informal.' He got into the Land Rover. 'What now?'

'If we weren't under orders not to bother Viscount Favon, I'd be straight over there to question this Reston creep. As it is, you're for the moors and I'm off to Newcastle MCU with the DCI.'

'Are you now? Good luck with that.'

Joni stared at the DS, but he didn't elaborate.

78

Joni spoke to Pete as Heck was driving them to Newcastle. He and his team up on the moors hadn't seen any sign of Suzana Noli. Except for a sheep.

'What?'

'Get this, ma'am. She – I'm presuming it was her as there's no one else up here – she killed the beast, skinned it and cut the meat off its back legs. We haven't come across a fire so I'm guessing she ate it raw.'

Joni thought about the Albanian girl. Desperate she might be, but she could clearly look after herself.

'Keep at it. I've asked the ACC for the Force helicopter. Apparently it's chasing some dope dealers on the A1, but it should be heading your way soon.'

'OK, ma'am, thanks.'

Joni updated Heck.

'Skinning sheep isn't straightforward, you know,' he said. 'She's handy with a knife, which is one of the reasons we have to catch her. Why do you think she went up on the moors?'

'Because it was the only option she had. You said the patrol car had its siren on, so the road was no good to her. The forest offered her cover.'

'You're probably right.'

'Probably?'

Heck laughed. 'There isn't much certainty in our line of work. Maybe she had a rendezvous up there with someone we don't know about. Maybe she's using the sun as a compass and heading in some particular direction.'

Joni shook her head. 'You're theorising, sir. Might as well say that a spaceship is coming to pick her up on the high ground.'

'Don't rule anything out, lass.' Heck paused. 'Oops.'

Joni groaned. They'd had more than one discussion about his use of patriarchal language. It was a never-ending struggle. She opened her file and looked at the notes on the Popi she'd taken from the internet.

'If the Popi were a law enforcement agency, they'd be the best in the world, sir. They're suspected – and much of this is hypothesis because they don't leave witnesses – of taking out much of the leadership and many soldiers of the Sicilian Mafia, the Camorra in Napoli, the Calabrian 'Ndrangheta, the Nuova Mala del Brenta in the Veneto, and the Sacra Corona Unita in Apulia. For example, the Popi lured twelve Sicilians to a meeting where cocaine and women were to be handed over and killed the lot. All twelve suffered post-mortem mutilation—' Joni stopped and took a deep breath. 'Their genitalia were hacked off and put under their arms.'

'Jesus,' Heck said, his face blanching.

'There's also a rumour that only four Popi were involved, along with some hired killers.'

'Now I come to think of it, Mrs Normal attended a conference at Europol headquarters last year,' Heck said. 'I read her report. The Albanians are turning to legitimate business as well as expanding their standard operations.'

'That squares with what I've read,' Joni said. 'They set up front companies, make sure they have top quality briefs and invest much of their black income in whatever legal activities are currently profitable.'

'Not much of those around here,' Heck observed. 'I haven't noticed many south European businessmen over the river in Ironflatts.'

'Actually, there are computer software and pharmaceutical companies in the new industrial zone. The ACC told me the Regional Economic Growth Forum's putting a lot of money and effort into attracting businesses to Corham. She spent an evening at some tedious presentation.'

'What was she telling you for?'

Joni shrugged. 'Female solidarity?'

'Aye, right. Then again we've had two murders, one of them Albanian on Albanian. Not a massacre like in Italy, though.'

'True.' Joni looked out of the window at the view down the Tyne. It was another clear day and the bridges formed a collage of different shapes. To her surprise she found herself impressed. The little she'd seen of the city since she'd arrived hadn't been to her taste.

The Toon MCU, as it was known in the trade, was on the fifth floor of the police building near the Central Station. DCI Young met them at the security door.

'Hallo, Lee,' Heck said. 'You've met Joni Pax.'

'Indeed I have. How's things?'

'Good enough, sir.' Joni had taken an instant dislike to the bulky man when she'd met him on her familiarisation tour. His type was common in the Met: hyper-ambitious, superficially charming, quick to stab colleagues in the back (Heck had confirmed that) and arrogant as hell.

'Good enough?' Young echoed. 'Seems to me you've got big problems with the Albies. Is that killer still on the loose?'

Joni nodded reluctantly. 'I hear you've got some Albanians here for us.'

Lee Young stared at her. 'Dunno where you got that idea from.' He grinned at Heck. 'You must have misunderstood me, old son.'

Heck bridled, but kept a grip on himself. 'You said it was complicated. How?'

Young led them to his office. A few heads turned as they passed and Joni knew she was being inspected. The chocolate DI who got herself attacked in London and took Mrs Normal's eye, she imagined them thinking. She wondered if it had got around that she had a Judo black belt. She'd be happy to demonstrate her abilities…

'Coffee? Tea?' Lee Young asked.

They both shook their heads.

'All right, here's how it is. There's a club called the Stars and Bars near the Baltic.'

'Don't know it,' Heck said.

'Used to be the Brass Monkey.'

'Oh aye. A real scumbag magnet.'

Young smiled. 'It's gone up-market – not a lot, but it attracts a better class of scumbag these days. It's owned by a company that's based in Panama, but it's run by—'

'Albanians,' Joni put in.

'Very good,' the DCI said condescendingly. 'Last night we got a call from them.' He looked at his desk. 'One Fatlum Temo.'

'Fatlum as in "wide chimney"?' Heck said. He and Young laughed, but Joni didn't.

'It seems friend Fatlum, who was on the door with a mate, was abducted the night before last by five local headbangers. The other Albie was beaten by baseball bats. Anyway, Fatlum managed to escape after doing some damage to one of the idiots. Guess what they did last night?'

Heck sighed, having seen Newcastle lowlife in all its tawdry lack of glory. 'They had another go.'

'Exactly. This time Fatlum saw them coming and called our lads in.' Young smiled. 'They're in the cells. Four of them, that is. The other one's in the Royal Vic with a throat wound. He's lucky to be alive.'

'He was the one hurt by Mr Temo?' Joni asked.

'Correct.'

'I take it you haven't held Mr Temo because he was defending himself. And he has a heavy duty lawyer.'

'You've got a smart one here, Heck.' Lee Young put his hands behind his neck. 'True enough, Tricky Dick Lennox is Fatlum Temo's brief. What do you do for an encore, Joni?'

'I prefer DI Pax, sir,' she said coldly. 'I'll tell you exactly what I'll do. I'll go down to the cells with my boss and question your headbangers.'

'Not without one of my officers present.'

Joni gave him a tight smile. 'What would be the point of that? You'll be watching us on screen anyway.'

Heck laughed. 'She got you there, Lee.' He stood up. 'Come on.'

DCI Young handed him a folder. 'You'll find their names and details in there. Along with the sheet on your headless man.' He glanced at Joni. 'Of course, I'm only too happy to help Force HQ with their enquiries, but I would ask that the prisoners are afforded every courtesy.'

Heck shook his head. 'Come on, Joni. I can't take any more of our host's wit.'

They were escorted to the cells by a uniformed officer.

'Give us a minute to get our bearings, lad,' Heck said. 'Oops, my patriarchal attitude strikes again.'

Joni raised an eyebrow. 'It seems DCI Young is contagious. You've suddenly become an even bigger—'

'That'll do. Well played about Lennox, by the way. Interesting these Albies, as Lee calls them, having the same lawyer as the ones in Corham.'

'And Alnwick.'

'Right.' Heck had opened the file and was running his eye down the list of names. 'These look to be your standard tossers: Kyle, aka 'Kylie' Laggan; Daryll Spencer; Edward 'Hot Rod' Miller, the one in hospital; Paul 'Pumpkinhead' Pearson; and John 'Jackie' Brown. Oh.'

'Never mind,' Joni said, shaking her head. 'I wonder why Daryll Spencer hasn't got a nickname.'

'I thought Daryll was a nickname.'

Joni laughed.

'This Kyle Laggan made a missing persons report two days ago. Gary Frizzell, 27 Harvey Street, Benwell. Height six-one, weight about twelve stone, hair brown and short – not much use to us – feet size twelve, lives with his mother, works as a park attendant. Last seen – get this – in the car park of the Stars and Bars nightclub on Friday night around two a.m., getting into a black Bentley Continental GT Speed. And guess who was holding the door open for him.'

'Fatlum Temo.'

'You really are good. DI Pax, that isn't a very ladylike gesture.'

'Ladylike is also off limits. Who are we going to talk to first?'

'Much though I'd like to see Pumpkinhead in the flesh, it's going to have to be Kylie.'

'I've heard that name somewhere.'

Heck stared at her to check she was serious. On further enquiry, he found that his DI really didn't have a clue about the owner of Australia's most famous backside.

<hr>

79

Close to the far side of the moor where she'd spent the night, Suzana heard the sound of the quad bike on the breeze. She recognised it instantly. Some of the local youths had bought such machines to drive like madmen down her village's narrow streets and across the fields. She was about fifty metres from one of the huge metal columns. She ran to take cover behind it. A barbed-wire fence made that impossible. Looking up, she tried to work out what the great propeller with red tips on the blades was for as it turned rapidly in the wind. There was a sign on the fence that she recognised – a jagged bolt with an arrow pointing downwards. Were they making electricity from these lonely giants? If they put them on the wind-blasted peaks above her village, they could light up the whole of Europe.

The angry buzz of the bike – 'sows' in her language – came closer and she looked round the circular metal wall. There was a single man wearing a black woollen hat, with a weapon – a shotgun, she thought – over one shoulder. He was coming straight for her column. She took out the longer of her knives and crouched down. Beyond the ridge was a steep and rocky slope. If she could make it there, the sow wouldn't be able to follow.

Taking a deep breath, she made a dash for it, trying to keep the column between herself and her pursuer. The sheepskin was tied round her neck with the dried blood outwards, and it occurred to her that the man might get angry when he saw it; perhaps he'd already found the carcass and it was his. She ducked as she heard the shot, the wind carrying the pellets away. Bastard. She started to change direction, running only a few paces before cutting to one side. Another shot rang out, the pellets whipping by, not near enough to hit her. He was trying to scare her into submission. The sow was getting nearer and the rocky chasm was still at least fifty metres away.

Suzana kept ducking and weaving, but the quad bike was close. She was about to turn and face the man when she was hit in the side by a boot and went crashing down on a piece of rough ground. The knife she'd been holding skittered away across the dry mud. Before she could get up, the man was on her, the stationary sow's engine sputtering. He straddled her, his weight forcing all the air from her lungs. He was talking but she couldn't understand the words. She struggled to reach the shorter knife inside the leather jacket. He understood she was up to something and grabbed her hand.

Aware of what was going to happen, Suzana forced herself to go limp. She had done that with Leka and it sometimes reduced his lust. This time it didn't happen. The man, heavy-faced, unshaven and probably in his forties, was desperate for her. He tore open the jacket and ripped at the clothing beneath. She lay still, averting her eyes. She knew that staring at the pigs only made them deal out more pain. His rough fingers found her breasts and pulled the nipples, then they went lower, tugging at her zip.

'Sheep,' he kept saying, 'sheep.' She couldn't understand why he was referring to her country, even though the pronunciation was way off. What did he care where she came from and how did he know that Albanians called the country Shqipëri? Or was he one of those foreigner-hating thugs who came to the slave house and swore at her as they penetrated her from behind?

Then she saw a blur to the right and heard a solid thud. The man on top of her crashed downwards, his face hitting the ground as she rolled quickly to the side. He was pulled away. Suzana sat up and looked into the eyes of a wet-mouthed and growling dog. Turning her head slowly, she saw another one. Then a man stepped up. This one was wearing a woollen hat that covered his face. He'd hit her attacker with a heavy piece of wood.

That was all she saw before her head exploded in a burst of stars.

80

Nick went up the steps to Favon Hall. The door was opened before he got to it.

'Ah, Nicholas,' Victoria said, smiling. 'How lovely to see you.

Michael not staying again? He really must have something against me.'

'Maybe he does,' Nick said, sidestepping his hostess. 'Evie's in the library, I suppose.'

'Where else, darling boy?'

Nick stopped and looked over his shoulder. 'I've turned eighteen so technically I'm not a boy any more. And as for darling…' He smiled harshly. 'I don't think so.'

Evie met him at the library door and caught sight of her mother standing like a pillar in the hall.

'What happened?' she asked, after they'd kissed.

'I might have said something she didn't like.' Nick told her what had happened.

Evie laughed shrilly. 'Oh Nick, good for you! That'll teach the old man-eater.'

He raised his shoulders. 'I didn't want to hurt her. I just think she's out of order.'

'What a sweet soul you are.' She kissed him again.

'I hope we're not doing slavery, torture and voodoo again.'

'No, I know you don't like that. I've made a vow to ignore my family history.' She gave him a crooked smile. 'Anything to keep hold of you.' She pulled him towards the table, jettisoning her crutch.

'Evie … I'm sorry about last night. I … you frightened me. It isn't right to hate your family so much. It's not your parents' fault that they have the house and estate. What do you want them to do? Sell it all off and give the money to charity?'

'That'd be a start,' Evie said, under her breath. 'You're right, Nick, you're right.' She put her hand on his groin.

Soon they were naked. Their limbs entwined and they both started to sigh.

Then the library door opened. From beneath the table they could see Lady Favon's black pumps and red-sheathed legs below the hem of her skirt.

The laughter was unexpected and coarse.

'Really, Nicholas, I hardly think this is appropriate,' Victoria said. 'I'll have to tell my husband.' She turned to go. 'And Rosie and Michael, of course.'

Evie sniggered after the door closed. 'What's happened to you? I've seen harder chocolate eclairs. Forget it. We're both over the legal age. Who cares if she tells?'

Nick looked away. He wasn't keen on his mother finding out, not least because she would demand that he revise at his desk in future. Gramps wouldn't be a problem. He had a woman himself somewhere, Nick was sure – he was forever disappearing on drives that were curiously vague. No, what really worried him was Lord Favon's reaction. Not on behalf of his daughter – as if he cared about Evie – but because of the other thing…

'Come on, handsome,' Evie said, grinning. 'I've been looking forward to the pole vault.'

It took some time, but she got her wish.

<hr>

81

'What do you reckon?' Heck asked, as he drove them back to Corham in the late afternoon.

'It's a bit hard to be sure without the head.'

'Aye, but that Kylie fella said Gary Frizzell had both his knees operated on three years ago.'

Joni nodded. 'Did them in playing football in the local leagues. You were right, sir. The problem is, we're no further on about what Frizzell, assuming it's him, was doing getting into a Bentley.'

'Lee said he'd interviewed the witness, a car mechanic, but he'd been stoned and pissed and couldn't remember the number.'

'Yes, but there can't be that many Bentleys of that model around here.'

'More than you might think, but I'm sure Lee will track them down.' He glanced at her. 'He's a decent cop.'

'But an indecent human being?'

'Something like that.'

Joni watched as the buildings thinned out and the dual car-riageway moved through the countryside. She felt a wave of relief. A few months in Corham had turned her into a bumpkin.

'I don't see why the Albanian who cut Hot Rod Miller's throat hasn't been arrested. So what that Lennox is his brief?'

'I'd guess Lee's playing a long game with the Albanians. His people will be keeping an eye on the Stars and Bars.'

Joni pulled down the sunshade. 'Do you think Frizzell was a dope dealer? The Albanians are into drugs, according to my ex-colleague down south. Maybe he crossed them and they took the kind of revenge that the Popi specialise in.'

'Maybe, but we'll have to leave Lee to sweat that out of the guys he's got in custody.'

'Smart move by the Albanians, wasn't it?'

'You mean not resorting to violence when the idiots went back? Aye, but it blows a hole in your idea about them being hyper-violent. Besides, what kind of an example is it when no one knows who he is?'

'Dr Volpert will confirm his identity from the notes on his knee surgery. It was laparoscopy, so the surgeon who did it can check his work.'

Heck nodded, taking the exit near the paper factory on the outskirts of Corham.

Joni's phone rang. It was Pete Rokeby. She listened, asked some questions and then hung up.

'What was that about?'

'No sign of Suzana on the moors, but the search team found an abandoned quad bike by one of the wind turbines. Pete ran the number. It's registered to an—'

'Oliver Forrest.'

'How do you know that?'

Heck tapped his nose. 'Hunch, instinct, call it what you will. I've got it in … nay, not really. I was at school with him. His father had the biggest sheep farm on the moors when I was a kid. Must have spent dozens of weekends up there. Ollie took it over when the old bugger died a while back.'

'Where are we going?'

'Up there. I should have been on that team myself. I know the moors better than anyone in it.'

Joni remembered what Ag had asked her to do, but kept silent. The truth was, she liked it when Heck was in the field.

∞∞

82

Oliver Forrest woke up, his head splitting. He couldn't see and he panicked, realising he was tied down by his wrists and ankles. Or cuffed, more like. He felt the metal against his skin. He shouted at the top of his voice, the sound echoing round an enclosed space. No one came. There was no sound apart from his ragged breathing. He inhaled deeply and picked up the smell of damp cut with something sweeter. Was it blood? No, more like perfume. How could that be? What had happened?

Forrest concentrated, blocking out the pain from his bone-dry throat. He thought back to the afternoon – was it the same day? He had topped the rise on the quad bike and stopped, standing up to scan the horizon. To the west the wind turbines strode away along the ridge. The surrounding landowners had got huge grants to erect the metal monsters and more were going up on the northern ridge. The great blades stood above the trees like medieval torture wheels; he remembered them from school history. To the east, his own land sloped away, the sheep in batches near the forest's edge, far from the remains of their fellow creature. Yes, that was it. He'd found one of his ewes butchered. The crows had made a mess of her, but he could see that some fucker had skinned the animal skilfully and hacked off the best of the meat. Yon was definitely a deid 'un.

So where was the butcher? He could be anywhere by now – the animal was stiff. The ground was very uneven. Streams cut through the heather and ancient rock faces broke up the grassland. Probably long gone. Ollie had sat down with a snort. Then his phone rang.

'Mr Forrest? My name's Detective Sergeant Peter Rokeby.'

'Oh aye?'

'I'm leading a search party on your land.'

'Search for what?'

'Maybe you've seen it in the news. Young Albanian woman killed one of her countrymen and injured another two?'

Ollie had seen that, but he played dumb. 'And you reckon this lass is on the moor?'

'We do. If you see her, don't approach her. She's armed and dangerous.'

'Right you are. I'll probably see you up here at some point.'

'Did you not see us yesterday afternoon, sir? I called at your house.'

'Nay, lad. The wife's car was in for service so I had to pick her and the lad up in Corham.' He cut the connection.

So, he thought, one of the tarts from the Burwell Street knocking shop was on the loose. He'd have to be quick if the coppers were already on the moor. He'd never had her – he stuck to the same tart, an older one who didn't care what he did. That didn't mean he couldn't have the young one now, knives or no knives. And if she'd slaughtered his beast, she was fair game.

He stood up on the bike again. Was that a black spot near the wind turbines to the west? His eyesight wasn't as good as it had been. Maybe his mother had been right about too much wanking. Yes, it was moving. Must be her. With a raging fire in his belly, Ollie gunned the engine and roared off. The other woman only knew a few words of English, most of them to do with shagging. He didn't care. He'd never been one for conversation with members of the fair sex, the wife included.

And he'd got her, he remembered, he was on top of her, pulling her clothes apart. Then he fell into a very dark pit.

Yelling again and pulling against his bonds, Ollie Forrest realised his roving eye had finally landed him in a sea of shit.

<hr />

83

Joni and Heck met Pete Rokeby by the wind turbines. It was early evening and the big Jeep bounced hard over the track from the farm. They had stopped there and Heck spoke to Ollie Forrest's wife, Lizzie. She hadn't seen him since early morning, when she had left for Corham with their son Jack. She'd spent the rest of the day in the bookshop where she worked.

'I wouldn't worry, Heck,' she said. 'You know what he's like. He'll be stalking rabbits.'

'It isn't safe,' Heck said seriously. 'There's a woman who has already killed on the loose. Make sure all your windows are closed and lock the doors. I'll leave an officer outside till we find him.'

They reached the truck on which the quad bike had been loaded, under supervision of a SOCO.

'Pancake,' Heck said, getting out. 'No sign of her?'

Rokeby shook his head. 'Not enough light for us to work by now.'

'Did that helicopter ever show up?'

'No, sir. There were other priorities.'

'I bet.'

Joni was walking around the areas marked by the SOCOs. 'Any prints or tracks?'

Heck groaned as a large red Japanese 4×4 pulled up. 'Here we go,' he said, under his breath. He watched as the hefty figure of Viscount Andrew Favon climbed down and walked towards him. He was in classic country squire attire – green shooting jacket, matching trousers and wellies. He also sported a large leather hat that reminded him of the one the missing Albanian girl had taken from Alice Liphook's shed, except this one was black and bore the family crest – a quartered shield supported by two fish-tailed men. Heck suspected Favon wore it to cover his bald crown. The unruly moustache compensated for it.

'That you, Rutherford?'

'In the flesh, Lord Favon.' Heck extended a hand. It was shaken briefly by a soft-fleshed and larger one.

'You look a bit seedy. Heard you were injured in the line of duty. Should you be back at work?'

'I'm all right.'

'What the hell's going on?' The viscount watched the SOCOs' van drive away.

'We're looking for an Albanian woman, a murder suspect.'

'I saw something about that on the news. You think she's up here?'

Heck nodded. 'We followed her through the plantation on the far side of the moor yesterday. It looks like she killed one of Oliver Forrest's sheep overnight.'

'Good God. So she's armed.'

'With knives. Were any of your people up here today? Ollie Forrest's quad bike was found abandoned here.'

Favon frowned. His eyebrows were long and sprouting. 'Forrest was probably drunk. How do you know he didn't fall over and damage himself on that ridiculous contraption?'

'Maybe the woman was here too, my lord.' Heck had learned the hard way how to address the landowner when he'd investigated a burglary at Favon Hall a few years back. 'We're taking the bike in. It's evidence.'

'I see. The fool. I've told him often enough to stick to his own part of the moor.' The aristocrat shook his head. 'Bloody man. Put in an objection to the wind turbines.' He smiled, showing yellow teeth. 'Not that it got him anywhere.'

Heck tried his luck. 'I'd like to search your grounds and check the estate vehicles.'

'What on earth for?'

'The Albanian woman might be in hiding down there.'

Favon laughed. 'Don't be ridiculous. You know how steep those cliffs are.'

'It's for your own safety.'

'I can look after my wife, daughter and myself, thank you.'

Heck considered telling him how handy Suzana was with a knife, but the pompous fool had refused him access so he wasn't going to play the Good Samaritan.

'We'll get off your land. You'll let me know straightaway if the Albanian woman is seen, won't you?' He handed over his card.

Favon stuck it in his pocket without looking at it. 'Or I'll ring your boss. Remarkable woman, Ruth Dickie. The next chief constable, I'm sure of it.'

Heck turned away with his head down – not in deference to the viscount, but because he was puzzled. Their conversation had been strange, even by the standards of that brusque blue-blooded creature. The problem was, he couldn't put his finger on what was bothering him.

84

'Where can Nick be?' Rosie Etherington was twisting a dish towel in her hands. 'It's almost eight o'clock. Why isn't his phone working?'

Her father-in-law tried to disguise his unease. 'Don't worry. He'll be back any minute. You know how enthusiastic he gets on his bike rides. He knows every bump in the road, even at night and with those inadequate lights. As for his mobile, he turns it off when he's in the saddle. Says he doesn't want to be disturbed.'

'What if he's had a puncture?'

'He'll turn his phone back on and call us.'

'Please, Michael, go out and look for—'

Then the house phone rang. Rosie moved towards it and then stopped, waving for him to answer.

Michael took the receiver from the wall and identified himself. After listening for a time, he felt the strength go from his legs and squatted down, his back against the wall.

'Are you … are you sure?' he asked, then listened again, avoiding Rosie's desperate eyes. 'I see. All right, I'll be over immediately.' With difficulty he raised himself to a standing position and put the phone back.

'What's happened?' His daughter-in-law's voice was almost a scream. 'Tell me, Michael!'

'The … the police…' He stepped over, legs like jelly, and drew Rosie close. 'There's been … there's been … an accident.'

Rosie was already crying. 'My baby, my boy … what's happened to him?'

'It seems … it seems he went off the road.'

'But he's … he's all right, my Nick, isn't he? Isn't he?'

The major general tried to extricate himself from her clutch. 'They want me there, Rosie. I have to go.'

'I'm coming with you.' She was holding on to the arms of his sweater. 'I'm coming, Michael, you can't stop me.' There was fire in her eyes, despite their dampness. 'It's Nick. He's all I've got left.'

He looked at her, his heart clattering, and nodded. The police would know what to do, they had experience with devastated parents. What he'd been through as a raw subaltern and later in senior command seemed useless now – a different life from this one.

'Come on, then,' he said, taking her to the Jaguar with his arm around her thin shoulders. It was still warm outside. There had been many such evenings in Bosnia and Kosovo. The mountains there were swarming with armed men, but it seemed those great peaks were no more dangerous than the gentle hills where he had grown up.

'Where is he?' Rosie demanded, her voice firmer. Michael had seen this with soldiers. They became calmer and more confident before they saw what had happened to their comrades close up.

'Near the bottom of High Edge, this side.'

He drove on to the road and went past the houses at 30 mph, discipline still in place. As soon as they were out of the village, he upped his speed, the car taking the corners smoothly. Neither of them spoke, but the tension was wound tighter than the armature of a generator. It increased when they saw the lights ahead. The police had cordoned off the nearside of the road.

Michael pulled up behind a police van. Before he could react, Rosie opened her door and dashed forward, evading a burly uniformed constable and ducking under the blue-and-white tape.

'Nick!' she screamed. 'Where are you, Nick?'

Michael went after her but she was a woman possessed, feinting to slip past a thin man in a suit he vaguely recognised and heading for an area lit by arc lamps. A second before he reached Rosie, the black woman detective came out of the trees in pale blue overalls and bootees. She clamped her arms around his daughter-in-law.

'I'm sorry, Mrs Etherington,' she said, 'you can't go down there.'

'Nick!' Rosie screamed. 'I'm here, Nick!'

Joni Pax held the distraught woman, looking past her to Michael. Rosie started screaming.

'Major General Etherington?'

He looked to his side and took in the haggard suited man.

'Detective Chief Inspector Hector Rutherford,' he said, extending a hand. 'We met at one of the rugby club balls.'

'Heck Rutherford, of course.' Michael took his hand. 'You were a hell of a number eight.' He looked to the front again. 'What happened here? The officer on the phone said my grandson had been badly injured.'

'I'm afraid it's worse than that. It's a pity his mother came out.'

Michael felt his hands tremble. 'I couldn't stop her. You mean … you mean that Nick's …'

Heck nodded. 'There can't be much doubt it's his body. There are name tags on his socks. Normally we would have waited for a formal identification – we still will if you prefer – but I thought you'd want to be involved from the beginning.'

'I … I appreciate that. But we'll have to do something about Rosie.'

'I have another female officer here. She can take her home.'

'She'll have her work cut out.'

'She knows what she's doing.' Heck signalled to a soft-faced woman and introduced DC Andrews to the major general. 'I need you to look after Mrs Etherington, Eileen. Take her home and keep an eye on her, all right?'

If Andrews resented being reduced to family support duty, she didn't show it. She went over to Rosie and gently prised her from Joni's embrace, speaking to her in a calm, low voice. When she had got her into a squad car, Joni came over, pulling off her latex gloves.

'What did you tell her?' Michael demanded.

'That Nick was killed in an accident.' She glanced at Heck. 'But that isn't the case.'

'What?' The major general's voice was faint.

'Force HQ received an anonymous phone call,' Heck said. 'A male voice, giving us the exact location and saying that a large black 4×4 had knocked your grandson off the road.'

'Have you found this black car?'

'We're doing what we can.' Heck dropped his gaze. 'But there's more.'

'Oh, Christ.'

'The officers who arrived first immediately realised they weren't dealing with a traffic accident or even a hit and run.'

'I want to see him,' Michael said firmly. 'Now.'

Heck and Joni exchanged glances. It would be useful to have a positive identification at this early stage. The injuries were such that they couldn't be sure, even though there was an Abbey School photo ID card in the victim's backpack.

'All right,' Heck said. 'You'll need to get suited up. It's a steep slope, but you look to be in good shape.' He gave a slack smile that wasn't returned. 'DI Pax will take you down. And Michael?' He hoped the use of the major general's first name wouldn't offend. 'Prepare yourself. It isn't pretty.'

Etherington nodded and followed Joni to the SOCOs' van. When he was kitted out and she had put on another pair of gloves, she led him to the side of the road. A rope had been tied to the tow bar of a Traffic Division Volvo. About three metres to the left, markers had been placed around a narrow tyre track on the verge.

'I imagine you've done this kind of thing before,' Joni said.

Michael nodded.

'Wait till I give you a shout.'

He watched as she stepped backwards down the surprisingly steep incline, moving her hands rapidly. The leaves and branches of the surrounding trees were lit up, as was a crumpled form in Lycra at the bottom. Michael took a deep breath and slithered down, the bootees giving him little traction. When he reached the end of the rope, he found himself held up by Joni's hands on his arms.

'Sweet Jesus,' he said, stepping past her. 'He's ... he's had his head smashed in,' Michael's throat was drier than it had ever been. 'Who ... who could have done this?'

Joni raised her hands. 'Slow down, sir. Please don't step near the markers. To start with, is this your grandson's bicycle?'

Michael bent over the twisted frame and nodded. 'That's his helmet too,' he said, pointing to the seemingly undamaged object in a bush to the right. He moved closer to the body. Nick was lying on his back with his arms and legs splayed. His face and head were a mass of red and grey.

'Sweet Jesus.' Michael Etherington squatted as close as he could get to his grandson. Such was the damage to his features that he couldn't be sure it was Nick. 'Can I open his top?'

'The doctor will do that,' Joni said, watching as a thickset woman in white coveralls picked her way past the markers and pulled down the zip from neck to lower abdomen.

'That's far enough,' the major general snapped. He extended his index finger. 'It's Nick all right. See those scars on his chest? He got raked on his debut for the first fifteen.' His eyes filled with tears. 'He should have gone to hospital, but he insisted on being patched up and sent back on. He scored a try and won the match for the school.' He took a deep breath. 'He was only fourteen.' He started to sob and stood up, pushing Joni away when she went to him. Then he dragged a sleeve across his face and there was a rapid transformation.

'Detective Inspector Pax, I confirm this is the body of my grandson Nicholas Michael Etherington. Do I have to sign something?'

Joni shook her head. 'We'll do the paperwork later, sir.'

Michael grabbed her arm and took her back from the corpse.

'Let go, sir,' she said, in a firm voice.

He stared at her and registered what he was doing. 'Sorry. Look, what the hell happened here? Why would someone do that to him?'

'It's too early to say,' Joni said, blocking out the pain in her arm.

'Who was it you thought he saw at the Albanian brothel? Is there a connection?'

It seemed likely there was, but Joni didn't intend to speculate now. 'I've no idea who your grandson might have seen. I only know he was lying.' She caught his eye. 'Do you know? Can you cast any light on why this might have happened?'

'Me?' The major general frowned. 'What would I know?'

'You live in the same house.'

'I don't know what you're getting at, DI Pax. He's ... he *was* a healthy eighteen-year-old. He took his schoolwork seriously, hoped to get to Cambridge—'

'Yes, he told me.'

Michael stared at her. 'Really? When? Oh, during your

interrogation.' He clenched his fists. 'You'd better be sure every-thing was done right because my lawyer's going to be combing through the paperwork.'

Joni didn't respond to the grief-stricken man's provocation. 'Did he have a girlfriend?'

'What, now you think one of his school friends did this?' Then his expression changed.

'What is it, sir?' Joni asked, immediately aware that some-thing had struck him.

'Oh, nothing. Look, can we do this tomorrow? I have to get back to Rosie.'

'Of course, sir.'

Michael Etherington looked around. 'What about his phone? Have you found it?'

'Not yet. He had it with him?'

'Never even went to the bog without it, though he turned it off when he was on his bike.' He took out his own and pressed a speed-dial button. There was no sound in the vicinity. 'The bastard who did this must have taken it with him.'

Joni stepped closer. 'Any reason why you think the killer is male?'

The major general's eyes opened wider than they might have. 'You think a woman could do that?' He glanced at Nick's body, then bowed his head.

Joni didn't answer. If pressed, she'd have said she doubted it, but she'd investigated domestic abuse cases where women had done equally terrible things to their abusive men. She sus-pected a female was involved in some way in the boy's death and that Michael Etherington thought so too; she'd noticed how he brushed off his question about Nick having a girlfriend. The trick would be to find out who she was – and get to her before the ex-soldier did.

85

Moonbeam Pax was sitting on her kitchen floor, head in her hands. She felt sick, but all she'd brought up in the bowl were strings of spit. What she had been told was terrible. Every human soul was precious, no matter what actions were committed by its bodily form.

She pulled herself to her feet, legs tangling in her robes. When she heard the news, she had been casting sage into the pot, her nostrils twitching as the combination of odours came right. She had been going to use the potion on her eczema, but now she didn't care. There would be no supper tonight either. Who could eat after such a vile act?

Gradually Moonbeam felt her troubled spirit slip back into the envelope of her flesh. Perhaps she would steam kale and boil potatoes. There was still some hot sauce in the larder.

No, what was she thinking? She had to call Joni – she would know what to do, things like this were her job. But Moonbeam stopped before she reached the phone on the wall. There was no need. Joni would be involved anyway. Despite the tragedy, her plan to bring her daughter on was progressing – if anything, it was now further ahead than she could have hoped. No, leave Joni alone. She would be more likely to accept advice later.

Moonbeam Pax leaned by the dirty chopping board, ignoring the ram's head that she'd bought at considerable expense – after the outbreaks of mad cow disease, heads and spinal columns were hard to obtain. The story of the headless man in the river had made her look through her grimoires. Previously she wouldn't have used such a thing in her spells, but it seemed she wasn't the only wielder of hidden powers in the vicinity now.

Looking out of the kitchen window across her garden, Moonbeam watched the bats flitting around. Innocent creatures, their spirits free and unspoiled. Why did man think he was superior to the animals, why did man harm the earth? The first of the wind turbine shafts had been erected on the hills. Soon there would be lines of metal giants along the ridges, their cross-shaped propellers trying to harness the wind. As if the wind could be tamed by man. She knew the landowners were despoiling the land to obtain government subsidies. That was one of many reasons to put pressure on them.

Moonbeam's face was still damp with tears. The struggle would be bitter and people were already paying the price.

86

Joni was sure she wouldn't sleep, but she'd gone to bed after having a shower on returning from the scene. It was too hot in her flat, even though she turned down the heating and opened the windows in the bedroom before lying naked on top of the duvet. She knew the ambient temperature wasn't high. The heat was coming from inside her, as if guilt and responsibility had become lava coursing through her veins. She knew Nick Etherington had been lying, she knew he'd seen someone significant in Burwell Street, but she hadn't been able to break down the barriers – those of an eighteen-year-old schoolboy, for God's sake. It hadn't helped that Morrie Sutton had acted like a pig at the beginning of the first interview, or that both Major General Etherington and his mother had been present at the second, but she was an experienced detective. She should have got him to crack. Now the poor boy was in the morgue, his fine features destroyed and his head smashed open. His killer was armed with a prodigious hatred, whatever other motivation there had been to kill him.

She heard the start of the dawn chorus and was about to get up and watch the light spread over the garden, when exhaustion hit her like a church bell and she dropped into profound sleep. Not for long. She remained unconscious but her senses, operating at a deeper level, were accessible to her. She could smell the sweat and semen of the brothel, she could hear the whispers of the figures ahead of her and, when they turned, she could see who they were. There was a bittersweet taste on her tongue like burnt sugar. It was cloying and she tried to lick it away. Then, aware that her heart was no longer beating fast, she reached out to touch the first figure. She made out her blanched grandfather, Ted, a steelworker who had spent the last five years of his life on oxygen – the tank on a trolley beside him. Julien, the bald Frenchman whom she had loved in Marseilles, strode ahead, never looking back, his head and upper body drenched in blood. Then Joni saw Aubrey Stein, one of her Oxford lovers as he was when they were together, curly hair on his shoulders. When he turned she saw the gaping wound in his throat – he committed suicide a couple of years into his career as an investment banker. She didn't have the nerve to attend the funeral in Golders Green. Others she didn't know crowded around. She understood they were the early and unjustly dead.

The last figure to appear was Nick Etherington. Unlike the rest, he was as he'd been before he'd left the surface of the earth. He stopped and let the others move on to a destination Joni did not know; perhaps there was none and the endless tramping was their fate.

Facing her, the young man spoke in a soft voice. 'You were right. I did see someone at the brothel.' He gave a sad smile. 'I'm sure you'll find out who. You know, I don't think I'd have got the grades for Cambridge. It was all for nothing.' He turned and moved away, fading into a curtain of dust or ash, and Joni was alone.

She woke with a start and put a hand on her heart. It was beating slowly, as if her body had been in some kind of suspended animation, and she felt the chill of dawn on her naked body. She pulled on her dressing gown, then closed the windows and got under the duvet. She knew she wouldn't sleep again, but she wanted to cling to the remnants of the spirits.

When the birds were in full voice and the traffic below the

Abbey was building up, Joni got ready for work with studied concentration. It wasn't all for nothing, whatever Nick might have thought. She would find out who killed him no matter what it took.

<hr />

87

Kyle Laggan was driven to Corham first thing in the morning. His face was grey before he reached the mortuary. He'd tried to fob the job off on Pumpkinhead, but the sod had kept his head down. Ha-ha. No, not funny. They hadn't found Gaz's head or hands yet. He hoped he could identify him from the scars on the knees. Mrs Frizzell had been told about the police's suspicions and refused to have anything to do with her son. She was a hard cow. No wonder Gaz had turned out the way he was.

Kyle, dressed in a blue jumpsuit and shoes without laces, was cuffed to a cop in the back seat. He couldn't understand why he and his mates were still locked up. The fucking Albanian was pressing charges and the useless lawyer they'd been assigned said they were in shit because the club's security cameras had recorded them when they'd gone in with the bats. Fuck. Maybe if he played ball with the cops now, they'd put in a good word for him. They'd been told Hot Rod was OK and would be joining them soon – in Durham Prison, not just the police cells.

What could he say to get them off the hook? The truth was, Gaz had been going off the rails. He hadn't showed up at the Grapes as often as he should in the last few weeks. Had he been working for the Albanians? It couldn't be dope. The first people Gaz would have tried to sell to were him and the boys. So what then? Gaz had always been a lady's man. He was a handsome fucker and he pulled more or less anyone he fancied. Was that what this was about? Had he been playing the fucking gigolo?

Kyle shivered, oblivious to the verdant countryside. Maybe

that's why his head and hands had been cut off. Had the jackass been knobbing some Albanian boss man's woman? Had his head and hands been chopped as a warning? He could see the head-bangers doing something like that. They had nailed a couple of local hard men's hands and feet to the door of an old warehouse to make a point not long ago.

A surge of vomit almost escaped his mouth.

'Don't you dare, sunshine,' the cop growled.

Kyle Laggan swallowed the foul liquid. If Gaz had been led by his dick, maybe the bastards had cut that off too. He'd have given anything not to be the one to identify his mate now.

<><><><><><><><><><><><><><><><><><><><><><><><><><><><><><><><><><><><><><><>

88

'All right,' Heck said. 'Pay attention, all of you. What DI Pax is about to say applies to both Corham and rural MCUs.'

Joni took a deep breath and gave a run-through of the Etherington case, rarely referring to her notes. The post-mortem would begin shortly. Traffic Division had so far found no large dark vehicle in the vicinity, though they were compiling a list of local owners and would be following them up, checking for scrapes or other damage. SOCOs were still on scene, but initial evidence suggested that a single person had clambered down the slope after the victim had been knocked off the road, the size ten and wide-fitting trainer print suggesting a male. The victim's helmet had either come off in the fall or, more likely, had been removed by the killer; but the only fingerprints on it were Nick Etherington's. Inspection of the extensive head and facial wounds had revealed fragments of stone, but no bloodstained rock had been found in the area. Further searches in daylight were underway. The likelihood was that the murder weapon had been removed by the killer.

Joni paused and looked around the faces of her colleagues

– all were serious, even the usually relaxed Morrie Sutton and Nathan Gray. 'Now I come to the issue of phones. First, the victim's mobile has not been found. According to his grandfather, he always had it with him so the likelihood is the killer took it too.'

'Unless it turns up in the search,' Pete Rokeby put in.

Joni nodded. 'We'll be contacting his service provider to find out who he was in touch with recently. We'll also be initiating tracking – apparently it was a recent model iPhone, which increases the chances of it being pinpointed. The second phone that interests us is the one used by the anonymous caller to report the incident – that is to report that a man had been knocked off his bike. It came in at 7.33 p.m.' She leaned forward and pressed a key on her laptop.

'Police Force of North East England emergency service. What is your name, please?'

'Never mind that, I want to report a hit and run.'

Joni watched as people's eyes narrowed and foreheads wrinkled. Not only was the voice neutral, the speaker holding some kind of filter over the device, but it was genuinely creepy. It seemed to be male, but was relatively high-pitched and almost sounded like a digitally produced sound.

'The location, please, caller,' said the duty officer.

'B5477, bottom of the east slope of High Edge. Guy on a bike was knocked off the road by a large black 4×4.'

'Caller, what is your name? Please stay on the scene until—' The officer broke off when she realised the call had been terminated.

'Any thoughts?' ACC Dickie asked.

'Could be the killer,' Nathan Gray said. 'Certainly sounds like a psychopath.'

'Why would the killer be alerting us?' Joni asked.

Gray shrugged. 'Wouldn't be the first time a nutter has taken on law enforcement agencies.'

'No, it wouldn't,' Heck said. 'But let's not stray too far from the facts at this time. The caller identified the location of the incident. The victim's bike is in the lab now and I'm hoping the techies will find traces of paint.'

'No other witnesses, I suppose?' DI Sutton asked.

Joni shook her head. 'Not so far. Obviously we'll be trying to locate this phone and its user details as well. The caller hadn't engaged the number withhold facility, which might suggest this is a genuine witness who was flustered.'

'Could it be a woman?' DC Andrews asked. Her face was puffy. She had stayed with Rosie Etherington until a family liaison officer took over in the early hours.

'Wouldn't like to meet her in a dark alleyway if she is,' Nathan Gray said, earning himself sharp looks from the ACC and Joni.

'We're sending the tape to a linguistics professor at Durham University,' Heck said. 'We used him when I was in Newcastle.'

'I reckon it's a man,' Morrie Sutton said, 'but I'm not sure he's a Brit. He could be speaking like a robot to hide an accent.'

'Good point,' Joni said, impressed despite her dislike of the DI. 'Anyway, we'll need to work out rosters for interviewing the victim's friends and relatives. Most of the former are at the Abbey School, so the Corham squad will take part.'

Heck nodded his agreement. Sutton and Gray didn't look unhappy to be involved in such a high profile case.

'Also,' Joni continued, 'there may be a connection between last night's murder and the incidents at the Burwell Street brothel. The victim was there; some of you may remember he was dressed as a traffic light. He claimed he saw no one he knew apart from his friends, but I'm not convinced he was telling the truth. He may have been killed to stop him revealing who it was.'

There was silence as people took that in.

'This Nick Etherington,' said Nathan Gray. 'He's related to the general.'

Ruth Dickie took a step forward. 'This is where things become problematic. As you all know, Michael Etherington is a big figure in the area, especially now he's retired and in full-time residence.' She glanced at Joni. 'DI Pax tells me she thinks he may be keeping information to himself and intending to act on it. That means it's even more important that interviews of the victim's friends are as in-depth as possible, but bear in mind that many are still at school and may be under eighteen. We need to follow protocol to the letter.'

'Especially since their parents are the local great and good,' Morrie said sourly. He had grown up on a council estate in Gateshead and wasn't good with the well-off.

'DI Sutton,' the ACC said, 'I sincerely hope I won't receive even a breath of complaint about your or any of your officers' conduct. Am I clear?'

'Yes, ma'am,' Morrie said meekly.

'Thank you.' Ruth Dickie glanced at Joni and Heck. 'From now on I'll handle relations with Michael Etherington.' She gave a tight smile. 'As it happens, I know him socially.'

Joni didn't feel particularly reassured by that admission. She saw Pete Rokeby raise his hand and nodded to him.

'We've just got confirmation, as far as that's possible, of the headless man's identity. A friend recognised the scars on his knees. He's one Gary Frizzell from Benwell.' He glanced at Heck. 'I understand DCI Young at Newcastle MCU is checking his background.'

Joni looked at her boss.

'That's right. I'll let you know if there's any link to our cases,' Heck said. 'One other thing. As some of you know, a farmer by the name of Oliver Forrest went missing on the moors yesterday, in the area where the missing Albanian girl Suzana...' He paused, looking helpless.

'Noli,' Joni supplied.

'Aye ... in the area where she was last presumed to be.'

'More on the headless man,' Joni said, glancing at her file. 'Dr Volpert's report says the victim had a bite on his lower neck, but she's unable to confirm whether it's human or animal because of the small amount of remaining tissue.'

'Oh great,' muttered Morrie Simmons. 'Cannibalism an' all.'

Ruth Dickie ignored that and took a step forward. 'I'm not ruling out the possibility that the brothel murder, the headless man, the disappearance of the farmer and the killing of Nick Etherington are connected, but we have to concentrate on the latter now.' She looked back at Heck. 'Assign some uniformed officers to keep up the searches for the Albanian woman and Mr Forrest, but concentrate on Nick Etherington.' She moved her eyes across the MCU personnel. 'He's the key, I'm convinced of that. DI Pax, after the post-mortem, you and I will interview the dead boy's mother and his grandfather.'

'Lucky you,' Heck whispered to Joni.

She looked unconcerned.

89

Ollie Forrest felt the cuffs on his wrists being opened. He opened his eyes and saw a figure whose face was covered in a black balaclava. That person rapidly stepped back and waved a cattle prod at him, before exiting and slamming the door. In the faint light from beneath it, Ollie saw there were things on the table next to the bed. He went through the open door to his right and found a small but fully equipped bathroom. He emptied his bladder and dashed water over his face. Then he drank from the large bottle of water and ate the thick cheese sandwiches that were on the table.

He lay back and tried to work out what the hell was going on. The side of his head still ached. He remembered the girl on the moor, then wondered what had happened to his quad bike. Had the shithead who'd hit him, most likely the same coward in the balaclava, nicked it? Surely the cops would be looking for him by now. He remembered the call he'd received. They had already been on his land, after the Albanian knife-woman.

Then Ollie thought of Heck Rutherford. He could rely on him to give the search priority. They'd been at prep and senior school together. Then again, they were very different. He was devoted to playing with himself, while Heck was a choirboy when it came to messing around. He shrugged off advances. There were others, like Ollie, who could tell when something was on offer. He'd never stuck his dick into another boy's arse, that didn't interest him, and he didn't let them do that to him – they didn't dare because he was strapping lad. At the minor public school they'd attended, things were different. The headmaster, a lecherous old git, had seen advantages in allowing girls into the sixth form. They didn't need accommodation because they stayed at home and no extra teachers had to be hired. Heck was on a full scholarship. Ollie and he shared a study for the last three years. Heck was a hell of a rugby player, the best school boy number eight in the county, and Ollie was a bullocking hooker. That was about all they had in common. Heck was smart and Ollie wasn't. Heck seemed to be satisfied with kissing the girls who hovered around him like butterflies in a flower garden. Ollie, already losing his hair and ugly as sin, sniffed out which girls were up for it and got stuck in. Heck had never said anything, but Ollie knew he disapproved.

Now Heck was a detective chief inspector, though he was lucky to be alive. They didn't meet often these days, but Ollie had gone to visit him in the Royal Vic after he'd had surgery for the horrible wound he'd taken. It looked like all the blood had been drained from him. Ag had been there, watching over him like a pocket prizefighter. She'd never been keen on Ollie, having seen how he was after he'd sunk a few at parties. He would have had her any time.

Then he heard footsteps outside the door, the light partially blocked. The key was turned and Balaclava Man came in again, cattle prod directed towards him. The business end hung a few inches above his chest as the fucker clicked the cuffs round his wrists again – Ollie had put them where they needed to be at speed. The guy pulled a balaclava without eyeholes over his head and moved away. A dim light in the passage was all he could see, then it went out.

In the darkness he sensed someone had come close silently. A whiff of perfume entered his nostrils through the wool and made him sneeze. He heard a sigh of what sounded like disgust. Then, to his amazement, a hand was on his groin, searching for his button and zip, and pulling his trousers and pants down to below his knees. He was hard in seconds. A leg went over him and he felt bare flesh on his outer thighs. He was unable to reach for the woman's breasts. He had a burst of panic when he thought it might be a man, then he felt himself being guided into a damp cunt.

The bitch rode him, she rode him hard, and when he came she pushed down on him, grinding against his groin until he gasped. Then she was off him and he felt movements he couldn't understand. She was still on the bed, he could feel her hair on his legs. What the hell was she doing?

90

Heck and Joni were standing behind the glass screen and looking down at the post-mortem that Dr Bertha Volpert and her assistant were carrying out on Nick Etherington.

'Bloody hell,' Heck muttered, as the mortuary assistant ran the electric saw around the skull. The top of the cranium, part of it damaged by the blows from the still unlocated rock, was levered off to expose the brain.

Joni thought of the boy's desire to go to Cambridge. All his thoughts, all his knowledge of French, history and maths, all his emotions were gone, leaving only defunct tissue and nerves. The studying, the efforts he'd made on the sports field, the friendships – all wasted. The laughter, the spirit that drove him to construct the traffic light he'd worn on that fateful night, the grief he'd felt for his father, had already dissipated.

'Lady and gentleman,' came Doctor Volpert's voice from the loudspeakers. She had come from Germany to study at Newcastle decades ago and married another pathologist. Her pronunciation, syntax and random use of idiom sometimes gave her away. 'Would you like a running report?'

Heck nodded.

'Cause of death, multiple and extensive penetrating trauma to the head and face. He would have died of shock, although damage to the brain may have shut his system down sooner. The time I estimated last night – no more than two hours at most before he was found – has, I gather, been further narrowed down by other factors.'

'The anonymous call was received at 7.43 p.m. and the first officers arrived on the scene at 8.01,' Joni said, into the microphone in front of her.

The doctor lowered her protective glasses and looked at the file on an adjoining table. 'I took the first of my temperature readings at 8.45. Do you think this caller without a name reported the incident immediately?'

'No way of telling that, doc,' Heck replied.

'I'd say he or she didn't wait long before calling.' The pathologist moved down the body and stood over the groin. She picked up Nick Etherington's distended penis. 'I checked last night – after his grandfather left – and took a fluids sample from inside the prepuce. There's no question that the victim had indulged in sexual intercourse not long before death.'

'Could you be more specific about the time?' Joni asked.

'You mean how long before death he had sex?' She shrugged. 'A few hours at most. We're running tests, but I don't think a prophylactic was worn. The characteristic ring mark at the base of the penis is not evident, though it may have already disappeared.'

'You'll be taking samples of the stone fragments from his face, of course,' Heck said.

Dr Volpert squared her shoulders, not deigning to answer.

'Any other wounds or injuries?' he asked.

'Recent ones? A twenty-two-centimetre gash on his left shin, caused, I would hazard, when he went through the branches at the roadside. Lacerations and contusions to both elbows.' She raised a finger. 'Note well – this shows that he went down the slope on his front. The killer turned him over before delivering the blows to his face, having first hit him at the base of his skull – there's a bruise and stone fragments externally. I'm sure I will find a haematoma shortly. That blow would at the very least have seriously disabled the victim. There are several older wounds – scarring to the upper chest, right ankle and left wrist.'

'He was a rugby player,' Heck put in. 'A bloody good one at that.' He'd seen the Abbey School team play several times.

'My friends,' the doctor said, lowering her voice. 'You must be careful. The force used to inflict the wounds was massive. I have rarely seen such damage except in motor or industrial accidents. The person who did this is almost undoubtedly male and equally undoubtedly in the grip of intense passion – whether rage, mis-directed lust, jealousy, I cannot tell, of course. This poor boy had an implacable enemy, you can be certain of that.'

Heck and Joni thanked her and walked out of the morgue.

'We need his phone,' Heck said, 'especially if he'd been with a member of the opposite sex. They'd have arranged a meeting.'

Joni nodded. 'He's bound to have used social networks. His computer will have to be examined. Right, I'm going to find the ACC and interview the mother and grandfather.'

Mrs Normal on the front line, Heck thought. How much more trauma did those poor people have to go through?

91

Michael Etherington was standing motionless in his grandson's room. Around him were the bed that Rosie had carefully made up, the desk covered in open textbooks and notepads, and the wardrobe with the door that never stayed shut. Inside he could see the Abbey School blazer and a row of white shirts, while there was a heap of footwear in the corner – black shoes, trainers, rugby and cricket boots, and a pair of running spikes. Nick had been school champion over four hundred metres and at the long jump for the last two years.

Michael went out of the room and down the passage. The door to Rosie's room was ajar and he opened it further. She was under the covers, breathing deeply. The district nurse had come during the night and given her a sedative. She'd be awake soon. He had already taken Nick's room apart and put things back so his daughter-in-law wouldn't notice. The police were bound to go through it soon. There was no sign of a diary; as far as Rosie and Michael knew, Nick hadn't keep one. His laptop would be taken, but Michael had already transferred all the files he could find to a memory stick and would download them to his own computer.

He went back into Nick's room and got down on his knees. Not to pray – the residual faith he'd taken from family and school had been burned away in Bosnia, where he had seen things which proved either that there was no god or that any such being was indifferent to humanity. He put his hands under the wardrobe, feeling for anything he might have missed. All he found was a wrapper crushed around a piece of desiccated gum. The idea that it had been in his grandson's mouth brought tears to his eyes. He put it in his pocket as carefully as if it were a holy relic.

Michael looked at the boxes that Nick had filled with his possessions. One was full of game cards, collected with devotion when he was younger; another contained pages cut from soft porn magazines; and another, programmes from rugby matches, including internationals at Murrayfield in Edinburgh – several of which they had attended together. He looked again at the bookcase on the other side of the fireplace. It was contained paperbacks ranging from Tolkien to Terry Pratchett. More recently, Nick had spent such free time as he had reading popular history – Beevor on Stalingrad, Hugh Thomas on the Spanish Civil War, Piers Brendon on the decline and fall of the British empire. Michael was glad Niall Ferguson's more positive book about the empire wasn't there. He'd seen the results of modern empire-making after the first Gulf War and in the Balkans, and had openly taken against it. That was why he'd been given a desk job during the Iraq and Afghanistan wars. He believed young men and women deserved better than the horrors they'd been thrown into. But none of that mattered now his grandson was gone. The only thing he wanted was justice.

The major general sat in Nick's chair and thought about how that could be achieved. Although he didn't much like Ruth Dickie or her black subordinate, he thought they were probably good at what they did. But what could that amount to? The people responsible for Nick's death would slither away, he was sure of that. Only death would be ample recompense for his grandson's life, so full of promise had it been.

Michael Etherington would act quickly and decisively. He didn't care if that cost him his freedom or even his life. There were tried and tested former brothers in arms he could turn to. Nick would be avenged.

92

Joni was waiting for the ACC in the entrance hall of Force HQ when her mobile rang.

'DI Pax,' came Mrs Normal's voice, 'I'm sorry, I've been called to an unscheduled meeting with the chief constable. You go on, but remember – leave the major general to me.'

It was only a fifteen-minute drive to the village. Joni prepared herself for what would be a difficult interview. The fact was, most murders were committed by family members. She had no suspicions that Rosie and Michael were guilty. On the other hand, the latter seemed to know something and to be prepared to act on it. She hoped Ruth Dickie would make him see how foolish that would be.

She pulled up behind the Jaguar, relieved to see that both it and Rosie's Saab were there, as well as a small Citroen that was presumably the FLO's. Michael Etherington answered her soft knock.

'DI Pax,' he said, his eyes narrowing. 'I hope you'll use more delicacy than you did when you spoke to Nick.'

So it was to be like that. 'You'll be relieved to hear that Assistant Chief Constable Ruth Dickie will shortly be arriving to interview you. In the meantime, I'll be talking to your daughter-in-law, with the constable in attendance.'

The major general's chest swelled. 'Rosie isn't up to it.'

'These are difficult times for everyone, sir,' Joni said, 'but you want to help us catch the killer, don't you?'

Michael Etherington stared at her and then took a step back. 'Very well. But she hadn't recovered from Alistair, my son's, death. She's hurting very badly now.'

Joni took a risk and put a hand on his sweater-clad forearm. 'I know. It isn't the first time I've done an interview on such occasions.'

That seemed to comfort him. He nodded and led her into the sitting room, full of floral covers and curtains. Rosie Etherington was on the sofa, a blanket around her. The FLO was holding her hand.

'WPC Kirsty Shearer, ma'am,' the thin middle-aged woman in civilian clothes said, rising to her feet.

Joni waved her to sit down, then turned to the major general.

'Thank you, sir,' she said, inclining her head towards the door. He went reluctantly, giving his daughter-in-law an encouraging smile. Joni pulled over a pouffe and sat on it, her head lower than Rosie's. She hoped it made her less threatening.

'Hello, Mrs Etherington,' she said, in a low voice, waiting until the damp-eyed woman looked at her. 'I'm so sorry about your son.' Again she paused, watching as more tears were shed. WPC Shearer whispered caring words and they gradually had some effect.

'Why ... why would someone ... someone do that to Nick?' Rosie said, wiping her eyes with a bedraggled tissue. 'He was ... he was only a boy.'

Joni nodded. 'I know, Mrs Etherington, it's an awful thing. But that's why I'm here. We need to find the person who did it.'

Rosie's gaze hardened. 'Why do you care? You didn't even believe Nick before.'

Joni absorbed the hostility, her eyes never leaving the other woman's. 'Your son was a wonderful human being, Mrs Etherington. I could see that the first time I spoke to him.'

'When you handcuffed him to the fence in front of that hell-hole?' There was more to the woman than Joni expected. She admired her spirit in adversity. It gave her hope that she might know something important.

'All I saw at that moment was a cardboard traffic light.' She hesitated, then decided to push harder. 'And a pair of beautiful brown eyes.' Rosie sobbed. 'Beautiful, *scared* brown eyes.'

'Nick ... didn't know fear. He was a fighter. You didn't see him on the rugby pitch. He never gave up, he fought to the end of every match, no matter what the score was.'

'I have no doubt of that, Mrs Etherington. But your son was murdered.' She didn't go into details of the injuries as she wasn't sure how much the major general had passed on. 'It's my job to find out by whom and why. More than ever, I'm convinced that his death is linked to something he saw in Burwell Street.'

'I don't know anything about that. He ... he didn't tell me. You'll have to ask his friends.'

'We're doing that. So how would you describe him after Sunday night?'

Rosie shot her another aggressive glance. 'Shocked. I don't know what you said to him.'

'Nothing to upset him, I can assure you. I apologised for handcuffing him and I think he accepted that. Did he talk to you about the man in the doorway who had been stabbed?'

'Not much. I don't think it gave him nightmares. He'd seen plenty of rugby injuries, not least his own.'

'How was he before Sunday? He must have been under pressure with A-levels coming up.'

Rosie shook her head, raising another tissue to her face.

'Mrs Etherington?'

'He ... he was coping.'

Joni played one of her aces. 'He told me he wanted to go to Cambridge.'

The hand holding the tissue dropped.

'Did he?' she said, surprised.

'Yes, it turned out he was studying the same subjects that I did.'

The second ace broke the last of Rosie Etherington's defences. 'Nick ... was different these last few days. Not in a bad way, though he may have been distracted.' She leaned forward. 'I think he was in love.'

Joni disguised her interest as best she could. 'With whom?'

'I ... I don't know if I should say. He didn't talk to me about it.'

Joni waited.

'My father-in-law will tell you anyway,' Rosie said. 'Evie Favon. Lord and Lady Favon's daughter. Michael drove him up to the Hall every day this week.'

Joni knew the Favons were local big shots, not least because the Force HQ building used to be in the family. She'd seen the man's unattractive face in the local press often enough, sometimes accompanied by his much more striking wife. She wasn't aware they had a daughter, but why would she have been?

'He was coming back from Favon Hall last night when he ... when he was attacked,' Rosie said, as if she only just made the connection. 'Michael drove him up and he cycled back.' Her hand flew to her mouth. 'You don't think...?'

'What?'

Rosie looked bewildered and didn't answer.

'I don't think what?' Joni nudged.

'Nothing. You'll be speaking to the Favons, won't you?'

'Of course. You know, Nick told me he didn't think he'd make the grades for Cambridge,' Joni said, playing her third card.

'Evie was helping him with the English papers. She did her exams last year. She was supposed to be in Africa on her gap year, but Andrew Favon reversed into her and both her legs were broken. Apparently she's made an amazing recovery.'

Joni scribbled notes. Heck would fill her in on the aristocrats. 'So Nick was studying hard,' she said, 'but he still got dressed up for May Sunday.'

'Yes. For some reason making that stupid traffic light engaged his interest.'

Joni considered telling her that she had rescued Nick from a backward flop into the river, but decided against it. Claiming too many links to her son might make the bereaved mother jealous. Besides, she'd just had a thought.

The conversation continued, but Rosie had little more of significance to add. Joni heard a knock at the front door and got up. She could see the ACC's car on the street.

'Thank you, Mrs Etherington,' she said, getting up. 'We'll need a formal statement, but that can wait for a day or two. Again, my deepest condolences.' She beckoned WPC Shearer to the door. 'ACC Dickie's just arrived.'

The FLO raised an eyebrow. Mrs Normal wasn't known for getting her hands dirty, even with murder cases.

Joni went out to buttonhole the ACC before she started on the major general. She was wrestling with her memory. Had it been Nick as traffic light who had led his friends to the brothel in Burwell Street? If so, he might have had something in mind – something involving the person she was sure he had seen there.

∞∞∞

93

Suzana had woken in the back of a vehicle that was being driven at high speed down a steep slope. She feigned unconsciousness, moving her hand against the pockets of the leather jacket, the movements disguised by the pounding of the car. Her main knives had gone. She could feel the small blue knife that she'd taken from the woman's hut in her knickers. She'd have to conceal it better at the first opportunity. Everything had been a blur under the great metal columns. The man on the sow had leapt on her, then he had collapsed from a heavy blow. She had lost consciousness too and was aware of a lump on the side of her head, having caught a glimpse of a red vehicle before the blackness took her.

The road had flattened out and the vehicle moved even faster. Keeping her eyelids almost closed, she saw only a large building with many windows. The man at the wheel, a heavy-shouldered pig with a woollen hat pulled over his face, drove round the back and turned off the engine. After he opened the back door, he grabbed her by the hair and dragged her out. She couldn't avoid a squeal of agony and he slapped her on the face, cursing her with words she had often heard. Dogs started barking and she saw two vicious creatures chained up in the back of the pickup. There were trees beyond the gravel-covered road, but she was trying to keep up with her captor by using her feet rather than be hauled along and her eyes filled with involuntary tears. Through the blur, she saw an older building made of large, weathered stones. It was tall and narrow, like the watchtowers that had dotted her country before the communists had brought them down and replaced them with concrete boxes set deep in the ground. In the mountains the clans rather than the army had used them.

There was a heavy metal door. She waited on the ground as the pig took out a key and opened up. She was dragged inside and thrown against the far wall. The door slammed shut. There was nothing in the place and the only light came through narrow slits in the walls. She saw a steep stone staircase to her left.

The man in the mask, who was wearing dirty jeans and a torn sweater, grabbed her arm and took her to the stairs. She started to walk up, his hands shoving her when she slowed at every corner. She counted four storeys, each with a single door dotted with metal studs. Then he grabbed her shoulder and unlocked the door on the fifth floor. The room was surprisingly large, but it was nearly empty – a bed in one corner, an empty table in the other and a blacked-out window. Another door was ajar, with bolts on the outside. She could see it was a bathroom that extended in a blister from the flat wall. The man nodded and she understood she was to use it. Then he started tearing at her clothes. She fought back, but she was tired and hungry, and, more important, she had to find a way of hiding her only weapon.

It didn't take Suzana long to realise that the pig didn't want sex. Once he'd pulled off her jacket and shirt, he ran his hands through the pockets before dropping them to the floor. She raised her arms and he gagged at the stink. That was good. He stepped away and she sat down to take off her shoes and socks. The stench grew worse and he cursed, turning away. That gave her long enough to undo her trousers and slide the plastic-covered knife into herself. Fortunately Leka had not made her shave down there, it didn't show at all. When she was naked, she stood up. Her nipples hardened in the cold. That was good too, unless the pig preferred men. No, he couldn't stop himself from looking at them as he patted her clothes. When he was finished, he pointed to the toilet and left through the main door, closing and locking it. In the dim light Suzana saw a hatch in the bottom of the door. She looked around. The walls were white and freshly painted, while the large stones on the floor looked old. She had the distinct feeling that she was not the first prisoner to be held in this place. What had happened to the others?

The stink from her body distracted her. Feeling her way, she was surprised to find that the toilet also contained a small shower cabinet. The water was warm. She scrubbed her entire body with the rough soap that was in a holder until the water went cold. As she was drying herself, she heard a clang. Going to the hatch, she realised that fresh clothes had come through the hatch. There was also a film-wrapped sandwich.

After she'd put on the loose-fitting blue leggings, denim shirt and heavy pullover, she stood by the window in her bare feet, wolfing down the food. There was a space where the black paint had been scratched away. She saw the corner of a lake and hills in the distance. Trees and birds were moving across a feathered sky. To her right was the other building, lower but bigger. There were no people.

Suzana cursed under her breath. She had lost her freedom and her good weapons. The pig didn't want her, at least until she was clean. She had the feeling he was only a servant, even lower in rank than Leka. She shivered. What if his master knew her countrymen? What if they were on their way to take their revenge on her? She thought about using the small retractable blade on her throat, letting her blood splash over the white walls. Or she could wait and take at least one more of the animals with her. She examined the floor and the surfaces. There was nowhere to hide the knife; besides, she wanted it close at all times.

She could hardly have it closer – in the place where she had been ruined and abused. Shame burned though her, shame and sadness. Her body had been so deadened that she was hardly aware of the knife's presence. Yes, she told herself, she would fight them to her last breath, slashing at them even after she'd opened her own arteries. That would be a death to be proud of. Beyond it there would be no more abuse, no pain … only peace.

94

'Ah, DI Pax. Anything to report?' Ruth Dickie spoke in a low voice, Michael Etherington having walked ahead of them towards the kitchen.

'Yes, ma'am. According to Nick's … the victim's mother, he recently fell for Evie Favon, daughter of—'

'Lord Andrew and Lady Victoria.' The ACC gave one of her tight smiles. 'I've met them several times at functions.'

'The victim was cycling back from Favon Hall when he met his end.'

'Interesting. Let's see if Michael Etherington can cast any more light on the matter.' Ruth Dickie gave Joni a cool look. 'You'd better sit in on the interview, but do *not* intervene without permission.'

They went inside and into the kitchen, where the major general was preparing a pot of tea. The ACC asked him if he minded Joni being present and he accepted with a shrug. When Ruth Dickie told him he could ask for a male officer to be present, he laughed emptily.

'I have no issue with women,' he said, glancing at Joni. 'As long as they know what they're doing.'

'Please accept my deepest condolences,' Dickie said.

'Thank you, Ruth.' Cups, saucers and teaspoons were laid on the table with precision. 'You know, neither I nor my daughter-in-law will ever get over this.' He sat down suddenly.

'I'm afraid it will be very hard.' The ACC waited until he raised his head. 'You'll appreciate that we need to act as quickly as possible to catch the killer.'

'I told your colleague everything I know last night,' Michael said, pouring the tea.

Ruth Dickie glanced at Joni. 'But you omitted to mention Evie Favon and the fact that your grandson was cycling back from Favon Hall when he was hit.'

Michael looked at them. 'I'm sorry about that. Shock, I

suppose. And Nick only started his fling with Evie a few days ago.'

The ACC held his gaze. 'Do you have any reason to suppose the Favons are connected with his death?'

'What? No, of course not. Why should they be?'

'I don't know, perhaps they didn't approve of Nick. Perhaps he said something to upset them.'

'Forgive me, Ruth, but that's ridiculous. You don't get killed for upsetting people, not that I can imagine Nick having done that. He's … was very mild-mannered.' A haunted smile appeared on his lips. 'Except on the rugby pitch.'

'How did you feel about this … liaison?'

'How did I feel? Good luck to the lad. Rosie was worried it was distracting him, but Evie was helping him with his English literature. She's a fine lass.'

The ACC nodded. 'I know. I've met her. Have you noticed any change in her since her father ran her over?'

'I couldn't say. I'm not close to the Favons. We move in some of the same circles, but I wouldn't say we're friends.'

'I see.' Ruth Dickie paused.

'What do you mean?' Michael said, in irritation. 'I suppose you've heard rumours that Victoria and I were involved. Well, the answer's no. I lost my wife under a year ago. I'm not interested in that tart.'

Joni watched him intently. She was impressed by Mrs Normal's technique. She'd successfully needled a self-assured man into blurting out potentially useful information. Then again, he was emotionally vulnerable. The ACC's lack of compassion was less of a surprise.

'What about Nick?'

'For God's sake, Ruth, what do you mean?'

'Was Nick interested in Lady Victoria?'

'He only had eyes for Evie.' Michael looked away. 'Besides, his exams were coming up, as was his last cricket match.' He paused, breathing deeply. 'Not that it matters now, but he took both work and sport very seriously.'

'Really?' Ruth Dickie managed to sound both sincere and disbelieving, a talent Joni wished she had. 'DI Pax?'

Surprised to be given the chance, Joni took up the questioning. 'I gather his school work had been slipping.'

'Who told you that?'

'Nick. He said he didn't think he'd get his Cambridge grades.'

The major general's expression was impassive. 'He never told me any such thing.'

Joni wasn't going to let that opportunity go. 'Maybe your relationship with your grandson wasn't as close as you imagine.'

'That's preposterous. Nick and I saw each other several times a day. We talked a lot.'

'But not about his studies.'

Michael Etherington looked from Joni to Ruth Dickie. 'I can assure you, he told me everything that was troubling him. He was completely fine, even after you lot hauled him over the coals on Sunday night.'

The ACC cut in. 'General, I'll be frank with you. I don't think you're being frank with us.'

Spots of red appeared on Michael's cheekbones.

'Other officers are interviewing Nick's friends about Sunday night as we speak, so we'll shortly have more information.' Ruth Dickie clicked her pen three times, as if that had some significance. 'We'll also be talking to the Favons. Surely you don't want us coming back every time we find out more about your grandson's activities. That would hardly help Mrs Etherington with the grieving process.'

There was a pause. Joni considered how limited her own interviewing technique was, as well as what a bastard Mrs supposedly Normal was.

'Have you found his mobile?'

'No. Do you think it will be useful to us?' Ruth Dickie spoke softly. She was skilful at modulating her tone.

'Maybe.'

'Is there anything else you can tell us, general?' the ACC asked.

He remained silent.

Joni decided to try a different angle. 'Your grandson's murder couldn't have any connection to you, could it?'

Michael Etherington's eyes sprang wide open. 'What do you mean?'

'He was outside an Albanian-run brothel, in which three Albanians were injured, one fatally,' Joni said evenly. She took a breath and went for the jugular. 'You served in Kosovo, general.'

At first she thought he was going to lean forward and grab her, such was the anger that twisted his features. ACC Dickie stood up and that put a stop to whatever he was about to do.

'What exactly is the relevance of that observation, DI Pax?' she asked, her voice marginally above freezing point.

Joni got to her feet too, still holding Michael Etherington's gaze. 'I wondered whether the general had antagonised Albanian criminal gangs when he was there. I understand the majority of the population of Kosovo is Albanian. Could you have attracted the attention of those notoriously violent clans? Did you command raids on such criminals?'

The colour had gone from his face. 'It was a very complicated situation, DI Pax. Freedom fighters and criminals are often the same people. However, we were there as peacekeepers, not as gangbusters. I can assure you, what happened to Nick has nothing to do with me.'

Joni and the ACC took their leave shortly afterwards.

'That was what the Americans call a curve ball, was it not, DI Pax?' Ruth Dickie said, by her car. 'Do you seriously think Albanian gangsters are getting at Michael Etherington via his grandson?'

'Anything's possible, ma'am. Maybe he's been involved with them in the bad sense since Kosovo and wants out. You don't retire from that business.'

'I'm without your capital city experience of such things. If you think it's worth investigating, do so.' She opened the door of her Audi. 'He was definitely prevaricating earlier.'

Joni nodded. 'I think he's going to take action of some kind himself.'

'I agree.' The ACC stayed standing and closed the car door. 'I'll go back in and give him a last chance to come clean. If he doesn't, I'll make clear to him the consequences of taking the law into his own hands.'

'Yes, ma'am.'

'Oh, and DI Pax? You came perilously close to crossing the line back there.' Ruth Dickie smiled emptily. 'Fortunately for you – and me – you stayed on the side of the angels. Just.'

Joni watched her go back to the door, unsure whether she'd been complimented or given a dressing-down. Possibly both. It had turned out that Mrs Normal was about as ordinary as a purple swan.

95

Morrie Sutton was enjoying this. The ACC was out, Heck Rutherford was out, Jackie Brown Pax was out, so he was in charge. DC Eileen Andrews had come into the MCU with a sheaf of notes from interviews with the dead schoolboy's friends and was transcribing them, not that she offered him anything more than an 'Afternoon, sir'. His own people were doing the same, those who weren't still asking questions. He didn't know where Nathan Gray was – the bugger wasn't answering his phone. He did that sometimes. Morrie reckoned he had a woman somewhere, probably married. His DS was a terrible shagger.

Morrie had spent the middle of the day with Nick Etherington's teachers. It wasn't the first time he'd been inside the Abbey School and the luxury of the place got to him. The poncey male teachers in their tweed jackets and college ties looked down their noses at him, as if his council estate background hung around him like a bad smell. The women were even worse – flowery skirts and shoes that were halfway between boringly flat and fuck me over the desk heels. They resented being taken away from their lessons and they didn't like talking about one of their pupils. The headmaster – a white-haired loon who rumbled about the staffroom like a St Bernard who'd lost his brandy cask – had asked them to cooperate, but that didn't mean they were going to spill their guts. He'd done the men, while DC Viv Stammers, a middle-aged woman with years of experience in the old Newcastle vice squad, did the females. He'd had a thing with her about a decade ago and it had led to the end of his less than stable marriage. That had been when things had begun to go really wrong for him, but they were looking up now.

The upshot was that Nick Etherington had been the school's golden boy: a hero on the sports fields, a smartarse at his studies, the kind who supposedly had no enemies – as if rich folk didn't get jealous. One of the fools, the vicar, had actually come out with the 'no enemies' bollocks, to which Morrie had responded that somebody had hated him enough to smash his face in. That didn't go down well; the truth rarely did. The teachers went all coy when he raised the question of the victim's extracurricular activities. They were taken aback when he said Nick had been taken in for questioning on May Sunday night, and even more astonished when he mentioned the Burwell Street brothel. He wasn't buying that. He was certain that at least one of them would have been a customer at some time, though they all claimed they were with their families last Sunday, indulging in the pre-bank holiday festivities. None of them struck him as a suspect for the murder, though he would be comparing the pupils' statements. It wouldn't be the first time that a teacher at a private school had been caught kiddie fiddling. Then again, the victim was a big lad who could look after himself on the rugby pitch. If there was cock-tugging going on, then he must have been involved voluntarily. But Morrie didn't think that was the case. He could sniff a lie as well as the next copper and he hadn't caught a whiff of illicit underwear business.

When he'd finished with the staff, Morrie went to the school secretaries' offices, where the victim's friends were being interviewed. Nathan Gray asked if he'd take over his list while he went for something to eat and he'd fallen for it. The fucker – he'd be having words with him when he reappeared. That meant he found himself across a desk from a pimply specimen called Percy Andrew Hurston-Woods. 'Call me Perce,' the cheeky bugger had said, showing off teeth that Tom Cruise would have been proud of.

'So, Mr Hurston-Woods,' Morrie said, 'you were a friend of Nick Etherington's?'

'His best,' the lad said, choking back a sob. 'I can't believe what's happened.'

The form was to allow people to catch their breath, especially when they were only giving preliminary statements, but Morrie didn't go along with that. 'Keep at Them' was his motto.

'You have to believe it, lad,' he said. 'Were you with him on Sunday night?'

The boy nodded.

'Brave lot, weren't you, supporting your pal when he was in need?'

'I ... I didn't want to get into trouble. My father...'

'Aye, I can imagine. So, any idea why Nick got himself killed?'

There was more sobbing. 'He ... I ... no, I can't imagine...'

Morrie groaned. 'Look, it's not a proposition from Wittgenstein,' he said. He had a hoard of Monty Python quotations that he liked to use in inappropriate situations. He was the only kid in his class who'd liked the comedians. He didn't know why, but their sense of the absurd chimed both with the unpleasantness of his childhood and the crazed bureaucracy of the old Northumbria force.

'What?' Perce said.

'Don't they teach you anything here? Come on, lad, I haven't got all day. Did Nick have any enemies?'

The schoolboy shook his head. 'No ... everyone ... everyone admired him ... loved him.'

'Oh aye? Anyone love him more than the rest?' He saw he'd hit a nerve. 'Come on, out with it. Who was he shagging?'

Percy Hurston-Woods blinked. 'You can't talk that way about—'

'I can talk any way I like, son. Answer the question.'

'I … he…'

Morrie drummed his fingers on the table. He'd found that it often made people spit things out.

'I don't know who she was, but he was … he was involved with an older woman.'

Bingo. Morrie Sutton sat back, making no effort to hide his satisfaction. 'Good for him, eh? What do you mean you don't know who she is? Young lads talk, we both know that. Tell me or we'll be taking a trip to Force HQ. You really fancy getting your old man to pick you up there after I've finished with you?'

Perce shook his head, his cheeks damp. 'I don't know,' he insisted. 'You have to believe me.'

Morrie did, but he wasn't letting him off the hook. 'Ever see him with her? Did he tell you where they met?'

The boy shook his head, kept shaking it until Morrie began to worry it would drop off and roll across the table.

'All right,' he said less fiercely. 'How long had this been going on for?'

'Since the beginning of the Easter vac.'

'Vac? What's that?'

'Vacation,' Perce said. 'He was very happy some days, then very down. I think … I think she was messing him around.'

'Did he tell you that?'

'No, he didn't say much. In fact, I hardly saw him over the va— holidays. He only told me after the first time that he'd been with an older woman … and that it was amazing.'

Morrie found himself remembering his own youthful adventures. Screwing older women was the number two sport after football in his part of Gateshead and he'd got more than one hiding for his activities. But, like everything else, it would be different for rich folk.

'Getting back to Sunday night,' Morrie said. 'He wasn't too busy with this lady...' he said the word sardonically, '...to build himself that traffic light costume. What did you go as?'

'A highwayman.'

'Stand and deliver, eh? Tell me, whose idea was it to go to Burwell Street? You don't get much of a view of the fireworks from there.'

'I'm ... I'm not sure.'

Morrie slammed his hand down on the desk. 'Don't lie to me!'

Perce's eyes bulged. 'Well ... I think ... no, I'm sure it was Nick's.'

'What were you going to do? Get your ends away? Fancied a bit of rough?' 'No,' the schoolboy said shrilly. 'There were girls with us, our friends.'

'Uh-huh. So why did Nick take you there?'

'There's a pub, well, more like a club, called the Green Onion. They have live music.'

'Anything else?' Morrie asked. 'Any illegal substances?'

Perce's cheeks went scarlet. 'I don't know what you mean.'

'Never mind,' Morrie said. 'I'm sure Daddy will understand.'

He let the boy go and went through a similar performance with the remaining three on Nathan's list – the bugger still hadn't come back from 'lunch'. They weren't as close to Nick Etherington as Perce and had nothing significant to add. Morrie went back to Force HQ. He was pleased with himself. He reckoned he knew more about the victim than Joni Pax did, even though it was her big fuck-off case. That would give the tosser Heck Rutherford something to think about.

96

A Traffic Division driver in plain clothes and an unmarked car had been tailing Michael Etherington since he left the village. Heck was about a mile behind in a squad car driven by a uniformed constable, ready to step in if things got rough. At the outset the general had stuck to main roads, but he'd recently turned on to a narrow B-road that led towards the National Park. There were tracks all over the place and he could easily slip out of contact if the tail wasn't careful. So far he was keeping in touch, but there was a danger Etherington would realise the same car had been behind him for some time and take evasive action.

Heck thought through his options. He had the general's mobile number and could stop this nonsense any time he wanted, but he was sure Michael Etherington would claim innocence. The question was, where was he going? There were only out-of-the-way farms and park rangers' cottages ahead. Further north there was a large army range but if he was heading for that he was taking a very long way round. Maybe he was just going fishing. There were good trout to be had in the streams up here.

'Target turning left,' said the tail over the radio. 'There's a sign to Whelper's End. Instructions?'

'Stay on the main road,' Heck said. 'It's a dead end according to the map. Looks like a cottage and a couple of outbuildings.' He called the MCU, asking for DC Andrews. 'Eileen, can you check the occupancy of a place called Whelper's End, west of Rothbury? Call me back ASAP.'

They drew up behind the tail car. Heck got out and went to speak to the driver. 'You're sure he didn't pick anyone up?'

'Positive, sir.' The officer was young and enthusiastic.

Heck was wondering if the general had tracked down his grandson's killer already. He couldn't risk waiting for Eileen Andrews to get back to him. 'Come on,' he said, waving at the driver of the other car. 'You go left, you right and I'll head for the door. Nail anyone who makes a break for it, OK?'

'Yes, sir,' the keen one said, his eyes gleaming. The uniformed officer, who was older and had seen plenty of bad things, nodded stolidly.

Heck walked down the rough track, avoiding damp patches the sun hadn't reached. There were trees on each side and a lot of shade. Looking ahead, he saw a small cottage with a roof missing some slates and a thin trail of smoke coming from the right-hand chimney. It was markedly chillier up here than on the lower ground. Michael Etherington's Jaguar was parked on the left, partially obscuring the windows on that side. On the right was a small green Renault that had seen better days a decade ago. There was an enclosed herb and vegetable garden that was in better shape than the lawn and flowerbeds nearer the house. A black cat slunk away under a bush near the first of two outhouses, which was in reasonable condition. The second had no roof.

Heck waited until the other officers had taken up position and then walked to the door, his thighs still hurting from the sprint after the Albanian. Dirty net curtains obscured the interior of the cottage. There would be little natural light in the place. He reached for his warrant card and knocked on the white-painted door.

A woman in her early fifties opened it. At least, that was his initial estimate of her age; as he took in the bird's nest of dyed red hair, the face untouched by make-up and the wrinkled neck, he upped it to late fifties. She had a good figure though, her top half sheathed in a tight-fitting, multicoloured blouse and bottom half in green leggings. She wore wooden-soled sandals and there were rings on all her fingers and both thumbs.

'Ah,' he said, at a loss as to what the general would be doing here. 'Police. DCI Rutherford. I wonder if I could come in for a moment.'

'Be my guest,' the woman said, with a wide smile. 'I was just making some nettle and basil tea. Would you like a mug?'

Heck followed her into a living room that was like no other

he had ever seen. There were what looked like religious shrines in three of the corners, the fourth containing the skeleton of a monkey, the bones yellowed and the lower jaw resting against the sternum. There were vases containing dead, or perhaps dried, flowers and grasses everywhere and the place smelled like a stable. Michael Etherington got up from a low sofa with stuffing coming through gaps in the fabric.

'Heck Rutherford?' he said, frowning. 'What are you doing here?'

'I was about to ask you the same…'

The woman reappeared, carrying a tray. 'DCI Rutherford?' she repeated. 'You must know my Joni.'

Heck was seriously discomfited. 'You're Mrs Pax?'

She laughed – a loud, almost braying sound. 'I'm not married. Moonbeam's my name. Or Pax. No fuddy-duddy titles, please.'

'Um, right.' Heck had heard from Joni that her mother was 'different' – that looked like a major understatement.

Moonbeam poured out a brew that smelled less than enticing. 'Oh, I know,' she said, with another stentorian laugh, 'but its reek is worse than its flavour.'

Heck kept the chipped mug at arm's length, trying to find a way to explain his presence. Eventually he settled on one. 'Mrs … Moonbeam. You may have seen in the news that—'

'I only watch nature programmes.' The hostess spread her arms wide. 'I live for the earth, its powers, its beauties and its gifts.'

'Right. Anyway, there's been a series of murders – one in Corham and another not far from here. In the River Coquet?' The woman stared at him blankly. 'We're looking for a young Albanian woman.' He described Suzana Noli and ran through what she'd done.

'The poor girl,' Moonbeam said. 'Only seventeen. She must have had her reasons for killing, but taking a life is the ultimate crime against nature. We are all receptacles of the spirits of earth, water and sky. None of us has the right to destroy any living being.'

Heck looked around the room. The body of what looked like a frog was splayed on a board, the extremities of its limbs pinned down.

'That was already dead,' Moonbeam said. 'I never kill the creatures I use in my spells.'

In her spells, Heck thought; then his phone rang. He got up and went outside. DC Andrews told him that the cottage was owned by Viscount Andrew Favon and that Moonbeam Pax had been registered for council tax there for nearly two years. There were no other declared residents. When Eileen linked Moonbeam to Joni, Heck cut her off. He went back inside, having waved the officers back to the cars.

Moonbeam Pax and Michael Etherington were leaning towards each other over a table. It was covered in sheets of paper with a curious, almost hieroglyphic script on them. Heck searched for a word to describe the way the pair looked. 'Complicit' was the one he found.

'So,' he said, sitting down again. 'Have you seen any sign of the woman ... girl?'

Moonbeam shook her head. 'If I had, I would have invited her in for sustenance. It's every good person's duty to help those in need.'

'In which case, as a good person, will you call me if you see her?' He handed over his card. 'Do you mind if I have a look in your outhouses?'

The woman drew herself up. 'Actually, I do. I have private things in them. I can assure you, the girl isn't there.'

'Have you checked today?'

'As a matter of fact, I have. I went out to fetch various ... utensils for Michael's consultation.'

Heck looked at her and then at the general, who raised his shoulders.

'Moonbeam has access to certain powers,' he said, looking at the table. 'I'm hoping she can identify Nick's killer.'

Heck wasn't buying that for a second, but there wasn't much

he could do to counter such a barefaced lie; except put Michael Etherington on notice. 'I see. You will, of course, share any such information with the police, general. It's a serious offence to take the law into your own hands.'

Michael met his gaze. 'Ruth Dickie has already made that very clear to me.'

Heck got up.

'You haven't drunk your tea,' Moonbeam Pax said, in dismay. 'It'll do your system so much good.'

'I'm on a restricted diet,' Heck said, which was true – Ag was into dietary planning for the whole family.

The woman followed him to the door. 'Give my love to Joni. Tell her to drop round.' She smiled mysteriously. 'I'll be expecting her.'

Heck looked into Moonbeam's green eyes. There was something powerfully sensual about her. He suddenly felt uneasy about leaving Michael Etherington there.

'Excuse me,' he said, stepping past her into the house. 'General, you should come with me. DI Pax told me she thought your daughter-in-law needed a shoulder to lean on.' He stood there until Etherington reluctantly got up.

'Michael, you're not leaving?' Moonbeam said.

'Another time,' the general muttered.

Heck watched him go towards the Jaguar and turned back to the woman. 'You will call me if you see the missing girl? She's armed and distinctly dangerous.'

'Don't be silly,' Joni's mother said. 'Nobody can harm me. I'm a force for life.'

He left her to that illusion.

97

'I don't believe you!' Evie Favon screamed. 'It can't be true.' Her face was drained of colour and she was trembling.

Victoria stepped towards her. 'Darling, I'm so—'

'Don't touch me!' Evie limped towards the kitchen door, stopping as she dropped her crutch.

'Here,' Andrew said, bending down awkwardly and handing it to her.

She snatched it away, eyes on her mother. 'Who told you?'

'Cheryl. She heard it on the radio.'

'I … I saw Nick on his bike. He was very careful.'

'Dangerous things happen on the roads,' her father said. 'Especially in the country and at night.'

'And the driver just … disappeared?'

Victoria nodded. 'Hit and run is what the reporter said.'

'How did he … how did he die?' Evie slumped to the floor. She raised an arm when her parents moved towards her.

Andrew glanced at Victoria. 'They didn't mention that.'

'I want to see him.'

'I hardly think that's appropriate,' her mother said.

Evie was panting from the effort of pulling herself up. 'You … you know a lot … about what's appropriate.' She limped to the door.

'I mean, you're not family. Think how Rosie and Michael will be feeling.'

'I loved him!' Evie screamed. 'And he loved me.' She burst into tears.

'Come on, darling,' Victoria said, stepping towards her.

'No! Leave … leave me alone. This is all … your fault.'

The door swung to after her.

'What did she mean by that?' Andrew asked.

Victoria lit a cigarette. 'I haven't the faintest idea.'

Her husband looked as if he was going to speak, but held his tongue.

'Are you going out?' Victoria asked.

'Meeting in Newcastle.'

'With the new investors?'

'Mm.'

'Make sure you keep them on board. That mess in Corham on Sunday might be making them jittery.'

Andrew laughed brusquely. 'I don't think these gentlemen do jittery.'

'Gentlemen?' Victoria shook her head. 'Your ancestors would be ashamed.'

'My ancestors, as Evie daily points out, were slave traders and owners. It doesn't get any worse than that.'

His wife blew out a plume of smoke. 'Do you think so, Andrew? Do you really think so?'

<hr>

98

Joni and Pete Rokeby were in the MCU, collating their notes.

'Where's the DCI?' she asked.

'On Michael Etherington's tail,' he replied, not looking up.

'What do you think of this for an idea? The general could have been at Burwell Street on Sunday night.'

Rokeby's eyes were immediately on her. 'His daughter-in-law gave him an alibi.'

'She seemed to be under a lot of strain when I spoke to her, even before her son's death. Maybe Michael Etherington coerced her.'

'What, and then got spotted by Nick, who he subsequently killed? I'm not buying that. Michael Etherington's a hard nut, but he'd never kill his own grandson.'

'I'm not suggesting he did. But maybe he saw the person who later killed Nick.'

'It's all a bit theoretical. How would he know that individual was the murderer?'

'I've no idea. That's why I'm going to ask Rosie if she lied to us. And find out if there's anything else she omitted to mention about her son and her father-in-law.' Joni stood up. 'If Mrs Normal asks, I've gone to join the DCI.'

'Yes, ma'am,' Pete said uneasily.

Twenty minutes later, Joni was back at the house. 'How is she?' she asked the WPC who answered her knock. 'And where's WPC Shearer?'

'Not great. I'm the duty FLO today – Mary Archer, ma'am.' For some reason the bulky middle-aged officer seemed to be amused by her own name.

'Who is it?' The bereaved woman's voice was weak. It came from the sitting room.

Joni identified herself.

'I'm not … I'm not up to more questions,' Rosie said. 'Can you come back another day?'

Although she didn't feel good about it, Joni played hardball. 'Mrs Etherington, if I have to come back, it'll be with a warrant for your arrest.'

'My arrest?' the white-faced woman on the sofa said. 'What do you mean?'

'I only need a brief chat.'

'Oh, very well.' Rosie reached for the phone. 'I think I'll call our lawyer.'

'That's your privilege,' Joni said formally. 'But if you do, this conversation will take place under caution at Force headquarters.'

'I … all right, sit down.' Rosie smoothed loose hair back from her face. 'What's this about? I've told you everything I know.'

Joni looked at her across the coffee table. There was a vase of wilting roses in the centre of it. 'I'm afraid I don't believe you.'

Whether the woman was still under the effect of tranquillisers or had been beaten down by grief, she made no response.

'In particular,' Joni continued, 'I think you gave your father-in-law a false alibi for Sunday evening.'

'I … what?' Rosie Etherington's eyes were wide, the pupils dilated. 'No … no, I didn't.'

Joni opened her notebook, for effect rather than necessity. She knew perfectly well what had been said. 'You stated that the general and you had a light dinner, played Scrabble and went to bed, your father-in-law having gone upstairs while you were making yourself a cup of cocoa.'

'He … he doesn't like cocoa. Nick does …' Rosie Etherington broke off, her eyes tightly closed.

Joni waited, watching as the woman felt for the box of tissues on the sofa and held one to her face. 'You also said that you never slept when Nick was out and that you would have heard if the general left.'

'That's … that's true.'

'Except he'd already left, hadn't he? After dinner.' Joni was out on a limb, but she was sure she was right.

'I … he…' Rosie Etherington glared at her. 'Why are you wasting time on this? Why aren't you out chasing Nick's … Nick's killer?'

'That's exactly what I'm doing.' Joni let her absorb the words.

'No,' Rosie said, with a whimper. 'Not … not Michael. He couldn't have…'

'I'm not suggesting your father-in-law killed Nick. Certainly not. But I do think he knows more than he's told us and that he went into Corham on Sunday night.'

'Why?' Rosie Etherington demanded.

'I was hoping you could tell me.'

'Me? I don't know anything about Michael's life. He may stay here, but he doesn't tell me things. He's a victim too, you know. He lost Christine as well as Alistair.'

'What does he spend his time doing?' Joni asked, changing tack.

'He still has army-related work – a regimental committee he chairs, a think tank he contributes to. I don't know, you should Google him.'

Joni had done so. As well as the activities Rosie mentioned, he was patron of a charity for service personnel who had been injured, both physically and mentally, in Bosnia. He wasn't involved in anything to do with Kosovo, but that proved nothing. He could be maintaining contact with people on a personal level.

'He did a lot of things with Nick since my husband died – fishing, hillwalking… they went shooting with friends of his once.'

That was another thing Joni had checked. Michael Etherington had a licence for a shotgun and a uniformed officer had visited the house to ensure he stored it in a secure location. Joni wondered if the weapon was there now – and if the general had souvenirs from the Balkans that he'd never declared.

'All right,' Rosie said, swallowing a sob. 'It's true. He said he had something to do after we'd eaten and that I was to say nothing about it. I don't know where he went, but he came back to pick me up when we heard that Nick was with you.'

'How long did it take him to arrive after you called him?' Joni knew the dispatcher had called Rosie to tell her about Nick's presence at Force HQ.

Rosie wiped her eyes. 'How long?' She gave that some thought. 'Half an hour, I suppose.'

Meaning the general could have been in Corham or even further afield.

'Is there anything else you'd like to tell me?'

Rosie shook her head slowly. 'I'd like *you* to tell me something, DI Pax,' she said haltingly.

'If I can, Mrs Etherington.'

The twice-bereaved woman looked straight into her eyes. 'How can I go on living?'

Joni felt the shock of the words. Then she did what seemed the right thing. She told her about what had happened to her in London and how she was struggling to cope with it. By the time she finished, Rosie Etherington looked at her in a different way.

'Can I call you Joni?' she asked, in a small voice.

Joni nodded, the weight she carried having lifted slightly. They spoke for another quarter of an hour before she left.

99

Ollie Forrest, his face covered, went to paradise again with the woman. Then he made a mistake.

'What's this all about?' he asked. 'I don't have to be tied down.'

Nothing happened for some minutes – he had no clear idea of time. Then she was over his legs and away. He heard low voices a few yards away, then heavy feet approached. His balaclava was pulled off, but the bulky figure before him was still wearing his. Before Ollie could move, the point of the cattle prod made contact with his bare belly. He screamed as his body arced upwards.

'You don't fucking talk to her,' the man said. His voice was low and contorted.

The point touched him again and Ollie screamed even louder than before.

'Got it? If you'd kept your trap shut, I'd have undone the cuffs. Now you can shit in the bed and lie in it for all I care.' He turned to go and slammed the door behind him.

Ollie blinked away tears. At least the prod hadn't been on a high setting, though if it had been he'd have lost consciousness, which would have been better. His belly was burning and he realised he'd wet himself. He shook at the cuffs vainly. Who was the woman? Some horrible cow who couldn't get a shag? He didn't have that impression from the lithe limbs that had been in contact with his. They told him nothing about her face. But why bother taking *him* prisoner? You could get fucked by any wide boy in Corham or Newcastle if you paid a few quid, even if you were a paper-bag job.

The scream from above interrupted his thoughts. It either

came from a woman or from a boy whose balls hadn't dropped. Surely it couldn't be the woman who'd ridden him. Was she a prisoner too? In that case the man in the balaclava was a seriously twisted tosser. He recalled the man's voice. He'd heard it before. Not in that form – it was being disguised, he was sure of that.

The second scream was louder, as his had been. Was the other prisoner being given the cattle prod too? What the hell was going on?

100

Joni was speaking to Heck. 'You're at my mother's?' she said, in astonishment.

'I'll explain later.'

'Listen, sir, Rosie Etherington's come clean. The general *did* leave after they ate on Sunday night. She doesn't know where he went, but he took around half an hour to come and pick her up when she told him that Nick was at Force HQ.'

'All right, he's here. I'll ask him about it.'

'Can you wait for me, sir? I'd like to be involved.'

'We'll bring him back to Corham.'

'No!' Joni almost screamed. 'I've got a strange feeling about this. I want to find out what my mother knows about him. Please?'

'All right, but get a move on.'

Joni did so. Her driving skills had improved since she'd moved north and her long-instilled London driver's aggression meant that she encountered few delays. As she went along the narrow country roads, she thought about Moonbeam. What on earth could Michael Etherington have been doing there? She immediately thought of sex. Her mother was shameless about getting men into bed, even in her late fifties, although the last Joni had

heard she was working her way through the local male population. She hoped they had joy of her. She suspected Moonbeam
took more than she gave between the sheets. Why wouldn't
she as that was her philosophy of life, no matter how much she
dressed it up in New Age flummery?

She went along the track, the Land Rover crashing up and
down, and stopped behind a squad car at the start of the track
that led to her mother's cottage. Heck and the general were
standing by the latter's Jaguar, talking animatedly.

'Sir,' Joni said to her boss.

Heck looked at her guiltily. 'Ah, Joni. We were minding the
times about ... er, Corham Rugby Club.'

'Uh-huh. This is a bit of a surprise.'

Heck nodded. 'I'm told your mother's using her powers to
help the general find his son's killer.'

'Her *powers*?'

'That's right,' Michael Etherington said. 'She has quite a
reputation.'

'You can say that again. You don't seriously believe in that
mumbo-jumbo?'

The general gave her a stern glance. 'I'm prepared to use any
means to locate the bastard who killed Nick.'

'We're the only effective means,' Heck said. 'Right now, something has come to light that DI Pax needs to ask you about. We
can do this informally or back at Force HQ.'

'Here is perfectly suitable,' the general said, with no sign of
concern. 'What is it you want from me?'

'The following,' Joni said, her eyes on his. 'Where were you on
Sunday evening?'

'You know that. At home with Rosie.'

Joni felt the words raise goose pimples. That was a recent
development. Before the disastrous Met operation, she hadn't
been physically affected by blatant lies.

'General, your daughter-in-law told me that you left home
after you'd eaten with her and that you needed half an hour

to come back to pick her up later.' She was glad to see that her words had an effect on Michael Etherington, making him jerk back as if she'd spat in his face.

He stood looking at her, his jaws working. Then he turned to Heck. 'It's a private matter.'

'There's no privacy in a murder case,' Joni said, 'especially not for close relatives of the victim.'

'What are you suggesting?' he said, eyes wide. 'That I killed Nick?'

Joni held her nerve. 'Your daughter-in-law gave you an alibi for *that* evening too.' Out of the corner of her eye, she saw Heck step closer. For a few moments, she thought the general was going to hit her, then the tension went out of his body and his shoulders slumped.

'I ... I did ask Rosie to cover for me on Sunday.' He looked at Heck, cutting Joni out of his confession. 'You see ... I ... there's part of my life that I ... that I don't ... didn't want anyone to know about.'

'What is it, Michael?' Heck said, in a low voice. 'We need to know.'

'Oh for God's sake, it's nothing to be ashamed about. When I ... when I was in Bosnia, I came to understand that my men were precious to me. I mourned every loss, every serious injury, I wanted to wipe the blood away myself...' He shook his head and tears flew into the air. 'I wanted ... I wanted to kiss them.'

Joni kept quiet, aware that any intervention from her would make him clam up.

'You're saying you're gay?' Heck asked, incredulity breaking through.

Michael Etherington nodded slowly. 'I didn't do anything about it until Christine died, but then I needed more than Rosie could give me in terms of emotional support. She was grieving for my fool of a son. So I ... I used an internet dating site and I met a man in Newcastle.' He smiled weakly. 'He's a lovely fellow, in his late thirties, calm and considerate. I was there on Sunday evening.'

'All right,' Heck said. 'I'm afraid I'll need his name and phone number. Address, too.'

The general opened his mouth, but then took out a notepad and wrote on it, tearing off the page and handing it to Heck. He didn't look at Joni at all.

She didn't care. She was going to have a serious conversation with her mother.

101

Pete Rokeby went back up to the moors to see if the SOCOs had found anything else. He knew it wasn't on his list of actions for the day, but he was disturbed by the farmer's disappearance and thought it wasn't being taken seriously enough. When he got out of the car, he was buffetted by the wind that was turning the turbine rotors rapidly.

'How's it going?' he asked Yates, the chief technician.

The middle-aged man was on his knees. He pointed to a tyre track. 'That wasn't made by the quad bike. I'd say it's from a pickup, the kind farming types use. The tread's heavy-duty, but the tyre isn't particularly wide. We should be able to get a decent cast.'

Pete Rokeby nodded and went over to the edge of a steep and rocky chasm. It fell a couple of hundred feet and, at the bottom, trees and bushes were thickly clustered around a burn. 'Think the Albanian woman or the farmer went down there?'

'Only if they were interested in suicide.'

'How else can you get off the moor?'

Yates pointed to the east. 'There's a track along the fence on this side, then the ground drops. Oliver Forrest's place is about a mile further on, but before it there are three roads running north.' Pete followed his arm. 'The first goes into the National Park, the second leads to the south end of the Favon estate and the third winds down to join the Rothbury road.'

'So we look for more tracks like this one and see where Forrest's attacker turned.'

Yates nodded, but he didn't look convinced. 'It's been pretty dry. The roads off the moor are all asphalt. We may not be able to follow him.'

'Or her. Maybe the Albanian woman laid into them both and took the vehicle.'

'Could be, DS Rokeby.' Yates grinned. 'I'm glad I don't have to work it out.'

Thanks a lot, Pete said, under his breath. He called Heck Rutherford, but his number was engaged.

102

'Right, Mother, what the hell have you been up to?'

'Good day to you, Joni.' Moonbeam smiled at her daughter across the festooned living room. 'It's lovely to see you.'

'What was he really doing here?'

'Who, the policeman? Don't you know? You work with him.'

'Not the policeman!' Joni yelled. 'Michael Etherington!'

'Sit down,' Moonbeam said, the smile still on her lips. 'You're disturbing the spirits.'

'The spirits.' Joni shook her head. 'Do you know what that man's going through?'

'Of course. He told me.' Moonbeam pointed to the papers on the table. 'I'm working on a spell to help him find the killer of his grandson. Murder always creates a black cloud and it follows the perpetrator around.'

'Really? That would explain why Hitler's executioners were all so effortlessly tracked down.'

Her mother ignored that. She had a limited knowledge of history. 'You're so set in your ways, Joni. Didn't that wonderful education teach you to open your mind? Of course, opening your mind isn't enough. You must also open your soul.'

Joni stepped closer to Moonbeam. 'You know how open-minded I am. For a start, I turned vegetarian decades before you did.'

'Ah, that was a terrible mistake on my part. I blame living in the big city. As soon as I came here, I realised how wrong I'd been.' Moonbeam gave a crooked smile. 'Then again, the men I was seeing all demanded meat, though not necessarily with two veg.'

Joni glared at her. 'I don't suppose you were extending your favours to Nick Etherington?'

'The dead boy? No, but I wish I had been. Michael gave me a photo of him for my work. He was beautiful indeed.'

'What about the general? Any hanky-panky with him?'

Moonbeam's laugh filled the room. 'Hanky-panky? Honestly, Joni, you sound like your grandmother. Do you mean Michael? I don't understand titles. Was he in the army?'

Joni had believed her mother concerning Nick, but she was less convinced about Michael Etherington, even after his confession. He'd been married for years. Maybe he was bisexual.

'Handsome man, though,' Moonbeam continued. 'Apart from the awful sadness in his eyes. He told me his son and then his wife died.'

'And now his grandson.'

'Life can be very hard for those who disregard the essential equilibria.'

Joni swallowed a laugh. 'The what?'

'There you go again, mocking forces you don't understand.' Her mother looked severe. 'Besides, I don't get involved with paying customers.'

'Very ethical. Who *are* you involved with then?'

'You've no business asking that, Joni.'

'You aren't usually so reticent. I spent my childhood being regaled with the virtues of numerous men, most of whom disappeared after a week or two.'

'Yes, well, things are different now. I've got a serious lover.'

'Really? What's his name? What does he do? Is he married?'

Her mother turned and walked into the kitchen. Joni followed, gagging at the smell from a large pot on the ancient stove.

'What's that?'

'Nothing that concerns you. This is turning into an interrogation. Take your nasty police attitude somewhere else.'

Joni removed a bunch of herbs from one of the two chairs and sat at the rickety table. 'Sorry. If you don't want to tell me about your new man, fine.'

'No, darling,' Moonbeam said, coming over and taking her daughter's hand. 'I do. I will. But not now. These interruptions have caused a disjunction between my being and the...'

'Essential equilibria?'

Her mother smiled, missing – or ignoring – the irony. 'If you'd only open yourself to the forces of the cosmos. Joni, I understand you. You're still hurting from what happened in London. I can help you get over it.'

Joni pushed the chair back hard. 'I have to go.'

'Don't be like that. Come over on Sunday. We'll have lunch and I'll introduce you to my man.'

'Sorry, I've got a prior engagement.' Joni was glad Ag's invitation meant she would avoid the nut rissoles and over-cooked greenery – some of it bizarre – that her mother would serve. 'I'll drop by in the late afternoon. In the meantime, keep an eye out for any strange young women and lock your doors.'

'Your colleague – Heck, was it? – told me about the Albanian. I'll sense her long before she comes close, don't worry.'

Joni raised her eyes to the ceiling and promptly wished she hadn't. What looked like a fisherman's net had been strung from the corners and was weighed down by decaying creatures. There were rats, crabs, a squirrel, even a bat.

'Lovely.'

'The physical envelopes of creatures who have passed on have a certain value to my craft,' Moonbeam said. 'If you're

271

wondering, they were dead when I acquired them. I told your colleague. You know, he has a great sadness in his eyes too and his body has been broken. I can help hi—'

'I know, Mother. You can help everyone. Unfortunately, when I was a kid, you forgot to help me.'

For once Moonbeam was silenced.

Outside, Joni looked around. She was tempted to go over to the outhouses – the nearer one had definitely been renovated since she'd last been there – but she didn't want another encounter with her mother. The sound of Joni Mitchell's plangent voice from the open window confirmed that decision.

103

Heck was up on the moor with Pete Rokeby and the SOCOs. He'd spoken to the DS and decided that what he was doing warranted support. Clouds had come out of nowhere and it was drizzling.

'Great,' he groaned. 'How are those moulds?'

'Don't worry about it,' Yates said. 'This stuff's waterproof.' They had located another tyre print a few yards beyond the first.

'Aye, but anything else'll be obliterated if this gets worse.'

'Something wrong, sir?' Rokeby asked.

'Well, I'm not exactly jumping for joy about the way things are going, Pancake.' Heck pulled the cord of his rain-jacket hood tighter. 'There's no sign of Suzana what's her name, Michael Etherington claims he's using a witch – Joni Pax's mother, no less – to find his grandson's killer and a chap I was at school with has disappeared.'

'This Forrest fella,' Pete said. 'I hear he has an eye for the ladies.'

Heck gave him a suspicious glance. 'Who told you that?'

The DS grinned. 'I need to protect my sources, sir.'

That got him a glare, but it was short-lived. 'Aye, well it's not exactly a state secret.' He shook his head. 'I was at prep and senior school with him. He was never one to pass up an opportunity to play with other boys' cocks. He moved on to girls as soon as he could and he's been playing away ever since. I don't know how Lizzie stands it. Then again, maybe he's changed. I haven't seen much of him since I hooked up with Ag. She took one look at him and knew exactly what he was. Won't have him in the house.'

'I was thinking,' Pete said, turning his back to the rain. 'Maybe he was chasing the Albanian woman. There wasn't a sheep anywhere near here yesterday.'

'You might be right, Pancake, but it doesn't get us anywhere. There's no sign of her and I don't fancy asking Lord Nose in the Air for leave to search his estate on the off chance. He's got friends in high places – including the chief constable.'

'Yes, but maybe one of the estate workers kidnapped your pal Forrest.'

'We can have a go at checking his people's vehicles when the prints are ready, though I doubt it'll be worth it. With the kind of legal firepower he can afford, we need much more evidence. It would be easy enough for an expert witness to cast doubt on how recent the tracks are. This is the first soak we've had in – what? – ten days.'

'Besides, according to Yates, two of the three roads lead elsewhere.'

'Exactly. I doubt Mrs Normal will want to go into battle with Favon unless we provide her with several pairs of armoured knickers.'

Rokeby laughed. 'Not a pleasant image.'

'Sod this. Let's get into the car.' Heck led him to the Traffic Division Volvo he'd commandeered. 'Listen, Pancake, I need to ask you something. You've met Michael Etherington, haven't you?'

'Not exactly. I've seen him a few times. I've got a mate who served with him.'

'Oh aye? What does he say about the general?'

'Nothing but good things. The best officer he ever worked for, tough but fair, always thinking about the men, cool under fire. I remember he was really pissed off when he heard General Michael had been taken off operational service. Said it was a disgrace and a terrible waste.'

Heck watched as the SOCOs collected up their gear and carried it back to the van. 'Speaking of disgrace, did your pal ever mention anything about the general's sexual um … proclivities?'

'No.' Rokeby stared at him. 'You're not saying he's gay?'

'What makes you think that?' Heck said, looking away. 'He could be a serial shagger like Ollie Forrest or an S&M type.'

'I'll tell you exactly why I think that, sir,' Pete said combatively. 'Because you're asking *me*.'

'Right enough. Don't get uppity, lad. I just wondered if you'd heard anything. Or noticed anything.'

'What, you think we have antennae that pick up signals from other poofters?'

'Er, not exactly.'

'Not exactly, but sort of?'

'Well, yes, I suppose so.'

Pete was shaking his head. 'No, my mate never said anything. No, I never clocked anything. And no, we don't have antennae – at least, no more than you heteros have when you zero in on women.'

'It's been a long time since I did that.'

'You're not getting away so easily, sir. Has someone told you that Michael Etherington's gay?'

Heck nodded. '*He* did, actually. Gave us the contact details of his lover in Newcastle too. DC Andrews is checking him out as we speak.'

Rokeby sat back. 'Does this have any connection with the death of his grandson?'

'It's how he explains what he was up to on Sunday night. Joni broke his alibi this morning. His daughter-in-law covered up for him.'

'Do you think he might be being blackmailed?'

'I don't know, Pancake. He didn't admit to that. Anyway, why would he care? His wife's dead and he's out of the army.'

'Maybe he was worried what Nick would think.'

Heck took that in. 'Good point. But I still don't buy that he was using Joni's mother to track the killer down.'

'That does sound weird.'

'You should see what she looks like.'

104

Joni spent the afternoon going through the statements made by Nick Etherington's friends. She was still puzzled about the walk they had taken to Burwell Street, apparently led by him. Maybe she was reading too much into it: youthful high spirits, drink (although his friends said Nick had only had three halves of bitter and she herself hadn't got the impression he was drunk), the desire to slum it, score dope and/ or listen to a covers band in a downmarket pub? Or could he and his grandfather have been up to something more sinister? Eileen Andrews had visited Michael's lover – a Julian Dorries – who confirmed that the major general was there until after ten on Sunday and that he'd left in a hurry after receiving a call from his daughter-in-law.

'Do you think he was lying?' she asked DC Andrews. 'The general talked Rosie into covering for him. Maybe this guy's doing the same thing. He isn't or wasn't in the army, I hope.'

Eileen shook her head. 'He's a freelance computer pro-grammer. If he was lying, he convinced me. I asked for some background to their relationship and he gave me a lot. Too much, frankly.'

'How long have they been together?'

'Three months. They met in a pub in central Newcastle after checking each other out on an internet dating service.'

'Is that how it works?' Joni asked. 'You check each other out?'

'Don't ask me. I've been married twenty years and I don't need any more men.' It was common knowledge in the MCU that Eileen Andrews wore the trousers in her marriage, her husband being a soft-spoken and very tall train driver. She gave a sly smile. 'Maybe you should try it, ma'am.'

Joni managed not to bite her head off. She knew the others thought it strange that she was without a partner. She went back to her desk. There were various reports in from the SOCOs and the labs. Curiously, there was no paint anywhere on Nick Etherington's bike or clothing from the car that had supposedly hit him. Neither were there any tyre marks on the road, suggesting that the killer slowed to a halt after driving the young man off the road and went back to deal with him, or that someone else smashed his head in. That got her thinking. How reliable was the anonymous phone call? Had Nick perhaps not been knocked from his bike at all? Had he stopped to talk to someone – maybe someone he knew – and been thrown down the slope and killed, and his bike smashed up afterwards? Only his fingerprints were on it, some of them smudged. His assailant had presumably been wearing gloves.

'Where are we with the victim's laptop?' she asked.

'There are three of us on it,' DC Andrews said. 'Plus a geek from Technical Services who's looking for any hidden files. He says Nick Etherington doesn't seem to have been much of a technical whiz – some games, a lot of schoolwork, and the usual email and social media sites on his browser, the latter not much used. I've been trawling his emails. Some of the teen stuff is hard to decipher, but I haven't come across anything that's set off alarm bells.'

'Have we got the records from the phone company yet?'

'Later today.'

'I don't suppose his or the anonymous caller's handsets have turned up.'

Andrews shook her head.

Joni looked round as loud male voices came through the MCU's swing door. Morrie Sutton was wearing a scowl the width of the River Derwyne, while Nathan Gray was ranting about football.

'Get your behind spanked?' Joni asked. Andrews had told her that Morrie had been called to the ACC to face the disgruntled parent of an Abbey boy he'd interviewed.

The inspector muttered something before looking at her. 'Nothing I couldn't handle, Jack. Found your murdering Albanian whore yet?'

Joni stared back at him, but she couldn't come up with a cutting response.

'Thought not,' Morrie continued. 'Not to worry, we've been doing your dirty work for you.'

'Aye,' said DS Gray, holding a file to his chest. 'Guess what's in here.'

Joni said the first thing that came into her head. 'Your transfer to Family Liaison?'

Gray's reaction was striking. His cheeks reddened and he glared at her, then lowered his head and whispered to his boss. Morrie Sutton shook his head and extracted the file from his grip.

'Nathan's wife has walked out on him and taken the kids,' the inspector said. 'That's no laughing matter.'

Joni shrugged. Nathan Gray's marriage had been creaking since she'd arrived at Pofnee, when he'd been having an affair with one of the catering staff. That had stopped when the woman's husband slashed Gray's tyres. She wasn't going to show any sympathy, especially since he seemed to care more about Newcastle United's defensive frailties.

'Am I supposed to get on my knees for the file?'

'Go on then,' Gray replied, trying to get it back from Sutton.

'Enough, Nathan,' Morrie said harshly. 'You can be a right tosser.' He handed the file to Joni. 'We've been following up on the men who were in the brothel on Sunday night, the ones whose fingerprints were on record.'

Joni flicked through the pages, the photographs ranging from a wide-eyed, pimply young man to a puffy-faced, shaven-headed older man whom she vaguely recognised.

'That's the one,' Gray said, putting a finger on the page. 'Alfred Peter Shackleton, also known as "Goat Skin".'

'What?' Joni asked.

'Don't ask me. He certainly doesn't smell too good.'

'I know why,' Morrie Sutton said. 'He used to go around in this manky coat he bought from a towel-head when he drove a VW van to Afghanistan with some pals in the seventies. The story is they brought back enough heroin to supply Newcastle for a month. Being a world-class waster, he pissed all the money away. Oh, and he got arrested for taking a dump in the Bigg Market on a Saturday night.'

'I saw him,' Joni said, recalling the man she'd seen first in Corham centre and then in Burwell Street on Sunday night.

'What, taking a dump?' Nathan Gray asked.

'Outside the brothel. He wasn't wearing a shirt and he's got…'

'The Toon colours tattooed on his belly.' Morrie nodded. 'That's him.'

'All right, so you interviewed him,' Joni said.

DI Sutton nodded. 'He didn't see any of the woman's knife work, though when we showed him her photo he said he'd screwed her a couple of times. Didn't like her, said she made him feel like he was raping her.'

Joni glanced at Eileen Andrews. 'Which he was.'

Morrie stared at her. 'He's got needs like all of us. Besides, you saw the size of him. His wife's a stick insect. It's not a happy home.'

The conversation was making Joni feel very soiled. 'Is there a point to this?'

DI Sutton gave her a thin smile. 'Oh, yes, DI Pax. You see, Goat Skin Shackleton might have been a regular at the knocking shop, but he wasn't just satisfying himself on Sunday night. He was checking the place out for one of the local gangs. They're pissed off with the Albanians and they want them out. He was quite happy to talk about them. Your scrubber ... I mean, stabber, did the Steel Toe Caps a good turn.'

'I want to talk to him,' Joni said. 'Where does he live?'

'Ah, there's the rub.' Morrie, a classic rock addict, had an old Wishbone Ash album of that name. 'His residence is in Ironflatts which, as you know, is within the boundaries of Corham.'

Joni sighed. 'All right, will you take me to him, please, DI Sutton?'

'In the spirit of inter-MCU cooperation, it would be my pleasure, Jack.' He raised a hand. 'Not you, Nathan. I'm sure DC Andrews has got something you can help her with.'

Joni followed him out, trying to get her mind back on the case. She felt disoriented, even out of her depth, remembering the sweaty fat man. Goat Skin Shackleton – what sort of a name was that? And the Steel Toe Caps? Worst of all, she was about to go south of the river, to the levelled industrial zone with its dilapidated tower blocks and cramped streets lined with thin-walled, two-up two-down houses. One of the few times she'd ventured there, the Land Rover had been pelted with rubbish.

Still, anything that might help save Suzana Noli from the retribution of her countrymen.

105

Ruth Dickie finished looking at her notes and called DCI Lee Young at Newcastle MCU.

'What can I do for you, ma'am?'

'What's the status of the four men you arrested for attacking the Albanian Fatlum Temo outside the Stars and Bars nightclub?'

There was a pause. As she'd expected, Young hadn't been expecting the question.

'They've been remanded to Durham Prison.'

'Having been charged with?'

'Assault occasioning actual bodily harm.'

'I see. You're aware they were trying to ascertain the whereabouts of the man now identified as Gary Frizzell, found without his head and hands in the River Coquet?'

'Yes, ma'am. I've been liaising with DCI Rutherford.'

'Have you interviewed Mr Temo about the alleged sighting of him with the dead man?'

'Yes, ma'am. He denied it and the witness, John Joseph, motor mechanic, also denied that he saw Mr Temo with the dead man.'

'Did you ask him why he lied to Frizzell's friends?'

'Yes. He said he was drunk and didn't know what he was saying.'

'Who's the Albanian's brief?'

'One of Richard Lennox's people.'

'What a surprise. Tell me, DCI Young, have you considered getting a warrant to search the Stars and Bars?'

There was silence on the line. 'Em, no, ma'am.'

'You're aware that an Albanian brothel was operating in Corham and that an Albanian working there was murdered?'

'Yes, ma'am.'

'Very well. Let me be absolutely clear. From now on we'll be operating a zero tolerance policy with Albanian-run businesses where there is the slightest suspicion of illegality. These gangs, or rather clans, are gaining a foothold in the north-east and I want them stopped. So, I might add, does the chief constable.'

'Yes, ma'am.'

'One more thing. I took the opportunity to speak to Kyle Laggan, the man who identified Gary Frizzell, when he was here. He struck me as a run-of-the-mill loud mouth, but not a professional criminal. Your background searches back that up, do they not?'

'Yes, ma'am.'

'So, although I in no way condone the serious charges that he and his friends face, I think your energies should be directed at the real criminals in this matter. That instruction has been sent to your commanding officer. Good afternoon.'

Ruth Dickie sat back in her leather chair. That would shake the Newcastle MCU up. She'd never liked DCI Young. He knew that and now he'd be wondering why she'd called him instead of his boss. It wouldn't take him long to work out the reason.

She had him in her sights as well as the Albanians.

106

'Why do you drive this old wreck of a Landie?' Morrie Sutton asked, as they left the Force HQ car park.

'Old wreck? Listen to the engine. I tuned it myself.' Joni swung the wheel hard left. 'See how she rolls? I replaced most of the suspension too.'

Morrie tried to disguise his admiration. He drove a beaten-up Mondeo and had no idea what went on under the bonnet and shell.

'Take the new bridge,' he said.

As soon as they were over the Derwyne, the urban environment changed. There were run-down parts in the north – Burwell Street and the area around the old sugar mill being prime examples – but they were nothing compared with Ironflatts. There was a narrow line of decent houses along the river, but beyond them was the industrial wasteland, only a small part of which had been revamped by the development zone commission. Over to the east stood the sixties blocks of flats, one of them empty. Nearer, two-storey office buildings of pale red brick and small business units in pastel shades of corrugated plastic stood behind a high fence.

'They're talking about electrifying that,' Morrie said, pointing. 'Thieves can get over it in seconds with expanding ladders and ropes. I reckon they go on training weekends with the SAS.'

Ahead of them was the large flat quarter where the steelworks had been. Grass had sprung up along the concrete tracks and, although it too was fenced off, there were piles of rubbish and rubble everywhere.

'Fly-tipper's paradise,' Morrie said. 'They get together, decide where they're going to cut the wire and go for it. They're in and out in minutes and there's bugger all we or the council can do about it. Puts companies off, even though the rents are rock bottom. Who's going to move to Corham when Newcastle and Sunderland have got secure facilities?'

'Pofnee did,' Joni said, glancing at the rows of houses that ran up the slope to the west.

Morrie Sutton laughed. 'Good one, Jack.' He looked at her. 'Does it piss you off when I call you that?'

'If I said it did, would you stop?'

'Probably not.'

'Directions,' she said, as they approached an incongruously large roundabout.

'Turn right. Ahead is Ironflatts West. Nice, isn't it?'

Joni had grown up in the urban squalor of eighties Hackney and seen much of the worst of London, but this was something else. The few shops had steel gratings over their windows and there were potholes in the road. Young women were pushing buggies along uneven pavements and dogs with their ribs poking through their coats tugged at the contents of toppled bins.

'Has Corham Council forgotten this place exists?'

Morrie shrugged. 'They did a bit here before the spending cuts, but they've got other priorities now. They're Tories, remember? They think the poor should get off their arses.' He looked at a couple screaming at each other, cigarettes attached to their lips. 'I voted Tory myself the last time. Look at those fuckers. They always have money for fags, don't they?'

Joni wasn't going to get into a political argument. She'd voted Labour when she was young and innocent, but she'd soon become disillusioned. Voting Lib Dem at the last general election had been another kick in the teeth. The lust for power had turned supposed radicals into well-remunerated lapdogs.

'Left here,' Morrie said. 'Goat Skin's dump is halfway up.'

She turned the Land Rover into a street that was scarcely wide enough for it. One side was full of clapped-out cars, but she found a space near the top.

'Am I going to have my wheels nicked?' she asked, looking around the deserted area. Some houses had their windows and doors boarded up, the roofs having collapsed.

'You could put your police sign under the windscreen.'

'Ha-ha.' Joni watched as a skinny youth wearing a baseball cap backwards emerged from a nearby house. She waved him over.

'Whatcha want?' he said sullenly.

'Make sure nothing happens to the Land Rover?' She smiled. 'I'll make it worth your while. Plus, I saw where you live.'

He scowled. 'How much?'

'I'll decide when I come back.'

'Why sh'd I believe you?'

'You've got nothing to lose. On the other hand, if my colleague here decides to get nasty…'

She followed Morrie down the road.

'You might get away with that,' he said, over his shoulder.

'I don't suppose you mind being cast as bad cop.'

'You don't suppose correct.' He stopped at a house. The small space between the front window and the wall by the pavement was piled with rubbish bags, which had been torn open by animals and birds.

'You sure he isn't called Pig Skin?' Joni asked.

'Jackie Brown!' Morrie grinned. 'That's racist.'

Joni rolled her eyes.

The door opened before either of them knocked.

'DI Sutton,' said the obese man in a Newcastle United shirt who filled the space. 'Didn't expect to see you again so soon.' He peered at Joni. 'Who's this?'

SAM ALEXANDER

'DI Pax,' Joni said. 'Pleased to meet you, Mr Shackleton.'

'Nice manners,' he said to Morrie, with a wink. 'Obviously not from round here.'

'Actually, we've encountered each other before,' Joni said. 'If you let us in, I'll tell you when.'

The big man went into reverse and beckoned them into the front room. It was surprisingly tidy, the furniture newish and a display cabinet full of thimbles and small ornaments in one corner.

'I remember,' Shackleton said, rubbing his shaved head. 'Sunday night.'

'Too cold to show off your tattoo today?'

'Aye. The wife doesn't like me putting the heating on during the day. Says I should be out looking for a job.'

Morrie Sutton laughed. 'You've got a job, Goat Skin. Mind, I can understand why you don't tell Muriel about it.'

Shackleton looked between Morrie and Joni. 'DI Sutton's always been a joker, DI Pax. Interesting name, that, for an officer of the peace.'

'Very good, sir,' Joni said. 'You're Catholic?'

'Very lapsed,' Morrie put in. 'Tell the lady what it is you do, Goat Skin.' He waited. 'No? All right, allow me. Mr Shackleton here is a leading light in the Steel Toe Caps…' He held up a hand as the fat man began to protest. 'Without him they'd have been given a good kicking by the other gangs this side of the river.' He smiled. 'Goat Skin gives quality kicking and he gets his retaliation in first.'

'I hear you were a regular at the Burwell Street brothel,' Joni said. Suddenly she had a flash of another man in costume who had been outside the brothel. She made sure her expression didn't change. 'And the Steel Toe Caps were planning on taking on the Albanians.'

Goat Skin looked at Morrie Sutton. 'Where's this little chat going?'

Joni shrugged. 'Nowhere unpleasant. You scratch our back…'

284

The big man grinned. 'Oh, it's like that. Well, you tell me what you want to know and I'll think about providing it.'

'OK,' Joni said lightly. 'Do you know Michael Etherington?'

Shackleton wasn't quick enough to disguise his surprise. 'Etherington? Yeah, he's that general who used to be on the telly from some Balkan shithole, isn't he?'

She nodded and waited for him to continue.

'He's from around Corham, isn't he?'

Another nod.

'His grandson got himself killed a couple of days ago, I saw in the *Bugle*.'

'You keep up with the news, Mr Shackleton.' Joni leaned forward. 'When were you last in touch with the general?'

'What? I don't—'

Joni raised her hand. 'No,' she said firmly. 'Don't waste my time. You spoke to him outside the brothel on Sunday night.' She was aware that Morrie Sutton was staring at her. 'Was that the last contact you had?'

'I don't know what you're talking about, lady.' Goat Skin turned to Morrie. 'You need to get your colleague under...'

'I saw you *and* him,' Joni said. 'He was wearing a monk's robe and half a beard. You left together.'

'Wha—' Shackleton broke off. 'Well, so what? It was May Sunday. Anything goes.'

'Including murder?'

'What murder?'

'This is the second time I've broken the general's alibi today. He's hiding something and so are you. Tell us now and I'll keep you in the background.'

The big man looked desperately at Morrie, who shook his head.

'For fuck's sake.' Shackleton turned back to Joni. 'It's in the records anyway. I served under the general – colonel as he was then – in Bosnia and Kosovo. I was a communications specialist and a decent one. He looked after me and I ended up a sergeant.' He raised his heavy shoulders. 'We've kept up, that's all.'

'You served together in Kosovo, where ninety per cent plus of the population is Albanian and you've been checking out an Albanian-run brothel on behalf of your gang. That sound like a coincidence to you, Morrie?'

'Not enormously, no.'

'Tell me what the general's up to.'

Shackleton looked down. 'Couldn't say.'

'Tell me!' Joni yelled, her spittle landing on the unshaven face. He wiped it away distractedly. 'Can't say.'

'Won't say, you mean.' Joni looked at her colleague. 'What shall we do him for, Morrie? Obstructing an inquiry?'

'Definitely.' He grinned. 'We can put him in the same cell as those two Albanians and all.'

'Good plan.' Joni took the handcuffs from her pocket.

'No, wait.' Goat Skin's face was a swamp of sweat. 'Wait! I don't know much, honestly. The colonel … he got messed around badly by the KLA – the Kosovo Liberation Army. It had links with organised crime, particularly a clan called the…'

'Spahia.'

Shackleton stared at Joni. 'How the fuck…'

'Never mind. Go on.'

'There are some other lads from the division in the Steel Toe Caps. The general's had us gathering information about the Albanians' operations up here. He couldn't bear that it was the Spahia again. They killed a bunch of non-combatants we'd been protecting for weeks. It was like they wanted to humiliate us, him especially.'

The tension in Joni's body slackened. 'OK, this is how I want things to be, if DI Sutton agrees. The Steel Toe Caps do nothing to incite the Albanians. No violence, you hear? And you tell Michael Etherington nothing about this conversation or I'll play him what you just said.' She lifted a recording device from her pocket. 'If you hear from him, call DI Sutton immediately and give him the details.' She nodded to Morrie. 'Let's go.'

Joni waited until Morrie had passed her, then stepped closer to Shackleton and kicked him hard between the legs. He bent forward, gasping in agony. She squatted down, head close to his. 'I heard you didn't enjoy the Albanian woman who's on the loose. I doubt she enjoyed you either.'

'Christ, Jack, what the hell was that about?' Morrie asked as they walked back up the hill. 'You're acting like that tart ... that girl's your sister.'

Joni recognised the truth of the observation.

'And how the fuck did you manage to put Goat Skin together with the general?'

'What I said was true. I saw them together – but I only realised back there that the man with half a beard was Etherington. A friend of mine shaved off half his beard when I was at uni. I was on the clean side and didn't recognise him for half an hour. It's surprisingly disorienting.'

The scrawny boy was leaning against the Land Rover. Joni ran her eye over it.

'Thanks,' she said, handing him a fiver.

He nodded and went back inside.

Morrie was shaking his head. 'You learn that in the Met?'

'Hardly. Saw people do it on the estate where I grew up.'

When they were seated and buckled up, Morrie Sutton turned to her. 'This is all very interesting, but where does it leave us?'

'I don't really know. Let's go and discuss it with DCI Rutherford.' She'd leave it to Heck to tell Morrie the general was gay. Surprises kept people on their toes.

107

Suzana had woken to the sound of the hatch in the door clanging open. She drank the flask of tea and ate the thick jam sandwich on the bed, shivering in the gloom. There were heavy footsteps on the stair, going down. It had been a man screaming, even though the sound was high-pitched. Who was he? Was this some kind of crazy prison? Then she heard a car drive away and the barking of dogs. She remembered the black creatures with their slavering jaws and clutched her legs with her arms. They were even worse than men. At least she could deceive the latter – draw them close enough to strike.

She went into the bathroom and removed the plastic-covered knife before taking a shower. She didn't want to re-insert it, but it was her only salvation. She hoped she wouldn't get an infection.

Suzana dressed and looked out of the gap in the darkened window. She made out the edge of a large garden and woodland beyond, then steep slopes. The house next to the tower was large, but she had seen no people. Maybe it was uninhabited. Had she exchanged her former place of captivity for one that was even worse – far from people, more secure, equipped for prisoners? She sniffed the air. It was fetid and damp, but there was something else. People had been hurt here, people had bled, perhaps to death. Was that what she had become? Bait for a monster?

Suzana stayed by the window. When the sun was near its zenith, she heard the crush of tyres on gravel and looked down. The red pickup screeched to a halt and a heavy-shouldered man with a moustache got out. She stiffened. Was that the animal from the brothel? No, it couldn't be. This one didn't have long hair, though she had sometimes thought that was a wig. The man was carrying a pole of some sort. She had a bad feeling about it.

The steps came up the stairs rapidly; the pig was obviously very fit. Then she heard bolts being pulled back and the key being turned. Dull light flooded in. The man entered, his face now covered by the black hat-mask. He held the pole out. When she didn't move from the centre of the room, he jabbed it forward and the tip touched her hand. She felt electricity crackle though her and found herself on the floor, screaming. The man was shouting and tugging at his clothes, though not removing them. She understood. She got up and started taking off her own. When she was naked, he stood staring at her, his eyes on her breasts and then on her groin. She hoped the blue plastic wasn't showing. Then he lunged forward again and she retreated into the bathroom. The door was slammed and she heard the bolts on the outside slide into place. She sat on the toilet, goose pimples all over her body.

Suzana had learned to focus on a single objective, as she'd done with the escape from the brothel. She was concentrating on getting out of the tower, with or without the help of her neighbour below, but there was one other thing she was going to do first: cut the throat of the man with the shock pole.

108

'Right,' Heck said at the morning briefing. 'The Nick Etherington murder. Where are we?' DI Simmons raised a hand. 'Morrie, you look unusually keen.' Then he saw the ACC at the rear. She didn't approve of first names in briefings.

'Yes, sir, I'm full of the joys of spring.' Simmons glanced at Joni. 'The victim had an affair with an older woman.'

There were several sharp intakes of breath. Joni glared at Morrie.

'My team interviewed the staff at the Abbey,' he continued, unperturbed. 'They were about as much use as chocolate lampshades. As far as they were concerned, Nick Etherington walked on water. The kids weren't much more use, except for the one who said he was the victim's best friend. Percy Hurston-Woods, Perce to his mates. He said the victim had been shagging … having sexual relations with an older woman during the Easter holidays. He doesn't know who she was.'

The ACC's eyes bored into Morrie. 'This would be the Percy Hurston-Woods whose father and lawyer we met yesterday afternoon, DI Simmons?'

'Er, yes, ma'am.'

'Why didn't you share the information about the older woman with me?' Ruth Dickie asked acidly. 'Or, for that matter, with DI Pax? Her thunderous expression suggests she didn't know till now.'

Joni bit her tongue. She was livid with Morrie – he'd deliberately withheld what could be vital information in order to upstage her at the briefing.

Morrie hung his head. 'I had to verify it.'

'And did you?'

'I tried, ma'am, but none of the victim's other friends knew about it. I called them all in the evening.'

The ACC let the issue go.

'Excuse me,' Joni said. 'There's nothing in the reports, but did the boy – or any of the others – say whose idea it was to go to Burwell Street on Sunday evening?'

Morrie stared at her. 'What … yes, he did actually. He thought the victim led them down there. Said something about a pub with live music. I reckon they were after scoring dope. He got nervous when I mentioned that.'

Joni made a note.

Morrie stumbled through the rest of his report. It was agreed that his team re-interview the staff and pupils who had been closest to Nick Etherington.

Joni caught Heck's eye. 'I've been collating the technical reports. Neither Nick's … the victim's phone nor the mobile used to make the anonymous call has been located. Neither has been used again. They've may have been turned off, dumped or destroyed. The companies' servers will show if they become active again. I've arranged for that to be flagged up, as well as lists of incoming and outgoing calls.' She glanced at Morrie Simmons. 'I'll extend that backwards by several months now. A search of the area has failed to locate the phones, the murder weapon or any other traces that might identify the murderer. We have the tracks of size ten, wide-fit shoes, now identified as

Adipower Howard basketball boots, with a modicum of wear on them.'

'A what?' Nathan Grey said.

'A fair amount,' Joni said, not bothering to look at him. 'There's been a preliminary report from the linguistics professor. He thinks the voice is male, but he doesn't exclude a female in the contralto range – don't ask, DI Grey.' No one dared laugh, given the ACC's presence. 'It's almost impossible to specify an accent because the voice was muffled, but he's going to do some testing on rhoticisation and frication loss.'

'Good idea,' said Nathan Gray. He didn't seem intimidated by the stare he got from Ruth Dickie.

'There are several other issues,' Joni continued. 'DC Andrews has been liaising with the technical team regarding the victim's laptop.'

Eileen Andrews stood up and said there was a lot of material on it to be examined, but nothing striking had been found so far. Nick Etherington hadn't used either Facebook or Twitter much – apparently he preferred to text.

'I'll assign you some help,' Heck said.

'And there's a report from the Traffic Division,' Joni said. 'DS Rokeby?'

'All large 4×4s and other vehicles with dark paint in the vicinity of the incident were checked,' Pete said, 'but as we know now, the bike wasn't hit. It's unclear how the victim ended up off the road.'

'What about the canvassing of the area?' Ruth Dickie asked.

'I've been looking at those reports too, ma'am,' Rokeby said. 'It's a pretty deserted road and no local residents saw a vehicle of that description at that time. It was dark, of course.'

'Did they see any other vehicles?' Joni asked.

Pete shook his head. 'I don't have that information.'

'Find out if the question's been asked,' Heck said. 'If not, get uniform to go back. Monitor that, please, DS Rokeby.'

'Suzana Noli,' Ruth Dickie asked.

'Still unaccounted for,' Joni said.

'The SOCOs have taken moulds of some tyre tracks in the vicinity of Ollie Forrest's quad bike,' Heck said. 'We're waiting for the results. The bike itself has been examined and has no suspicious damage or marks. Ollie's – Mr Forrest's –fingerprints are on record following a bar brawl years ago. They are the only ones on the machine.' He looked around the room. 'Oliver Forrest is still missing.'

Joni wanted to mention what the ganger Garston had told her and Pete about the Spahia clan and Dan Reston, Lord Favon's employee, but she decided to discuss it further with Heck. The ACC wouldn't like the aristocrat's name being tossed around in the briefing.

'I gather there have been some unexpected developments with General Etherington,' Ruth Dickie said. She raised her hand. 'Those can remain confidential to DI Pax's team for the time being. I presume you'll be following them up and talking to him again?'

Joni nodded. 'I'll be asking him about the older woman his grandson was seeing too.'

'What about the Steel Toe Caps?' Morrie Simmons asked hurriedly. 'Some of them are connected to the general as well. Do you want me to talk to them?'

'The Steel Toe Caps?' the ACC asked.

Joni filled her in.

'Another link to the Albanians,' Dickie said. 'Interesting.' She stared at Morrie. 'No, DI Simmons, I expressly forbid you to have further contact with those individuals or anyone with ties to them. I want a full report on their activities so far by eleven o'clock, understood?'

Morrie nodded glumly.

'As regards Gary Frizzell, the headless man,' the ACC said. 'Since he was from Newcastle and was last seen alive there – even if that testimony has since been denied – I've assigned the case to DCI Young's team. I'm confident he'll come up with the goods.'

There was an uneasy silence.

'Right, DIs Pax and Simmons, here are your tasks,' Heck said, handing out stapled sheets of paper. 'We need results, people. Results and arrests.'

The meeting broke up.

<hr>

109

Evie was in the library, the door locked. She'd hardly slept and had got up at dawn.

'Darling, are you all right?' her mother had called after nine. 'Come and have breakfast, won't you?'

'No!' Evie shouted, the single word covering both questions.

Her father tried too. 'Evie, at least let us see how you are.'

'No!' she replied again. She knew Andrew had been put up to it by Victoria. If left to his own devices, he wouldn't have shown that he cared.

Evie got under the table and lay face down, taking in the smell of the old rug she and Nick had lain on. There was the faintest trace of him and she inhaled it. It was cold comfort but at least there was something of him in her again.

'Nick,' she said under her breath. 'Where are you? What happened to you?'

She stayed there for some time and then couldn't take any more. She had to distract herself. If she'd been mobile, she'd have gone to stay with a friend. She suspected her parents wouldn't drive her anywhere when she was in a state, as Victoria referred to the dark moods that had afflicted her since she became a teenager. No, she had to find something to take her mind off her dead lover. She got up and sat at the table. There were plenty of books to look at, but she turned to the catalogues. When she'd first started working on her history of the family, those heavy tomes had been her way in. There were hundreds of handwritten pages, the first volume completed by the original librarian, Dr Rodney Costello, who served until 1843. He may have died at his work, as the final entry, 'Bullingdon, George – A Description and History of the Sugar Plantations of Barbados, Milton of St Paul's, 18…' was incomplete, the downward scrawl of the nib going off the page. Some months later the entries were taken up by a more certain hand, that of Joshua Hilfer MA, who was replaced by Arthur Plain Esq. and, finally, by Doctor Steven Horsley. After he stopped work in 2000, there were no more entries. Her father rarely bought books and obviously deemed a librarian surplus to requirements, despite the size and significance of the collection. Evie had been its sole recent reader.

And she had learned much. Now that Nick had passed to the realm of spirits, she felt the proximity of the slaves' old gods. The *loa* were whispering around her. Baron Samedi and the others deliberately used language that frustrated her – words that were almost comprehensible but lingered between conscious thought and dream. She caught glimpses of his top hat and bony white face, and heard the rattle of bones as he took his pleasure with Maman Brigitte.

Evie was the last of the Favons and she knew her parents would have preferred a boy. Still, she was responsible for what had been done in her name. However, her injuries had kept her to the Hall for months. She wasn't forced to work, but the removal of freedom was the basic condition of the slave and so, although her ancestors had owned thousands, myriads of slaves, she had become one herself. Victoria and Andrew were too stupid to understand that, let alone the danger. If they had, they would have realised that people deprived of their freedom revolt. There were plenty of descriptions of slave rebellions in the books. She had to make a stand against her parents and their secrets. Some were already partially in the open. She was sure there would be others. It was up to her to find them, as well as to get justice for Nick.

Evie got up and limped to the door. She unlocked it, but didn't go out. The library was her haven, the place where she had reached levels of joy with Nick that she had never believed possible.

◇◇

110

'What do you think of that, sir?' Joni asked. She and Heck were in his glass box.

'Which bit?' he said, with a scowl.

'DCI Young.'

'Not sure. I think Mrs Normal's got his balls in a vice, but I'm pissed off she took the case away from us.'

'And then there was Morrie's little bombshell. I could kill him. I was on my own with him in Ironflatts and he never said a word.'

Heck leaned back in his chair. 'An older woman. It's probably nothing. Over and done with.'

'It's only a few weeks since the Easter holidays. We have to look at it.'

'Aye, we do. Means talking to the Etheringtons again.'

'Though they may have known nothing about it.'

'Michael drove Nick up to the Favons every day this week, didn't he?'

'Yes, he was doing revision with their daughter.'

'Wonder if that was all they got up to.'

Joni saw the lines on his forehead. 'Do you know the daughter?'

'Evie? Not in person. I've seen her at local events with her parents over the year. Her father ran over her last autumn and broke both her legs.'

'Really?' Joni felt a frisson of anticipation. 'We need to get a statement from them about Nick's visits.'

Heck raised a hand. 'Hold your horses. I'm waiting for the SOCOs' report on the tyre tracks on the moor. Oh-oh, here's trouble.' He stood up.

Joni did the same when Ruth Dickie came in.

'Sit down, both of you. I just had a phone call from Lord Favon, DCI Rutherford.'

'Been badmouthing me, has he?'

'Not exactly.' The ACC glanced at Joni, as if she was considering whether to eject her. 'To tell you the truth, I wasn't too impressed by his tone myself. His hand couldn't have been heavier. As far as he's concerned, his estate's off limits to everyone, including us.'

'Even if there's an armed killer on it,' Heck said.

'Apparently. Do you think he has something to hide?'

'Everyone has secrets. Then again, Andrew Favon's on the board of almost every major company and charity in Northumberland, as well as having close contacts in most of the councils. His more than ugly mug is in the *Bugle* at least three times a week.'

'As is his wife's,' Dickie said.

'Hers is rather easier on the eye than his,' Heck said, the smile dying when Mrs Normal frowned. 'She's on all sorts of boards and committees too.'

'Why are these people so important?' Joni asked.

'They're Northumbria's main aristocrats apart from the chap in Alnwick,' Heck said. 'Andrew Favon lost his seat in the Lords when the hereditaries were cut back, but he spent most of his time up here before that anyway. Old family, old house – they've got a medieval tower next to the main hall – and old-fashioned ideas about the likes of us. We're servants, theirs first and then the public's.'

Ruth Dickie nodded. 'That characterisation strikes me as pretty accurate.'

'Do they know Michael Etherington?' Joni asked.

'Now that *is* a good question,' the ACC said, turning to Heck.

'Oh yeah,' he replied. 'I've seen them together at the Corham Sevens.'

'Maybe we should investigate their relationship,' Joni said.

'And others,' Heck said. 'Lady Favon's been known to grant er … favours to deserving men. A few years back, she was caught coming out of the deputy leader of Corham council's weekend cottage at dawn, when his wife and kids were in the Canaries.'

'All right, do it,' the ACC said, 'but go gently. We'll need good grounds before we question them. His lordship's friendly with judges and magistrates as well.'

'Nick Etherington was on his way home from Favon Hall when he was killed,' Joni said.

Mrs Normal chewed her lip. 'That might do for a start.'

'Also, Garston the ganger said he dealt with the Favon estate via one Dan Reston. I suspect he was in the red pickup on the other side of the road when Suzana Noli was trapped.'

Dickie looked even less convinced by that angle.

'And we're waiting for the techies' evidence from the moor,' Heck said.

'Very well.' The ACC turned on her heel and left.

Heck caught Joni's eyes. 'See what I mean. Andrew Favon may look like a double-chinned fool, but he knows how to pull people's chains.'

'Not mine, he doesn't.'

111

Later that morning Heck got news that made him curse. Michael Etherington had managed to shake off his tail in the back roads south of Alnwick. He wasn't answering his phone and he wasn't at home – two uniforms were sent to check and were allowed to look round the house by Rosie. Julian Dorries, the general's lover, was brought in. Heck asked Joni and Pancake Rokeby to do the interview, this time formally. The man, pale-skinned and short-haired, waived his right to a lawyer. Heck watched the CCTV feed.

'Mr Dorries,' Joni began.

'Julian, please.' The interviewee smiled broadly, revealing gleaming and even teeth.

'Mr Dorries,' Joni repeated. 'What time did Michael Etherington arrive at your flat on Sunday night?'

'I told the other officer. Just after nine.'

'I see. How do you explain sightings of him by several witnesses in Corham around that time?'

'Who are these people?' Dorries demanded, self-assurance in tatters.

'I'm one,' Joni said, looking at him sternly.

After a few moments, the interviewee looked down. 'Well, maybe I made a mistake about the time. Maybe it was later.'

'Maybe is unacceptable. This is a serious issue and I'll charge you with wasting police time if you're not more forthcoming.'

Julian Dorries raised his gaze. 'Forthcoming about what?'

'The nature of your relationship with General Etherington.'

'He told you that himself, didn't he? We're lovers.'

'Uh-huh. DS Rokeby?'

'According to our records you're married, Mr Dorries.'

'Separated. When my wife discovered I was meeting men, she threw me out. That was over a year ago.'

'We'll be asking her to confirm that, sir.' Pete Rokeby ran an appraising eye over the other man. 'Perhaps you could give me the names of some gay pubs and clubs in Newcastle.'

Spots of red appeared on Dorries' cheeks. 'I … I don't go to those places.'

'But you must know some of them, even by reputation. We all do.'

It took Julian Dorries some moments to realise what Rokeby was implying. His gaze dropped again. 'I told you, I don't go out to meet people. Like I said to your colleague, I use an internet service.'

'Could you give us its name?'

'I … why should I? My private life's none of your business.'

Joni intervened. 'Michael Etherington's grandson was murdered, Mr Dorries.'

'I know that. What is this? Am I a suspect?'

'We could make you one.' Joni leaned forward. 'That's enough bullshit. I don't care whether you're gay, bisexual or hetero, but I know you've been lying about the general. Tell us the true nature of your relationship with him. Did you give him a false alibi because you became friendly when you did contract work for the Ministry of Defence's computing division?' Eileen Andrews had discovered that juicy piece of information on an obscure website.

'I'd like a lawyer now, please.' Dorries' voice was almost inaudible.

Joni terminated the interview. She and Rokeby left him on his own.

'What do you think, Pancake?' Heck asked, when they gathered in the MCU.

'It's not something you can measure with a ruler, sir, but I doubt he's gay.'

'And I doubt Michael Etherington is,' Heck said. 'But Dorries will have signed the Official Secrets Act so he's a dead end, at least as regards the MoD angle.'

'Still no sign of the general?' Joni asked.

Heck shook his head. 'There's an alert out for him and I've got uniforms at both ends of the village. Trails are going cold all over the place. The Albanian girl…'

'Suzana Noli,' Joni supplied.

'Aye – she still hasn't shown up anywhere. And neither has Ollie Forrest.' He looked at his watch. 'I've got a logistics meeting. You'd better go and talk to Rosie Etherington. See if you can get anything more about her father-in-law.'

Joni nodded. But there was something else she planned on doing first.

112

Ollie Forrest was eventually released from the cuffs by the goon in the balaclava. He thought about nutting him, but the man was no fool. He was holding the prod close to Ollie's chest and, if he fell on him, he'd be jolted to Newcastle and back. Food and drink were left. Ollie gorged himself. He hadn't been given anything but water for a long time – at least a day, he reckoned. Then he walked around the dark room, holding his hands before him, and got the circulation going in his extremities.

No sign of the woman who'd milked him for sperm. He'd worked out that was what she was doing. She was standing on her head afterwards to get one of the little swimmers to stick. What he couldn't understand was why he was being kept in captivity. He'd happily have serviced the cow all day and all night. Then his hands touched a wall and he stopped.

Shit. Several pennies had dropped. The cuffs had been on the bed when he was first brought here. That suggested he wasn't the first, especially since he'd been a chance victim. He thought back to the girl on the moors. What had happened up there? The copper had told him she was Albanian and a killer. It seemed likely her own people would be after her. In that case, why was he still alive? No, it had to be someone else who had caught him. Someone who had reason to be on the moor. It wasn't hard to imagine who that could be. And the woman – well, she had a track record as long as his own.

He tensed as screams rang out from above. What was the fucker in the balaclava doing to the Albanian, assuming that was who the female captive was? Not hard to guess. Christ, this was all about shagging. Normally he'd have been up for that in a big way, but there was more. The woman who'd straddled him hadn't shown up. If that went on, what kind of future did he have?

Ollie Forrest thought of Lizzie. He'd treated her like shit, going off to the tarts in Burwell Street and getting pissed on the nights he stayed home. She'd stuck with him. At first he'd assumed it was because of their son Jack, but now he understood she really did love him.

There was another shrill scream, only partly deadened by the heavy walls. He had to get out. That poor girl didn't deserve what was being done to her. For the first time in years, Ollie Forrest felt good about himself. He was going to rescue her and get them both out of this shithole. If that meant nailing Balaclava Bollocks, he'd be happy to oblige.

113

Joni watched as Heck left the MCU. She was working on her computer and taking notes about a different world. At Oxford she'd seen the scions of the aristocracy at a distance, heard them braying at each other across quads and marching around in dinner jackets, but she'd never had much contact with them. Viscount Andrew Favon and his wife were the real thing, the kind of people who would have been the parents of the chinless loud mouths at Oxford. At least Evie Favon wasn't like that.

She checked an online register of the aristocracy and quickly got lost in a welter of names, dates and cross references to other families. Andrew Peter Dobie Draconis Massingberd Favon had succeeded to the title as seventh viscount in 1999, when he was thirty-one. He'd attended Eton and the Royal Agricultural College. In 1992, he had married The Honourable Victoria Flavia Stowe-Warner, born in 1974, elder daughter of a lesser peer. Following links, Joni found a photograph of Lady Favon shortly after her marriage. She was stunning – above average height, with a full figure and fine legs, her hair auburn and her eyes a piercing green. By contrast, her husband already had a paunch and his mouth was slack and unattractive. He had combed his hair over a large bald patch.

Before checking the online archives of the *Corham Bugle*,

Joni ran a search on the Favons. The first site that came up was the family's own, the home page showing the family coat of arms and photographs of Favon Hall. Going back to the search engine, Joni scrolled down the entries. Most were from the *Bugle* and other local rags, but there were some links to national newspapers and magazines. Lady Favon had appeared in the gossip columns early in her marriage – she attended a lot of parties, often without her husband, who was described by one hack as a 'huntin', shootin', borin' type'. That didn't stop him being involved with many public and private organisations. Lady Favon's name was also to be found on several charitable foundations.

Joni went to the *Bugle*'s site and typed in the name Favon. The most recent entry was from the day before. She clicked on to the article, which covered the opening of a new supermarket in north Corham. Victoria Favon was holding scissors, in the process of cutting the ribbon that had been strung across the entrance. Her eyes were wide and her smile crooked. She looked like she wished she was somewhere, anywhere else.

'Ma'am?' Eileen Andrews was standing in front of her desk. 'Shouldn't we get over to Mrs Etherington's?'

'Are we going together?'

'That's what the DCI told me.'

Joni logged off her computer, wondering what Heck was up to. Using Andrews to keep her in line? Maybe he was just showing who was in charge. Either way, she was unimpressed, though she didn't make that obvious.

In the Land Rover Joni didn't speak.

'How do you want to play this, ma'am?'

Joni glanced at her. It was hard to be angry with the round-faced woman, especially as she wasn't at fault.

'All right, Eileen, how about this? I'm hard and you're soft.'

The DC laughed. 'I can't argue with that.'

Their smiles faded as they arrived at the village. The idea of facing the grieving mother and widow was less than attractive. Michael Etherington's Jaguar was nowhere to be seen.

Joni knocked softly on the door. It was opened surprisingly quickly.

'Hello,' Rosie Etherington. 'I heard your Land Rover. It has a … distinctive sound.'

Joni decided against responding to that. It wasn't her fault if everyone else ran their Landies with faulty tuning.

'I suppose you have more questions about … about Nick.'

'Yes. You remember DC Andrews?'

Rosie nodded. 'Come in.'

They followed her into the sitting room and sat down on the sofa opposite the one their hostess had taken.

'Mrs Etherington…'

'Rosie, please.'

The invitation to informality made Joni feel worse about what she was about to say.

'Rosie. There's no other way to do this, so I'll dive straight in. Were you aware that your son had a relationship with an older woman during the Easter holidays?'

It was hard to read the woman's face. It was expressionless, only the eyes blinking more frequently than normal.

'I … we had … suspicions.'

'The general and you?'

Rosie nodded, but didn't speak.

Joni glanced at Eileen.

'What prompted these suspicions?' the DC asked.

'Oh … he would go off on his bike, fired up like he was before a rugby match. He…' Rosie stifled a sob and Eileen Andrews handed her a tissue. 'He looked … so happy. Even more when he came back. I thought he was meeting a girl, but Michael said he'd seen him with a woman. He wouldn't tell me anything else.'

'Why was that, do you think?' Joni asked.

'To … to protect me. Michael's been doing that since Andrew died.'

'Do you think the woman could be someone you know?'

Rosie wiped her eyes. 'Maybe … I didn't care. I just wanted my boy to be happy. Of course, it didn't last.'

Andrews took over. 'You mean it was broken off?'

'Yes … not by Nick, I'm sure. He was upset for a few days. Hardly came out of his room. I think … I think Michael talked him round. By the beginning of term, he was much better. Concentrating on his work…'

Joni stood up. 'Where is your father-in-law, Rosie?'

'I … I don't know. He was gone by the time I woke up.'

'And you have no idea where?'

'No … I told you. Michael lives here, but I don't know what he does with his time.'

'How was he last night?'

'I … I didn't see him. I was in bed, but I heard him on the stairs. I don't know what time.'

Joni nodded. She believed the woman and didn't want to make her feel worse.

In the Land Rover Eileen Andrews said, 'I'd better check Nick's computer for the Easter holidays. The phone records should be in later.'

Joni nodded.

'Oh, and by the way, ma'am, I think this machine makes a lovely noise.'

They both laughed.

'Not that I know anything about cars.'

114

Moonbeam Pax had a predilection for outdoor sex. Even when she lived in London, she'd taken every opportunity to drag often unwilling partners to Epping Forest, Hampstead Heath, even Green and Hyde Parks on several memorable occasions, one in broad daylight. That was the reason she was in a clump of trees off a minor road north of Corham. Of course, taking a lover in the embrace of nature was a way of worshipping the old powers and she always made sure they received a libation from the bodily fluids that were exchanged.

She hard a car pull up and a door slam. Her heart began to beat faster.

'Sorry, I'm late. Lot going on at work.'

'That's what you always say. I made the effort to come all the way down here.'

'I'm ready to show my appreciation. Here, I brought a blanket.'

'I told you, I like to feel my skin on the ground.'

'Up to you. Hope there aren't any nettles … or other prickly bits.'

'I can see one prickly bit. You *are* a big boy.'

'That's what they all say.'

'No, not yet. Put it here.'

'If you insist. Aaaah…'

'Slow down. I want you inside me.'

'Oh, all right. Aaah. That's … better.'

'Yes, but take it slowly. And touch me … there.'

'You know, you're in very good shape for your age. Ow!'

'You don't even know my age. Keep going.'

'I … don't … think … I … can…'

'Useless man. I'll do it myself.'

'Ready? Ready?'

'Yes! Yes!'

Eventually the panting stopped.

'I've got to go.'

'So have I.'

'You know, you should get a grip on your daughter. She's a real ball breaker. Ow!'

'Like mother like daughter.'

'I promise I'll never mention her again. Fuck!'

'I doubt you can manage it again so soon.'

'Not after you dislocated my knackers.'

Moonbeam watched him buckle himself up and leave, giving her a rueful smile. She put her hand between her legs and wiped the stickiness on to the grass.

<hr />

115

Heck was with Joni and Pancake in his office. They were looking at the SOCOs' report on the tyre track from the moor.

'BF Goodrich 235/70 R16,' Rokeby said. 'Standard all-terrain model often used on pickups and 4×4s. This one's almost worn to the legal limit.'

'Lord Favon had a red Japanese 4×4 up on the moor – a Toyota Land Cruiser,' Heck said. 'But it looked in pretty good nick. Even if the tyres weren't, he saw the techies taking the prints. If he grabbed Ollie Forrest, he'll have changed his tyres by now.'

There was a knock on the glass door and Eileen Andrews came in, holding some printed pages.

'Vehicles registered to Favon Estates Ltd – three tractors, a combine harvester...'

'Not farm equipment, Eileen,' Heck said impatiently.

Joni had the impression that DC Andrews was playing to the gallery. She didn't blame her as she'd done the donkey work.

'Right, sir. One Toyota Land Cruiser, red, registra—'

'The one Andrew Favon had on the moor,' Heck said. 'Go on.'

'One Mazda Miata, black—'

'I've seen Lady Favon in that in town,' Heck said. 'Go on.'

'One Suzuki Grand Vitara, black—'

'What?' Joni said. 'As per the anonymous phone call?'

Heck nodded. 'Interesting. Is there more, Eileen?'

'Yes, sir, there's a Hilux Invincible, 2007—'

'Colour?' asked the other three, in unison.

DC Andrews smiled. 'Red.'

'Like the pickup that disappeared up a side road after monitoring Suzana Noli in the wood,' Joni said.

'I wonder who was driving that,' Heck said, turning to Eileen. 'Can you get a list of the Favons' staff?'

'Should be able to from National Insurance records.' The DC left the room.

'Do you think this will persuade Mrs Normal?' Joni asked.

'I...' Heck frowned and picked up his phone. 'Right away, ma'am.' He stood up and looked at Joni. 'Speaking of the devil seems to work. We're required upstairs. Not you, Pancake. Lucky bug ... Sorry.'

Rokeby shrugged.

Ruth Dickie was waiting for them impatiently.

'Listen to this,' she said. 'DCI Young just told me that the Stars and Bars club in Newcastle has been destroyed in an explosion.'

Heck and Joni looked at each other.

'No casualties as it happened when the place was closed. Fortunately they weren't stocking the bars or cleaning.'

'Does DCI Young have any suspects?' Joni asked.

'Well, Gary Frizzell's mates are still in Durham Prison, so they're ruled out.'

'No doubt he had other mates,' Heck said.

The ACC nodded. 'Though I doubt they know much about explosives. The Bomb Squad is still working the scene, but they seem to be sure this was a sophisticated device linked to numerous barrels of petrol.'

'Does Lee think one of the local gangs had a go at the Albanians?'

'It's a possibility. They could have hired an expert.' Dickie paused. 'Do you have any thoughts?'

'Michael Etherington,' Joni said.

The ACC's face was blank.

'He's involved with the Steel Toe Caps,' Joni continued. 'And he has a grudge against the Albanians from his time in Kosovo.'

'Plus he's been out of contact since last night,' Heck said.

'I understand him wanting revenge for his grandson's death, but what would the Albanians, especially those in Newcastle, have had to do with that?'

Joni glanced at Heck. 'Perhaps the black 4×4 that ran Nick off the road was driven by an Albanian.'

'Motive?' Dickie demanded.

Joni thought about that. 'Not sure.'

The ACC turned her attention to Heck. 'I'm going over to the Newcastle MCU shortly. You should come with me unless you have more pressing business.'

'I think I do,' he said, laying out the SOCO evidence about the tyres and Andrews's researches into the Favon estate's vehicles, as well as the fact that the ganger Wayne Garston was in contact with Dan Reston, Lord Favon's factor.

'I doubt even this will get us a search warrant, given the viscount's friends in high places,' Ruth Dickie said.

'Maybe not, but it's enough to justify a visit and some questions.'

'Very well, but keep it short and polite. Lord Favon can cause a lot of trouble. And if it arrives on my desk, I'll be passing it down.'

'Great,' Heck said, under his breath. 'I'll get DI Simmons and his team to check where the Steel Toe Caps were last night.'

The ACC handed him a report. 'This is what DCI Young knows.'

'A couple of pages,' Heck said, after a quick look. 'That much?'

Joni stifled a laugh as they turned away.

116

Evie was lying beneath the table in the library. She felt feverish, having not eaten or drunk much since she'd heard about Nick's death. There was a rattling noise in the sky. She could feel them gathering around, entering her, filling her weak and damaged body. Except they, the spirits of *vodoun*, didn't think it was damaged. They loved it, caressing it with their invisible fingers and running their tongues through her veins and organs. What was it they were telling her, their voices low and sombre? That the earth was waiting to feel her feet on it, the winds to blow through her hair, the sun to warm and the rain to purify her. Had she not seen them, the messengers of the *loa*? Pigeons on the rooftops, sparrows venturing high up the old tower to peck at the walls, the blur of a peregrine as it plucked away a sparrow...

And what about the smells? Fruit, some rotting after the long journey from the islands in the west; goat flesh, high and greasy, but glorious; dried fish from the bright blue waters of home. And, above all, sugar, bringer of life and death, of wealth and desecration, of power and deviancy: glistening molasses, dark demerara, moist muscovado. Her exploiter ancestors refined away the goodness, making Europeans addicted to the supposedly pure variety that matched their skins. Sugar built and sustained empires, sugar ruined the teeth and bellies of those who consumed it. Sugar was what she would throw in her parents' faces. She'd read enough of the family history. Until recently she'd thought she would be able to escape unaided. But now the spirit voices were telling her of a new future...

Evie heard cars on the gravel of the front drive. She came out of her trance and crawled out. She got to her feet, then limped to the door and opened it. There was a high window on the other side of the passage. She recognised some of the people who had arrived. She decided to play the spy. She knew all the hidden passageways and secret places that her forefathers had built into the Hall for their nefarious purposes

117

Joni drove the Land Rover to Favon Hall, with Heck in the passenger seat. Pancake was in a separate vehicle behind, followed by a SOCO van. They were going to try their luck without a warrant.

Joni glanced at Heck. 'Morrie Simmons told me that Viscountess Favon – Victoria – has a reputation for affairs.'

'Aye, she does. The last I heard, she was knocking off a joiner in Ponteland.'

'Was he young?'

'A friend of a friend told me he was in his mid-twenties. Couldn't believe his luck.'

'Victoria Favon's thirty-nine,' Joni said. 'Her biological clock's ticking pretty loudly.'

Heck frowned. 'What are you saying?'

'Maybe she's going with young men in order to get pregnant. They do have higher sperm counts.'

'You think she might be the older woman Nick Etherington was with at Easter?'

'It's a possibility. And the anonymous caller might be leading us by the nose. He – or she – told us where the incident happened, but that doesn't mean the rest of the information is true. Maybe a red Toyota Land Cruiser was involved.'

'You do have a vivid imagination,' Heck said. 'Then again, the Favons have a black 4×4 as well.'

'True. I'm not finished being vivid yet. Are there any rumours about Viscount Favon?'

'You mean about playing away from home?' He looked at her thoughtfully. 'Actually, he does have a bit of a reputation. He was caught during a raid on a brothel in Newcastle about five years ago. Friends in high places got him out without charge. The senior investigating officer – nice fella called Donnie Pepper, he's retired now – was very pissed off. One of the women said the noble lord hurt her with nipple clamps and the like.'

Joni's jaw dropped. 'And this only occurred to you now?'

Heck ran his hand across his thin hair. 'Well, yes. What, you think it's important?'

'Can you call this Donnie Pepper and ask him for more information? If Favon's a brothel-user who's into S&M, he might have been a regular at Burwell Street.'

'Bloody hell.' Heck sat back and searched for his phone. When he found it, he called and left a message.

'There's something else,' Joni said. 'The Favon family needs a male heir. I checked the line of succession. If they remain without a son, the house and the estate will pass to a cousin in Canada.'

'Can't see Andrew Favon being too happy about that,' Heck said. 'He always goes on about how his ancestors have lived there for centuries.'

'Yes,' Joni said, 'I read a speech he made to Corham chamber of commerce in which he said exactly that.'

Heck looked out at trees on both sides of the drive leading to the Hall. He'd spoken earlier to the viscount. He wasn't enthusiastic, but he agreed to see them.

'Are you going to be diplomatic?' he asked.

'I doubt it.'

'Why am I not surprised?'

'Someone's got to do the dirty work.'

Heck thought about that. It was one thing playing hardball with armed gangsters, and that was bad enough. But people who could ruin your career with a single phone call were an entirely different matter. To his shame, he found himself afraid again, just when he thought he'd got his nerve back after tackling the Albanian.

118

Suzana knew she was getting to the man in the woollen mask. He had made her strip again and she had started to scream. Her hope was that she'd provoke him into some careless action, giving her a chance to use the knife on him. Instead, his reaction was strange. He threatened her with the shock stick, but this time he didn't force her into the bathroom. He stared at her with wide, bloodshot eyes, taking in her breasts and the triangle between her legs. She'd expected him to make a move on her and was ready. Her screaming must have put him off. He shouted something she didn't understand and then left the room after throwing a flask, a wrapped sandwich and an apple on the bed. It was a victory of sorts and it raised her spirits.

But not for long. Suzana had been thinking. Why was she being kept in this dark room? Why was she being fed? At first she'd expected one or more of her countrymen to come through the door, armed and fired up for vengeance. As time went by, that began to seem less likely. She kept up her guard and slept lightly, ready to draw the knife from inside herself. She thought about the man she'd heard screaming below. It was hard to count the hours, but she knew it was at least a day since his voice had come through the floor. Had he gone? Had he been killed? Why were they holding a man and a woman? The pig Leka would have had her working on her back by know, so it didn't seem she was being prepared for prostitution. But if not that, then what?

Suzana stood beneath the blacked-out window and listened to the wind. She heard the songs of birds in the distance and they reminded her of her village. These were country birds. Was the big house far from others? Was that a good thing? At least she wasn't being penetrated by men. Yet.

She made a decision. The next time the man with the stick came, she would attack, even if it cost her life. She wanted her freedom again. The days in Cor-ham and in the fields and hills had brought her back to life. She wasn't going to let anyone control her again. Now that she had made up her mind, she felt better.

Suzana slept.

<hr />

119

Lord Favon met them on the front steps of the Hall, a building Joni took an instant dislike to. Apart from shaking her hand loosely, he paid no attention to her. Even Pete Rokeby got more attention, which struck her as interesting. The viscount seemed to find women difficult.

Lady Favon greeted them inside the entrance hall. In contrast to her husband, she gripped Joni's hand tightly and gave her a warm smile. At Oxford Joni had been in a tutorial pair with a female student from an aristocratic family and hadn't enjoyed the experience. The young woman had been friendly enough at the start, but frequently put her down in front of the don. She was later reported to have referred to Joni as 'that poor black bitch', the first of the adjectives referring to her early years in poverty rather than suggestive of sympathy.

The Favons led them into the large drawing room.

'So, DCI Rutherford and sidekicks,' Victoria Favon said, her green eyes flashing in the sunlight coming through the leaded-glass windows. 'What is it you want to talk to us about?'

Heck had his stern expression on. 'Do you know General Etherington, my lord?' he asked.

'Michael? Of course.' Favon looked at the faded oriental carpet. 'Terrible thing. First his son, then his wife and now his grandson. He must be feeling very inadequate.'

That struck Joni as a remarkably ill-chosen thing to say and she stored it away. His lordship evidently had a talent for inserting his foot in his mouth.

'Have you seen him recently?' Heck asked conversationally.

The heavy man thought about that. 'At a dinner a few weeks ago,' he said, after several moments. 'Maybe more recently. Can't put my finger on it. Why?'

Heck didn't answer.

Joni looked at Lady Favon. 'Perhaps it would be easier if your husband left the room. DCI Rutherford has various things to discuss with him.'

'None of that,' Andrew Favon said, voice booming in the open space. 'We have no secrets from each other.'

Joni took in the couple's body language. They were seated about five yards apart and Victoria Favon, dressed in an immaculate dark blue skirt and jacket with a string of pearls round her neck, was leaning away from her husband. The latter's bald head gleamed like a pink moon.

'Of course not,' she replied, smiling but not at Andrew.

'Very well,' Joni said. 'Lady Favon…'

'Victoria, please.'

Joni didn't respond to the offer of informality. 'Were you conducting an affair with Nick Etherington around Easter time?'

Victoria didn't look away, but she did laugh lightly. 'Conducting an affair? That sounds like something out of an old-fashioned novel.' She took a cigarette from a silver case and lit it. 'I'm sorry, would anyone else like one?'

The three police officers said nothing.

'As a matter of fact, I was.' Victoria Favon blew smoke out elegantly and glanced at her husband. 'We have what people call an open marriage, don't we, darling?'

Joni looked at the lord, who nodded and gave a tight smile. 'Thank you,' she said. 'Can you tell me when and why the affair finished?'

Victoria Favon's expression darkened. 'Yes … yes, I can. It was shortly before Nick went back to school. I didn't want to distract him before his A-levels. And, to tell you the truth, he'd become rather needy. I felt it best to draw a line under things.'

'How did he react?'

'He was shocked at first. He called and texted me. But I was firm and he saw the light.'

Joni finished writing. 'When was the last time you saw Nick?'

Victoria blew smoke out again. 'Wednesday evening, I think. He was here revising with Evie and left on his bike.'

'Lady Favon,' Heck said, 'we have made frequent appeals across the media for witnesses and information. Why did you not come forward?'

'Because she knows nothing about the boy's death,' Andrew Favon said gruffly.

'Please allow your wife to answer,' Joni said.

'I … I heard the broadcasts, of course,' Victoria said, her eyes on Joni. 'I didn't think I could say anything relevant.'

'We like to be the judges of that kind of thing,' Heck said.

'When you were with Nick, where did you meet?' Joni asked.

'Oh, various places. I used one of the 4×4s.'

'The black Suzuki Grand Vitara?' Pete Rokeby asked, breaking his duck. 'Registration number NO11 WDH?'

'It's round the back if you want to take a look,' Victoria said.

'Thank you,' Pete said, getting up. 'May we inspect all your vehicles, my lord?'

Favon didn't look overjoyed, but he nodded.

After Rokeby had left, Joni continued.

'How many times did you and Nick have sex?'

'Is this really necessary?' Andrew Favon protested.

'Yes,' Heck said.

'It's all right,' Victoria said. 'Six, at least.' She smiled sadly. 'He was such a sweet young man. I feel terrible about what happened to him.'

'Have you any idea who smashed his face in?' Joni asked, with deliberate brutality.

'Now, look…'

Lady Favon raised a hand and her husband was instantly silenced.

'I can't believe anyone could do that,' she said.

'What other vehicles did you use?' Joni continued. So far the woman's responses had been convincing.

'Once I took the estate pickup, a…'

'Red Hilux Invincible, manufactured in 2007, registration number NL69 SMG.'

Joni read from her notebook.

'Yes,' Victoria said. 'Our factor Dan Reston usually has the use of it, but one of the places we met is particularly rough and I didn't want to make a mess of the Vitara.'

'Did you use the red Land Cruiser at all?' Heck asked, watching her husband.

'No, that's Andrew's. He keeps it very much for himself.'

'And you would have sex in the vehicles?' Joni asked.

'Actually, no. I'm rather a fan of al fresco.'

'Wasn't that uncomfortable?'

'I've become a tough country lass,' Victoria said, looking at her husband. 'Haven't I, darling?'

He laughed hollowly. 'I should say so.'

Lady Favon smiled, showing straight white teeth. 'You *have* been doing your homework, DI … Pax, was it? Unusual name.'

Joni kept her cool and changed the subject. 'Major General Michael Etherington. What's the nature of your relationship with him?'

Lady Favon laughed and stubbed out her cigarette. 'You mean, did he and I have sex, as you put it? No, he was very attached to his wife. And for years he was away being a hero.'

'He was a desk jockey in the MoD at the end of his time in the army,' Andrew Favon said dismissively.

'When did you last see him?'

'Wednesday. He brought Nick here.'

'Man's turned into a frightful bore since he retired. Keeps talking about his service in those God-awful Balkan places. He has a real bug in his bonnet about them.'

'Bee,' said Lady Favon.

He stared at her uncomprehendingly.

Joni caught the woman's gaze again. 'Do you think the general knew that you'd chanced your hand with Nick?'

'Chanced my hand?' Victoria Favon's laughter was a high trill. 'You really must read a lot of romantic fiction. I fancied him, that's all. It was nothing to do with Michael. The boy was over age.'

'Do you have dogs?' Heck asked.

'What?' Andrew Favon said, taken aback by the handbrake turn in the questioning. 'No. I get asthma if animals are in the house.'

'There must be some on the estate.'

'Of course, man. The shepherds have their collies, no doubt some of the tenants have pets. What are you getting at?'

A decision had been taken not to publicise the marks on what remained of Gary Frizzell's throat.

'No guard dogs?' Heck looked around the room. 'You must have plenty of valuable things and burglaries of big houses are on the rise.'

'This is a hall,' Favon said stiffly. 'If you look outside, you'll see that there are burglar alarms on the walls. They have been quite satisfactory.'

'What about your man Reston?' Heck asked.

'What about him?'

'Does he have dogs?'

Lord Favon hesitated. 'I don't think so. He's more of a machine type.'

Joni noticed the delay before he answered. The questioning moved on to Ollie Forrest. Neither of the Favons had seen him recently and both twisted their lips at the mention of his name.

'I'd like to interview your daughter, Evelyn,' Joni said.

'Out of the question,' Andrew Favon said.

'I really must agree with my husband,' Victoria said. 'Tell Ruth Dickie that Evie's off limits, at least for the time being. She'd grown very friendly with Nick recently. She's still terribly upset.'

Heck and Joni got to their feet. Lady Favon said her fare-wells at the main entrance, while her husband took them to the garages. There they watched as the SOCOs ran tests. The prints from the moor did not match any of the vehicles' tyres.

'We need to talk to Daniel Reston,' Heck said to Favon.

'Well, you'll have to wait. He's on leave.'

'Since when.'

'The day before yesterday. He took his wife, Cheryl, to visit her family on the train. I ran them to Newcastle Central. I'm afraid I don't know where they were going exactly. Somewhere in the south-west.'

'I presume Mr Reston lives on the estate,' Heck said. 'We need to check his house.'

'Now, look here, Rutherford, I've played the white man.' If Andrew Favon cared about using that expression in Joni's pres-ence, he didn't show it. 'But this is too much. I'm not letting you go through a man's home and mess up his things when he isn't there, especially without a warrant. What have you got against him anyway?'

Heck ignored that. 'Give me his mobile number, please.'

The viscount did so, with ill grace. It squared with the one found on the ganger's phone.

'One more thing,' Heck said. 'Do you know a Wayne Garston?'

Andrew Favon looked blank. 'Never heard of him. Who is he?'

Heck smiled and didn't answer. Soon afterwards they left the estate. Pete Rokeby stayed behind with the SOCOs. It wasn't long before the ACC was on the phone. Heck turned on speaker mode.

'I've just had a call from Lord Favon,' Ruth Dickie said. 'He wasn't happy.'

'I took very accurate notes,' Joni said.

'I'm glad you did, DI Pax. Did you find out anything useful?'

Joni filled her in.

'I hope you think it was worth it,' the ACC said. 'If I get the chief constable on my back, you'll be the first to hear.'

'I don't know why he would complain,' Joni said.

'Favon mentioned intrusive questioning.'

'His wife was quite willing to answer everything I threw at her.'

'I don't think we went far enough,' added Heck. 'I wish I'd asked the noble lord about his interest in nipple clamps.'

There was a loud sigh. 'I suppose I should count myself lucky then.'

Joni and Heck both laughed after she broke the connection.

'Good old Mrs Normal,' Heck said. 'Mention nipples and she has a hot flush.'

Joni shook her head. 'Have you heard of political correctness, sir?'

'Isn't that what the government's full of?'

She let that go. 'What did you make of them?'

'Victoria Favon is as cool as a … you know what I mean. I don't think she's a killer, though.'

'No, I agree. Her man's more in that mould.'

'No, he's all bark – even though he isn't a dog fan – and as toothless as an old wolf.'

'He drew the line about giving us access to Reston's house.'

'We haven't got enough for a warrant. Hang on, I'll call the man himself.' Heck did so. There was no reply, the call transferring to voicemail without a personalised message.

'What now?' Joni asked.

'Back to Corham. Maybe Michael Etherington will have turned up.'

'Or maybe he'll have blown something else up.'

Heck shook his head. 'Jumping to conclusions is a bad idea.'

'The one about Victoria Favon and Nick Etherington worked out all right.'

'Aye, but where has it got us?'

Joni needed to think about that.

120

Skender Spahia stood at the armoured windows at the rear of the house in Holland Park. Like his neighbours, he'd installed wire and broken glass on the top of the two-metre walls round the garden, as well as electronic alarms and CCTV. Unlike his neighbours, he also used armed clan members to watch the screens and check the equipment daily. He'd bought the house from a Greek shipowner who tried one insurance scam too many and made a rapid exit from the UK. The name Spahia appeared in none of the deeds or transaction records. He was the clan's leader in the country and he answered only to his father, who had a thousand-acre estate in upstate New York. The old man had been unwell, a cancer gnawing at his belly, but he was still as sharp as an assassin's blade. Fortunately he trusted Skender, the eldest of his four sons and heir apparent to the criminal empire. Unlike his brothers in Italy, Germany and France and his cousins in less profitable countries, Skender had both an analytical mind and two degrees in business management. He had invested in hedge funds and in both traditional and new technology companies. That was the future.

Except the old ways of doing things couldn't be ignored. The money that fuelled the legitimate business interests came from the clan's well-established activities – drugs, people trafficking, whoring, pornography, smuggling, kidnapping, luxury car theft and so on. The operation he headed in Britain was a pyramid. He smiled at the thought. Millions of his countrymen had lost their life savings in a pyramid scheme partly run by the clan a decade ago. That had been his first taste of the profits that could be made by appealing to people's basest instincts – greed and lust. Fear was the other member of the triad. Between him at the top and the street-level operations that brought in the cash there were several layers of management, all of them connected to the clan and all with particular areas of expertise. As a business model it couldn't be improved upon. Computers made running

the varied operations easy, while the exercise of extreme violence by clan members made the structure impenetrable. No
Spahia clan member had ever given information to the authorities or been turned. Everyone knew what would happen to them
and their families if they did.

All of which made the reports Skender had been receiving from Northumberland disturbing. One clan member dead
and three in police custody largely because of the actions of a
seventeen-year-old prostitute, who was still missing. In practi-
cal terms, there was nothing to worry about. The three members
would never talk and the lawyer, Richard Lennox, was paid well
to look after them. The whore would know nothing of the clan's
organisation – it was standard operating procedure to keep the
women separate and fully disciplined. This one was obviously a
rogue. He'd considered having her family back in the homeland
brought over as bait, but that had its own risks. They would be
killed later, when the bitch had been caught and could watch
their long-drawn-out deaths on a satellite feed before her own.
No, the issue was that of example. The clan code was clear. Any
breach of security had to be punished in a way that terrified
both insiders and outsiders.

And now a clan nightclub in Newcastle had been blown up.
Losing face in such a public way was far beyond acceptable.
Lennox had no idea who was responsible, despite the police-
men he paid. The Bomb Squad had so far kept their conclusions
to themselves, apart from saying that the explosive device was
sophisticated.

Spahia turned as his secretary opened the door and ushered
in two members of the Popi. They were not his family – what
family would want such men in their midst? – but they had
pledged their allegiance to the clan by killing one of their own
relatives. They did this because they would be paid premium
rates and to show that nothing was more important than their
master's wishes. The original Popi had been a band of brigands
who harassed the Ottoman occupier for centuries, slaughtering

his troops, stealing his possessions and dying in droves when the columns of Janissaries eventually caught up with them. Contemporary Popi received one of the curved daggers their predecessors had used to cut the throats of the enemy when they made their first professional kill.

'Gentlemen.' Spahia spoke in English because he wanted to see how well the assassins spoke the language. He had used them before – and been impressed – but their handling had been delegated to his senior deputy. This time he wanted a more hands-on role.

'My leader,' they answered, lowering their heads.

'You've been examining the situation in Cor-ham.'

'Yes, my leader.'

'How do you recommend we proceed?'

The elder of the men stepped forward. He was of average height, but even the well-cut suit failed to disguise his muscular frame. His feet were large and sheathed in black cowboy boots.

'The men who've been caught do not represent any risk. The whore is also of little importance. The clan network will track her down and she can be dealt with at your pleasure.'

Skender Spahia raised a hand, then adjusted his silk tie. The white polka dots provided a pleasing contrast to the dark blue pinstriped suit that had cost him over three thousand pounds. 'Do I understand that you discount the woman?' he asked, the high forehead furrowed beneath his combed-back, raven hair.

The older Popi nodded. 'Yes, my chief. We believe the priority is for a strong message to be sent to the local gangs who will attempt to profit from the enforced closures of the brothel in Corham and the nightclub.'

'Both those matters can be handled by clan members in Newcastle.'

'We would be happy to help.'

Spahia smiled. 'No doubt.'

'But, excuse me, chief. We also feel an important message should be sent by striking at the police detectives who are hunting the woman. This will have the added benefit of bringing into line the businessmen, landowners and local politicians with whom the clan is dealing.'

This time Spahia didn't smile, although he found the killer's advanced grammar almost surreal. Whoever they were paying to teach them English was in line for a bonus. He didn't smile because he took the proposal seriously, even though killing police officers was never a course of action to be taken lightly. And because he'd had an angry call from one of the people he was in business with in the north.

'I approve the idea in principle,' he said, sitting down at the wide mahogany desk. He knew better than to invite the Popi to take seats – the master-servant relationship did not include comfort for the latter. 'However, if there is any danger of the clan being implicated, I will not sanction the murder of police officers, particularly senior ones, by Albanians – and that includes you.'

The younger Popi stepped forward. His face was unusually smooth and his eyebrows thin and arched. 'We anticipated this, my leader. We have carried out background checks into two officers. It is possible to have them executed by persons unconnected to the clan.' He took out a folded sheet of paper and handed it to Spahia.

'Interesting,' he said. After reading it, he put the document in the top drawer of his desk and locked it. 'You have located these individuals?'

'Yes, chief,' the elder Popi said. 'Both were very enthusiastic, even before we discussed payment. We will meet them when we go north before finalising the agreement.'

'And you are convinced that using them will send the message with sufficient force?'

'We will instruct them. Although the woman is on her own, she has a mother who lives in the area. As to the man, he has a wife and children, and his father lives in the same house. They will provide audiences.'

'And you are sure your operatives will manage to kill them in front of their families and get away unrecognised?'

'If they don't, we will step in.'

Skender Spahia knew what that meant – no witnesses left alive. He sat back in his leather chair and spun it towards the garden. His daughter Roza was playing in the garden with a small dog that he hated. She was two and a half, her dark hair in a pink bow, her chubby legs in traditional tight trousers. He waved at her and received a wide smile.

'Very good,' he said, turning back to the Popi. 'I want this affair concluded by Sunday at the latest.'

'Yes, my leader,' the men said, bowing their heads again and making for the door.

Spahia went over to the humidor and selected a Havana, chopping the end off with a cutter. As he held his gold lighter under the cigar, he felt his heart rate return to something akin to normal. He couldn't help it. He was a child of the rock fathers, the snow-glorious peaks of his homeland. Killing remained in his blood, no matter how many multi-million dollar deals he made. Even talking about it was exhilarating.

121

When Heck left the MCU, Joni was still at her desk. Morrie Simmons and Nathan Gray had hauled Goat Skin Shackleton in and were grilling him about his whereabouts and those of his fellow Steel Toe Caps before the bomb went off at the Stars and Bars. He insisted he'd been at home – with not even his bingo-playing wife to give him an alibi – and that he hadn't seen Michael Etherington. Neither had anyone else. Either the general had gone to ground or he was in the ground. Heck shook his head. He liked Etherington and he was holding on to an ever-shrinking hope that he wasn't mixed up in the bombing. But why wasn't he answering his phone? Maybe he'd gone fishing somewhere remote…

On the drive home Heck thought about Joni. She'd handled herself well with the Favons, though she'd trodden close to the line. She was predisposed against the aristocrats, no doubt because of her very different upbringing. Which reminded him: Michael Etherington and Joni's mother – he found it very hard to believe the general wanted a spell from her. Then again, he could hardly believe that the dead boy's grandfather was gay.

Passing trees in numerous shades of green, Heck thought about Joni again. There was something different about her, something beyond her colour and Met service. She was amazingly intuitive. It was as if she could see connections the rest of them couldn't. Or was it just that she had more objectivity? Perhaps he and his colleagues had been taken in by the Favons' status. No, he didn't think that was the case. Then there was the missing Albanian woman. Joni seemed to be on a mission to find and save her from the brutes who had abused her. That was understandable given their shared gender, but was it affecting her judgement? He had the feeling that Joni's interest in the Favons was dictated by the fact that Suzana – he'd remembered her name! – had last been seen on the moor that bordered the family's estate.

Heck forgot Joni as soon as he pulled up in the driveway. Luke was stroking a tennis ball against the garage door with a cricket bat.

'Hiya, Dad. Wanna bowl to me?'

Heck kissed his son on the crown of his head. 'All right, kiddo. But you fetch the balls.' The back garden was long enough for a makeshift wicket but if Luke creamed anything loose it would go into the fields. He'd once managed to land the ball in an old teapot that Ag had hung on the fence at backward square leg. They'd both collapsed in hysterical laughter; until his wife appeared and saw the damage to her pansies.

'School OK?' Heck asked, as he rolled his arm over, feeling

the muscles in his chest stretch. He was relived to find that he had no spasms in his lower abdomen.

'Aye, Dad,' Luke replied, playing a slick cover drive into a rhododendron. 'Did you know the Spartans sent their kids – boys and girls – off to live in barracks when they were seven? They went about the place naked and beat the … fought each other all the time.'

'Sounds a bit like the schools I went to.' Although they could have afforded it, at a pinch, he and Ag had decided against private schools for Kat and Luke. They wanted to see them grow up day to day – to watch over them, truth be told. That didn't mean Luke would escape the usual rugby injuries; just that he'd get them at the club rather than school.

'Come on, Dad!'

Heck came back to himself. There was something lurking in the depths of his mind that he couldn't dredge up. He bowled to Luke and this time the ball was hoisted high in the air. He kept his eye on it and, rather to his surprise, took the catch.

'Howzat!' He was handed the bat by his son and took guard. Luke had been working on his bowling. The first delivery was a fast yorker that he struggled to dig out. The second was a bouncer he couldn't resist pulling. The ball rocketed into a clump of early rose blooms.

'Stop that, you silly boys!' Ag shouted, from the back door. 'Come inside, your tea's ready. And wake up the old man, will you?'

Heck and Luke exchanged guilty smiles, the latter going over to the rear extension and shouting, 'Tea!' through the letter box David had insisted on, even though the postman delivered everything to the front of the house.

The three of them walked across the lawn.

'All right, lad?' David asked.

'Aye, Dad.' Heck liked being addressed that way, even though he felt far from young. 'You?'

David grinned loosely. 'Ag dropped me off in town. I went to see Maisie Lang.'

'Yuk,' Luke said, running ahead.

Heck shook his head. His father's appetites were amazing, especially compared with his own. 'Tea and crumpets?' he asked, smiling despite himself.

'More of the latter,' the old man said, pulling his trousers higher. 'She's gagging...'

'Hello, petal,' Heck said, giving his father an admonitory look. He put his arm round Kat, who had come to the back door. 'How are you doing?'

'OK, I suppose,' she said moodily.

'Boys?' he asked, looking at Ag.

'They're so stupid,' his daughter said.

'You can say that again,' Ag said, carrying a platter of pork chops into the dining room. 'They're only interested in balls.'

The atmosphere improved at table. Luke went off on one of his rambling stories about the geography teacher, who was as gaff prone as Buster Keaton. There was a lot of laughter.

'What have you been up to, Heck?' Ag asked. 'Apart from battering my flowers.'

'Sorry.'

'I'm only joking,' his wife said, with a smile. 'They can take it. Honestly, you men. You think you're ace jokers, but we can do for you any time, eh, Kat?'

'Ace jokers?' Luke said. 'Is that supposed to be clever, Mum?'

Heck laughed. 'Sharp as a tack.'

'Thick as a brick,' Kat said, grabbing her brother's arm and squeezing. 'Submit?'

'That'll do on the gender war front,' Ag said. 'Well, Heck? Caught any bad men?'

He shook his head and then, without warning, what he'd been trying to remember came back to him. 'The Corham Sevens. You were all at them, weren't you?'

'Yes,' Ag said, 'you were feeling poorly so I took the others.'

'Aye,' David said. 'I had my pipes. There was a – what do they call it?'

'Jam session?' Heck hazarded.

'That's right – round the back of the stand. Plenty of whisky flowed.'

'So you obviously didn't see much of the rugby, Dad.'

'Luke and I did,' Ag said. She glanced at her daughter. 'Kat and her friends were off boy-hunting.'

'We were *not*!'

'Where were you sitting?' Heck asked.

'Near the top of the stand,' his wife replied. 'So Luke could get a good view.'

'Yeah, it was great, Dad. I told you when we got back, don't you remember?'

Heck had no recollection. He'd still been tired in March and spent most of the weekends in bed. 'Remind me, lad,' he said.

'The Abbey School team was amazing. They nearly lost in the quarter finals, but they destroyed the Colts in the final. Nick Etherington was...' Luke broke off. 'Dad, is it true someone killed him? I heard it on the news.'

Heck tried to ignore the hostile look he was getting from Ag. 'He came off his bike, son. We're still not sure what happened.'

'Oh.' Luke instantly returned to his cheerful self, rattling on about the final and the tries the dead boy had scored.

Heck changed the subject as soon as he could. The evening passed calmly enough: baths, homework, half an hour of gin rummy. When the old man was back in his hutch and the kids in bed, Heck settled down to watch the news.

Ag joined him on the sofa a few minutes later. 'What was that about the rugby?' she asked. 'Luke could have been upset.'

'Aye, I'm sorry,' he said, taking her hand. 'The Etherington case, it's doing my head in. I spoke to Andrew and Victoria Favon today.'

Ag raised her eyes. She wasn't anti-aristocracy, but she had no time for that particular family.

'Did you see them at the Sevens?'

'Yes, they were right in the middle of the stand.'

'What about Michael Etherington? Did you see him?'

Ag thought about that. 'Yes.' She turned to him. 'Yes, I did. He was just behind Andrew Favon. Victoria presented the cup.'

'Victoria Favon presented the cup to Nick Etherington?'

'Yes, that's …' Ag stared at him. 'No. Surely not.'

122

Evie was in her room, the door locked. After the police officers had left, she went back through the passage that ended in the basement. One of her lunatic ancestors had built it so he could slip out of the drawing room through a panel. The wood was thin and she heard every word that was said. She bit down on the fingers she'd stuffed in her mouth and tasted blood after her bitch mother admitted she'd had sex with Nick during the Easter vac. She sobbed, but managed to keep the noise down, even though she wanted to scream and push the panel open and claw her mother's eyes out.

After holding her damaged hand under the cold tap and wrapping it in a hand towel, Evie managed to get her breathing under control. She lay on the floor, trying to visualise Nick as he lowered himself over her, into her – but he wasn't there, she couldn't bring him back. Her mother had destroyed even her memory of him. Evie wept for a time, and then pulled herself together. She went to her bedside table and picked up her notebook and the Parker pen Nick had left behind on the first day they made love – they didn't 'have sex'. She hadn't had the chance to give it back to him. Then she wrote down what she could remember of the police questions. The fact that her parents had refused to let them speak to her made her suspicious.

But not as much as what they'd said about Dan and Cheryl Reston. For a start, her father hadn't taken them anywhere.

Cheryl had been cleaning in the Hall that morning as usual, and she'd seen Dan drive the red Hilux to the old tower. Then there was the lie about the dogs. It was true that Andrew had asthma. What he hadn't said was that Dan Reston had a pair of vicious Dobermans he took with him on his drives round the estate. He kept them down at the old dowager house where he and Cheryl lived. It was obvious why her father had refused to allow the police to search the place.

Evie looked out the window. It was on the rear of the Hall and had an uninspiring view of the outhouses. Only the sandstone trunk of the old tower to the right provided some interest. It struck her that there had been more coming and going than usual recently. Mostly at night. There were no lights in the vicinity, so she hadn't seen anything when she'd peeked between the curtains. But she was sure she'd heard the heavy steel door clang to several times. What was going on? As far as she knew, the building was full of old furniture and farm equipment, and had been declared unsafe.

She had two options. The first was to rat on her parents to the police; she had no qualms about doing that – they deserved everything they got. The second, which was more attractive, was to find out what was going on herself. She owed that to Nick. She was sure he'd been seduced by her lascivious mother and hadn't been able to resist.

Before she left for uni, Evie was going to have a reckoning with Andrew and, especially, Victoria.

123

Joni was still in the MCU when Pete Rokeby came in.

'You look pleased with yourself,' she said.

'Found stuff in the Hilux that the factor Reston drives.'

'What sort of stuff?'

'The floor of the cargo area is scratched all over and the bars behind the cab have regular dents in them, like from chains. And there were scratch marks on the paint on the cargo area and tailgate.'

Joni didn't get his drift. 'And?'

'There were short black hairs on the metalwork. I took samples and gave them to the SOCOs, but I'm pretty sure what they are.' He grinned. 'Bow wow.'

'So Favon lied about Reston.' Joni checked her notes. 'Or maybe. What he said was he didn't think Reston had dogs.'

'Could be an honest mistake.'

'Could be. But he was very keen we didn't go to the factor's house.'

Rokeby sat down. 'Let's do some theorising.'

Joni smiled. 'My favourite. But not Mrs Normal's.'

'Too bad. She'll be off at some function with the local big heads. Or wigs. How about this? Reston's dog – I'm thinking a big, fierce mutt – tore out Gary Frizzell's throat. Then Reston cut off his head and hands, and dumped the body in the Coquet.'

'What's missing is a…'

'Motive. I know. Here goes. The victim's tall and handsome – we've seen photos. Maybe he was involved with Lady Favon.'

'She's got the track record. But as far as we know she hasn't killed any of her previous studs.'

Pete Rokeby gave her sceptical look. 'As far as we know. This time the victim's mates kicked up a fuss. Plenty of people don't have friends or relatives who care.'

Joni raised a hand. 'Leave that for the moment. The initial witness report said Frizzell was put into a Bentley behind the now burnt-out Stars and Bars by the Albanian Fatlum Temo…'

'Some memory, ma'am.'

'Thanks – on Friday night around two. If Frizzell was a lover of Lady Vicky, that suggests the Favons have links to the Albanians.'

Rokeby nodded. 'We already know they do – or at least Reston does. Wayne Garston, whose company is owned by the Spahia clan, told us Reston used his labourers.'

'On behalf of the Favon estate.' Joni leaned back in her chair. 'Maybe we're looking at this the wrong way, Pete. Maybe Reston is the main player, not his employers.'

'What, he got his Albanian friends to bring Frizzell to him in a Bentley?'

'Maybe his wife likes a bit of footballer. Hm, it isn't too convincing. Does Lord Favon give you the impression of being able to manage an estate that size?'

Rokeby laughed. 'I doubt Lord Favon can tie his own laces.'

Joni looked at him. 'Going back to Reston's wife. What do we know about her?'

'Not much. She works in the Hall, I think.'

'Has she been checked in the databases? Has Reston?'

'Yeah, he has. Nothing. I don't know if Eileen looked at the wife. May I?' He slid his chair closer and tapped at the keys. Soon a file appeared on Joni's screen. 'Cheryl Reston, maiden name Duncan. Bloody hell!'

'She isn't very attractive, is she?' Joni peered at the data. 'Not only that, she's got twenty-three convictions for soliciting and … shit! … she served two years for inciting child prostitution. All that in Bristol, where she was born.' She looked at her colleague. 'Maybe that's why Lord Favon was so jumpy about the Restons – she's the problem, not the husband. Or they're both in it up to their necks. We need to do a door-to-door on the estate and in the vicinity.'

'Favon's tenants may not say much.'

'We'll try the local pubs. If the Restons are dodgy, someone will have a bad word to say about them.' She pressed Print and put the report in her bag. 'Come on, then.'

'What, now?'

'Yes, now.'

'Oh, ma'am.'

'Call me Joni when we're on our own.'

The ACC appeared at the door. 'Working late?' she said. 'Most commendable.'

'Thank you, ma'am,' Joni said. 'Actually, we're off for a drink. Would you like to join us?' She heard Pete's sharp intake of breath.

'No, thanks. I'm taking work home with me. You will make sure you stay under the legal limit, won't you?'

'Bitter lemon for me,' Joni said.

'I'm an alcohol-free lager man, myself.'

Ruth Dickie stared at them disbelievingly. 'Good night, then.' She went to the stairs.

'Jesus,' Rokeby said. 'What if she'd said yes?'

Joni smiled. 'It'd have been your round.'

124

Donnie Pepper was half asleep in front of the TV when the phone rang.

'Aye,' he mumbled.

'Bad time?'

'Is that you, Heck Rutherford?'

'It is. How the hell are you, you old fart?'

'Surprisingly sweet smelling.'

'Uh-huh.'

'I've never spoken a truer word. What do you want?'

'Lovely. I ring up a former colleague and I have to want something other than ask how he is?'

'I'm fine, if bored. The wife's still working so I have to make the dinner every day.'

'I thought I saw a stick woman in town the other day.'

'Ha! Actually, I'm a dab hand. Tonight we had coq au vin.'

'This is a family show.'

'Idiot. Let's have it then.'

'If you insist. Lord Andrew Favon.'

'Fucking shit-headed nose-in-the-air arsehole.'

'Let me try and draw that.'

'No, seriously, Heck, I hate that pillock.'

'Tell me more.'

'Must have been a couple of years back. We raided one of Billie Forman's knocking shops. It was the last time anyone saw that pillock alive. Lots of half-naked women and men pulling up their suit bottoms.'

'Classy place then?'

'Classier than most. Anyway, I went through a door on the top floor and who should I find but his nobbing lordship. Still nobbing. Either he's deaf or he was in transports of delight. I hauled him off and yelled. He had two pairs of nipple clamps wired together. One set was on his – what do the youngsters call them?'

'Man boobs. Moobs.'

'Impressive.'

'My kids know all the choicest patois.'

'What?'

'Jargon.' Heck had picked up the term from Joni.

'Well, anyway, his nobship had attached one set to himself and the other to the poor woman. She was young and she was crying in pain. I unclamped hers carefully and then pulled his off with extreme prejudice.'

'What happened?'

'The bastard grinned.'

'S&M freak.'

'Aye. I arrested him under the Sexual Offences Act and made him get dressed. You'll never believe this. His brief arrived before we got him to the van. Wanker must have had someone monitoring the police channels.'

'Who was the brief?'

'That bastard Lennox.'

'Richard Lennox?'

'Is there another one?'

'Interesting.'

'No, it bloody wasn't. He rang the senior magistrate and got the fucker excepted from the haul of dishonour. He never went to court.'

'Friends in, et cetera'

'Bastards. I hate the way they look after each other. But that's not all.'

'Let's have it.'

'The girl – she was only seventeen – was taken to hospital. She had serious injuries to her breasts. I went to take a statement the next day, but one of Lennox's sidekicks was hanging about. The girl wouldn't talk. It was pretty obvious money had exchanged hands.'

'It's a brave new world.'

'Fucking cowardly old-world thieving wankdogs.'

'Wankdogs? Haven't heard that one before.'

'Me neither.'

'Anything else on Favon?'

'Nay, lad. I retired a year later. Things weren't the same after that night. I reckon Lord F. pulled some senior officer's chain.' Donnie Pepper paused. 'How are you, Heck? Over that op?'

'Getting there. Been back at work for a bit. I thought Corham MCU would be quieter than the big city. It was until last week.'

'I've been following the stories. Getting anywhere?'

'This conversation's been a help.'

'I'm glad. Listen, Heck. I didn't want to bother you with this, but since you're on the line – I heard from the lads I keep up with in the Force that Ned Sacker's fuckwit brother's got it in for you in a big way.'

'Not So Lucky?'

'Aye, Ian to his mam. He's been heard saying he's going to get you for banging up his brother. Pissed, of course.'

'Not So Lucky hasn't got the balls, Donnie.'

'I wouldn't be so sure. He's got some nasty friends, inherited from that evil bastard Ned. At least that reptile won't be out for a very long time.'

'Hey, Donnie, you heard anything about Albanian gangs moving north?'

'I doubt I know more than you do, Heck. They're here and they're staying.'

'Mm. Even Lee Young said that much.'

'Lee Young? DCI Balls of Wafer? You don't want to listen to anything he says. He's dirtier than … dirt.'

'I don't suppose you've heard who's been cosying up to him.'

'Oh aye.'

'Who?'

'The foreigners you just asked me about.'

'Shit.'

'In a very large sandwich.'

125

Morrie Simmons and Nathan Gray were in the Kettle and Vulture between Corham and Newcastle. The former still lived in Gateshead, while his DS's place was near the airport, north-west of the city.

'Well, that was a waste of time,' Gray said. 'All the Steel Toe Caps have got armour-plated alibis except Goat Skin and he's suddenly lost his voice.'

Morrie downed his pint and signalled for another round. 'Fuck's sake, Nathan. You don't think that's a wee bit suspicious?'

His subordinate shrugged. 'Who cares? We did what we had to do.'

'There's one very large problem. The sodding general.'

'Aye, I wonder where he's got to.'

'So do I. None of the tossers claim to have seen him since

the weekend.' Morrie took another deep drink. 'Course, there's a related problem.'

'What's that, boss?' Gray was drinking orange juice. He'd nearly lost his licence the previous year and had only escaped being charged by getting Simmons to pull strings with the uniforms.

Morrie sighed. 'Etherington will have friends in the SAS and such like. The Steel Toe Caps are boot boys. He'll be keeping his serious operatives in reserve.'

'We can't find what hasn't shown itself.'

'Easy for you to say, Nathan. You don't have to stand up in the briefing and tell that wanker Rutherford we got nowhere.'

'Don't worry, boss, you'll get his job soon enough. Anyone can see he hasn't got over the scalpel in his belly.'

Morrie emptied his glass. 'He looks better every day. I remember in the old Newcastle MCU. Lee Young had his nose in every case, but Heck would mope around until something big came up. Then he turned into fucking Sherlock Holmes.' He punched his DS's arm. 'Anyway, you're forgetting the bitch Jackie Brown.'

'How did I manage that? I'd really like to...'

'You'd really like to stick your cock into the old bag behind the bar, Nathan.'

'Come on, boss. You'd do her if you got the chance.'

'Jack? Not my type.'

'What *is* your type, then? I've never seen you with a bird.'

Morrie glared. 'Doesn't mean I'm not doing it with a lady.'

Nathan frowned. 'What?'

'Before your time, lad. Anyway, don't underestimate Jackie B. She hasn't only got film-star looks. She's sharper than you and me put together.'

'Black and brainy. Bollocks to that.' Gray grinned. 'And to her.'

'Don't worry, I'll sort her out with Rutherford. Then the whole MCU will be ours for the taking.'

Nathan Gray looked at his watch. 'Got to go. Something

moist waiting for me. But you've forgotten the main player. Mrs Normal.'

Morrie's face fell. 'True. Imagine having to report directly to her.'

'Exactly. I heard on the grapevine she's got Lee Young's nuts in a vice. Seems she's unhappy about what went on before the Stars and Bars turned to dust. The headless man's mates?'

'Is that right? I'd better extend feelers.'

Gray laughed. 'Speaking of which.'

Morrie Simmons watched him go. His DS was a lazy, shagging tosser, but he was well connected. The headless man's mates had beaten the shit out of an Albanian from the club and been charged. DCI Young had been warned about crossing the line before. Had he done that with the Albanians? Selling your soul to the devil would be a picnic compared with that.

<hr>

126

Rosie Etherington had hardly slept. Now, in the first light of day, she couldn't sit down. She moved from room to room, upstairs, downstairs, into the garage, through what had been the pantry to the larder and out again. She went into Nick's room and touched the bed, then bent to smell the pillow. She hadn't changed it, but the smell of him was fading. One wall was covered in framed photos of rugby and cricket teams. There he was, caught in time, never growing older. She choked and wished she could cry. Even that small relief had been denied to her over the past twenty-four hours. It seemed she was growing a shell, a carapace that shielded her from everything that had been thrown at her. The problem was that it also blocked emotions she knew were dangerous – anger, disgust, the lust for revenge.

She went into Michael's bedroom. It was little more than a guest room, with a bed and a single chair. He kept it very neat and didn't allow her to clean it. She opened the wardrobe. His uniforms hung inside clear plastic covers. The bright red mess jacket, the dark green formal uniforms he'd worn at the Ministry of Defence, battle dress … but no camouflage gear. She was sure there had been two sets.

Curious, Rosie went downstairs. Michael's hiking boots were not in the drying room. Then she had another thought. She walked to his study. Again, it was preternaturally tidy. The police had taken his desktop computer the day before, but she hadn't said anything about his laptop. For some reason he'd never explained, he kept it behind a row of large books about the Balkans on the bottom shelf of his bookcase. She looked. It wasn't there. The police hadn't found it as she'd been given a receipt for the other computer, so Michael must have it with him. She didn't know what to make of that, anymore than she had any idea where he was. His mobile was permanently on the answering service. She'd stopped leaving messages asking him to contact her.

Rosie kept on moving, up and down the corridor on the ground floor. Then her stomach somersaulted. She went up to her bedroom and dug her fingers under the corner of the carpet. The key was where she'd put it after her father-in-law moved in. He'd insisted she take it, 'in the remote chance some bastard tries to break in when you're on your own. You need to be able to defend yourself.'

She went back down and towards the drying room, her heart galloping. The tall steel locker was in the far right-hand corner. She put the key in the lock and turned it. She immediately saw there were weapons missing. She didn't know much about guns – her husband had never fired one in his life – but she knew there had been a hunting rifle that Michael took up to the Highlands for the annual deer cull on a friend's estate. It wasn't there. There had also been two pistols, illegal as Michael said, but souvenirs from his time in the service. One of them was gone. And there had been two knives – combat weapons, he'd said. Now there was only one. She pulled it from its leather sheath and moved it from side to side. The light glinted off the polished metal. She touched the edge and blood bloomed on her finger.

Rosie closed and locked the door. Then she went up to her room and lay on the bed, holding the point of the knife to her throat. She let pictures of Nick cascade before her, moving, ever moving until darkness came to claim her.

127

Heck was early into the MCU, though Joni was already there. He took her into the glass cube to tell her what Donnie Pepper had told him, omitting the parts about Not So Lucky Sacker and Lee Young.

'More evidence against Favon,' Joni said.

He shook his head. 'He wasn't even arrested. It's only hearsay. I'll tell Mrs Normal, but I'm not bringing it up in the meeting.'

'He's involved in this to the hilt, I'm telling you, sir.'

'You may well be right, but we need more.'

'How about this?' Joni recounted what Pete Rokeby had told her about the hairs that he'd found in the Hilux.

'Interesting. Let's wait and see what the techies come back with.'

Joni opened her mouth.

'What?'

'Nothing,' she said, looking away. 'I've got some notes to write up before the briefing.'

Heck watched her go, aware she wasn't being straight with him. Women. Then he thought what Ag would say to that and felt embarrassed. Not for long. He had a decision to make. Should he tell Mrs Normal about Lee Young's alleged dirtiness or not? He'd never liked the guy, but they'd worked on several big cases in the Newcastle MCU and he couldn't fault Young. The bugger was good at politicking too. But there had been whispers about where he got some of his leads. No one had proved anything, although some detectives reckoned Young was on the take, fitting up gangs on the word of the opposition. If he was in with Albanians, he could have vital information. He called the ACC and was in her office two minutes later.

Ruth Dickie listened without interrupting, her fingers in a pyramid beneath her snub nose. 'This man Pepper,' she said, when Heck finished. 'You trust him?'

'Yes, ma'am. But he's out of the game now, so his sources might not be reliable.'

'No, I think they are.'

Heck failed to disguise his surprise.

'You see, I've had a close watch on DCI Young since the headless-man case was linked to the Albanians. This is highly confidential, of course. If Lee Young gets wind of this, I'll know who to blame.'

Anger coursed through Heck. 'I brought this information to you, ma'am. I'm hardly likely to tell Lee.'

'Stranger things have happened, but all right. The chief constable is aware of this, by the way.' She glanced at her watch. 'We should go down to the briefing.'

She led him down the stairs. 'I hope you're getting somewhere with the various cases,' she said, over her shoulder.

'So do I,' he said, under his breath.

The MCU was full. They walked to the front and Heck began. 'The missing Albanian girl?'

'Nothing further, sir,' Joni said.

'Oliver Forrest is still unaccounted for, too. General Etherington?'

'His Jaguar hasn't been seen by Traffic Division,' Pete Rokeby said. 'No sightings of the man himself.'

'Nick Etherington?'

'Canvassing of the houses further from where he was found has drawn a blank,' Joni said. 'No black 4×4s have been found with any damage, but that's a dead end anyway, given that his bike has no paint residue on it. The likelihood is that he swerved when the vehicle came close and went off the road.'

'And then someone stoved his face in,' Morrie Simmons said.

Joni gave him a sharp look. 'Traffic Division hasn't found any skid marks. It appears the car came to a halt without braking hard, then went back so that the driver or passenger could commit the murder.'

'Nasty,' Nathan Gray said.

'Professional,' Joni riposted. 'At least it could be.'

'Less speculation, please,' Ruth Dickie said.

'Nick's phone has still not been recovered.' Joni looked across the room. 'DC Andrews?'

'We've got the records from his service provider. There are calls to Evelyn Favon's mobile and to his home number in recent days. Nothing else that sticks out, but I'm checking back further.'

Heck raised a hand. 'The Steel Toe Caps?'

'Apart from Goat Skin Shackleton, who's in a cell downstairs, their alibis are as tough as Corham Steel,' Morrie Simmons said. 'Then again, look what happened to that.'

There were a few titters.

'Spare us what you fondly imagine is wit, DI Simmons,' the ACC said. She turned to Heck. 'This is going from bad to catastrophic, DCI Rutherford.'

Before he could speak, Joni butted in.

'There have been some positive developments, ma'am. DS Rokeby?'

'Although the tyre prints taken from the moor near Oliver Forrest's quad bike didn't match any of the Favon estate vehicles, I found some hairs – probably animal, the lab's checking – in the cargo compartment of the red Hilux. It may be the vehicle that was spotted near the wood where Suzana Noli was last seen.'

Ruth Dickie's face had hardened when the name Favon was mentioned. Joni saw that and pressed on.

'Lord Favon told us that his factor Dan Reston and his wife

Cheryl are on leave. We ran a check on them. Reston himself came up clear, but Cheryl has numerous prostitution charges going back to her youth in Bristol, and later she served two years for inciting child prostitution.'

There was silence in the room.

'Where does that leave us, DI Pax?' Heck said sharply. He was unimpressed about having been kept in the dark.

'I haven't finished, sir. DS Rokeby and I went up to the area around the Favon estate yesterday evening. We split up and asked questions about the Restons in the local pubs. They aren't popular, to put mildly.'

'How about putting it meaningfully?' Heck said.

Joni kept her eyes off him. 'Dan Reston has been barred from two of the places. He gets violent when he drinks and threatens people. No reports of actual violence.'

'There was talk of him abusing women in the labour gangs that work on the estate,' Pete added. 'Though he seems to have stopped that in recent months. He orders tenants around and gets any who talk back thrown out by the noble lord.'

'Is this going anywhere?' the ACC asked, her expression grim.

'Cheryl Reston doesn't go to the pubs, but she does have a reputation for picking up senior schoolboys. Nothing's been reported as the boys are too scared to talk. Some parents got it out of them and complained to Lord Favon last winter. He said Cheryl's duties would be confined to the estate. She hasn't been seen outside much since then.'

'So, we have a bully and a sexual degenerate,' Ruth Dickie said. 'Hardly unusual and not directly connected with any of the cases we're investigating. Haven't you got anything better to do with your time, DI Pax?'

Morrie Simmons and Nathan Gray exchanged grins.

'As a matter of fact I have, ma'am,' Joni said, with a cold smile. 'Lord Favon was caught in a raid on a Newcastle city-centre brothel two years ago. He used his contacts to escape arrest.'

'That's enough,' the ACC said. 'DCI Rutherford, DI Pax, in

there.' She pointed to Heck's office. 'What exactly is going on here?' she demanded, when the door closed behind them. 'I told you to leave the Favons alone.'

Heck glanced at Joni. 'We haven't been in further contact with them, ma'am.'

'I'm glad to hear that, but why did you authorise DI Pax and DS Rokeby to question people in the local pubs? That'll get back to Lord Favon, you can be sure.'

Joni was about to speak, but Heck cut her off.

'I'm not convinced he's being straight with us, ma'am. He says the Restons aren't there, but he flat refused to let us go to their house.'

'But what can any of this have to do with the Albanian girl – a firm murder suspect, I might remind you – and Nick Etherington's killing?'

'The Favons have business connections with the Albanians,' Joni said.

'You mean via the ganger? Hardly very incriminating.'

'Suzana Noli was last seen on the moor adjoining the Favon estate,' Heck said. 'And Ollie Forrest was up there too.'

'Maybe he abducted the girl.'

Joni and Heck looked at each other.

'Maybe he did,' the latter said. 'Ma'am, Lord Favon is into S&M. He hurt a working girl badly in that brothel in Newcastle. It has to be a possibility that he was in the Burwell Street brothel last Sunday night.'

'We don't deal in possibilities, DCI Rutherford. Leave the Favons alone. We'll never get a warrant with so little evidence.'

Pete Rokeby knocked on the door. Heck waved him in.

'Sorry to interrupt, but I thought you'd want to hear this. The SOCOs confirm there were dog hairs in the Favon Hilux. Dobermans, to be precise. Two of them.'

The ACC sighed. 'So Dan Reston has dogs. Perhaps Lord Favon didn't know.'

'Perhaps,' Heck said. 'But a Doberman could have ripped out

Gary Frizzell's throat. Pete, ask Dr Volpert to compare what remains of the wound to a Doberman's bite pattern.'

'Sir.' Rokeby left.

'This is getting more confusing by the minute,' Ruth Dickie said. 'Put together whatever kind of case you can, but don't take action without my permission. It's Friday. We all need the weekend to reflect on this.'

'We should be on the estate looking for Dan Reston,' Joni said.

'We need more evidence,' the ACC said. 'Lord Favon said the Restons aren't there. I can't accuse him of lying without due cause.' She turned and left.

Joni looked at Heck. 'Thanks for…'

'Don't ever do that again, Joni. You didn't tell me you were going to the pubs up there and you didn't tell me what you heard. You hung me out to dry.'

'I appreciate the support, sir. It won't happen again.' Joni's eyes flashed. 'But you know Favon's dirty.'

Heck ran his hand over his hair. 'I don't know whether it's Friday or a scrambled egg.'

128

Michael Etherington had crawled to his position behind the hedge before dawn, having left the Range Rover he'd borrowed from an old army friend three miles away up an overgrown track. He was wearing camouflage fatigues and matching hat, as well as his walking boots. As the sun rose, he took in Favon Hall and the old tower behind it through the scope on his rifle. The formal garden in front of the main building was in surprisingly poor condition, considering the place would be open to the public in under a month. Maybe Andrew was making less from the estate and his investments than he used to. Plus there was the fact that there was a leech attached to him.

He moved the rifle left and right, but there was no movement in or around the buildings. Too early for nightbirds like
the Favons. He wondered if they'd been out the previous evening
and whether they'd been together or on individual pursuits.
Andrew's red Toyota was parked at the side of the Hall, but Victoria's black sports car was right in front of the main entrance. It
looked like it had slewed to a halt as though the hounds of hell
were after her. Maybe they were. He knew they had sold shares
in some of their businesses, especially in high-tech and paper,
to the Albanians. Julian Dorries had managed to identify the
ultimate owners even though the Spahia clan was using front
companies.

He thought about what he'd been told the previous day. The
woman was a fool –what kind of person called herself Moonbeam? – but there was more to her man. At first he'd found it
hard to believe he was serious. How could a relatively minor
player like him be successfully blackmailing a big figure like
Andrew Favon? Because he could, was the answer – he obviously had good sources of information. He knew himself that
Andrew had secrets he didn't want in the public domain, but *this*
– this was incredible. The man said he'd been following Victoria
and had seen her and a man he couldn't identify run Nick off
the road. Michael had gone to meet them to obtain information,
after he'd got a call saying 'I know who killed your grandson' and
directing him to the mad woman's cottage.

He hadn't believed it, but he was so desperate that he went.
The blackmailer had disappeared as soon as the police officers
approached and, quick as a flash, Moonbeam made up the story
about him consulting her about Nick's killer. It wasn't so far from
the truth, he reflected afterwards. Except he had to think on his
feet too, feigning that he was gay and phoning ahead to Julian to
back up the story. The police were ahead of him, breaking that
alibi too. He was unlucky that the striking black policewoman
had recognised him from Burwell Street with Goat Skin, despite
his efforts to disguise himself. Julian had invoked the Official

Secrets Act, which had bought him time – that was one of the reasons he'd involved the techie. Julian would be under pressure now. At least his wife would confirm that she'd thrown him out. He was bisexual and good luck to him.

On the general's insistence, everyone in the Steel Toe Caps and his group of ex-SAS men had multiple pay-as-you-go phones. Goat Skin had told him what the police said. They'd agreed it would be sensible to pay heed and leave the Albanians alone for a while. But if they stuck their noses back into Corham, they'd feel more than just toe caps. And all the time, Julian Dorries would be collecting information about the Albanian clan's activities. The police had been after the Steel Toe Caps again about the Stars and Bars explosion. They all had solid alibis, except the idiot Goat Skin, who would keep his mouth shut whatever happened. None of them knew the explosives men, who had become ghosts after leaving the SAS.

Eye on the scope, Michael Etherington thought about the actions he'd taken since he got confirmation that the Spahia clan had extended its operation into the north-east three months ago. Recruiting had been easy, as he'd kept in touch with reliable former soldiers in the area. Shackleton had let himself go, but he was still a useful man in a fight, as well as having communication technology skills that would be essential if they had to stop using mobiles. There were four other hard men. They had been in Kosovo at the same time as him and they knew how vicious the Spahia were. The Albanians didn't only kill in the heat of battle, but as a point of principle. It would almost be admirable if their principles weren't so repulsive – pimping, people trafficking, smuggling, kidnapping, drugs. Michael remembered the men, most of them old, and the women and children they'd found massacred on that April morning in the forest near the Kosovo border with Albania. The clear air was cut with the stench of corruption. The dead hadn't just been executed, they'd been mutilated. He was sure the younger women had been raped before being killed. He swore to himself that he wouldn't let it rest. His superiors saw his rage and withdrew him, letting him shuffle paper for five years before giving him the push. He'd spent the time planning, organising and equipping. His intention had been to strike at the Spahia in London, but their expansion northwards coincided with his own move home. The battle lines had been drawn. If that whore – the poor, desperate girl – hadn't justifiably gone crazy in the brothel, the Steel Toe Caps would have dealt with the Albanian pimps the following weekend. He'd planned to torture the men to find out more about the clan's activities in the area. Now he was reduced to stalking a callous man-eater to find out what she'd been up to with his grandson. Moonbeam Pax's man hadn't been accurate – he didn't actually *know* who killed Nick as he'd reversed away when the black 4×4 stopped. Michael had paid him the five thousand he wanted anyway.

He thought about his grandson. He'd known about the affair with Victoria, having spotted her drop him off at the end of the village one evening. He had seen Nick receive the Sevens cup from Victoria before Easter and, with hindsight, there had been a spark between them. She'd spoken to him longer than a local aristocrat normally would to a dirty adolescent rugby player. Andrew Favon was next to her and he had his usual distracted air. Victoria had come on to him once, not long after Christine had died. Deep down he'd been flattered, though he told her to behave. He should have realised she'd get back at him by bedding Nick. He hoped Nick had enjoyed the experience, even though it had brought unhappiness too –Victoria had toyed with him, leading him on and then rejecting him. Had that been another way of revenging herself on Michael? It seemed likely she'd been jealous of Nick's feelings for Evie. But what kind of monster killed a young man for loving her daughter?

He would wait until Andrew went off on his daily round of meetings and go down to the Hall to find Victoria. If he suspected she was lying and that she did have something to do with Nick's death, he would break her bones one by one. The combat knife would be useful too. He'd also find out exactly why Andrew was being blackmailed. If he was the one who had killed Nick, Michael would wait for him and then execute them both. His only fear was Evie. He would have to lock her up somewhere.

Michael heard a noise and saw a red pickup come round the corner of the hall from the old tower. He made out the figure of the Favons' factor, a gorilla by the name of Reston. He remembered him scowling at one of Andrew's shoots when he had to hand the whisky round. Two large animals were running next to the vehicle. He zeroed in on them. They were Dobermans, spittle lathering their flanks. Then one of them stopped and sniffed the air. The other did the same and their smooth heads turned in his direction. They started to bark at the same time and then tore across the unmown lawn, ears back, heading straight for him.

129

Sergeant Moody brought a large brown envelope up to Heck's office. 'Some kid from the *Bugle* tossed this on the front desk and scarpered.'

'Probably worried you'd take the paper's crap reporting of police work out on him, Len.'

'Aye, I could believe that. Won't be long till Mrs Normal's round there bashing heads.' The sergeant paused. 'Don't take this the wrong way, sir, but are you all right? You look like…'

'Death after thirty seconds in the microwave?' Heck emptied the envelope's contents on the desk. 'I get that a lot.'

'Yes, but should you be back at work full-time?'

Heck looked up. He'd known Len Moody for years and knew he meant well, but he was getting sick of people offering sympathy. 'Listen, I might look like shite but I didn't have brain surgery. Get out of here.' He waited until the sergeant had reached the door. 'And don't refer to the ACC that way ever again.'

They managed to confine their laughter to a couple of barks.

Heck spread the photos over his desk. Gary Hext, the sports editor at the *Bugle*, had played in the Corham second row for years and was used to having Heck's head in close proximity to his arse. He complained about printing out the photos, but Heck insisted. His eyes got tired staring at digital images, not that he'd be telling Len Moody.

He'd asked only for shots of the presentation ceremony. Gary said he was lucky the photographer hadn't wiped his card, whatever that meant. There were forty-six images, but most were of the younger age groups that had preceded the main final. Victoria Favon was caught smiling, but it was obvious she wasn't enjoying herself. Andrew was grim-faced, not bothering to acknowledge the lads who climbed the short flight of steps. Behind them Michael Etherington seemed happy enough – one image showed him chatting animatedly to his neighbour, a middle-aged man Heck didn't recognise, and another clapping enthusiastically. He'd often sat in those seats himself – every season until this one – and had enjoyed seeing the young uns showing off their skills. Then again, he was a rugby addict, as was Michael Etherington, while the Favons definitely weren't.

He looked at the images of the final presentation. Nick Etherington really had been a fine figure of a lad – tall and straight-backed despite the hard matches he'd played over the afternoon, and smiling broadly. His grandfather looked as if he would burst with pride, while Andrew Favon gave the boy a snooty look. The big difference was in Victoria. Her ladyship had been transformed, her eyes wide and her face animated. She was holding Nick's muddy hand in several shots, while he tried to keep hold of the trophy in the other.

Heck leaned forward and scrutinised the last photo. What was Nick Etherington doing? His right hand was either going into or coming out of the pocket of his shorts. Had Victoria slipped him something? He looked at the other images, but none was similar. Had she slipped him her number in front of her husband and hundreds of other people? The way she looked was the giveaway. This was a woman who had the hots for Nick in a big way.

The question was, what had that to do with his murder seven weeks later? Then he had another thought. Michael Etherington was still missing. He'd known about his grandson's affair. Perhaps he'd noticed the way Victoria behaved towards him at the Sevens. Had he found a connection between her and Nick's murder? If so, he was capable of doing major damage.

130

The Popi were in a windowless room in central Newcastle, sitting on one side of a cheap metal table. The older Albanian was wearing a black polo neck and jeans and the younger was in an ex-German army jacket. The man opposite wore a denim jacket and matching trousers, his brown hair cut high at the sides, with a thick swathe lying across his forehead. There were several objects on the table.

'We never use real names,' the older Popi said. 'I am Jackal, my colleague is Hyena and you are Gazelle.'

'Gazelle? Why can't I be a meat-eater too?'

'The names are randomly generated,' the younger Popi said. 'The memory stick, please?'

Gazelle, a white man in his late twenties, felt inside his jacket and placed a blue 4GB stick on the table.

'Your computer is secure?'

'I use an iPad with enhanced protection. As soon as the wrong password is entered, all the files are immediately turned into gobbledygook.'

'Good. Give us your suggestions for the operation.'

Gazelle laughed. 'Operation? What is this, the SAS?'

The Popi looked back at him, their eyes blank.

'Sorry. Right, the operation. Detective Inspector Joni Pax.

Hitting her at the weekend is definitely the way to go, and Sunday's best. She's less likely to be working than on Saturday – the woman works more overtime than your tarts. As for taking her out in front of her mother, this Moonbeam weirdo – yeah, why not? I was thinking of putting the fear of a large knife up her and getting her to call her daughter, saying she's ill and needs looking after.'

Hyena raised a hand. 'You're aware that the target and her mother have a troubled relationship. Maybe she won't go.'

Gazelle grinned. 'I think I'll be able to make it convincing.'

'It's risky,' Jackal said, lighting a cigarette with a gold Zippo. 'Even though they appear not to be close, the daughter may realise her mother's under duress and call for reinforcements.'

'Under duress?' Gazelle said. 'Where did you guys learn English?'

There were more hollow stares.

'Anyway,' Gazelle continued, 'you want me to cut Joni Pax up badly.'

'While she is still alive,' Hyena said.

'I'm on my own, the briefing said. Joni Pax is a big woman and she knows judo. I'm not saying I can't handle her, even with her mother present, but I'd rather she walk to her final resting place than I have to drag her there.' He paused. 'I'll kill her in Moonbeam's cottage – Jesus loves me for a moonbeam, ha ha – which is in the middle of nowhere.'

'That is up to you,' the older Popi said. 'We would prefer the detective to be found in her apartment in Corham, but it's a town-centre location and the risk for you is greater.'

Gazelle smiled. 'No problem, I'll work it out.'

'You'd better,' Hyena said. 'If *we* have to clean up, we clean up everyone. You follow?'

Gazelle looked less sure of himself. 'I follow.'

'You've been paid a substantial sum of money, which will be doubled on completion of the operation,' Jackal said. 'Do you have any questions?'

'No, no.'

The older man smiled, but there was no trace of humour on his face. 'Have a good time, my friend. But be careful. I think you know we can reach anyone in the British prison system, maximum security units included. Should you talk, sooner or later you will die choking on your own reproductive organ.'

Gazelle put his hands on the table to show he wasn't trembling. 'What's all this gear, then?' he asked.

Hyena ran through the equipment, his fingers hovering over each piece but never touching. There was a Daewoo DP51 semi-automatic pistol and two clips with nine 9mm Parabellum rounds, a KA-BAR seven-inch fighting knife and sheath, and a mobile phone with six SIM cards in small clear plastic bags, each with a number between one and six written on it in indelible ink.

'The account linked to each card has five pounds credit and is strictly for single use,' the younger Popi said. 'You have memorised our contact number, yes?'

Gazelle parroted it without hesitation.

'Good, but we do not expect to hear from you except in extreme emergency. When you have made a call, remove the SIM, destroy it and insert the next in the series. Do not use your own phone, which should already be turned off and the battery removed.'

'Yeah, yeah,' Gazelle said, 'I read all that in the briefing.'

Both the Popi leaned forward.

'I emphasise it,' Hyena said, 'because in our experience communication systems are a weak link. We would prefer you to be completely out of contact, but that has its own dangers.'

'What, like you might change your minds about the operation?'

Jackal laughed, deep in his throat. 'There's no chance of that. By midnight on Sunday, DI Joni Pax will be in the state you're required to arrange, whatever happens.'

Hyena pushed a large plastic bag towards Gazelle with the toe of his work boot. 'Balaclava – keep it on at all times. Waterproof jacket, trousers and boots. Wear them when you cut her, then stand under the shower in them.'

'You've got this all worked out,' Gazelle said, looking at the clothing. 'How many times have you done it?'

'Goodbye.'

'Oh, right. Bye.'

The Popi waited until he had gone.

'Will he do?' the younger man asked, in their language.

'Probably. It's the other one I'm less sure about.'

Hyena looked at him thoughtfully. 'Shall we do it ourselves?'

'No, he will be satisfactory. The policeman has not fully recovered from abdominal surgery, his father is old, his wife is small and his children are young. Leopard will kill him in front of them.'

The younger Popi nodded. 'He is very angry.'

'Anger is good. Up to a point.'

'True.' Hyena stood up. 'There is one thing we have not decided. Which of us will watch over Gazelle and which over Leopard?'

Jackal got to his feet, standing on the cigarette end he had dropped. 'Are you ready for the policeman and his family?'

'Uncle, you insult me by asking.'

The men laughed and embraced each other.

131

Joni drove to the Etheringtons' village on Saturday morning. No further progress had been made on the cases on Friday and, though she was off duty, she wanted to keep an eye on things. The uniformed officers watching the roads in and out had seen no sign of General Etherington. His daughter-in-law hadn't left home, but had been visited by two women separately. Both gave her baskets of food and neither stayed long. Joni considered going in to ask Rosie if she'd heard from Michael. In the end she didn't. The idea of having to admit that they were no nearer to catching Nick's killer put her off.

Later she drove to the field where Wayne Garston's foreign labourers had been working. They were back, even though it was the weekend. The overweight ganger was leaning on the gatepost. He didn't look happy to see her.

'No rest for the innocent?' Joni asked, getting out of the Land Rover.

'Eh?'

'Your work force. Don't they get time off?'

'Tomorrow. Look, I'm not supposed to talk to you. I'm calling Mr Lennox's office. Oy, where are you going?' Garston hurried after her into the kale field.

'I'm going to talk to the women, Wayne.' Joni gave him a slack smile. 'Find out if you've been having it away with any of them.'

The look on his face was as good as a signed confession.

'You sleazy pus bag,' she said, drawing up her shoulders. 'I'm going to break your back.' She went into a fighting stance.

'You canna do that,' the ganger said, taking a step back. 'There are witnesses.'

'Who'll all testify that you attacked me.' She grinned. 'Or do you want to take a chance on that?'

It was obvious Garston was no fighter.

'What do you want?' he said, eyes down. 'The Albanians will rip my tongue out if they find out I've talked.'

'I'm not interested in the Albanians,' Joni said, straightening up. 'I want to hear about Dan Reston and his wife.'

'Haven't seen him recently. Or spoken to him.' He glanced at her. 'I keep away because of Cheryl. She's even crazier than he is.'

'You wouldn't happen to have heard that they're away on holiday?'

Garston laughed. 'Them? They never go anywhere. Dan runs the estate. The Favons can't do without him.'

'And what about Cheryl? Can they do without her?'

He shrugged. 'Dunno. Last I heard she was doing stuff in the Hall.'

'So why is it you keep away from her exactly? What did she do to upset your sensitive soul?'

The ganger's eyes were down again. 'She raped me.'

Joni blinked. 'What?'

'You heard me? She tied me down one night when I was in their place. I can't remember where Dan was, we'd been boozing. He was probably shagging a sheep. Cheryl got on top of me and bounced up and down until ... you know.' He turned away. 'Jesus, it was horrible. Not just because she's heavy and ugly as sin. She bit me on the neck. It didn't heal for weeks. Here, look.' He turned down his collar.

'Nasty,' Joni said, taking in the rows of deep indentations. She pulled out her phone and took a photo before he could react.

'What's that for?' he said, covering himself up.

'Comparison purposes,' Joni said. 'Anything else you want to tell me about the Restons?'

'Well ...'

'It'll be good for you if we arrest them with your help.'

'I'm no rat.'

They all said something like that. 'Of course not. But I've had bad reports about them. Besides, if Reston goes down, the factor's job would be up for grabs. You're already halfway there with the workers you supply.'

Wayne Garston looked as if he'd been kicked up the arse. 'I never thought of that.' He came closer and Joni's nostrils filled with the stink of old and new sweat. There was something worse in the wind: the reek of greed. 'Now, Dan, he's a cunning bugger and a careful one. But he's got a weak point. You promise to put in a good word for me if I tell you?'

Joni nodded, fingers crossed in her mind.

'All right. He was ill last year. Cancer, I heard. Did something to his ...' Garston pointed to his groin. 'He can't get it up any more.'

'I wasn't hoping he'd come on to me, Wayne.'

'No, not that. He's got even nastier since then. I heard he kills animals by hand. And he eats bits of them raw …'

Joni swallowed bile.

'A friend of mine saw him take down a sheep,' the ganger continued. 'His dogs were with him, of course.'

'The Dobermans?'

'You know about them? Make sure you don't let them get anywhere near you.'

Joni walked away, calling Heck. They had to nail the Restons before someone else's throat was ripped out.

<hr />

132

Evie Favon heard the dogs barking. She went to one of the windows at the front of the Hall and watched the Dobermans run across the grass towards the hedge at the bottom of the slope that led to the moor. It was early in the morning and neither of her parents was up. She went into the hallway and took the binoculars from her father's shooting jacket. Back at the window, she saw Dan Reston – the man who was supposedly on leave in the south with his wife – drive the red pickup over the uncut grass. When the dogs reached the hedge, they leapt straight in and disappeared for a time. Then they reappeared in open ground, heading for a clump of silver birches. They flew backwards before the sound of the shots reached her. She moved the binoculars and saw a figure in camouflaged hat and clothing move up the hillside. The man – she presumed the figure was male – was carrying a rifle and had a pack on his back.

Dan Reston had driven up to the hedge, got out and pushed himself through. She heard his wails as he approached the dogs' motionless bodies. He ran towards the armed man and then stopped when the rifle was pointed at him. She focused on

the camouflaged man's face and saw with a quiver of surprise
that it was grotesque. Then she realised that different coloured
stripes had been painted on it. She couldn't make out the features, but she saw the lips move. Dan Reston walked backwards
to the Dobermans. He dropped to his knees and cradled their
shattered heads. When she looked again, the shooter had disappeared into the pine forest that covered the hillside to the
east.

'Did I hear shots?' Victoria asked, from behind her.

'I don't know, did you?'

'Grow up, Evie. You know what I mean.' Her mother was in a
white kimono with black zigzags across it.

'I heard two.' She handed Victoria the binoculars.

'Oh God, Dan's dogs. Did you see who did it?'

'Yes.' Evie clammed up.

Victoria grabbed her arm. 'Tell me!'

'Calm down. Yes, I saw him. No, I don't know who he was.'

Her mother lit a cigarette. She was even paler than she usually
was in the mornings. 'Dan will be impossible now. Those dogs
meant everything to him. Especially since…'

'What?' Evie demanded, when no more words were
forthcoming.

'Since his operation. Prostate cancer. He was lucky to survive,
apparently.'

'I didn't know that.'

'You had physical problems of your own in the winter, darling.
We didn't want to bother you.'

Evie took the binoculars back. The factor was now lying
on the ground between the Dobermans, his face and clothes
covered in blood.

'Yuck.'

'Let me see. Oh, hell. I'd better wake your father.'

'So he can go and roll in the gore too? Is that another quaint
family tradition?'

'You really can be a pain in the arse.'

'You think so?' A dark curtain descended over Evie. 'I wonder why. My mother told the police she'd fucked my boyfriend.'

Victoria wasn't taken aback. 'Before you were with him, darling.'

'So? Now I know why you were eating him with your eyes when he was here this week.'

'Get a grip, girl. I finished with him before he went back to the Abbey for the summer term.' Victoria smiled crookedly. 'I'm surprised Nick didn't tell you about it.'

Evie slapped her mother's face hard. 'Bitch.' She lifted her crutch and pointed it at Victoria. 'Stay away from me!'

'You're overwrought, Evie. You need some time in a home.'

'Fuck you! That wasn't all I heard. You and Father lied to the police. You said Dan and Cheryl weren't here. Why? What have you done?'

'What have *we* done? The Restons are the ones the police want to talk to.'

'But you're protecting them. Why?'

Andrew Favon appeared at the end of the corridor. His remaining hair was tousled. 'What on earth are you two screaming about at this hour?'

'Look,' Evie said, handing him the binoculars and pointing.

'Good God!'

'I'll handle him,' Victoria said, walking away. 'Take Evie's crutch and lock her in her room.'

Andrew looked surprised, then did as he was told.

Evie was no match for him physically. As soon as the key turned, she started to think about how to get out.

133

'I can't hear you!' Heck yelled into his phone. He was on the Roman Wall west of Cawfields and the wind was strong. He ducked down behind an escarpment. 'That's better. What were you saying?'

Joni told him what Wayne Garston had told her about the Restons.

'Lovely pair,' he said. 'What do you want to do?'

'I just called Big Bertha. She confirms that the bite on the headless man is from a Doberman.'

'At least Reston didn't kill him.'

'Maybe he drank his blood.'

'Look, Joni, you know this isn't going to get Mrs Normal to give the go-ahead for a warrant to search the Hall and estate.'

'What if the Restons have got Suzana Noli and your friend Forrest?'

'There's no evidence to suggest that.'

Joni paused before speaking. 'I've got a bad feeling about this, sir.'

'I'm not exactly over the moon about it myself, but we have to work by the ACC's rules. Listen, go home and have a quiet evening. I promise you a lively lunch tomorrow, OK? And we can slip away to talk things over.'

Joni accepted that with ill grace and cut the connection.

Heck clambered down the slope and took refuge in a stand of trees. A teenage couple, cheeks red and laughter shrill. There was no doubt what they'd been up to. The girl didn't look much older than Kat. Heck shuddered. The idea of his daughter being pawed by some callow youth was awful, but he could never make it clear to her. Contrary as she was, she would run straight for the nearest pair of arms.

Sitting on a fallen tree, Heck tried to get his head together. There was a dull pain in his belly, as so often after he'd been walking. Tackling the Albanian had only been a stage in the fight to overcome his fear. Since the operation, he had gradually learned to trust his being as a whole, accepting that the physical and the mental were intertwined. Now he could see that his work – especially the murder cases – was testing and gradually improving his resilience. A lot of the time in the MCU he felt he was floundering as people pulled him in different directions. Joni was convinced the Favons and their employees were at the heart of things. Morrie Simmons put everything down to the Steel Toe Caps and their opposition to the Albanians. He himself was trying to coordinate their efforts. Pancake Rokeby, who'd drawn the short straw for Saturday, had called him from the office earlier. Michael Etherington's phone records had arrived, by some miracle given it was the weekend. He was collating incoming and outgoing calls, but had found nothing suggestive so far. The general's computer was also devoid of anything significant, apart from the contents of his grandson's computer, which suggested he was set on finding out who killed the lad. Things were at a standstill. Then he had a thought. The reason for that was Mrs Normal. The chief constable would be in on it too. They didn't want their crony Andrew Favon investigated unless convincing evidence of wrongdoing came to light. But how were he and his teams to find evidence if they weren't allowed to work the way they would with ordinary people? Fuck the rich and powerful.

Heck got up slowly to avoid straining anything. He reckoned they had most of the information they needed, but putting it all together was proving difficult. He would call Dan Reston again when he got home, but Favon's man had been keeping his head down. That made him uncomfortable. He had a feeling something bad was about to happen and Reston was his, and Joni's, prime suspect – but the bugger had vanished. As had Michael Etherington. Was there a connection?

As he walked on the Wall, Heck came out of his black mood. Luke would be waiting to bowl him some leg breaks and Ag would produce the usual Saturday high tea, cream cake and iced buns included. Tomorrow Joni would come to the family Sunday lunch. The rest of the weekend would be good.

<hr />

134

Suzana was hungry. No food had appeared for what she guessed was close to a day. Water wasn't a problem as she could drink from the tap in the bathroom. She lay on the bed in the dark, listening carefully. Occasionally there were shouts – a man's voice – from below. Perhaps he wasn't being fed either. What had happened to the pig in the woollen mask? She had heard wheels moving across the gravel outside and had screamed, but nothing had happened. Were they being left to die? As she dropped in and out of consciousness, it came to her that this wouldn't be such a bad way to reach the end of things. At least the pig hadn't done more than peer at her when she was naked. If he kept away and she didn't have to use the knife on him, she might never have to bear a man's weight on her again, feel a man inside her.

The knife. She put her hands between her legs and eased it out. The other option was to use it on herself now. That would guarantee her escape from captivity, from the world. She slid the blade out from the plastic casing and put it against her throat. One swift movement, that was all it would take. She shivered as the longing for death gripped her. She heard seductive words – no more suffering, no more running, no more abuse. She gripped the knife harder and made a small cut on the side of her neck. She felt a warm trickle and put a finger against it. Then she got up and went to the bathroom. There was no mirror and the light from the blacked-out window was minimal, but she could see a contorted image of her face on the showerhead. She drew a line of blood across her forehead, then dabbed spots and dashes on her cheeks and nose. She smiled and the witch-like creature grinned back at her malevolently. For the first time in many months, Suzana laughed.

The blood from the cut soon dried up. She washed the blade and put it in her pocket. She no longer felt the need to hide it inside herself. She wasn't going to commit murder on her own body. The pigs, so many of them, had done what they wanted to it. She had endured that and she wasn't going to give up now.

The man in the mask might not come back, but if he did he would regret it – in the seconds before death pulled his soul from the gaping wound she would make in his flesh.

135

Joni slept badly again. This time she wasn't bothered by dreams or visions, but her body seemed to be out of control. When she went to bed, she started shivering and had to wrap an extra duvet round herself, even though the night was warm enough. Later, she woke to the sound of an owl's calls and found herself bathed in sweat, despite the fact that she'd kicked off both duvets. She thought she must have a virus and took her temperature with a digital thermometer. It was normal. She drank two glasses of water and sat looking out over the dark space of the garden, the lights from the Abbey to her left. She opened the window and heard the soughing of the wind through trees planted by monks in the Middle Ages. Suddenly she felt very far from home.

As if she had a home. She'd never been back to Hackney after she left for Oxford. She would arrange to meet her mother in the centre of London, usually in art galleries, though her taste in art had outstripped Moonbeam's permanent miring in the sixties. Likewise Oxford: it wasn't a place she liked revisiting, and certainly not on the gaudy nights intended to extract funds from alumni. She hadn't been in Bari or Marseilles long enough to feel attached to them, and they were tainted by the love affairs that had ended when she left. As for the flats she'd owned in south London, they never felt like home, mainly because of the hours she worked. So where did she belong? In Corham? She'd only been there for a few months and, though she found the town pleasant enough, she hadn't begun to put roots down.

Joni felt a hollowness in her abdomen and a quickening of her pulse. She thought she could hear faint voices on the breeze, voices speaking in a strange form of English. She closed her eyes and saw a figure in dark clothes, his face unnaturally white. When he came close enough that she could smell the decay on his breath, she saw that the cheeks and forehead had been smeared white, and the mouth was wide in a lipless grin. She was shocked to feel her libido rush back. She slid the fingers of one hand under her T-shirt and played with nipples that were already hard. Her other hand moved under the waistband of her sweatpants, past the scarring, and found the wetness she hadn't experienced since she'd left London. In a matter of seconds she shuddered in a prolonged climax. As her heart rate returned to normal, she was sure she heard laughter fading into the dark.

She sat there until the cool of night finally got to her, then closed the window and went back to bed. Sleep refused to arrive, so she lay there thinking about what had happened. She felt pleasantly sated and distinctly more alive than she had been. She shouldn't have cut herself off from her body for so many months. But then her conscious mind began to reassert itself. She thought of Suzana and the missing farmer, of Michael Etherington – was he really going to avenge Nick? And the Favons – haughty and high-handed, but plagued by the same weaknesses as lesser people. And Dan Reston. Was he the key to all the mysteries?

The thoughts continued to swirl, some of them making sense, some of them bordering on the fantastic. Joni didn't think her new-found clarity was only because she'd relieved months of sexual tension. Something she was near to understanding was going on. Near, but still it eluded her...

Joni slept for a few hours and then couldn't sit still. She

arrived at Heck's place half an hour early to find him, his father and the kids in the back garden, throwing a tennis ball around at speed. Even the old man had a good eye, moving his body as soon as the yellow sphere headed in his direction. Joni watched them over the fence for several minutes before Kat spotted her.

'Joni!' the girl cried, throwing the ball hard at her brother then running towards her. 'How are you doing?'

'I'm fine,' she replied. 'You?'

'Oh, you know – school, boys, my idiot brother.' Kat liked Joni because she took time to talk to her on the few occasions they'd met. 'Nice blouse.'

The men arrived at varying degrees of speed, Luke hanging back behind his grandfather.

'Wow!' Heck said. 'I've never seen a fruit salad blouse before. Is it from Hawaii?' He ran an eye over her. 'Wherever it was made, you look spectacular.'

'Hello, lass,' David said, holding out his liver-spotted hand. 'Come away in.'

'Hiya, Luke,' she said, smiling at the twelve-year-old.

He nodded, eyes down. If ever there were a case of early teenage lust, this was it.

'Joni!' Ag called from the house. 'Come and help. As usual I'm left to slave in the kitchen on my own.' She looked sheepish. 'Sorry, I shouldn't have used the "s" word.'

Joni smiled. 'Slavery isn't confined to people of colour.'

'True enough. Have a white wine, orange juice and soda spritzery thing.' Ag filled a glass from a jug. 'I've made a mushroom lasagne. Can you sort out the salad?'

Joni nodded, sipping her drink.

'Those heathens demand meat,' Ag said, 'so you're going to have to live with the scent of rib roast.'

'It's fine. You shouldn't have bothered with the lasagne. I could just have eaten the vegetables.'

Ag frowned. 'I invited you. I'm not going to give you nothing and three veg.'

Joni laughed.

'You look well. Are you settling in at last?'

'I wouldn't say that exactly. No time. We've been very busy.'

'I noticed.' Ag moved closer. 'Is my man coping? He's come home every day in a state of exhaustion.'

Joni nodded. 'The DCI's doing fine.'

'He's called Heck, Dad or Son in this house. Take your pick.'

'OK,' Joni said, as her boss walked in. 'Can we … can we have a few minutes?'

'No!' Ag commanded. 'It's Sunday, it's nearly lunch time and shop talk is banned.'

Heck opened his hands helplessly, then poured two glasses from the jug. 'I'm looking forward to seeing the old man get this down. He thinks white wine is the work of the devil.'

'He'll also drink anything that contains alcohol,' Ag said.

They moved to the front room, where Kat and Luke were playing with the long-suffering pets. Adolf was sitting on the back of the sofa, peering at the boy through narrowed eyes, while Cass was standing against Kat on her hind legs. Joni felt a shiver run up her body as a high-pitched sound entered her ears. She looked round and saw Heck's father sitting at the table, Northumbrian pipes on his lap. He started on a fiendishly complicated air, accompanied by his son on the bodhran. Joni clapped when they finished, even though the music had made her uncomfortable. It had reached a part of her that classical music didn't. She found herself thinking of the laughter that had floated away on the wind in the middle of the night – the laughter and the skeletal figure she had glimpsed.

Lunch was loud and delicious. Joni had been put between David and Luke. While the old man would happily have talked to her without interruption about the larks he and his friends had got up to when they were young, she tried to engage the teenager in the conversation. He was interested in rugby and cricket, two sports she had never seen the point of – she'd never cared for teams, preferring to test herself against her own personal best with the javelin rather than bother with the opposition. But Luke's enthusiasm was infectious and she found herself asking him about the complexities of the scrum. He wanted to be a number eight, whatever that was – like his father had been – but apparently he needed to put some inches and pounds on.

'Aye, Heck was the man,' David said, shaking his head. 'When he had the bit between his teeth, he could get the ball over the line with half-a-dozen defenders hanging off him.'

The meal finished with a spectacular homemade ice cream cake.

'All right,' Ag said, after coffee had been handed out, 'I can see Heck and Joni are bursting to get to work. Half an hour in the study and then rounders in the garden, OK?'

Joni nodded gratefully and followed her boss to the small room on the first floor, where he had a desk piled with paper and no computer.

'Let's have it then,' Heck said, after she sat down on the low sofa.

She made her case for searching the Favon estate for the Restons – as well as for Suzana Noli and Oliver Forrest.

'But Dan Reston and his wife have done a bunk,' Heck said, fumbling for his phone. He clicked on a number and waited for a reply. 'Still going straight to voicemail.'

'He hasn't done a bunk, sir,' Joni said. 'I'm sure of that. He's on the estate somewhere and Lord Favon's knows it.'

'What do you suggest we do? It's still all conjecture.'

'Not if we get the SOCOs to go over the whole pickup instead of just the tyres.'

'At best that might put Reston in the frame for the headless man's death, though he could easily claim the dogs got loose.'

'But someone cut off Gary Frizzell's head and hands. If we squeeze him, maybe he'll put Favon in the frame.'

'All right, I'll talk to Mrs Normal tomorrow morning.'

'Not today?'

'Lay off, Joni. I've only called her on the weekend once. She was at a lunch and wasn't happy. Besides, getting a warrant on Sunday afternoon is a tough ask.'

'People's lives may be at risk.'

'All right! I'll call her later so we can at least get the paperwork ready.'

Joni wasn't impressed – it didn't work that way in the Met – but she had to accept the ways things were done in the north. Soon Ag opened the door and ushered them out.

Joni proved to be a useful rounders player, hitting the ball so hard that it took Luke a couple of minutes to find it in the neighbouring field. He grinned as he ran back, shyness gone.

It was close to four when Joni left. She had to visit her mother and her stomach was already clenching at the prospect. She felt things were coming to a head with Moonbeam and their relationship would never be the same again. Ag kissed her on both cheeks as did David, more sloppily. Heck pecked her once, then Kat gave her a hug and Luke did the same. They were sweet moments.

'Come again!' Ag called, as Joni was climbing into the Land Rover. 'Come next Sunday.'

Joni waved but didn't speak. She could only look ahead a matter of hours. As she pulled away from the Rutherfords', she saw a figure in the wood across the road. For a moment she wondered who it was, but the thought immediately left her mind as she concentrated on her mother.

<hr />

136

The man known as Gazelle had been outside Moonbeam Pax's cottage since midday. He was fifteen feet up an old oak tree and had a viewpoint that was both safe and panoramic if he shifted the branches. He didn't need the binoculars he'd brought in his backpack. He'd parked the car about three hundred yards further down the road, in a concealed turn-off that led only to the gate of an empty field. There was just an old Renault outside that he knew went with the house. Smoke was rising from the chimney on the right side of the low building and the woman with the crazy name didn't come out until mid-afternoon. She spent some time cutting from plants in a fenced patch of ground, then went back inside. Her hair looked like a buzzard had been nesting in it and her clothes were hippy but definitely not chic. He could imagine she'd once been an attractive woman. It was hard to see in the small windows, but he reckoned she was on her own. When he was watching her in the garden he thought he heard the door to one of the outhouses bang, but he must have imagined it. There had been no sign of anyone else.

After eating a sandwich and an apple, his back against the gnarled trunk, Gazelle looked at his watch. Nearly four. The sun was still up in the west, but a chill was beginning to settle. He saw no reason to wait any longer. He took the pistol and ammo clips out of his bag, slapping one in and racking the slide. Then he slipped the sheathed knife into the pocket of his dark green combat jacket. One pocket was already stuffed with plastic restraints. After pulling the balaclava over his face, he was ready to rock.

Dropping down from the tree silently, he went to the door and knocked three times. If the woman wanted to know who he was before opening up, he would say he was a police officer, but that turned out to be unnecessary.

'Wha—,' Moonbeam Pax said, the smile dying on her lips.

Gazelle had the pistol raised. 'Inside. No noise, no pissing about.'

The woman backed into the cottage. He glanced into the room on the left past the open door and saw only heaps of cardboard boxes.

'Christ!' he said, gagging as he followed her past the foot of the stairs and into the other room. 'What *is* that?'

'A herbal remedy for gout,' Moonbeam Pax said, showing less fear than he was used to.

'Sit down,' he said, pointing to a wooden chair by a rickety table. She did so and he quickly secured her arms and legs with ties.

'What do you want?' she asked. 'I have nothing of value, at least to those who do not believe in nature's powers.'

Gazelle slapped her hard on the left cheek. He was wearing thin leather gloves and the blow made a loud crack.

'Why … why did … did you do that?' she asked, her eyes wet.

'Because you're a stupid cunt.' He pressed the muzzle of the pistol against the side of her head. 'Now start taking deep breaths. In a few minutes you're going to call your daughter and tell her you're feeling poorly. You need her to look after you, got that? You need her now.'

Moonbeam Pax nodded slowly as she tried to control her breathing.

137

Michael Etherington was wedged in the braches of an old oak at the top of the wood. Favon Hall was over a mile to the west. He'd watched as Dan Reston, covered in blood, had dragged the dogs' bodies through the hedge and loaded them on to the Hilux. His head was down and his shoulders slack as he lit a cigarette. It was too far to hear, but it looked like he was bellowing. Then the factor's body language changed. He straightened up and pounded his fists against the bodywork. He got in and drove at speed across Andrew Favon's lawns, heading for the old dower house on the other side of the gardens.

The general considered his options. If he went home, he'd have to find a secure place to hide the camo gear and his weapons – the police would no doubt take him in for questioning about the explosion at the nightclub. He could go back to his friend's 4×4 and drive as far away as he could, but there was no honour in that. No, he had to go to the Hall and question the Favons about Nick's death.

He got down from the tree and made his way through the wood to the eastern edge of the gardens. He was surprised that the shots hadn't brought Andrew to the door, but maybe he was still pissed from the night before. Although booze wasn't too high on the list of his vices… Then he heard the roar of an engine and saw the red Hilux speed across the gravel. It swung round the edge of the Hall and drove towards the medieval tower. He raised the scope and watched as a figure dressed in black – no sign of blood – got out. A balaclava had been pulled over the face. Moving quickly, the man took a cattle prod from the back of the pickup and opened the steel door. He disappeared inside, leaving the door ajar.

Michael Etherington had a bad feeling. As far as he knew, the tower was full of junk and was also unsafe. One thing he was sure of – there weren't any cattle in it. So what was the prod for? Jesus, he said, under his breath. Has the mad fucker locked Andrew and Victoria up in there?

He broke cover, running in a crouch. There was open space between the wood and the tower, but he had no choice.

138

The man with the codename Leopard was getting impatient. He'd been among the trees across the road from Heck Rutherford's house for nearly three hours. He'd seen Joni Pax arrive and the whole pack of them go inside for a lunch that seemed to last forever. Then they reappeared and played rounders in the garden, their leaping, running forms visible from his hiding place. He looked at his watch. At last it was nearly time. He checked his clothing. It was all brand new, bought with cash from different shops: a black cagoule and waterproof trousers, black hiking boots that pinched. He hoped he wouldn't have to run further than the stolen car he'd been supplied with and had parked down the road.

Leopard had his weapons in a shooting bag: a Benelli M4 Super 90 semi-automatic shotgun, with seven 12 gauge rounds already inserted and another twenty in his pockets; a Korean pistol which he only intended using in the last resort; and a combat knife. He didn't want to inflict any more damage than he had to, but he would do anything to punish Heck Rutherford. The Albanians had discovered how much he wanted revenge, even though he thought he'd concealed it from all except close family. The money was great too, but it was the icing on the cake. Slaughtering the bastard Rutherford in front of his family was motivation enough.

At last the black cow left – he'd been given strict instructions not to start until she'd gone – and Leopard checked his gear. He pulled on thick latex gloves and rolled down his balaclava. This was it. Payback in blood and guts. He moved to the edge of the wood, checked the road in both directions and headed for the front door. The westering red sun made him blink, but only once.

<hr />

139

Evie was at the rear-facing window of her bedroom when the Hilux drove up to the tower. Was that Dan Reston with a balaclava over his face? Why was he taking a cattle prod in there? The way he moved, it was frightening. Could there be someone else inside? She made her mind up – it was time she got out. She wedged a chair under the door handle so her parents would have a struggle to get in. Then she stripped the bed and pulled off the sheet and under sheet. She twisted the fabric and then tied the ends to make a form of rope that would at least get her close to the gravel-covered ground below. There was a basement that increased the distance.

Andrew had forgotten about her second crutch. She smashed it against the worn wooden frame, breaking as much glass as she could, then threw the duvet over the jagged edges. After securing one end to the leg of a chest of drawers, she threw the rope out and sent the crutch after it. She took a deep breath and climbed out. Her upper body strength was good after using the wheelchair for months, but she still almost lost her grip as she went down and had to pull her legs up to prevent further damage. She straightened them until her feet reached the gravel and stood panting before she picked up her crutch. The silver-coloured metal had taken a battering, but it still held her weight. She limped over to the tower, stopping when she heard what sounded like a man scream. Then she started moving again, her heart pounding.

As she passed the pickup, she had a thought and looked in the window. The key wasn't in the ignition.

'Bollocks,' she mouthed.

There was nothing else for it. She had to go in. It would be the first time in her life. The old building had been out of bounds since she was a small child. She smelled the musty air. There was something else in it – something animal. As she started on the first set of stone steps, she heard another scream, this one more highly pitched. She glanced at her crutch. She had the feeling it wasn't going to be anything close to adequate as a weapon.

140

The call came when Joni was about five miles from her mother's. She immediately knew something was wrong.

'Joni? I'm … not well, darling. Can you come and … look after me?'

Moonbeam's tone was almost the standard mixture of laid-back charm and neediness, but Joni caught the tension in it. She didn't say she was on her way, as arranged, because she knew her mother wouldn't have forgotten that.

'What's the matter?' she asked, as evenly as she could.

'Oh, I've got this bug. I've … I've thrown up twice already and I hardly have the energy to get to the loo.'

'That doesn't sound good. All right, I'll be with you in half an hour.'

'Thank you, darling.' The connection was cut, too quickly Joni reckoned, but she'd bought herself some time. She drove on, trying to work out what was happening. A burglary, a home invasion – or something worse? She called Heck. The landline was engaged and his mobile switched to voicemail. Parking about five hundred yards before Moonbeam's track, she found Pete Rokeby's number.

There was a lot of noise in the background when he answered.

'It's Joni, Pete. There's something going on.' She explained the situation.

'You think your mother and DCI Rutherford are in danger?'

'I don't want to take any chances, given what we know the Albanians can do. I'm calling uniform to both places, but I want you to get to Heck's … to the DCI's, as quick as you can. Where are you?'

'Restaurant in Corham. It's a friend's birthday and I've been drinking.'

'Too bad. Get over there now.' She terminated the call, called the uniformed branch and then got out of the Land Rover. She had a toolbox under a blanket in the back. She knew she should wait for backup, but she couldn't leave her mother in danger, for all their problems. She put a screwdriver in one jacket pocket and took a two-foot socket wrench in her hand, before cutting across the fields and approaching the cottage from the rear. She reckoned backup from Alnwick would be at least twenty minutes. She stooped as she approached the back window of the main room. Raising her head cautiously, she saw her mother sitting on one of the chairs at the table. The white restraints round Moonbeam's wrists and ankles immediately caught her attention. She looked around slowly. A figure in dark clothes and a balaclava was standing behind the door that led to the small hall. The height and bulk suggested it was a man. He was holding a pistol in his right hand and what looked like a combat knife in his left. He couldn't be seen from the front windows. If she knocked at the front door, she'd make a large target.

Joni rocked back on her heels. She was seriously outgunned and there was nothing she could do about it. Moonbeam hated shooting and certainly wouldn't have any firearms about the place. Maybe there was something useful in the outhouse, the one her mother had been so snippy about being searched. Joni headed there and dropped to her knees to look through the keyhole. It was blocked on the inside. She tried the door and it opened immediately. She stared up in amazement at the familiar figure rubbing sleep from his eyes. Getting to her feet, she pushed him back and closed the door.

'Morrie? What the hell are you doing here?'

'Had a bit of lunch with your mother. She very kindly drove me up here so I could hit the home brew. I was having a snooze till you woke me up.'

Joni's eyes were wide. 'Never mind. There's a man with a pistol and a knife in the cottage and he's tied her to a chair. I got a call from her that I realised was made under duress. She knew I was coming this afternoon.'

'Did she now? Oddly, she didn't mention it to me.' Simmons smiled. 'Looks like she was going to introduce you to her new man.'

Joni tried to ignore that. 'I don't suppose there are any weapons in here? Backup's on its way but I don't want to wait.' She looked around the small room. It had been refurbished as a kind of bedsit, with a single bed along the back wall and a desk at the shuttered window. There was some kind of altar in the far corner. The mingled smells of fruit and herbs filled her nostrils.

'There's a garden fork outside,' Morrie said. 'That might make him fill his shorts. Besides, I know how to look after myself.'

'Really?' Joni said doubtfully. 'OK, here's what we'll do. I'll knock at the front door. When he goes to open it, you get in the back. Is the door locked?'

'Wasn't when I went out an hour ago.'

'He might have secured it. If he has, break the kitchen window and get inside as quickly as you can.'

'There are plenty of knives in the kitchen,' Morrie said. 'You sure you don't want *me* to go in the front?'

Joni shook her head. 'She's my mother. You don't have to do anything if you don't want to.' She caught his eye. 'Then again, it sounds like you have an interest in her.'

'You could say that.' Morrie followed her to the door and went to the rear of the cottage with unexpected stealth.

Joni dismissed the thought of her mother and Morrie Simmons together. She went to the front door, crawling beneath the window, and stood up. Holding the socket wrench behind her back, she knocked with her left hand.

'Mother? It's me.'

There was a pause, then the door opened quickly. The pistol was pointed directly at her face.

'Inside, you stupid bitch.' She recognised the voice immediately and her stomach clenched. The man holding a gun on her was Marcus Ainsworth, the armed robber who had crippled Roland Malpas during the raid in south London and managed to escape.

'You!' she said, expelling breath rapidly.

A smile appeared on the mouth in the balaclava slit. 'Me. Show me what you've got in your right hand. Slowly!'

Joni brought the socket wrench round and dropped it. She was struggling, so shocked was she by the reappearance of the vicious piece of shit who had stabbed her after she'd taken Roland Malpas's place.

'Come on,' Ainsworth ordered, the pistol aimed at her abdomen as he backed into the main room.

'Joni!' her mother wailed from the chair. 'He forced me to phone.'

'What's this about?' Joni demanded.

Ainsworth laughed. 'You've pissed off some powerful people. They're smart as well. Hired me to get rid of you.' He glanced at Moonbeam. 'It'd be a good idea if you don't tell your mother who I am.' He laughed emptily. 'Otherwise I'll have to kill her too.'

Joni was suddenly aware that Morrie was behind her captor, crouching with the garden fork held horizontally.

'Leave her alone,' she said. 'I don't care what you do to me.'

Marcus Ainsworth stared at her. 'What's happened to you, woman?' He glanced at Moonbeam. 'Didn't you like what I did to you down south?' Then his head cracked to the right as the curve of the fork's tines hit the left side of his skull. He crashed to the floor.

'Fucker,' Morrie said, leaning over the motionless man and pulling off the balaclava. He started emptying his pockets. The knife and pistol were pushed out of range and more plastic restraints tossed out. 'Secure his hands behind his back, Jack,' he said. 'I'll tie his ankles together. Come on. He could wake up any second.'

Joni, who had been replaying the scene outside the warehouse, came back to herself. In seconds she had Ainsworth's hands fastened. Blood was flowing from four lines on the side of his head, but he had a pulse. His face was still covered in the acne she remembered.

'Good job,' Simmons said, going over to release Moonbeam.

'That was a terrible thing you did, Morrie,' she said. 'No living creature deserves to be treated like that.'

Joni burst out in laughter bordering on the hysterical. 'Mother,' she said, when she'd calmed down, 'that's Marcus Ainsworth, the bastard who nearly gutted me. He was going to kill me – you too, probably – but you're more worried about offending the essential equilibria?'

'Didn't have much choice,' Simmons said, his arm round Moonbeam's shoulders.

'Is that really <u>him</u>?'

'Yes, Mother,' Joni said. 'Did you think he was after your dope stash?'

'It … it must have been terrible for you, to be confronted by him again.'

Joni couldn't believe what she was hearing. Her mother had never shown such empathy before. Maybe Morrie Simmons was good for her. No, that was too hard to believe.

'Why was he going to kill you?' Moonbeam asked.

Joni sat down. 'The cases we've been working on – Michael Etherington's grandson, the dead man from the brothel in Corham – there's an Albanian clan involved. They don't take prisoners.'

'But he's no Albanian,' Morrie said, glancing at the comatose figure.

'They used him to make it worse for me, I suppose. And to cover their tracks.' She took out her phone. 'I'd better call the DCI. Is this some kind of a joke, Morrie? Are you cosying up to my mother to get at me?'

Moonbeam's laughter was like a peal of large bells. 'I was the one who cosied up to him.'

Morrie Simmons shrugged. 'Mutual attraction.'

Joni shook her head. Then threw herself to the floor as multiple gunshots turned the windows into lethal fragments.

141

Heck was settling down in front of the TV to catch up on the sport when the doorbell rang. His old man was asleep on the other sofa, Adolf on his lap, while Ag was in the kitchen, Kat in her room texting her friends with Cass no doubt flopped on her bed, and Luke playing some computer game involving balls – he was banned from anything overtly violent. Heck groaned and went to the door.

'What the…'

'Shut up.' The man with the balaclava covering his face jabbed at Heck's belly with a shotgun. 'In the front room and sit down.'

'What the fuck…'

The butt of the Benelli was slammed into Heck's belly and his face creased in agony. 'No talking, right?' His assailant glanced at David and then went to the kitchen. He returned with Ag in front of him. 'Get the kids down here,' he said. 'If you screw up, they die.'

'Do … do as … he says … pet,' Heck said from the sofa, doubled up. He wasn't sure if he'd sustained internal injuries. Worse, he was trembling. The fear had returned and it was more debilitating than ever.

Ag stayed calm and called the children. Kat started to sob when she saw the weapon, while Luke ran to his father.

'What have you done to him, you shite?' he yelled.

'Keep the noise down or it'll be much worse.' The gunman herded the woman and children towards the inner of the two sofas. 'Wake the old tosser up. He may as well hear what I've got to say.' The landline started ringing. The intruder picked up the handset and pressed the End Call button. Heck's mobile on the coffee table started to buzz.

'Leave it,' he ordered. 'In front of the fireplace, Rutherford. The rest of you sit down.' The shotgun was pointed at Heck's chest, but it quickly moved towards Ag, Kat and his father. They crammed on to the sofa.

Heck pushed Luke gently towards his mother.

'What is this?' Ag demanded.

Heck peered at the man in the balaclava, then turned to his family. 'Don't worry, we'll sort this out quickly enough.' He opened his arms. 'Why don't we go outside and talk this over?'

The intruder stared at him, then shook his head. 'No chance. You're going to die in front of your family.'

Kat and Luke gasped and started to cry.

Ag put her arms round them. 'Don't you da—'

The last word was lost in the roar of the shotgun. Plaster crashed down from the ceiling.

'That got your attention?'

Ag, David and the children glared at the masked man, but kept quiet.

'You want to tell me what this is about?' Heck asked, his arms still wide.

'It's about you dying in agony, shithead.' The shotgun swung towards the others. 'Keep still or I'll blow the lot of you apart.'

Heck had taken courses in handling armed assailants. The important thing was to keep them talking.

'Whatever it is you think I've done, it can be sorted out.'

'Like hell,' the gunman scoffed.

There was something about the rough voice that was familiar, but Heck concentrated on getting his family out of the danger zone.

'Let the others go into the kitchen, and you and I will sort this out between us.'

'Fuck...'

There was a loud hammering at the door.

'DCI Rutherford? Heck?'

'Stand still!' the man in the balaclava ordered. When Pete Rokeby's face appeared at the window, he loosed off another shot then racked the slide. Kat was screaming.

'Listen to this before your guts spill over the floor, Rutherford. Ned Sacker. This is for him.' He pointed the shotgun at Heck's midriff.

'No!' Ag shrieked, leaping forwards.

At the same time, Pete Rokeby reappeared at the window and threw a hand-sized stone at the gunman, glass flying inwards after it. The stone hit him on the side of the head and he staggered back, the shotgun wavering. Heck leaped towards him and grabbed the weapon. Pete came through the window and helped him wrest it from the man in the balaclava, who had one hand on the side of his head and the other inside his cagoule. It came out holding a black pistol, which he pointed at Heck's head.

'Out of my house!' the DCI said, the shotgun to his shoulder. 'Out!' He glanced at Rokeby, who was on his knees with his arm wrapped round the intruder's legs. 'Let him go, Pancake.'

The gunman swayed, the hand holding the pistol unsteady. He backed towards the door slowly, eyes wide open in the balaclava slit. Then he went round the corner and out of view. The sounds of the front door opening and closing were clearly audible.

Heck kept the shotgun raised and followed as far as the sitting-room door.

'No!' Kat said, gulping for breath. 'Don't, Dad!'

Heck made sure the street door was firmly closed. 'Right, all of you behind that sofa, heads down. We don't know this is finished. Pete, come with…'

There was a shot from outside, but the house wasn't hit.

Heck went to the front door and lifted the flap of the letter box. 'Jesus,' he said, under his breath. Then he listened as a high-powered motorbike revved and raced away to the east.

Rokeby was already calling for backup and an armed response unit. Heck waited for a couple of minutes, then opened the door. He looked out cautiously, and then went over to the body in the grass on the other side of the road. There was no more gunfire and he lowered the shotgun. When he got to the man who had threatened to kill him, he saw that he was done for. He'd been shot in the neck and the blood was coursing between his fingers. He knelt beside him and pulled off the balaclava.

'Not So Lucky,' he said. 'I thought I recognised your voice.'

Ian Sacker coughed, blood wetting his lips. 'Fuck … you.'

'This was all about your brother? You were going to kill me because the tosser's inside?'

'You … deserve … it,' Not So Lucky panted, then his hand fell away. The blood coursed unimpeded over his chest and on to the grass.

'You were going to kill me in front of my family because of your headbanger of a brother?' Heck said, then he realised. 'It was the Albanians, wasn't it? They put you up to this.' He leaned closer. 'Give me your contact. At least you won't have thrown your life away for nothing.'

Sacker tried to spit in his face but his breath and blood ran out, and he died.

'The Albanians turned *him* into a hit man?' Pete said from behind, in astonishment.

Heck waved Ag and the others back inside. 'Yup. And when he failed, some bastard on a big boy's bike shot him to make sure he kept quiet.' He stood up, keeping hold of the shotgun.

'He was a fuckwit, though,' Pete said. 'Lucky for us.'

Heck nodded, then caught a glimpse of a fast-moving object in the corner of his eye. The motorbike was returning. 'Back to the house!' he said, grabbing Rokeby's arm. Shots from a machine pistol kicked up asphalt and earth as they made it to the front door. Heck slammed it shut and slid the bolts. The roar of the motorbike was followed by the screech of tyres outside.

'Everyone upstairs,' Heck shouted.

The rhomboid window in the front door was smashed and bullets thudded into the carpeted steps. 'Shit! On all fours, into the kitchen, everyone! You too, Pancake. We'll see if we can get out the back.'

'Shouldn't be long till the ARU gets here,' Rokeby said.

Heck grinned at him ruefully. 'We haven't got long. Come on, everyone!' He waited by the sitting-room door as the others crawled to the rear of the house. 'Pancake, we'll try and block the way with the sofas.'

They did their best to manhandle the heavy furniture to the door, but a rattle of shots came through the already broken window.

'Forget it!' Heck said, on his knees. 'Get in the back.'

The two of them made it to the kitchen as more shots drilled across the floor.

'This lunatic isn't giving up,' Rokeby said.

Heck closed the kitchen door. 'That's the problem. From what Joni said, the worst of the Albanians are like the Terminator.' They shoved the table against the door. 'Let's see what's going on outside. Everyone stay on the floor, hands over your heads.' He went to door that led to the garden and opened it slightly. Splinters of wood flew past his face.

'Bloody hell. Either there's more than one of them or he knows exactly what we're doing.' Heck pulled Pancake down. 'Kitchen cutlery drawer's over there. Get the big knives out.'

Ag looked up. 'Heck, why don't we wait for the other officers?'

'Because we aren't going to be allowed to. He or they have made enough noise to wake up even the doddery old couple down the road.' He smiled reassuringly at the kids. 'You two, in the larder with Granddad. Go on, now! Lock the door and get on the floor. Don't worry, it'll be all right. Ag, you too.'

'No chance. You need all the help you can get.'

A fusillade of shots came through the windows and they were sprayed with glass and wood fragments. Fortunately no one was hit in the face.

'How about playing dead?' Pete said. 'Then we nail him when he comes in to make sure.'

'Aye, good idea.' Heck looked at the gashes on the backs of his hands. 'But we need more blood.'

Ag opened a low cupboard and took out a plastic bottle of tomato ketchup.

'Genius,' Heck said, as she slid it across the debris-littered floor. He squirted it on his head and upper chest, then passed it to his colleague.

'How are we going to get him?' Pete asked, when he was equally drenched.

'Leave that to me,' Ag said. She waited until another blast of shots came, then scrambled on to the Raeburn. It was only a foot from the back door. Above the stove hung a row of long-handled, cast-iron saucepans.

'You realise that if there's more than one, we're dead,' Heck said.

'Thanks for pointing that out.' Ag pressed her back against the wall and took down a heavy frying pan.

There were more shots, this time through the door. Heck and Pete lay still as they were spattered by more splinters. Then there was a light step outside and the door was pushed slowly open. Heck knew this was the worst moment. If the killer decided to shoot them in the head before coming any further, at least it would be a quick death.

But he didn't do that. Looking down at Heck and Pete, a machine pistol in his hand, the young man in the tatty German army jacket and black motorbike helmet seemed satisfied. Then came a loud thud as Ag played a perfect square cut against the right side of his head. The machine pistol dropped to the floor and the gunman crashed sideways. He was pulled down by Heck and Pete, the latter holding a carving knife to his throat below the helmet.

The sound of a siren came closer up the road. Heck grabbed the machine pistol and waited to see if anyone else took the plunge. As uniformed officers ran around the house and entered it from front and rear, he realised that, after Not So Lucky Sacker, the partially conscious man on the kitchen floor had been their sole attacker.

'And what's the moral of all that, Pancake?' Heck said, as he helped Ag down and embraced her. 'Women. Don't go up against them.'

'You'd better not.' Ag nudged her husband in the ribs and went to get the kids and David.

Heck shook his head in admiration. Then he realised two things. One, his belly hurt like hell but, two, he'd lost his fear. This time he didn't think it would be back.

<hr>

142

Victoria Favon was at the kitchen window.

'Andrew!' she cried. 'Come here, now!'

Her husband arrived, newspaper hanging from his hand.

'Evie managed to get out of the window. She's in the tower.'

The paper fell to the floor.

'What?'

'Don't just stand there, you fool!'

Andrew was looking out of the window. 'I shouldn't worry. The Hilux is there. Dan will handle her.'

'That's what I'm afraid of. Get over there immediately.' As he reached the door, she added, 'And take your shotgun. You saw how distraught Dan was about the dogs. God knows what he might do. I don't care about the slut you've been fattening up or that oaf of a farmer, but I'd prefer Evie to remain alive.'

'I don't suppose you're coming with me.'

'You don't suppose correctly. I'm going to talk to our Albanian friends. We need professional help.'

'For heaven's sake, Victoria, we owe them enough already.'

'Get over there!'

Lord Favon beat a retreat.

Lady Favon went to her bedroom and called the number she'd been given. She smiled when she was told that a man was already in the vicinity.

143

From the floor Joni looked at the others when the shooting stopped. By some miracle she hadn't been hit. Her mother was clutching her right shoulder, while Morrie Simmons was on his back, blood oozing from several chest wounds. Moonbeam stared at her in agony and Joni put her finger to her lips. The ARU and backup would arrive soon. Two things occurred to her. The shooter, who must have a machine pistol or an automatic rifle, was the real thing compared with Marcus Ainsworth. And, being a pro, he was going to make sure that at least she was dead. As she crawled towards Ainsworth's pistol, she had another thought. Maybe there was more than one of them. She glanced at Morrie. He was breathing, but he'd been hit by at least three bullets. She called 999 and directed an ambulance to the cottage. Then she waited for their assailant. He was a Popi, she was sure.

There was a shadow at the window. Joni waited until it darkened, catching sight of a stocky man in black leather jacket and cap. She was behind the door so he couldn't see her, but the comatose Ainsworth, her mother and Morrie were visible enough. She heard a metallic object hit the paving stones outside the window and then the slap of another magazine being loaded. She'd been on a firearms course at the Met, but it had only been to familiarise officers with the weapons they would come up against – specialist firearms units did the actual shooting. There was a small lever on the right side above the butt of the pistol that Ainsworth had dropped. She pushed it down to reveal a green dot. She was surprised he had the safety applied, but what bothered her now was whether there was a round in the chamber. She bet there would be, moved out of cover and emptied the magazine at the window. The noise made her ears ring and at first she couldn't tell if her shots had provoked a similar response. Grabbing the garden fork, she crawled to the front door and stretched up to open it slightly. There was the roar of a car heading away to the right of the cottage. Had she actually scared off the bastard?

Then Joni made out another sound – the wail of a siren. She let out a gasp of relief and looked outside. There was blood on the grass beyond the paving stones. She had hit the shooter at least once.

'Are you all right, ma'am?' said a constable, who came running towards her.

'Yes.' She got to her feet and dropped the empty pistol. 'If any of you guys know first aid, there are three wounded people inside – but don't waste your time on the one in restraints. I've already called an ambulance.'

Three more uniforms arrived, one of them a sergeant. She gave him a brief run-down of what had happened. Then a black van appeared and men in combat fatigues jumped out. The Armed Response Team leader came over.

'Chief Inspector Bonnett,' he said, glancing into the house.

Joni introduced herself and told him what had happened.

'Do you have any idea where he might be heading, DI Pax?'

'I imagine he'll be going back to Newcastle. The Albanians are there in numbers.'

'We haven't got much to go on,' Bonnett, 'given you didn't see his vehicle. I'll liaise with uniform about closing off the roads in the vicinity.'

Joni nodded and left him with the sergeant. She went inside the cottage. One of the officers was kneeling by Morrie Simmons, head close to his chest. He looked up as she drew close and pursed his lips.

'He's been hit badly, ma'am. I'm doing what I can, but let's hope the paramedics get here soon.'

Joni knelt down on the other side. 'Come on, Morrie,' she said. 'Stay with us.'

He blinked, his breathing rapid. 'Sorry … Jack … fucking … hell…' His voice trailed away.

Joni looked up and saw that his eyes had closed.

There was a pounding of boots as the paramedics arrived. They took charge immediately. Joni stepped back and went to her mother.

'Is he…' Moonbeam choked.

'He's still alive, I think,' Joni said, looking at the wound in her mother's shoulder. 'We need attention here too.'

One of the paramedics, a short young woman, raised her head and took in Moonbeam's condition. 'I'll be with you in a minute.' She was attaching a drip to Morrie's wrist.

'Hold on, Mother.' Her phone rang and she went outside.

'Joni, thank fuck.' Heck sounded desperate. 'You OK?'

'I am, yes.' She told him about Ainsworth, and what had happened to Morrie Simmons and her mother.

'They tried to get me as well,' he said. 'Thanks to Ag and Pancake, we're all OK. The brother of an evil fucker I put away was going to kill me with a shotgun in front of the family.'

'Jesus Christ, Heck.'

'Someone – an Albanian, I'm guessing – took him out and nearly did for the rest of us. He's got a serious concussion. What happened to your second shooter?'

'He drove off to the west. Could be miles away by now and I didn't see the vehicle.'

'OK, hold fast. I'll talk to the ACC and see if the helicopter's available. We might pick your gunman up if he's driving like a lunatic.'

Looking to the right, Joni made up her mind. 'I've got to go. See you later, Heck.' It was only as she cut the connection that she realised she'd called her boss by his first name twice. She'd resisted doing so when she was at his house despite Ag's stipulation. She watched as one of the paramedics and a uniformed officer carried Morrie, another holding up the drip. Her mother followed, a blanket round her and the female paramedic leading her by her good arm.

'Joni, you'll … you'll follow … us to the hospital?' Moonbeam sobbed.

'I'll be there,' Joni said, squeezing her mother's wrist.

'We'll secure the scene, ma'am,' the sergeant said.

'Such as it is after we've stomped all over it,' Joni replied. 'Do what you can. I need to go to the hospital.'

Back down the lane, Joni got into the Land Rover and checked the map. Just as she'd thought, if she carried on past the turn-off to her mother's cottage, she'd reach Favon Hall in about ten minutes. Something was going on there, but she knew Heck would forbid her to approach without approval from Mrs Normal. By the time a team was organised, it could be too late. She was sure Suzana Noli and Oliver Forrest were there – perhaps even Michael Etherington. She also reckoned the gunman was on his way to the Favons.

She drove past the cottage turn-off, seeing CI Bonnett turn and stare. He would pass on the direction she'd headed when asked. It was the opposite to that taken by the ambulance, but there were plenty of junctions between here and the Hall. She picked up her phone and turned it off.

Joni felt as if some strange power was directing her. She didn't usually feel this way before cases broke. Then again, she wasn't usually the target of two hit men in one afternoon.

144

Suzana heard the roar of an engine and the rattle of gravel. Then there was a clang as the door below opened. She listened to the ascending footsteps. Would they stop at the man below or come straight to her? She thought of putting the knife up her sleeve, but it would be seen if she was forced to strip, so she left it where it was. The footsteps stopped and then started again almost immediately. Suzana took a series of deep breaths, remembering what she had done to Leka and the others in the slave house. She had a flash of the mountains around her village, the forests and the high pastures, then shook her head. There was no going back. She had to find a new world, and dealing with her latest captor was the beginning of it.

The sound of heavy boots grew louder. Suzana considered

standing by the door and trying to wrest the shock pole from the pig, but decided that it would be better if she let him come close. She could do the most damage if she looked like she was beaten. She sat on the bed, her shoulders and head down. When the key rattled in the lock, she relaxed, her breathing even and her heart rate steady. Let him come.

The door burst inwards and the pole appeared, followed by the masked man. He shouted at her. She didn't know the words, but she understood what he wanted – his eyes, wild as a rutting boar's, were on her body. She took off her clothes slowly. She left her pants on – they were grey and over-sized, not in the least sexy, and her captor signalled to her to take them off, the pole wavering as he stepped closer. She stepped out of them and flicked them away coquettishly with one foot. The pole was laid down and a hand grabbed her left breast. She moaned and that made him breathe heavily. He came closer, both hands now on her breasts. Suzana sighed and moved her hand downwards. Then she tugged the knife out of herself, pressed the blade forward and slashed at the thin strip of skin beneath the woollen mask. As he staggered back, gasping, she bent down and picked up the pole. She hit him on the hand and then the head, unsure if the shock was as effective through clothing. He jerked backwards, one hand to his throat, blood spilling between his fingers. Suzana used the pole to drive him towards the bathroom. He stumbled against the step and fell backwards, his head striking the rim of the toilet. He lay still. She shoved his legs into the small room and turned to go. Then she was overwhelmed by curiosity. What did the pig look like? She squatted over her captor, knife held forward. Then she pulled off the mask and gasped. The pig in black was a woman – middle-aged, heavy and unattractive. Her hair was brown and greasy. The bitch. Suzana slammed the metal door shut and slid the exterior bolts. She dropped to her knees, panting. She was free.

When she got her breath back, Suzana dressed and put the knife in her trouser pocket. The pig had a larger knife in a sheath on her belt, but she wasn't going to open the door to grab it. Her former captor might be pretending to be unconscious.

Suzana took the shock pole and ran out on to the narrow landing. Before she went down the worn stone steps, she removed the keys from the door. She glanced at the stone walls. What was this? A castle? She banged on the door.

'Hel-lo?' she called softly. Maybe there were more pigs nearby. 'Hel-lo? I op-en.' She drew the bolts and tried the keys in the lock. Finally one turned. She swung the door inwards, holding on to the handle.

'Hel-lo?'

At first she didn't see anyone. The bathroom door was open, so she assumed the captive was hiding in there. Then she saw movement to her left. A big man was coming at her. She raised the pole and hit him on the hand. He yelled. Then she touched him again, this time on the neck. He fell back and lay motion-less. She looked at his face and recognised him – the man who had jumped on her from the sow bike, the pig who had ripped at her clothes. She retreated, pulling the door to and locking it.

Suzana wiped the sweat from her face and went down the steps, holding the pole in front of her. She could smell cool, fresh air. This time she really was free.

Then she heard a man outside shout and her hopes turned to dust. A second later, she was confronted by a young woman with short brown hair. In her hands she held a metal object like the shock pole she herself was carrying.

They stared at each other, motionless as the shouting came nearer.

145

'Andrew!' Michael Etherington had yelled several times.

Lord Favon finally turned to him, his eyes widening. For once he wasn't wearing a hat and his bald patch glinted in the sinking sun.

'Michael? What are you doing? Put that bloody rifle down.'

'No, Andrew. The shotgun, on the gravel. Now!'

'I … oh, all right.' Favon complied, standing up again with his face red. 'What the hell's the meaning of this? Was it you who shot Reston's dogs? Why are you dressed like a bloody soldier?'

The general walked closer. 'Because that's what I am. You think I stopped when I retired? I'm fighting a new war now.'

'Don't be ridiculous, man. Who's the enemy?'

'Your friends, the Albanians.'

'What?'

Michael looked beyond him. 'It's all right, Evie,' he said, picking up the shotgun. 'Who's your friend?'

The two young women stared at him, then the one in ill-fitting clothes dropped the cattle prod and rushed at Andrew Favon, raking his face with her nails and screaming words in a language that Etherington recognised, even though he couldn't speak much. The pair collapsed and the woman stayed on top. Suddenly there was a small blade in her hand and she started slashing at Favon's head and neck.

Evie seemed to have been turned into a statue, her eyes fixed on the spectacle in front of her. Michael Etherington went over and handed her the shotgun after checking that it was loaded.

'You know how to use this?'

Evie twitched and came back to herself. 'Yes.'

'Cover me while I sort this out.' The general put down his rifle, stepped forward and grabbed the woman by the scruff of her neck, knocking the knife from her hand. Then he told her to stand still and be calm– that much he could say in Albanian. He pulled Andrew Favon to his feet and examined his wounds. There was a lot of blood, but he couldn't see any serious cuts.

'Come on,' he said, 'let's go to the Hall. Victoria will clean you up.'

Favon didn't reply. He looked like he was in shock.

'What happened, Evie?' Michael asked, as they went to the back of the Hall.

'I … I don't know. The girl was in the tower, I think she'd been locked up. Why did she do that to my father?'

'Not sure. Anyone else in there?'

'I don't know. I met her on her way down. She was holding that cattle prod. I spoke to her, though I'm not sure she understood. She was worried about my crutch until she realised what it was. She was scared by the shouting.'

The general glanced at the young woman. She looked in control of herself now, but he'd seen the frenzy on her face when she attacked Favon. He knew why as well, but he wasn't going to tell Evie. He'd seen her run out of the brothel on Sunday night. She was Suzana, the murder suspect the police had been looking for. It was obvious that Andrew had been a customer, no doubt a demanding one.

The basement door opened.

'What on earth's happened?' Victoria Favon demanded. 'Andrew, are you all right? What are you doing with that shotgun, Evie? Give it to me immediately.'

'So you can lock me up again? No, thanks.'

'Lock you up?' Michael said. He looked at Victoria. 'Is this true?'

'Don't intrude in family matters. How dare you shoot Dan's dogs?'

The general's jaw jutted forward. 'Because they were about to rip my throat out. Besides, these aren't just your family matters, they're mine too. What did you do to Nick?'

Victoria took a step back. 'To Nick? Nothing whatsoever.'

'Let's go inside,' Michael said. 'Evie's tired and your man's about to collapse.'

'My man!' Lady Favon said scathingly.

146

Ruth Dickie was not happy, primarily with herself. Although no one could have predicted there would be assassination attempts on DCI Rutherford and DI Pax, she knew how dangerous the Albanians were. The second man at Heck's house wasn't talking, but he was swarthy – Ag Rutherford's word – with curly black hair. She was pretty sure he was one of them. If Richard Lennox or one of his sidekicks arrived to represent him, that would clinch it.

She should also have listened to Joni Pax. Her suspicions about the Favons had seemed fantastical, but she'd kept beavering away. The ACC would be recommending to the chief constable that a warrant to search the Hall and other premises on the estate be sought.

'Cup of tea, dear?' her husband asked.

'I'm working,' she said, in a steel voice.

After he'd closed the door behind her, Ruth Dickie rested her head on a hand. Today could have been a disaster. She was lucky the casualty count was so low. How had the Albanians discovered so much about her officers? She had a suspect in mind – DCI Young. Although he hadn't yet been caught in contact with them, she was sure he was taking their money. Tomorrow morning she would squeeze him until he leaked blood.

The Force helicopter was on its way to Favon Hall, along with the armed unit that had been at Joni Pax's mother's cottage. It was clear to her that DI Pax had gone to the Hall on the assumption that the gunman who had escaped was headed there. What worried her most was that Joni wasn't answering her mobile. She was a good detective, but she was rash. That could have got her into very deep water indeed.

The ACC called Heck Rutherford. She was concerned he would be having a reaction to what he'd been through – she had seen something approaching fear in his eyes in the weeks since he came back to work. When she told him of her concern, he said he would set off immediately for Favon Hall with Pancake Rokeby.

Ruth Dickie hadn't known the DS's nickname. Maybe a girl-friend had given it to him.

<hr>

147

There was no one in the estate's outer fields as it was Sunday. It took Joni seven minutes to reach the ornamental gate to Favon Hall, having forced two cars into the ditches that lined the narrow road. There was a pair of cones across the entrance, but she ran the Land Rover over them without braking. The long driveway meandered between lines of copper and silver beeches so thick that the light was almost shut out. Then she came into the open to the left of the Hall. There was no sign of any other cars. The medieval tower was to the rear on her right, the red Hilux parked outside the building's open door. Joni considered going there, but decided against it. The tower looked like it was ready to collapse. She saw vehicles at the front of the Hall – Lady Favon's sports car and her husband's red Land Cruiser. There was no sign of the black 4×4. As she got nearer, she realised that the wheels on the nearside of both vehicles had burst. When she got out of the Land Rover, she saw the spatter of shotgun pellets. Her heart began to beat more quickly.

The main door was open. Joni went up the steps and into the entrance hall. Standing still, she listened but there was no sound of people. Joni could see the sitting room where she, Heck and Pete Rokeby had interviewed the aristocrats, but there was no one in there. She checked the other rooms on the ground floor – dining room, kitchen, study, breakfast room, TV room, unim-pressive picture gallery, and the magnificent old library – but there was no sign of anyone. She went down the stairs behind a green baize-covered door and past a laundry room. Beyond it most of the rooms were filled with dusty old furniture and junk. Then she came to a door that led outside. It was half open. She looked down and noticed drops of blood on the step outside. Turning round, she saw more on the passage she had walked along.

'Shit,' she said. She'd potentially contaminated a crime scene. She went back the way she'd come, keeping close to the wall. The drops grew less frequent, as if a bandage or the like had been applied.

Back on the ground floor, Joni ran up the wide staircase. She took in the large portraits on the walls showing heavy, self-satisfied men in the clothes of days gone by, medals and other decorations on their frock coats and swords at their belts. In the background of each painting were fields and plantations. Looking closer, she saw the bent bodies of black men and women, the former wearing nothing but loincloths and the latter in white dresses and headbands. Each portrait's subject had a table in front of him, bearing a tea service with an especially large sugar bowl heaped high with white grains. Sugar – the gold of the Caribbean and source of Britain's empire. Joni knew enough about history to make that connection. She took in the haughty faces again – slave traders, exploiters, thieves. The Hall had an unhealthy air and she felt her lungs constrict.

She stopped on the landing and listened. She could hear voices coming down a corridor. The walls were pale pink, with elaborately carved doors and frames on either side. As she approached the open door at the end, there came a scream that turned into heart-rending sobs. Joni remembered the screwdriver in her pocket and grabbed it.

'No!' came a woman's voice. 'For God's sake, no!'

Joni entered the room and took in the scene. There were five people in the sitting area by the high window looking over the garden to the edge of the moor. To the right was a large bed. Andrew Favon had a towel over his head, and another round his neck. The skin on his face and forehead was torn and there was a lot of blood. He was breathing heavily.

'DI Pax,' said Michael Etherington. 'Just the person.' The muzzle of his hunting rifle was against the side of Victoria Favon's head. She looked terrified, but her expression quickly changed.

'Put down the weapon, sir,' Joni said, aware that the screwdriver made her look ridiculous. 'You do the same with the shotgun, Ms Favon, please.'

Neither complied. She examined the thin figure in outsize clothes crouching beside an armchair.

'Suzana?' she said. 'Suzana Noli?'

The young woman looked at her blankly and then gave her a weak smile. 'Pax? Jo-ni Pax?'

'Are you all right?' Joni asked, in Italian. 'We've been looking for you everywhere.'

Suzana replied in ungrammatical Italian, speaking quickly. Joni glanced at the others. The general was still aiming the rifle at Lady Favon, while her daughter had gone to Lord Favon. At first Joni thought she was going to comfort him. Instead, Evie put a hand in his jacket pocket and took out several orange cartridges. She slipped two of them into the shotgun she had broken, then snapped it shut and pointed it at her mother. Eventually Suzana stopped talking and ran the back of a hand over her lips.

'What did she say?' Evie asked.

Joni shook her head. 'That she was attacked by a man on the moor, who is locked in a room in the tower, as she was. There's also a middle-aged and, in her words, "ugly and fat" woman in the bathroom.'

'Cheryl,' Evie said. 'I saw her go in, but I thought it was Dan. She was wearing a balaclava.'

Joni nodded. 'Suzana was brought to the tower by a heavy-shouldered man with a moustache. He had two large and vicious dogs.' She looked at Lord Favon. 'That would have been Dan Reston. You didn't take him to Newcastle train station, did you?'

Favon mumbled something incomprehensible.

'Who's the man in the tower?' Joni asked.

Lady Favon had recovered her poise. 'Oliver Forrest. My husband's been at loggerheads with him for years. He finally lost his cool.'

'Vick!' Andrew gasped. 'What … what are you saying?'

'He had that Albanian tart under lock and key too.' Lady Favon laughed harshly. 'Pampering her so he could do the things to her that I stopped letting him do to me years ago.' She moved her head against the rifle muzzle. 'Michael, now there's a police officer here, perhaps you would consider removing the weapon?'

General Etherington gave that some thought and said, 'No. Not until you've answered my questions.'

'And mine,' Evie said, limping forward.

Joni had gone to Suzana and helped her to an armchair. She saw a carafe of water on an antique table and filled a glass for the young woman. She smiled at her and then turned to the others.

'The weapons,' she said. 'Please lower them.'

The general looked at her and nodded. He put the rifle on the floor behind him. Evie did the same with the shotgun and went to sit on the window seat.

'Thank you,' Joni said. 'Lord Favon, are you badly injured?'

'Only flesh wounds,' he said, with more spirit than she'd have expected.

Joni looked around the well-appointed room. 'Why are you here rather than downstairs?'

'My daughter's idea,' Victoria said suavely. 'She thinks there are hidden secrets in my room.'

'Well, aren't there?' Evie shouted. She turned to Joni. 'I heard them lie to you about the Restons.' She let out a sob. 'And I heard her say she had sex with Nick.'

'Before you were with him, darling.'

'Let's talk about Nick,' Michael Etherington said. 'He's why I'm here. I knew you had an affair with him, Victoria. He told me. Fortunately he soon got over it.'

Lady Favon's carefully made-up face clenched.

'But you wanted him again when he started visiting Evie, didn't you?' The general stepped closer. 'Didn't you?'

'Calm down, Michael. And what if I did?'

'You wanted to take him from me,' Evie said, her voice breaking. 'You … you couldn't stand … to see me happy.'

'You were in the Suzuki that drove Nick off the road, weren't you, Victoria?' the general said.

Lady Favon looked at Joni. 'Shouldn't you be asking the questions, Detective Inspector?'

'I think he's doing an excellent job,' Joni said, wondering how Michael Etherington had found out who was in the 4×4.

'Who killed him?' the general yelled. 'You weren't driving. Was that bastard Reston at the wheel?'

Victoria Favon looked down. 'Yes, he was. I just wanted to teach Nick a lesson. I stopped him after he left Evie that night and told him how much I wanted him. The impudent boy told me that he loved Evie and, besides, I was too old for him.'

'Teach Nick a lesson?' Michael repeated. 'By running him off the road? You could have killed him straight off.'

'Dan said it was soft ground there.'

The general's face was red. 'So who took the rock and smashed the life out of him?'

'Certainly not me.'

'There were prints from size ten Adipower baseball boots,' Joni said. 'I'd say Reston was wearing them.'

'Thank you, DI Pax,' Victoria Favon said.

'But you didn't stop him,' Etherington said, his spittle flecking her face. 'Perhaps you even incited him.'

'I didn't have to, Michael. Dan Reston's been jealous of the men I've been involved with for years – ever since I stopped seeing him.'

Lord Favon's head dropped, while Evie gasped in disgust.

'He's impotent after his prostate operation,' Joni said. 'Did that make him even angrier?'

'Indeed it did.' Lady Favon smiled gratefully.

Joni caught her gaze. 'At the very least you're guilty of aiding and abetting a murderer,' she said.

'In that case, so is my husband. He was very keen that something happen to Nick. The boy recognised him at the brothel in Corham on Sunday night, despite the ghastly wig he was wearing.'

Joni nodded; it was as she had suspected. 'How do you know all this?' she asked the general.

'I have a reliable source.'

'The bugger who's been blackmailing me?' Andrew Favon asked, raising his head.

'Correct,' Michael said. 'You're both in well over your heads and you're going to pay for it.'

Joni had a good idea who the blackmailer was. She looked at Lady Favon, remembering the research she'd done. 'You knew soon after you were married that Lord Favon was infertile.'

'Before, as a matter of fact. I didn't care. The deal was that I produce an heir to the title – it didn't matter who the sperm donor was.' Victoria Favon smiled sadly. 'Evie's father was a pleasant if dim electrician but after that nothing stuck, so to speak. It wasn't for lack of trying, I can assure you.'

'You wanted a male heir,' Joni said.

'Needed one, more like,' Victoria said, glancing at her daughter. 'I'm sorry, darling, but you won't inherit. Some lumberjack in Ontario will be the next Lord Favon unless I can get pregnant.'

'You won't have much chance of that in prison,' Evie said, surprisingly calm.

'Anything's possible if you know the right people.'

'And if you have the money,' Joni said. 'But you're in trouble financially, aren't you?' She looked at Andrew Favon.

'Don't ask me,' he said, head down again. 'I only sign the cheques.'

Michael Etherington was staring at Lady Favon. 'It was you, wasn't it? You were the one who got in with the Albanians.'

She shrugged. 'Something had to be done. The estate's been

haemorrhaging money for years. The financial crash was a disaster for us. The Albanians…'

The stutter of machine-pistol fire made Joni dive to the side. Suzana and Evie also hit the carpet, but Victoria sat perfectly still. Plaster fell from the ceiling in snow-like flakes.

'There you are,' the lady of the house said. 'Couldn't you have made an appearance earlier?'

The man in the black leather jacket and cap smiled. There was a bandage round his upper left arm. Joni realised he was the one whose shots had hit her mother and Morrie Simmons.

Lady Favon twitched her lips. 'What are you going to do with these miserable creatures?'

'Kill them, of course.' The gunman's English was precise, the accent neutral and almost robotic. 'The police officer Pax has already escaped death twice today. The whore Suzana Noli should be fucked to death, but there isn't time for that. No doubt more police are on the way. I presume you want me to kill your man.' He glanced at Lord Favon, who was staring at him, mouth agape.

Victoria Favon's brow furrowed. 'Do you have a better idea?'

'In normal circumstances, he would be a useful hostage – to make sure you deliver the profits on our investment as you promised. But this is an exceptional situation and…' The Albanian broke off and gave the viscountess a slack smile. 'And you are not a normal mother.'

Something in the tone of his voice alerted both Joni and Lady Favon. The latter stood up and moved towards him.

'Stop,' he said, pointing the gun at her. 'You are not at all a normal person. You are unreliable and you know too much.'

Victoria screamed but, before her killer could pull the trigger, there was a single, loud shot. As the Albanian fell back, a gaping wound in his chest, the machine pistol moved to his right. An oblique line of wounds ran from Michael Etherington's right shoulder to the left of his groin. He crashed to the floor and didn't move again.

Evie and her mother shrieked, while Lord Favon sat motionless. But Suzana was smiling as she got to her feet.

'He was a Popi,' she said, in Italian. 'They all deserve death.'

The distant sound of a siren cut through the ringing in Joni's ears. Backup had arrived and it was too late. Or was it?

※※※※※※※※※※※※※※※※※※※※※※※※※※※※※※※※※※※※※

148

The Armed Response Unit had been delayed behind a car that had swerved off the narrow road and blocked it. Heck and Pancake arrived as they finished pushing it into the ditch, the driver waving his arms like he was sending an irate message in semaphore.

'Where's that fucking helicopter?' Heck said, as he drove past the ARU van, holding up his warrant card.

'On its way from Sunderland. Boy racers in a stolen Merc.'

'Brilliant.' He drove over a couple of crushed bollards into the Favon estate and slammed the accelerator to the floor.

'Sir!' Rokeby yelled. 'Let's get there in one piece.'

'Shut up, Pancake. Joni's up there with a houseful of maniacs.'

'Ah, my shoulder!'

'Take it like a man. Nearly there.'

Heck swung across the drive, gravel spraying all over the place. 'Come on!'

They ran towards the main entrance of the Hall. As they got to the top of the steps, Evie Favon appeared, her face pale and her limp more pronounced.

'Where's Joni?' Heck yelled. 'DI Pax?'

Evie shrugged listlessly.

'She's with that Albanian whore,' Lady Favon said, putting on a leather coat.

'Pancake, look after the ladies. Make sure they stay here.'

Victoria Favon sighed and Evie laughed bitterly.

'How do, my lord?' Heck said, as he ran into the drawing room. 'Jesus, what happened to you?'

'Eh? Whisky and soda?'

'Where are they?' Heck yelled.

'What? Oh, upstairs, last room on the right.'

Heck took two steps at a time, feeling fitter than he had since his operation. This was about Joni. She was what mattered. He pounded down the pink walled hallway, realising as he got closer to the open door that there was a strong smell of gunsmoke.

'Fuck!' he said, slowing to turn into the room.

The bodies were sprawled in a welter of blood.

'No!' he screamed. 'Joni? No!'

<hr />

149

'This way,' Joni said, leading Suzana along the passage to the basement stairs. She opened the door. A dark blue BMW was parked near the house, presumably the assassin's. About two hundred yards beyond, there was a thick line of trees.

'You go first,' Joni said, in Italian. She felt for the Albanian girl, but she didn't want to sacrifice her career. 'I'll pretend I'm chasing you in case anyone sees us.'

Suzana nodded and hared away. Joni gave her ten seconds and followed, not running as fast as she could, but making it look as if she was. Once she reached the trees, she saw Suzana waiting.

'We don't have much time,' Joni said. 'Listen to me. I know how dangerous it would be for you in prison and I think you were right to do what you did to those bastards in the brothel.'

'Slave house,' said Suzana.

Joni looked into her grey eyes, bottomless pools of pain. 'You were right to defend yourselves against the fools in the park, too. And against the piece of shit with the motorbike. I'm so sorry for everything that's happened to you.' She glanced back towards the house. There was no one in the vicinity.

'I see your photo in newspaper,' Suzana said, smiling shyly. 'You are more beautiful in real.'

Joni's heart broke, but she concealed it. If Suzana was to get away and survive, the girl – because that was what she was – had to stay tough. She took out her wallet and handed over all the cash. 'Stay away from big cities. Use the public libraries to learn English.' She let out a sob. 'Oh, Suzana, I wish I could help you more.'

'Is all right,' the Albanian said. 'I can look after me.' She smiled again. 'I will become great businesswoman, you will see. Not any more slave.'

Joni nodded, her eyes damp, and leaned forward to embrace Suzana. Then she watched the slim form move through the trees until she disappeared in the gloom. Did Suzana have a chance of staying below her countrymen's radar? If so, it wouldn't be much of one.

When she returned to the back of the Hall, she turned on her phone. She had missed numerous calls and it immediately started ringing. There was also a text from Mrs Normal: 'Do NOT go 2 Favon Hall.' Too late for that. She put the device on the floor as if she'd lost it and went upstairs. The entrance hall was full of people, including several ARU men; Pete Rokeby, who gave her a huge smile; and Heck Rutherford, who ran towards her with surprising speed and grabbed her in a tight hug.

150

Heck set about organising a search for the people Joni told him about. Because there may have been other armed men around – Albanians, Dan Reston, friends of General Etherington – the ARU took the lead. They found Cheryl Reston in the small bathroom on the top floor of the tower and Oliver Forrest in the room below. The former had lost a lot of blood, but was sta-bilised by paramedics, while the latter was still jittery from the touch of the cattle prod.

'What the hell happened, Ollie?' Heck asked.

'You won't believe me when I tell you.' The farmer described his experiences in the darkened room – the woman who covered him, as he put it, the way she stood on her head afterwards; the bastard in the balaclava who had cuffed him to the bed and jabbed him with the prod; the crazy-eyed girl who had used it on him before he was rescued

'You know who the woman was?'

Ollie Forrest looked at the Hall and the grounds. 'Lady Vicky, eh?'

'Looks like it. Apparently she was desperate for a kid.'

The farmer laughed. 'Well, she won't have got any little swim-mers from me. Lizzie made me have a vasectomy a couple of years back.'

Heck sent him to the paramedics for a check-up, then allowed him home. He'd ask him what he was doing on his quad bike on Lord Favon's side of the moor, and why Suzana laid into him, another day.

His radio crackled. 'CI Bonnett here. We've surrounded the Dower House. I'm watching Dan Reston through the window. You'd better get down here.'

Pancake Rokeby was sitting outside the entrance to the Hall with Joni Pax. Heck waved to them. Seconds later they were in the Land Rover, Joni driving it deftly down an unmetalled road. The ARU van was blocking it, about fifty yards from the old building. An armed operative guided them to the team com-mander's location.

'Take a look,' Bonnett said, handing Heck his binoculars.

The image was blurred and Heck rolled his finger over the focus wheel. 'Jesus!' he said. 'Has he had a bath in blood? Are those bodies he's got his arms round?'

'Dobermans, as far as I can tell,' the CI said. 'He's crying.'

'Wonder what happened to them,' Pete said.

'The general shot them this morning,' Joni said. She'd been speaking to Evie Favon. 'Apparently they were about to rip his throat out.'

'Gary Frizzell,' Heck said.

Joni nodded. 'I think Lady Favon got the Albanians to bring him out here.'

'Maybe he was in the tower before Ollie.' Heck told them what the farmer had said. 'We'll need to question Reston and his wife – if she survives – to find out what happened.'

'Another victim of Suzana Noli,' Pete said.

Heck looked at Joni. 'You reckon?'

She raised her shoulders. 'No more than she deserved since she and her husband locked Suzana up.'

Heck and Rokeby exchanged glances.

'The helicopter's trying to locate her, you know,' Heck said.

Joni took the binoculars from him. 'It'll be dark soon.'

Shortly afterwards, the ACU went in. Dan Reston hardly registered their arrival. He struggled briefly when he was separated from the dogs, then allowed himself to be taken outside.

'You killed Nick Etherington,' Joni said, leaning towards him.

Reston's eyes were wide and bloodshot. He looked as if he was many galaxies away.

It didn't take them long to find the evidence. A six-inch-wide stone in a plastic bag had been stuffed behind cans of food on a shelf in the filthy kitchen. There was blood on it, and visible fingerprints. Pete Rokeby opened the fridge.

'Fuck!' he said, swerving away.

Heck and Joni took deep breaths and opened the door wider.

The head, on its side, and hands were on a platter on the top shelf. Despite the loose skin and agonised expression, there was no doubt that the head, at least, belonged to Gary Frizzell. Fingerprints would show whether the hands did too.

'Whose else would they be?' Pete asked, his face pale.

'In this hellhole, anything's possible,' Heck said. 'Right, out. The SOCOs are in charge here now.'

It was almost full dark by the time they got back to the Hall. A powder blue Mercedes was parked as near the steps as the driver could get. Heck and Joni went into the drawing room. A uniformed WPC was at the door.

'Ah, DCI Rutherford,' said the tall man sitting next to Lady Favon. His hair swept back from his patrician features in blonde waves.

'Mr Lennox,' Heck replied. 'Not a surprise to see you.'

'Ha! I take it this is the famous DI Pax.' He stood up and ran an appraising eye over Joni. She ignored the hand he extended.

'Terrible day,' the lawyer said, resuming his seat. 'By the way, I'm representing Neritan Dibra, the man who was hit on the head at your house. I do hope he isn't seriously injured.'

Heck took a deep breath. When he spoke, his voice was low and controlled. 'They came into my house, him and that bird-brain Ian Sacker. You represented his brother. This is personal now. My wife and kids, let alone my old man, aren't targets for your fucking clients, you...'

'That'll do, Detective Chief Inspector.'

All eyes turned to ACC Dickie. She was wearing full dress uniform, braided hat under her arm. She regarded Richard Lennox with undisguised disdain.

'I understand Lady Favon is an important client, but you might need to revise your priorities.'

'Why would I do that?' the lawyer asked, with a wide smile.

'Because DCI Lee Young is currently being questioned by officers from Professional Standards. He's being extremely cooperative.'

Richard Lennox's smile disappeared. He leaned over to Victoria Favon and whispered to her, before getting up and leaving.

Mrs Normal beckoned to Heck and Joni to follow her. They went into a huddle in the entrance hall.

'I gather Michael Etherington has been killed,' the ACC said.

'Yes, ma'am,' replied Joni. 'He shot the Albanian assassin then was hit himself. Suzana Noli told me the man was a Popi. He was going to kill Lady Favon.'

'Interesting. The Albanian connection is going to take a lot of working out.' She gave a fleeting smile. 'But Lee Young's spilling his guts, as I believe the Americans say.'

Heck was impressed, Joni less so.

'We should have searched these premises and the estate days ago, ma'am.' There was little respect in her tone.

'That's as may be, DI Pax. I appreciate your work today and I understand your mother was injured, but you acted irresponsibly by coming here on your own and out of contact. Plus, you let the Albanian girl go.'

'Excuse me, ma'am,' Heck said. 'That isn't the case. I saw Suzana...'

'Noli,' Joni supplied.

'Aye, her ... I was at a back window down the corridor and I saw her run like a hare into the woods behind the kitchen garden. Joni ... DI Pax made a valiant effort to catch up with her, but she couldn't manage it. Once the Albanian was in the trees, there was nothing she could do.'

Ruth Dickie gave him a searching look. 'Very well. I'll expect to read that in both your reports. DI Pax, you should go and check on your mother.' She turned on her heel and went back into the drawing room.

'Thanks,' Joni said. 'Did you really see me?'

Heck grinned. 'Oh aye. Pancake did too.'

Joni shook her head and smiled. If she hadn't been so tired, she'd have danced the tango with her boss over the black-and-white tiles. Then she remembered Rosie Etherington. She had volunteered to tell her about the general's death. The prospect was as attractive as an evening walk through Ironflatts.

151

Joni met Eileen Andrews at the edge of the Etheringtons' village.

'Glad to see you're in one piece, ma'am,' the DC said, getting out of her Escort.

'Call me Joni when there's no one else around, Eileen. Under the surface I'm a wreck. I hope I can get through this.'

'I heard your mother was hurt.'

'She's had surgery and is all right. It's touch and go with Morrie Simmons, though.'

Eileen nodded, but was discreet enough not to ask what the head of the Corham MCU had been doing at Joni's mother's place.

'You know the gist of what happened?'

'Yes, m'a— Joni. I spoke to Pancake. Pete.'

'I'm going to call him Pancake like everyone else. He doesn't seem to mind.'

'He's a good lad. Shall we get this over with? I'll drive you down to the house.'

Joni went along with that. When they arrived, she looked at herself in the mirror. 'Shit. Have you got a tissue?' Her face was dirty and her hair all over the place.

'Have a comb too.'

When Joni was ready, they headed for the door. There was only a single light on, in the kitchen. The light above the door came on before it was opened.

'DI Pax,' Rosie Etherington said. 'And DS...'

'Andrews,' Eileen said, with a soft smile. 'Can we come in?' She pushed Joni gently forwards.

'Have you got any news?' Rosie asked, running an unsteady hand over her hair. In the days since Nick's death, she had suffered a rapid decline. Her clothes were crumpled and deep lines had appeared on her face.

'Shall we go into the kitchen?' Eileen said.

The other two women followed her, walking slowly.

'What is it?' Rosie asked, when they were on opposite sides of the table. There was a half-eaten biscuit on the tabletop, no crockery in sight. 'What's happened?'

'I'm so sorry,' Joni said.

'Just tell me!'

'Major General Etherington is dead.' Joni told the story, leaving nothing that was relevant out. Rosie listened intently, her breathing uneven. When Joni finished, she wiped her eyes with the sleeve of her brown jumper.

'I don't … I can't take this in,' she said, her lips trembling. 'Victoria Favon got her factor to run Nick off the road and he took a rock to him because he was jealous?'

'Nick rejected her; he wanted Evie. And Reston was jealous of Lady Favon's lovers.'

'But that … that's ridiculous. You don't … you don't do something like that because you were … rejected…'

Joni stretched across the table and put her hand on Rosie's. 'Also, Nick saw Lord Favon coming out of the brothel on Burwell Street last Sunday night.'

'You mean … you mean Andrew was involved too? But we … we know them socially. Michael…' The words were overtaken by a rush of sobs.

Eileen sat by Rosie, passing her tissues.

'Poor Michael,' the bereaved woman said. 'He knew … those horrible Favons were involved in Nick's death. I wish he'd killed *them*.'

Joni was struck by the irony. Michael Etherington had given his life to save the woman who had brought about his grandson's death.

'I'll stay overnight, ma'am,' Eileen said, putting her arm round Rosie's collapsed shoulders.

Joni mouthed her thanks and went quietly out. On the way back to the Land Rover, she tried to get her thoughts in order. It was pointless. Her mind was a maelstrom. Then she remembered Suzana's face before she turned away in the wood. The girl was exhilarated by her freedom. That was something to hold on to.

◇◇◇

152

'How's Joni?' Ag was at the wheel. They were on the way to her sister's in Bardon Mill, the Cherokee packed with clothes and other gear. The house was full of SOCOs, drafted in from Newcastle, and the damage to the windows and doors meant it would need work before they could go back. The kids and David were in a squad car behind them.

'I called her before we left. She sounded knackered, which is hardly a surprise. Moonbeam's OK, but they're keeping her in for a few days. She's had an operation on her shoulder.'

Ag laughed. 'I still can't believe someone would choose that ridiculous name.' She glanced at Heck. 'What on earth was Morrie Simmons doing at her place?'

'Shagging her, apparently.'

'Lovely, Heck Rutherford. But you don't sound very convinced.'

'I don't know. There's something strange about the whole thing. According to Joni, Michael Etherington knew that Andrew Favon was being blackmailed.'

'And you think it was Morrie?'

'There isn't going to be any evidence, especially if Morrie doesn't make it. He's still in surgery.'

'I never liked the man, but he seems to have acted pretty heroically.'

'As did Joni, more than once.'

'She's a remarkable woman.'

Heck put his hand on her thigh. 'So are you. I'll never forget the hit you landed on that scumbag's helmet.'

'Lioness defending her kin. You're no slouch yourself, mind.

You were in full command while the shots were flying. I was impressed. How's your gut? That was a heavy blow you took.'

'Weirdly, it feels better.'

'Away with you.' She put her hand on his. 'Though if that's really the case, the night is ours.'

'You fancy messing about?'

She laughed. 'You take your time, but you get there in the end.'

'Uh-huh. Given your sister's married to a vicar, you'd better keep the lead vocals down.'

Ag stopped her elbow just before it made contact with Heck's lower abdomen.

∞∞

153

The morning briefing, Tuesday, 14 May.

Heck Rutherford was at the front as usual, with ACC Ruth Dickie at the back, looking mildly pleased with herself.

'DI Pax?'

'Thanks, sir. We've still got a way to go with the details of the Etherington-Favon-Albanian clan case, but here's where we stand now. Suzana Noli. There have been no sightings of her since Sunday. Her description has been passed to all neighbouring forces north and south of the border.'

'I don't suppose she could have doubled back,' Nathan Gray said. With Morrie Simmons still in intensive care, he was acting chief of Corham MCU.

'If she has, you'd better make sure she doesn't slip through your fingers, DS Gray,' Mrs Normal said. 'That wouldn't look good at all.'

Heck suppressed a smile. He knew the ACC was actively looking for a replacement for Morrie. If he recovered, his career was in jeopardy because of the suspicion he'd been blackmailing the Favons.

'Lord Favon has been released from Corham General,' Joni continued, 'and is being held in the cells here. Along with his wife, he's been charged with kidnapping and false imprisonment – their fingerprints are all over the beds in the old tower – as well as aiding and abetting a murderer. On advice from Richard Lennox, neither is talking. Lady Favon claims that everything she said when Michael Etherington was holding a gun on her was a lie. However, her daughter Evie is keen to testify on that and other matters.'

'We won't need her,' Heck said. 'We've got enough evidence to send Lord and Lady F down for years. And that's before the fraud squad has crawled all over their business interests. They've developed close ties to companies potentially linked to the Spahia clan.'

'As for Dan Reston,' Joni said, 'his prints were found on the stone that was used to kill Nick Etherington. A pair of Adipower Howard baseball boots whose soles match the prints found in the proximity of Nick's body was found in his house.'

'Has he started talking yet?' Ruth Dickie asked.

'No, ma'am. He's still in the psychiatric ward. The doctor in charge told me that he's suffered a major psychotic breakdown and it may take months, or even years, to bring him back to reality.'

'What about his wife?' Eileen Andrews asked.

'Cheryl's at the opposite end of the spectrum. She shouts and swears at anyone who comes near her and has refused representation. The wound in her neck wasn't as deep as it initially looked. Her prints have been found in the tower and on Greg Frizzell's head and hands. She's been charged with false imprisonment, and aiding and abetting his murder. More charges, some of them pretty nasty, will follow.'

Heck put a hand on Joni's arm. 'Ollie Forrest told me the person who cuffed him and brought him food and clothes always wore a black balaclava. I reckon Dan and Cheryl Reston took turns to play warder and use the cattle prod. Ollie also said it was Dan Reston who clobbered him up on the moor.'

'Delightful people,' Pete Rokeby muttered.

'You have several other men to account for, DI Pax,' said the ACC.

'Yes, ma'am. Marcus Ainsworth, who tried to kill me in my mother's cottage, was, as you know, the man who attacked me in London. There's no way we can link him to the Spahia clan unless he talks – and he may not even know the clan name – but it's a reasonable assumption that they hired him.'

'You and DI Simmons dealt with him effectively enough. The Albanians obviously didn't trust him since they had backup on the scene.'

Joni nodded. 'My research showed that outside contractors are often used, as I told you. They are often killed to silence them. As for Ian Sacker, I think he's DCI Rutherford's special subject.'

Heck smiled grimly. 'Some of you'll remember a sick gangster called Ned Sacker. I put him away for a long stretch when I was in Newcastle. His brother Not So Lucky thought he'd have a go.'

'He really was not so lucky,' Nathan Gray said, grinning.

Nobody laughed.

'As for the Albanian killed by General Etherington,' Joni resumed, 'he was carrying no ID. According to Suzana Noli, he was a Popi, their unofficial equivalent of the SAS.'

Ruth Dickie walked to the front, but didn't speak.

'Michael Etherington ran an organisation dedicated to fighting the Spahia clan, with whom he'd clashed in Kosovo.' Joni looked at Nathan Gray. 'Have you got anywhere with the Steel Toe Caps?'

'Em, not really, ma'am. They've all done a bunk. Even Dorries, the computer nerd.'

The ACC shook her head. 'You let them get away? That's not very impressive, DS Gray.'

Nathan's head dropped.

'That's all, ma'am,' Joni said. 'DI Rokeby?'

Pancake looked as uncomfortable as ever, but he stepped

forward. 'DCI Rutherford asked me to talk to DI Pax's mother, Moonbeam. She's still in Corham General. She told me that she and Morrie had been … together for over a month. She said she knew nothing about the blackmail General Etherington mentioned and was adamant that he had visited her for a spell consultation to help find his grandson's killer.'

Ruth Dickie cleared her throat eloquently.

Pancake went on. 'Ms Pax also said that DI Pax knew nothing about her relationship with Morrie … DI Simmons, or about anything else.'

Heck looked at Joni. She was holding her head high, but he could tell she was mortified.

'Thank you, DI Rokeby,' the ACC said. 'Now, I want to make something crystal clear. Some of you will have heard that DCI Lee Young of Newcastle MCU has been arrested on corruption charges that directly relate to these cases. He has admitted to receiving bribes from Albanians belonging to the Spahia clan, both for supplying information and for protecting their illegal activities. As a result, Newcastle MCU is being thoroughly investigated by Professional Standards. If anyone in this room has relevant information, it must be reported to me in person by end of shift today. Am I clear?'

There was a lot of nodding, but no one spoke.

'One last matter. The chief constable and I are committed to driving the Albanians out of Force area. This is our number one priority. I expect all of you to respond appropriately.' Mrs Normal headed for the door.

After Heck had allocated duties to both MCUs, he called Joni into the glass cube.

'Nice one by your mother.'

'I'll kill her.'

'Don't be stupid. She's protecting you.'

'Huh.'

Heck took his suit jacket off and sat down. 'There are still some things we have to clear up.'

SAM ALEXANDER

Joni nodded. 'Such as, who made the anonymous call about Nick Etherington being forced off the road by a black Suzuki?'

'Aye. What do you think?'

Joni sat down opposite him. She was wearing a scarlet blouse, no longer committed to white for work. 'It must have been Morrie. He was on the Favons' backs already about Andrew using the brothel. Nick's death would have made him even more greedy.'

Heck was looking out of the window towards Ironflatts. 'You're probably right. Professional Standards will be over his house and his accounts like beagles after a fox.'

'You used to work for them.'

'Doesn't mean I like them. Then again, I don't like dirty cops either. If Morrie was one of those, he can go to hell.'

'He saved my life.'

'I know. The question is, where has Morrie hidden his stash?'

'Oh, Christ.' Joni smacked her forehead.

'What?'

'My mother. The money's probably at her place.'

Heck smiled. 'That would explain why she covered your backside and every other part of your anatomy.'

'Maybe they won't think to look there.'

'Don't bet on it. I won't drop them any hints.'

'Stupid cow. It's so like her to mess things up for me.'

Heck opened a file. 'Here, guess what? Kyle Laggan and his mates have been let loose. The charges against them have been dropped as the Albanians concerned seem to have left the area.'

'They were lucky. If they'd been in prison much longer, the Albanians would have got to them.'

Heck nodded. 'Do you think the Spahia clan will leave them and us alone?'

'It's not their style.'

'No, but Mrs Normal's on a mission.'

'Rather them than me.' Joni yawned before she could get a hand over her mouth.

416

'Come on, lass, you're out on your feet.'

'Lass? What kind of patronising…'

'Take the day off. That's a direct order.' Heck grinned. 'Go on, bugger off. And don't give me any bollocks about homophobic language. I love Pancake dearly.'

Joni gave up and went home

154

Joni slept into the early evening. Her dreams weren't as vivid as they had been the previous two nights – they didn't wake her – but she relived the most heavy-duty scenes from what had turned out to be one large interlinked case: the stabbed Albanian in the brothel, the body in the river without head or hands, Nick Etherington's bloody, crushed features, the shootings in her mother's cottage and the deaths in Favon Hall. The last sight was of Gary Frizzell's putrefying extremities in the Restons' fridge. That did rouse her.

She went into the sitting room and put on a CD of Mozart's clarinet concerto. Sitting by the window, she looked at the birds swooping around in the twilight. She felt curiously relaxed – Heck had been right to send her home. She considered going to visit her mother, then decided against it. She and Moonbeam had quarrelled the previous evening and she didn't trust herself to keep calm after what Pancake had said in the briefing. Her mother always thought Joni had some kind of special powers and that she was denying them by cutting herself from black culture. Joni had always resisted, but now she felt less determined – which was paradoxical, given that there was scarcely any black culture in north-east England. The truth was that she herself had always felt she was special – not in terms of powers, but intellectually. Suddenly she understood how arrogant she had been. She thought of the portraits of the previous viscounts in Favon

Hall, the slaves bending earthwards in the background. The latter were her ancestors, at least on one side. She shouldn't have ignored black history and everything that went with being black for so long. The insult one footballer had used about another came back to her – she was a classic choc-ice and that couldn't be good. She got up and changed the CD to one by Duke Ellington. A friend had given it to her for her birthday years ago and she'd never even opened it. She found herself enjoying the music from the first notes. That would show Moonbeam.

Her mother was recovering from the wound in her shoulder. The bullet had damaged only muscle and the surgeon expected her to regain full mobility in her arm in time. She told him she would treat herself when she was allowed home, which went down like a lead jumbo jet. Joni hated to imagine the animals – already dead, of course – that would be chopped up and boiled to make poultices.

Her mobile rang.

'DI Pax,' said a female voice tentatively.

'Evie? I told you call me Joni.'

'Em, Joni. Could we … could we meet?'

'What, now?'

A pause. 'Yes.'

'All right. How about Old Mother Mary's Tea Shop? It stays open till ten.'

'I … I'd prefer not to be seen in public. Could I … could I come to your place?'

Joni felt a twinge of concern. Inviting people connected to ongoing cases into your home was a no-no for police officers, especially detectives. But the girl had been through so much and sounded so broken that she decided to make an exception. She gave her the address and Evie said she'd be there in ten minutes.

Joni studied her in the entry-phone screen. She was leaning on one crutch, a bag over the other shoulder, and she looked like she was about to collapse. Joni went down to let her in.

'You're all in,' she said, taking the girl's arm. 'Sorry, there's no lift, but it's only the first floor.'

'I'll … I'll manage,' Evie said, but she didn't try to shake Joni off.

They went into the flat and Joni led her to the sofa.

'Lie down if you like. What can I get you? Have you eaten?'

Evie shook her head.

'Hold on.' Joni made her a mug of coffee and a cheese sandwich. Both disappeared in a few minutes.

'Thanks,' Evie said, wiping her mouth.

'More?'

'No, I'm OK now. I'm sorry…'

'There's no need to apologise. I'd say you're in at least mild shock.'

Evie picked up her crutch and rested it against her thigh. 'I don't know … I might be, but the thing is … I don't care what happens to my parents. They … they disgust me.'

Joni sat down in the armchair facing her. 'Shall I turn the music off?' she asked, suddenly aware of the big band.

'No, don't.' Evie gave a small smile. 'I listen to a lot of black music. Not just jazz, but blues and reggae too.'

'Really? How come?'

'Well, for a start, I like it. And then … there's the fact that Favon wealth was built on the exploitation of slaves.'

Joni nodded. 'But you aren't responsible for that, Evie.'

'No, but I still benefited from it – private schools, ponies, dance lessons, whatever I asked for. I don't want anything to do with the estate or my parents. From now on I'm going to pay my own way – student loans, bar work, whatever it takes.'

'Good for you. I finished university when grants still existed. Actually, I'd probably have had my fees paid. I was a serious smartarse with a single parent in Hackney.'

'Nick told me you went to Oxford. That's amazing.'

'I told you, I was a swot. A bluestocking too, not that I ever wore those.'

'Well, I want to be like you, not the offspring of aristocracy.'

'I can understand that, Evie.' Joni studied her. 'You know, your parents might be in prison for a long time.'

The girl nodded. 'And I won't be visiting them. They're so … immoral, so grasping. I'll never forgive them. I sometimes think my father ran me over deliberately. He was angry about paying towards my gap-year trip.'

Joni shook her head, though nothing would have surprised her about the Favons. 'There's no benefit in thinking like that. They're human beings like the rest of us. Everyone makes mistakes.'

'You can't defend them,' Evie said, her eyes flashing. 'Not after everything they did.'

'No. I'm just saying we all have weaknesses. Theirs were worse than ours.'

'And they had the influence and wealth to do what they liked.'

It had become clear that the Favons' finances were in free fall, but there was no point telling Evie that.

The girl stood up. 'I … I wanted to say thank you, Joni. I probably won't see you again.'

'There's the trial.'

'Of course. I'll come back and tell the truth, the whole truth and nothing, et cetera.'

'Come back?'

'I'm going down to Exeter later this week. I'll find a room and a job before uni starts.' She smiled, this time less reservedly. 'Maybe learn to surf. Being in the water'll be good for my legs. I still believe I'll get full movement back, even though the doctors don't.'

'I'm sure you will.'

Joni went down with her. At the door they embraced – awkwardly at first and then with real warmth.

'You're a brave lass, as my boss would say.'

'So are you.' Evie kissed her on the cheek and took a folder from her bag. 'These are copies of notes I took from old books in the family library. I did some writing of my own based on them. You should read it. There's a lot about how black people were treated.' She turned away and limped towards the Abbey.

Back upstairs, Joni flicked through the thick file. There were passages on how the slaves were shipped to the Caribbean, the work they were forced to do, the punishments they endured and the gods they brought with them. She sat down and started to read. She had ignored her heritage for too long – and it wasn't only a question of heritage. Slavery, whether in the plantations in the Caribbean or the brothels and fields of Europe, destroyed people's humanity. Lethal acts, carnal acts like those of the Favons and the Albanians were still part of life in every supposedly civilised country.

Through the window came a strange wheezing noise that made her start. She looked down and saw a small bird standing on a fence post at the back of the garden.

The little owl turned its head 180 degrees.

Suddenly Joni Pax felt enlightened. Although the weight of the past, both distant and recent, was oppressive, for the first time in months she realised that she could be happy in the future. That lifted her enough to make her laugh out loud. The owl was startled and flitted away. Something from her went with it into the warm darkness.

155

Heck thought about Ag as he drove into work. She was doing a great job of making Kat and Luke feel safe after the terrors of Sunday. And she'd done a great job on him. Ag had the gift of joy. His old man was drinking more whisky than usual, blaming himself that he hadn't done enough to help during the attacks, but Heck had embraced him and told him to stop talking bollocks. The previous evening they'd gone fishing and David had hooked a beaut of a trout. Neither of them felt the need to talk further about what had happened.

After the morning briefing – nothing significant had come to light – he went down to the Crown Court for the arraignment of Lord and Lady Favon. It was a formality, but he wanted to be there. Joni and Pancake came with him. They stood outside the golden stone Victorian building, talking to the CPA solicitor. A crowd was building up and the press was there in a swarm, cameras and microphones at the ready. The narrow streets of central Corham meant that the vans carrying the defendants – one each to prevent them communicating – had to pull up at the front entrance, beneath the wide steps that led to the pillared entrance.

'Are there enough uniforms?' Joni asked.

Heck looked at the inspector who was marshalling the officers. 'I reckon Mac Albert knows what he's doing.'

The first van arrived and backed down the tunnel formed by lines of uniforms. Boos rang out as Lord Favon was led up the steps, his face and bald head still covered in dressings. His eyes were down and he looked years older.

The van moved away and the second one took its place. This time the jeering was louder. Both local and national media had gone to town on Lady Favon's activities. As usual in such cases, someone in the Force or the CPS had succumbed to the lure of lucre and leaked. Heck wasn't hugely concerned.

'Whore!' a woman shouted, as Victoria Favon climbed down. 'Murdering bitch!' yelled another.

Lady Favon was dressed immaculately, her hair in a chignon and understated make-up on her eyes and lips. She looked around haughtily as she was led up to the entrance.

The first shot hit the right side of her head, removing most of the ear. The second ruined her profile and the third penetrated her upper back, passing through her left breast and heart.

Heck and Joni pushed through the crowd, the former almost falling as the screaming crowd fled. It soon became obvious that they didn't need to rush.

Rosie Etherington had dropped her father-in-law's pistol and was kneeling on the ground, eyes filled with tears and the faintest of smiles on her pale lips.

'Jesus Christ,' said Heck.

Joni caught sight of Evie in the middle of the square. She was leaning on her crutch, her face expressionless. Then she turned and walked slowly away.